nothing feels better

ALTERNATIVE COVER EDITION

BRIT BENSON

Nothing Feels Better

BRIT BENSON

Cover Design: TRC Designs by Cat

Editing: Rebecca at Fairest Reviews Editing Services

Proofing: Sarah at All Encompassing Books

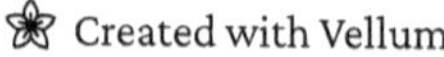 Created with Vellum

*To any mom who has ever felt like you've lost a part of yourself.
It's never too late to say, "Welcome back."*

Live a Little – FOOL
Easy On Me – Adele
Classic – MKTO
GIRL – Maren Morris
Summer On You – PRETTYMUCH
Head in the Clouds Remix – Naïka, TeaMarr
Magic In The Hamptons – Social House, Lil Yachty
Butter Remix - BTS, Megan Thee Stallion
Wave of You – Surfaces
In the Water – CAL, Quinn XCII
Love Some – Pikoe
CHAMPION – Bishop Briggs
Good Thing Go – Quinn XCII
Something Good – Austin Riddle, Luther Lizama
Cherry On Top – Olmos, Kyle Reynolds
love ride – Christian French
Come With Me – Surfaces, salem ilese
superstars – Christian Fench
Blue Hundreds – Holy Mattress Money
Fly You to the Moon – mike.

hold me, baby – We Three
To Hell & Back – Maren Morris
Underneath the Covers – Alex Di Leo
Ghost – Justin Bieber
fools (can't help falling) – Foster, Sody, Sarcastic Sounds
if we never met – John K, Kelsea Ballerini
Put It to Bed – Jhart
Slow Dance – AJ Mitchell, Ava Maxx
Nothing Feels Better – Pink Sweat$

For the extended playlist, visit the Brit Benson Spotify

*content note from
the author*

Please be aware: this book contains references to some difficult topics that could be upsetting for some readers.

Topics that take place on page are: alcoholism, verbal abuse, physical abuse, gaslighting, manipulation, and stalking.

Topics that are referenced but do not take place on page are: addiction, sexual assault, life threatening accident involving a child.

If you or someone you know is experiencing domestic violence or intimate partner abuse, I encourage you to contact a professional who is trained to help. Call the **National Domestic Violence Hotline** at **800-799-7233, chat with someone online** at **thehotline.org**, or **text START** to **88788**. Someone is available to talk 24/7/365.

Everyone deserves healthy, loving relationships free of DV.

MOM SAYS EVERYONE HAS A SUPERPOWER.

She has one. My brother Jude has one.

Even my dad has one, but I still don't know what his is.

Mom says my superpower is that I'm *observant.*

She says I see things. Things other people don't. Things even the grown-ups miss. It doesn't feel very super to me, though. Sometimes, I wish I didn't have it at all. Maybe it would be better if I could actually say the things I see, but I'm not good at that yet.

Mom says it's important to figure out other people's superpowers.

She says the right people, with the right superpowers, can change your life for the better. She says it's how we find our family.

When Jesse from next door started coming around, I learned his superpower right away. I didn't tell anyone because I didn't know how. I couldn't say it, but I *felt* it. I *saw* it.

When I realized I should probably say something, because none of the grown-ups were figuring it out, I told my brother.

He's still a kid. He can't keep a secret. He's better at being loud, at being the center of attention. I thought he would say it so I wouldn't have to, and then my life could change for the better. Then Jesse could be part of our family.

I should have just done it myself.

By the time everyone else figured out what I already knew, it was too late.

ONE

jesse

"YOU 'BOUT READY?" my roommate Kelley asks from where he's leaning on the kitchen counter. He already has his jacket on and he's typing something on his phone, probably sending an update to the group chat about our ETA.

"Yeah. Just finishing this up," I mumble as I work with my needle to close off the latest knitted hat I've been working on. I'll attach a pompom to the crown later. I drop my stuff back into my basket and stand from where I've been working on the couch.

"How many is that?" Kelley asks, nodding to the box of colorful knitted hats sitting next to the coffee table.

I snag my coat off the back of the recliner and slide it on. "That would be number forty-three," I state proudly, flashing him a grin. Once I get to fifty, Ivy, Kelley's girlfriend and one of my best friends, offered to wash and bag them for me. Then I'll take them to the Knots of Love collection location.

This will be my eighth box of fifty hats since July.

That's four hundred knitted hats in eight months.

I don't mean to brag, but I'm a beast.

"Damn," Kelley says as he follows me out, "this box filled up fast."

"No shit. Interviews had me keyed, and the wait was killer." The more pressure I've got on my shoulders, the faster I knit. Needless to say, the entire med school application process is to thank for my successful hat production.

"All worth it now, though, yeah?" He grins at me as we slide into his Jeep.

"Hells yes." I grin back.

We pull up to Ivy's apartment complex, and I wait in the car while Kelley runs in to grab her. And to also probably bang one out on the couch since Bailey, V's roomie and another of my good friends, is already at Riggs's place. I swear, Kell and V never stop boning, but they gotta make up for all the years they spent pining, I guess.

When I see them coming back to the car fifteen minutes later, I jump into the back seat, so V can ride shotgun.

"How many?" I ask them when they're buckling up.

"How many what?" Sweet V asks, her innocent baby blues blinking at me from the front seat, and I choke on a laugh, just as Kelley throws up two fingers.

"Two," I shout, pretending to be appalled. "A whole quarter hour and *only two?*" Kelley fights laughter, and Ivy shakes her head, finally catching on. "Shoulda picked me, V," I joke. "I'd have made you come *at least* three times."

Ivy and Kelley laugh it off; they know I'm just kidding. Those two are grossly perfect for each other, and though I was feeling V for a bit when we first met, I backed off pretty quickly when I saw how she and Kell were together.

I knew they were gone for each other even before they did.

"I got seven more, V, then I'm ready for you," I change the subject, and Ivy whips around with a smile.

"Dang, Jesse, that was fast," she praises, and I mime dusting off my shoulders. "Are you going to want me to take them to Mrs. Gunther or are you going to do it?"

"I'll do it," I tell her. "You know she likes me better."

Ivy rolls her eyes at my jibe. Mrs. Roxanne Gunther, the nice older lady who runs the Knots of Love collection site near the Butler University campus, likes Ivy just fine, but she fucking loves me. Roxanne is about ninety years old and drives her late husband's 1976 Ford Mustang Cobra to deliver her Avon orders. She always has some sort of pie and fresh sweet tea at her house, and she's got a new badass story to tell me every time I drop off a box of hats for donation. I fucking love that lady.

"You better watch it, or she'll ask you to be husband number four," Kelley says with a laugh, and I waggle my brows.

"I'm down. You know I like the older women." I say it jokingly enough, and while Kelley chuckles, I don't miss the way Ivy's lips purse slightly. She's the protective mama bear of our group, and she's still not over the bullshit that went down last summer. I'm not quite over it, either, but I don't tell her that. It's going to take her some time. I reach up and squeeze her biceps lightly, and she flashes me a soft smile before taking a deep breath.

Kelley pulls up to the curb, a block down from Riggs's townhouse. I can already hear the music pumping from the building and see people milling about on the front lawn. Riggs Stanton, Butler University's star pitcher, has been dating Bailey since around Christmas. They had a rocky as hell start, but things are going good now. He even hangs with me and Kelley on nights when V and B are doing secretive girl shit that we're not invited to.

"Damn, is the whole campus here?" Kelley muses as we hop out of the Jeep. He slings his arm over Ivy's shoulder, and we make our way to the house. "Bet Riggs loves this."

I snort, because we all know Riggs does *not* love this.

If Riggs could go the rest of his life without having to attend another raging house party, he gladly would. Bummer for him, his roommate Dylan was selected to play in the MLB Draft League, so the whole baseball team decided to throw him a party. And since Riggs is the unofficial team captain and campus stud, he's hosting. Dude's fucking *thrilled*. Not.

When we walk into the house, we're greeted almost immediately by Bailey and Riggs. Ivy must have texted to let them know we were here.

"Hi guys!" Bailey shouts over the music, then she links her arm with Ivy's and starts to pull her away.

"Kelley," Riggs greets as he shuttles us in, then he turns to me. "Slipper Dick," he says, lips tilted in a small smirk, so I wink at him.

"It's *Doctor* Slipper Dick to you," I say, and his grin breaks through, just as Bailey shouts at us over her shoulder.

"You're not a doctor yet! If someone gets hit by a car, we're still calling 911."

I flip her off just as she flips me off, then she and V disappear into the house.

"This place is packed," Kelley says, and he gestures for my coat, so I shrug it off and hand it to him. "You want these in your room?" he asks Riggs.

"Yeah, just toss them on the bed." Kelley heads up the stairs with our coats, and I follow Riggs into the kitchen, weaving in and out of the insane crowd of people on the way.

I'm reaching into the fridge and grabbing three of the fancy beers when someone bumps into me. I step back to find Riggs's roommate, Dylan, blitzed off his ass and grinning like an idiot. It's his party; he can dude bro if he wants to.

"J Dawg," he shouts and pulls me into a drunk hug.

"Hey," I say with a smile, giving his back a few pats before pulling away. "Congrats on the Draft League, man. That's fucking awesome."

"I know, right?" he slurs. "And what about you? You got into Harvard Med!"

I can't resist the in, so I grin and say, "What, like it's hard?"

Dylan scrunches up his face in disbelief. "Yeah, bro. It's fucking *Harvard*."

"*Legally Blonde*?" I ask, brows raised and eyes wide. Is he messin' with me?

"Dude." He blinks. "This is my natural hair color."

"Never mind, man." I shake my head. "Super excited for you." I pat him on the shoulder once more as I shuffle around him. "I need your autograph before you leave."

I push my way back through the kitchen and small dining area until I find Kelley and Riggs in the living room. Their girlfriends are nowhere to be found, so I stroll up and offer them each a beer.

"Beer pong in the garage?" I suggest.

"Let's do it," Kelley says. "I'll grab Zay."

I point a finger at Riggs. "You're going down."

"Not this time, SD." He takes a pull from his beer bottle, eyes narrowed, then turns and stalks toward the door that leads to the connected garage. *SD*. Short for Slipper Dick. Because the first time Riggs and I met, I was knitting a pair of slippers. I chuckle to myself. The nickname still cracks my ass up.

The beer pong table is already set up when we walk into the garage, and Kelley and Zay, Riggs's other roommate, are filling the red plastic cups with water. Some people fill the cups with beer, and then you have to down it any time the opposing team makes a shot, but not us. We've got douchey-refined palates, so we fill the cups with water and drink from our fancy beers. That, and we were sick of having to fish dirt and junk out of the cups from the nasty ping pong balls. I shudder at the memories. I'm not a germaphobe, per se, but when you can actually see shit floating in your beverage? Yeah, no thanks.

Kelley and I stand on one side while Riggs and Zay stand on the other. I hold back a laugh at Zay's blank face.

"Calm down, Zay," I chuckle, "I know you're excited, but you're embarrassing us."

He just arches a brow and takes a pull from his beer. I think I saw the corner of his lips twitch, though. Maybe. I swear the dude is a robot, but I'll wear him down eventually. I wink at him, and he rolls his eyes.

"Toss off?" Kelley asks, and Riggs shakes his head.

"Nah. You guys go first." He grins at us. "We kicked your asses last time. It's only fair."

"You'll regret that," I say smugly, then take my first shot. It plunks right into the cup with a plop. Kelley whoops, and I take a dramatic bow.

Riggs pulls out the ping pong ball, dumps the water from the cup and sets it on the ground, then takes a drink from his beer bottle. He tosses the ping pong ball back to Kelley, and Kelley takes his shot. We go back and forth, sinking more than we miss, until we're down to two cups left on each side. Kelley's gloating when the door opens and Bailey and Ivy strut in.

"There you guys are," Ivy chirps, and slips her hands around Kelley's waist as Bailey sits down on the big cooler next to the table. "Been looking for ya."

"Hey, babe." Kelley smiles down at her. "You just missed my shot."

"Rim job." I wink, and Bailey huffs out a laugh. Some parties let you try to scoop out a ball when it circles the rim of a cup, but Riggs's House Rules only let you try to blow it out. It's way harder. Zay wasn't fast enough, so he had to drink. "I didn't know he was good at the butt stuff, V."

"Oh my gosh, Jesse." She gasps and buries her face in Kelley's chest, and I see the tip of her ears turn bright red.

"Don't be shy, babe," Kell teases, and I have to look away from the flare of heat in his eyes. Fucking hot, those two.

I chuckle, then turn my focus on Bailey. "'Bout to make your king cry."

"Quit flirting with my boyfriend, Hernandez," she says with a roll of her eyes. "Get your own."

"I tried, but Zay won't laugh at any of my jokes." I push out a not-so-pretend pout. The dick's stony face definitely wounds my pride a little.

"Maybe he doesn't think you're funny," Bailey snarks, and I whip my eyes to Zay and clutch at my chest.

"Z, say it isn't so!" He smirks. I'll take it.

"His name starts with an X, ya dummy," B pipes in, and I jerk my head back.

"It does?" I must look shocked as hell because everyone laughs, and Bailey legit cackles. Douches, all of them.

Zay shrugs. "Xavier," he says, emphasizing the X at the beginning of his name.

"Huh." I had no idea. I blink at him and take a pull from my beer. "I feel like I don't even know you anymore."

I catch some movement out of my peripheral and zone back in, just in time to see Riggs's ping pong ball bounce on the table and Kelley swat it across the garage with a growl.

"God of Thunder!" I roar in my best Thor voice. "Cheap shot and you *still* couldn't sink it."

"Just moving the game along, SD," Riggs taunts as Bailey and V crack up from where they've perched themselves on the cooler.

"In a hurry to get your ass kicked, Thor?" I ask with a grin, and Riggs smirks at the nickname. I call Riggs, 'Thor,' because, well, he's fucking huge and has long Thor hair.

"More like in a hurry to *get* some ass," *X*-avier mumbles under his breath, and Kelley and I both bark out a laugh. The man of few words himself has some great zingers when he deigns to speak. Riggs just shrugs and flicks his eyes toward Bailey with a dumbass grin, and B groans and covers her face with her palms.

"You guys are all a bunch of horn dogs. I'm gonna get a boner from all the sex pheromones floating around." I'm met with a chorus of laughter, then Bailey throws a beer cap at my head, so I toss an empty plastic cup at hers.

"Children," Riggs scolds, and I throw up my hands.

"She started it!"

"Did not!"

"Yes, you did, ya little liar."

Bailey sticks her tongue out at me, and I mirror the gesture, which sends Ivy into a fit of giggles. I clamp my lips together and narrow my eyes, and when Bailey's smile slips first, I fucking beam. Victorious.

Zay sinks his shot, then Kelley sinks his. When it's my turn again, there's one cup left in front of Zay and Riggs. I hold the ping pong ball lightly and practice flicking my wrist a few times.

"This one's for all the marbles, boys," I say in my best Christopher Walken impression, then I take a breath and let the ball fly.

Plunk, into the cup it goes.

"Fuck yes," I shout, then jump into Kelley's arms. We sing "We Are the Champions," and he does a victory lap around the garage—it's only a little wonky, because I might be 6'4", but he's still a beast—then drops me back down at the table.

"Suck my fat one, you cheap dime store hood!" I shout, finger pointed at Riggs.

"Not more movie quotes," Bailey complains, and Riggs crosses his arms over his chest and hits me with a grin.

"Who told you, you had a fat one, Hernandez?"

"Biggest one in three counties," I finish, and the girls laugh.

"Good grief," Ivy breathes out, "we've created a monster."

A few hours later, I've come down off my beer pong victory high and am sitting in a lawn chair in the smallish back yard with Kelley, Ivy, and Zay. I mean **X**-avier. With an X.

What the hell?

He doesn't even look like an **X**-avier. Why did I think his name was Zack? Zay isn't a typical nickname for Zack. Isaiah, maybe. **X**-avier. With an X. What the actual hell?

Riggs and B disappeared a while ago, and I doubt we'll see them for the rest of the night. It's chilly out here, but the fire pit in the middle of our lawn chair circle emits just enough heat to make it comfortable.

My weekends have changed drastically since my friends got all loved up. V used to be my wing woman. We'd troll bars and help each other land *company* for the night, but we haven't done that in months.

I went from wild hookups every weekend to fifth-wheeling at movie nights and Pictionary parties. Weird how that shit happens. I feel like maybe I should be upset about it. Maybe I should miss the partying and the sex and the carelessness of it all. Maybe I do. Maybe I don't. I can't really tell.

When Zay gets up to head inside, I glance across the fire toward Kell and V. Their eyes are closed, and she's perched on his lap with a blanket draped over their legs. He's running his fingers through her hair, and they're probably nice and toasty and comfortable and content. In more ways than one.

I fight off a pang of something like jealousy. Not because I've got feelings for either of them—nothing but the strongest platonic love—but because of that *thing* that they have.

That B and Riggs have too.

That I *don't* have. *Didn't.* That I was so fucking wrong about.

My gentle foot shaking switches to quick leg bouncing, but I resist the urge to slip my hand into my coat pocket and grab on to the object inside. If Ivy or Kelley knew I was still carrying it, well... That's a conversation I'd rather avoid.

I love Ivy, I do, but I don't feel like being on the receiving end of one of her interrogations. *Again.* I'm still recovering from last summer's shit storm. I wince at the onslaught of memories, at the replay reel of fuck-ups that tries to invade my head. Since going to the gym isn't an option right now, and neither is losing myself in a knitting project, I attempt a mental redirect.

Instead of a small, outdated kitchen or a metal desk or potted ferns, I picture a knitting pattern. The stuffed elephant I'm making for my mom. She's obsessed with elephants. I only have three of the four legs done right now, so I picture the steps for finishing the fourth. I move my fingers, like I'm casting yarn on a knitting needle, and I can almost feel the soft navy-blue cotton worsted on my fingertips. I'm about 20 imaginary stiches in when something stabs me in the arm, and my whole body jerks with alarm.

"Ahhh," I shout, and swing my head in the direction of the fucker who jabbed me. I'm expecting Dylan or another of the drunk goons from inside, but instead, I see a tiny human dressed as a pirate.

The kid's just a smidge over three feet, so he's probably around four years old. He's wearing a black plastic vest and Spider-Man underwear. On his head is a plastic pirate hat, on his feet are a pair of Spider-Man rain boots, and in his hand is a fucking sword.

It's made of cardboard, but it's still a fucking sword.

And the kid is scowling at me. What the hell did I do? He's the one who stabbed me. With a fucking cardboard sword.

"Ahoy there, Dread Pirate Roberts," I say in my best pirate voice, but the kid doesn't say anything. I don't even know if he's blinked yet, but his eyes are kind of big. Even with the way they're narrowed in my direction, his eyes are easily the biggest thing on his tiny kid face.

"How fair the seas?" I try again. "Cap'n Blackbeard says he saw some merpeople off the coast...somewhere..."

He blinks!

"Seriously, though, kid, aren't you cold?"

Nothing.

"Where's your, like, parents? Or grandparents? The people in charge of you, where are they?"

He still doesn't speak, so I stand and start to shrug out of my coat.

"Here, kid, take my jacket and we'll find your, uh, crew? First mate?" I move to drape my coat over his shoulders when a woman comes rushing up behind him.

"Jude," the woman yells, her voice equal parts angry and relieved. Then she drops down on her knees in front of the kid and throws a blanket over him. "Jesus, Jude, you're gonna freeze your toes off." She stands then picks him up. "What did I tell you about leaving the house?"

"Not. Jude," the kid growls out, and I watch as the woman closes her eyes and takes a deep breath, the creases between her eyebrows prominent in the glow of the fire.

"Captain Meatball," she says tightly, and I have to hold back my laugh. "What did I tell you about leaving the house?"

"Don't do it without you or Doonie."

"Correct. So why are you out here? It's eleven at night and forty degrees. You're supposed to be in bed."

Captain Meatball shrugs and points to the fire pit behind me. "I wanted 'mores."

The woman looks up to see what he's pointing at, but her eyes run straight into mine, because I'm staring. Hard. Her eyebrows shoot up, as if she didn't even realize I was standing here until just now. I give her my most reassuring bedside-manner smile, the one I use on patients when I'm volunteering at the hospital. She visibly relaxes, and my smile grows.

The orange flames from the fire pit create just enough light that I can make out her features. I can't tell what color her eyes are, but they're big, just like the kid's. Her face is shaped like a heart, and her upper lip looks like it's got a perfect Cupid's bow. Her nose is tiny and slightly upturned. When she blinks, her eyelashes add to the shadows on her cheeks, and her dark hair is thrown up on top of her head in one of those crazy bun-things that Bailey and Ivy like. I quickly let my eyes scan the rest of her. She's wearing a huge purple hoodie, grey sweats, and flip flops. Basically, she's dressed like most of the students on campus during finals week.

"Sorry," I say smoothly, "Meatball didn't ask for s'mores. I could have found him some."

"No," she stutters, then squeezes her eyes shut and gives her head a little shake. "It's fine. I'm sorry if he bothered you."

"I didn't!"

"He didn't." The kid and I protest at the same time.

"Still," she says, "he shouldn't be out here."

"It's fine, really," I assure her. "I've never met a real live pirate before."

I flash the kid a grin and he gives me one right back, nose scrunched up in that fucking adorable way only kids can pull off. The woman laughs, and the sound hits me deep in my chest. It's not a tinkling sound, like Ivy's laugh, and it's not a sarcastic bark like Bailey's. It's more...I don't know. *Full*. Musical. And kind of raspy. And kind of tired. She only does it once, and I have to swallow the urge to make her do it again.

She gave me one note, but I want a whole scale.

"Right, well," she says on a sigh, "Meatball needs to go back to bed." She nods toward the fire. "Enjoy your night."

The woman, with the miniature pirate still hoisted on her hip, turns and walks toward the neighboring townhouse—not the one Riggs's house is attached to, but the one just across the yard. The kid waves at me with his sword, and I salute him. His smile makes me chuckle.

I watch until the woman reaches the dimly-lit cement patio and opens a sliding glass door. She steps into the house, and just before she slides the door closed, she smiles softly and sends me the wave that I didn't know I was waiting for. I smile and wave back, then sink down into my lawn chair.

"Who was that?" Kelley asks, and I look up to find him and Ivy watching me. Ivy's got a little smile on her lips, which has me realizing I've got one on mine too. I shrug it off and play it cool. "Captain Meatball and his first mate, I guess."

"She was pretty," Ivy adds.

I hum in response, just as Dylan comes stumbling from the house and throws his drunk ass into a lawn chair.

"Dyl, who is your neighbor?" Kelley asks casually, gesturing to the townhouse across the yard.

Dylan squints toward the house. "You mean The Hot Mom?"

"The Hot Mom?" I repeat. It didn't register that she could be the kid's mom. I assumed babysitter or something, but the eyes... Those big eyes that they both had. It makes sense.

"Yeah," Dylan pushes out as his eyes drift closed. Dude's gonna pass out. "Moved in last month. Zay and Riggs helped her unload a U-Haul."

"Huh," I say, and flick my eyes back to the house. The lights are all off but for a soft glow coming from a second-floor window.

I bet that's her room.

The Hot Mom.

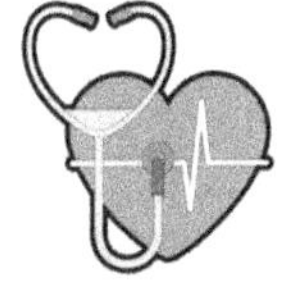

jocelyn

"MOVE YOUR BOOTY, June Bug. We're gonna be late."

Jude giggles from his spot at the tiny kitchen island, which I suppose is technically more like a peninsula, given that it's attached to the wall.

"You said move your booty to her," he mumbles with a mouth full of waffle, and I reach over and boop his nose with my finger.

"Eat your waffles, Jude." He huffs into his plate, so I smile and correct myself. "Eat your waffles, *Captain Meatball*." He beams.

"This isn't waffles, Mom, this is pirate food from the ocean."

"Yeah? Is it tasty?"

"Yeah, it's really good and mermaids eat it too."

"That's very cool," I say, my tone full of excited awe. I'm always amazed by the depths of his imagination. It's endless.

"Can I wear my pirate vest today?"

"Not today. It's in the wash."

He groans loudly, and I stifle a laugh at the dramatics. The most expressive four-year-old in the world, I think.

"You can wear it tomorrow, okay?"

"Promise?"

"Promise."

Just as I'm putting June's peanut butter and jelly sandwich into her Wonder Woman lunch box, she rounds the corner and slides onto the stool. I watch as she silently pulls her plate of knock-off toaster waffles in front of her, then throws me a pathetic, pleading look.

"Don't even ask it, June." I shake my head and turn to pour the last of the milk in a glass for her. "You have to go. You've only got a few weeks until summer, anyway. So, you're going. Learn all the things, get a nice big brain, and before you know it, ten years will pass and you'll be eighteen and graduated and will never have to go back."

She huffs and shoves a forkful of waffle into her mouth. I glance at her outfit. Jeans and an oversized-green sweatshirt.

"You got a t-shirt on under that?" I ask, even though I already know the answer. She shakes her head and continues eating. "It's supposed to warm up this afternoon. You sure you don't want to layer in case you get hot?"

She shakes her head again, and I stifle a sigh. I don't want to push her. But it's difficult not to. I smooth my frown into a smile when I feel Jude's eyes on me.

"Is today Wednesday?"

"Yessir, it is."

"Can we visit my friend?" he asks, referring to the boy he met next door. I'm not sure what they talked about, but he made an impression on Jude. It's been nearly three weeks, but he won't stop bringing him up. *The boy with no s'mores.*

"Not today, bud. We don't even know if that boy lives there."

Boy? Is that right? Something about it feels awkward on my tongue. Like tripping over a lie, or a secret you tell to protect yourself from the truth. He certainly didn't look *that* young, not that I could really tell much in the darkness. But since this whole cluster of townhouses is full of college students, it's a safe assumption that the kid was probably around eighteen. I was worried when I signed this lease that we'd be living in some frat-row nightmare, but the rent was so reasonable and the house was so nice, I took the chance. It also helped that Stanton Property Management, the company that owns all the townhouses, assured me that we could break the lease early if the area wasn't to our liking.

"Can we knock and see?" Jude continues, and I take a big gulp of my coffee. We've been out of creamer since Monday, and we just ran out of milk, so the taste is bitter in my mouth. Overpowering. Almost nauseating. But like most unpleasant things, I'll get used to it after a few more sips, tolerate it, and then ignore it all together.

"Not today, Jude," I repeat. "We're already running behind for school, and you guys go to your dad's tonight."

"Will you be very late?" June chimes in, and when I look at her, she's got her pleading eyes on again.

"You know I work," I say softly. "But I can be there after, okay?"

"Thanks," she whispers, then snags her lunch box and walks out of the kitchen.

The kids are supposed to stay the night at Patrick's every Wednesday, but so far, that's only happened a few times. June doesn't want to be there, and I get the impression Patrick doesn't want them there, either. Cramping his bachelor style or whatever. Sometimes I feel like I should force it, but honestly, I sleep better when they're with me.

"Let's go, Captain," I say to Jude as I put his and June's dirty plates in the sink. I'll have to wait until tonight to wash them because we're running late. Again.

June is already buckled in the back seat when Jude and I

walk into the garage. I get Jude strapped into his car seat, then I climb into the front.

"Okay," I say before pulling out of the garage, "Jude, it's your turn to be DJ."

"Stories!" he shouts, like I knew he would. I pull up the story time podcast on my phone and push play, and the dulcet tone of the podcast's hippie librarian host plays through the speakers of my trusty Camry. Today, she's reading us a story about a girl named Stephanie and her ponytail. We've heard this one before, but I like it. It teaches a good lesson, and I flick my eyes to the rearview mirror to see if June is paying attention.

I let the kids take turns with the radio. Jude always chooses stories, and June always chooses music. Specifically, BTS on repeat. And usually, after I drop them at school, I'll forget to change the radio back to something I would choose.

At this point, I'm not even sure I know what I would choose. Silence, probably.

I could scan for the local pop station, but I would probably only recognize the songs by BTS. My brow furrows at the realization.

Do I really not know what I would listen to if given free rein of my own car radio?

Before the kids, what did I like to listen to? When I was young, one of my foster dads would play classic rock and conservative talk radio. By the time I was sixteen, Patrick was driving me everywhere, and he put himself in charge of the music. He always had a country station on, and I never complained, but damn if I can recall a single artist or song.

In fact, the more I think about it, the more I realize I never actually *liked* any of it.

If I did, wouldn't it have stuck? Been memorable in some way?

I suppose it's my own fault for not speaking up. For just

going along with everyone else's choices. For being a chameleon and confusing Patrick's likes as my own. It hits me like a ton of bricks as I pull into the elementary school parking lot—another part of myself I didn't know I'd lost.

I drop June off with a few words of encouragement. I remind her that she's brilliant and strong and that I love her. She just rolls her eyes with a mumbled *love you too* and walks into the school. When we get to Jude's preschool, I attack him with kisses and hugs, and fight off the nagging reality that, someday soon, he'll be too cool for this kind of sendoff. I steal two more kisses and one more long hug before I leave.

I climb back into the car, and before pulling back onto the road, I take out my phone. I open my music streaming app, find a random "popular music" radio and push play. I might not know what kind of music I like, but now is as good a time as any to find out.

I add it to the list of things I didn't know were missing.

The list of things I would like to rediscover.

"You look like shit," Meryl greets me as I scan my badge.

"Thanks, Meryl." She's always so blunt.

"You just came back from two days off, but you look like you just got off a twelve-hour shift." I can feel her surveying me, assessing my weaknesses, and I do my best not to look at her. "Honey, when is the last time you slept?"

"Four years ago, right after I had Jude," I say with a tired laugh, only half joking. I don't tell her it was because I was passed out from blood loss. "No rest for with wicked, right, Meryl?"

"There isn't a single wicked thing about you." She gives me a sympathetic smile before continuing, and I shove my bag in my locker. "Mr. Murphy in 402 coded two nights ago, so his room is empty."

I'm not surprised about that, but my heart still aches at the news. Mr. Murphy had been with us for a while in the assisted-living facility, but his family recently put him in hospice care. He was a kind and gentle man, and I'll miss seeing his smiling face.

"And you've got a new resident on your hall in the rehab wing," Meryl says, breaking into my thoughts.

"Oh?" I'm getting my things in order as she fills me in on what I missed. The inpatient rehabilitation wing is a revolving door of residents coming and going. Sometimes they're here for months, sometimes for weeks, but there are always new faces.

"She'll probably be around six weeks. Recovering from surgery to repair a hip fracture. She was over at Indianapolis General for a week and a half before coming here. Real spitfire."

I open a five-hour energy shot, drink it in two gulps, then meet Meryl's eyes with a smile.

"The spitfires are my favorite."

"I know they are," she says with a laugh.

I knock lightly on the open door of room 108. I can hear the TV playing Family Feud somewhere in the small, studio apartment-type room.

"Come on in," a voice calls, and I walk in to find a small, red-haired lady in a black, silk night gown, sitting upright on the bed.

"Hi, Mrs. Gunther." I smile brightly. "I'm Jocelyn. Welcome to Harvest View."

"Jocelyn is a gorgeous name," she says, then quickly narrows her eyes at me, "but Mrs. Gunther was my third mother-in-law, and she was an insufferable bitch. You can call me Roxanne."

I hold back my laugh. "Well, it's nice to meet you, Roxanne."

"I suppose you're here to dress me and feed me like an infant?" She scowls.

"I'm here to assist you if you need it, yes."

"Well, I don't need it," she states matter-of-factly. "I'll tell you the same thing I told the man from yesterday and the day before that: I am perfectly capable of dressing myself, feeding myself, and I sure as hell can wipe my own ass. The only reason I'm here is because they had to jam pins in my hip, and my doctor wouldn't let me go home after surgery."

I nod, understanding completely. It's a dignity thing. An independence thing. I see it all the time with the rehab residents, and I *get it.*

"I hear you loud and clear, Roxanne. I'm here if you need help, but I won't force it."

"Thank *God.*" She heaves a dramatic sigh of relief, then turns a charming smile on me. "But you can help me up."

I chuckle and walk to the bed, maneuvering her walker so that when she's standing, she can use it immediately. I pull her covers back and help her to her feet.

"Tell me about yourself, Jocelyn. You're young and beautiful. I'll relive my youth through you."

"Oh," I laugh, "you might want to choose someone else." I lean on the wall and look out the window as she moves her walker to the dresser and digs through her drawers. She might not want to be here, but she's wasted no time making herself at home.

"Nonsense," she huffs, tossing clothes on the bed, "I remember being your age. Time of my life, some of those memories."

I shrug. There's nothing exciting about my life, but I don't want to disappoint her so soon after meeting her, so I tell her about the only good thing I've done.

"I have two kids. June and Jude. They're eight and four." I smile. "They're brilliant, actually. Jude has the biggest imagination, and he's absolutely fearless. He's really into pirates right now. And June. She's so smart. She doesn't miss a thing. So quick-witted too. She's always reading."

I avert my eyes, in an effort to give her some privacy, as Roxanne gets dressed, though she doesn't seem to care at all that I'm here. I can't go far in case she struggles, but she gets her...*flowy pleather pants?*...on without incident. The physical therapist at the hospital probably made sure she could dress herself before they discharged her to our facility.

"Oh!" I add. "And June is part of BTS Army."

"Oh, honey, me too," Roxanne says as she does up the last button on her leopard print blouse. Pleather pants and a silk, leopard print blouse. The woman has more character in her pinky toe than I have in my whole body. "Those boys are delicious. That Jungkook has a jawbone that could slice through glass. The jaw alone converted me to a K-pop Stan."

I can't contain my laugh, and she smiles when she sees my wide, amused eyes.

"What? I'm old. I'm not dead." She pushes her walker to the window and lowers herself onto the chair in the corner. "Your children sound lovely."

"Thank you," I say honestly. "They are."

"And their father?" she asks, innocently enough, but I wince slightly anyway.

"He's around." Roxanne takes the hint and moves on.

"And what about you?"

"What about me?"

"Well, you've told me all about your kids," she says with a

raised brow, "now tell me about you. What do you like? What do you do in your free time? What makes your soul happy?"

I'm speechless for a second, chin bobbing aimlessly, then I clear my throat.

"My kids make my soul happy. I don't have much free time, I suppose. I work here, and I'm in a nursing program online. To be an RN."

"Ah, and nursing is your passion?"

"Maybe. I get to help people." I smile at her. "I get to meet great new people like you."

Her answering laugh is full and melodic. "Yes, well, I'm sure it's never boring."

"Never." I furrow my brow as I continue, "and as for what I like..." I trail off, then lift my shoulder. "I guess I don't really know anymore. I used to want to travel, but I've never left Indiana." I think for another few seconds. "And I used to like taking pictures..." In high school. Ten years ago. "But now..."

I'm just desperately trying to remain functional.

I grow quiet, that same feeling from earlier lingering in my mind. The reminder that there is nothing remarkable or unique about me. The reminder that I'm barely my own person, if I ever was. Roxanne nods, as if she is reading my thoughts.

"I had a daughter with my first husband. Her name was Marie. I remember those early years being some of the hardest. I read a book not too long ago by a woman named Chimamanda Ngozi Adichie. I wish I would have had it when I was a young mother. Adiche says it's easy to lose yourself in motherhood. Easy and understandable. For a time, even necessary. It's a priceless, beautiful gift, being a mother, but it's also important to be a full person. To remember the woman you were before, and the woman you will grow to become."

I stare at her, her words settling heavily on my chest. Do I even know how to do that? Do I even know where to start?

It's not until I'm leaving the room that something else she said resonates. *Was.* She said her daughter's name *was* Marie. She said she *had* a daughter.

"Roxanne?"

"Yes, dear?"

"What happened to Marie?"

Her smile is true, but her eyes are sad. "That's a story for another time."

When I get home that night, after the kids have been picked up from Patrick's and tucked into their own beds, I take out a pen and paper and sit at our small kitchen table with a glass of wine.

My eyelids are like sandpaper, and my body feels heavy, like I've been walking up a never-ending spiral staircase with a kid on my back. And I have, haven't I? That's basically my life right now. A never-ending spiral staircase, and I just have to keep climbing, because if I stop, even just for a second, I risk falling. Tumbling all the way back to the bottom. Back to Patrick. Back to that life. And my kids will be casualties.

I rest my chin on my fist. Tap the base of the wineglass with my fingers.

Is this how twenty-eight is supposed to feel? Bone-tired and bleak?

I stare at the pen and paper for a few minutes. Pick the pen up, just to drop it back down again. I take a sip of wine. Then another. I breathe in and out.

Who am I outside of June and Jude? Who am I outside of Patrick?

I take mental inventory of my body, my personality, and I don't like what I find.

Bone-tired and bleak. Unremarkable. Valueless.

A sardonic, hollow laugh escapes me. Distressed furniture, distressed jeans, vintage everything. There's a whole market out there that centers around buying something new and putting in the work to make it look old. But when it comes to people? When it comes to *women*? Distressed is unacceptable. Everyone always wants to trade out and up.

But I can't trade out myself. I don't think I want to. All I can do is strengthen and cultivate. Find value in what I have. For myself, and for my kids.

"Be a full person," I say to myself.

Then I pick up the pen, and I write.

I start simple with a task I've already begun: find _my_ music. Something that isn't influenced by Patrick or the kids. Something that I like. Then I jot down photography. It's fresh on my mind from today's conversation with Roxanne. I move on to things I've always wanted to do but never could. Like get a tattoo. Patrick said tattoos on women were disgusting. Said they diminished a woman's beauty and worth. Never mind he has an entire sleeve of ink. After that, I can't stop. I'm on a roll. Every interest, every desire I had that Patrick stomped out, I put on the list. Making my own friends. Being more physically active. Patrick didn't like when I worked out.

Who you fucking working out for, Lyn? You got side dick?

Sex.

I write it almost before I think it, and it surprises me.

Patrick is the only man I've ever slept with. The only man I've ever done *anything* with. I don't like that he owns that part of me. It still feels like it's his, and I don't want it to be.

I laugh at myself. Drag my hand through my hair. Out of all the things on this list, that one might be the most terrifying.

My phone rings next to me, and my shoulders tense. I don't have to look at the Caller ID to know who it is, and it makes me want to cry. I let it go to voicemail. It rings again. I let it go to voicemail again. It rings once more, followed by a loud banging on the front door. I squeeze my eyes shut and fight the sting, then I shove the list in a drawer and move toward the door.

If I don't, he'll get louder. He'll make a scene. He'll wake up the kids, the neighbors.

So, like every time before, I let him in.

Baby steps.

jesse

"JESSE," Dr. Rana greets with a smile Sunday morning, "how's your week been?"

"Good," I say, trying to tamp down my excitement. Dr. Parisa Rana is an emergency room physician at Indianapolis General, one of the largest Level I trauma centers in the state, and I get to shadow in her emergency department today. She's also a good friend of my mom's, which is how I managed to score such a coveted gig. I've known Parisa since I was in diapers, so here's the proof that it pays to know people. "Thanks again for letting me do this, Dr. Rana. I really appreciate it."

"Of course, Jesse." Her smile is warm, and I can tell she must have one hell of a bedside manner. I bet patients dig her. If I didn't know her already, that smile would make me want to trust her with my life. "Have you been signed in?" She gestures to the nurses' station, and I tap on my name badge.

"I have."

Dr. Rana nods, then gives me a tour of the department. Labs and diagnostic imaging, trauma rooms, treatment rooms, pediatric care, acute care, waiting areas—she points and rattles them off with efficiency as we speed walk down the halls. Dr. Rana can't be more than five foot two, but her legs move at lightning speed. Usually, at six-foot-four-inches tall, I have to actively take smaller steps when keeping pace with someone, so I don't leave them in my dust, but not Dr. Rana. She takes six and one-half strides for every one of mine—she's practically jogging—and she's not even winded. It's probably an unspoken prerequisite for being a successful ER doc. Swiftness and a calm sense of urgency.

"Vanessa says you've been volunteering over at Kindred," Dr. Rana says, pulling me from my thoughts.

"Yes, ma'am. Kindred Spirit Hospital is where I've been volunteering since last year," I say as we loop back toward where we started. "I was able to do some shadowing over there, too," I add. Kindred is a smaller hospital, and its focus is long-term acute care, so I've been able to get a lot of great patient interaction. The cardiac care and recovery departments were my favorite. It's mostly older people, and I fucking love old people.

We stop at the intake desk and Dr. Rana flips through the pages of a clipboard on the counter. "Wonderful," she says, and I watch her scroll through something on the digital tablet she's carrying. "Have you been able to shadow Vanessa at all?"

I lean on the counter and nod. My mom, Dr. Vanessa Hernandez, is a nationally renowned plastic surgeon. She specializes in reconstruction after trauma and is well-known in the plastic surgery world as being a complete badass.

"I have," I say with a proud smile. "It's pretty amazing to see her work."

"She's one of the best," Dr. Rana agrees. "Are you still thinking you're going to go that route? Reconstructive surgery?"

"I am. Probably craniofacial, but we'll see."

She hands me a clipboard and then grins. "Well, you're in my house for the day, so let's get to it."

For the first half of the morning, Dr. Rana sets me up with an ER nurse named Stefan to do triage. I watch as Stefan takes vitals and categorizes patients by severity of condition: immediately life-threatening, urgent but not life-threatening, and less urgent. He's definitely one of the most informative and helpful people I've shadowed over the last year. (Except for my momma, of course.)

By lunch, I've seen lots of abdominal pains and chest pains, one tooth ache, some minor cuts and contusions, one gnarly skin infection, and a guy who shot his own foot with a nail gun. Twice. Thanks to that last one, I've had the staple gun scene from *Home Alone 2: Lost in New York* playing on repeat in my head. The one where Kevin booby traps the doorknob with a staple gun, and Marv ends up with industrial-sized staples in various parts of his body. Makes me laugh every damn time. Good stuff. I'm gonna have to make my friends watch it with me soon.

I feel like an ass for complaining. I shouldn't wish emergency situations on anyone, but I'd be lying if I said I wasn't hoping for a little more excitement. Maybe a car accident or a gunshot wound or a random stabbing or something. I mean, I don't *want* anyone to die or have life-altering injuries, but shit like that comes through this hospital all the time. If it's gonna happen, I wouldn't mind being present for it. And I definitely wouldn't mind being a little less...*bored*.

Things do pick up a little once I join Dr. Rana for the second half of the day. Namely when she has to suture up a pretty nasty laceration and relocate a shoulder joint. She does both without wincing, and I'm pretty sure I even saw a little spark of glee in her eyes when she popped that shoulder back into place.

Dr. Rana might be a bit of a freak.

I'm here for it.

"Alright," she says around 4:30, after a quick scroll through her tablet. "You're technically done for the day, but I've got a four-year-old with a potential broken arm, if you want to tag along. I know you said you've not had a lot of experience in Peds."

"Yes, definitely," I say. "Thank you."

I've had almost no experience with pediatrics, and exactly zero with any patient under the age of sixteen. Most of the patients I've met at Kindred are at least late-thirties, and my favorites are all sixty plus. I like kids. I think. I like Ivy's younger brother Jacob. He's a cool kid. He's twelve and can kick my ass in Mario Kart.

And once in high school, I helped a girl babysit twin boys.

Well.

By helped, I mean I showed up after she put the kids to bed and then I felt her up on the couch until the parents came home. Rounded third base and then slipped out the back door before midnight. Alison.

Or Abbey.

Ashley?

Whatever. Anyway, zero experience with pediatrics.

I follow Dr. Rana into the patient's room and scan for a parent, but instead, I find a familiar tiny human sitting upright on the bed. He's not wearing a pirate hat, and the cardboard sword is thankfully missing, but I'd recognize those freakishly large eyes anywhere.

"Cap'n Meatball, my man," I blurt with a grin and step closer to the bed. "What'd ya do, kid? Go to battle with a sea monster?" Meatball gives me a small smile, and I notice dried tear tracks on his dirty face just as Dr. Rana clears her throat. *Whoops.* Almost made it the whole day without a fuck-up.

"Mr. Hernandez," Dr. Rana chides, eyebrow arched. She looks more amused than offended.

"Right," I say sheepishly. "Sorry, Dr. Rana. I got excited. This is my friend, Captain Meatball. Captain Meatball, this is Dr. Rana."

"Captain Meatball?" She glances down at her tablet. "I must be in the wrong room, then. The little boy I'm looking for is named Jude Thompson."

"That's me," the kid says with the most adorable fucking lisp. Jude. I like Meatball better, but Jude is good too.

"Ah, well, nice to meet you." Dr. Rana gives him a warm smile. "I'm going to call you Jude for now. Is that okay?" Jude nods once. "Good. Now, it says your father brought you in. Where is he?"

"Smoking," a small voice answers, and Dr. Rana and I turn toward the chair in the corner. On it sits a young girl, maybe seven or eight, with big eyes, long dark hair, and cheeks full of freckles. She's got her knees pulled up to her chest, her arms wrapped around her legs, and her chin resting on top. It's like she's trying to shrink herself down, to become as small and unnoticeable as possible. It almost worked. I had no idea she was even in the room until she spoke. I wonder if Dr. Rana knew she was here. "Dad went outside to smoke a cigarette and call Mom," the girl clarifies.

Mom. That's right. The *Hot* Mom. I glance at the door.

"I see." Dr. Rana sends one of her smiles toward the girl, and I watch as the girl's muscles grow less rigid. And that's on bedside manner. I need to take notes. Would it be weird to ask Dr. Rana to record a short clip of her smiling? I should practice in the mirror. "Well, my name is Dr. Rana, and this is Mr. Hernandez. He's helping me out today. Are you Jude's sister?"

"That's my sister, Doonie," Jude chimes in from the bed, and the girl's face flames red as she narrows her eyes at him.

"It's *June*," she stresses, then averts her eyes to the floor. June and Jude. Well, that's just adorable.

"It's nice to meet you, June," I say, and she forces a grimace-like smile, but doesn't look back up. Dr. Rana turns back toward the bed and asks the kid how he's feeling, just as a guy—the dad?—walks back into the room, reeking of Swisher Sweets and coffee. He's wearing jeans and a Colts sweatshirt, and his hair is buzzed short. He's broad shouldered, and even with the sweatshirt, I can tell he's built. But I'm taller than him, and that makes me smile.

"Ah, y'all are here," he says when he sees us, flashing a smile. I can tell it's fake. "I had to step out."

"Sorry for your wait," Dr. Rana says, as diplomatic as ever. "My name is Dr. Parisa Rana and this is Jesse Hernandez. He's shadowing me today. Is it alright if he's present during our examination?"

"That's fine," the guy says with a nod of his head. "I'm Patrick Thompson. Jude's dad." He's all smiles and respect, but I don't miss the way he doesn't mention or even look in the direction of the girl, or the way he speaks more to me than he does Dr. Rana.

"Is Mom comin'?" June asks from her chair in the corner, and her dad flicks his eyes toward her dismissively.

"She'll be here soon."

"Alright, well, how about you tell me what happened? I hear you had a pretty bad fall," Dr. Rana says to Jude, redirecting the conversation. The kid nods.

"I climbed." He says the *l* like a *w*.

"Are you supposed to climb?" the dad interjects sternly.

"No," Jude whispers, then looks up at me through his lashes. I have to hold back a laugh. He reminds me of a little puppy who just pissed on your rug and is trying to use its cuteness to get out of trouble. I don't know if it's working on the dad, but it's definitely working on me. I wanna scratch his head and give him some treats.

Dr. Rana goes on to ask Jude about the fall and how much it hurts, then she does a physical examination of his arm, prodding it and moving it gently. She tells him she's ordering some x-rays, then addresses the room.

"Mr. Hernandez is going to take Jude down for x-rays and will bring him back when they're finished," she tells the dad and June. "You are welcome to wait in here."

"My wife is on the way," the dad says. "Will she be able to come back here?"

"I'll tell the front desk. They'll bring her back when she arrives."

"You ready, Captain?" I ask Jude after he's seated in the wheelchair a nurse brought. His entire body fits on the seat, just his little feet hanging off, and he wiggles his toes. He nods and cradles his arm to his chest. I roll him out of the room and head toward x-ray.

"It hurts," he whispers, and I hear him sniffle. Ugh, my heart aches for this kid.

"I know, buddy. But we're gonna get you an x-ray and then we'll have you all fixed up in no time." I keep my voice soft but try to infuse it with encouragement. "Just hang in there, okay? You're doing so good."

"What are they gonna do?" he asks. His voice is small, but I don't hear fear. Just curiosity.

"They're gonna set you up next to a big machine and take pictures of your arm, so Dr. Rana can see if you need a cast or not."

He wiggles his toes some more. "How will she know?"

"The picture is going to show her. It's gonna be a picture of your skeleton." I add quickly, "your bones."

"How's it gonna show my bones?"

"Well, it's really cool, actually," I tell him. "The machine emits a fractional amount of ionizing radiation that passes through your skin and tissues and is captured on another device to produce a two-dimensional image of the internal structure of your body."

"Oh." Jude goes quiet for a second, tiny feet wiggling in Spider-Man socks, then asks, "Like magic?"

I chuckle. "It's better. It's *science*."

He tilts his head up and looks at me with a smile, giant eyes all lit up and glowing. I mentally fist bump myself. *Nice job, Hernandez.*

"Does it hurt?" he asks as I wheel him to the x-ray room.

"Nah," I tell him honestly. "Not any more than it did when you fell." His eyes get even bigger, his face falls, and his little chin bobs. *Shit.* "Nah, Captain," I scramble to fix it, "you'll be alright, and it will be over quickly. Just be brave."

He clamps his mouth shut and jerks his chin. "Kay."

The x-ray tech takes over, and I move behind the barrier window to observe. Jude takes it all like a champ.

"I was brave," he beams when I step back into the room. His *r* sounds like a *w* too. *Bwave.* Fuckin' adorable.

"Dude, you were *so* brave. You did better than some adults, you know?"

"I did?" His little feet wiggle once he's situated back on the wheelchair. "I didn't cry even once. Only a little bit. But I stopped fast."

Own-wy. Wittle. I just want to ruffle his hair or pinch his cheeks or something.

"Wow," I say with surprise. "I would have cried. I had a pretty nasty fall when I was younger, and I cried a lot."

"Really?" Jude gasps, then adds incredulously, "boys don't cry. It's not brave."

"Sure they do," I say honestly. "I cry. My dad cries. My best friend cries. I've even seen my papa cry, and he's the bravest man I know. He used to fly the helicopters that put out wildfires. Boys can cry too."

As I round the corner with Jude, I see Stefan and nod my head. He's got an armful of something, but he nods back before walking into one of the treatment rooms. Nurses work their asses off, and I've got mad respect for them. My dad is a nurse anesthetist—that's how he met my mom—and I've heard some crazy-ass stories about his experiences climbing the ranks. He started as a certified nursing assistant and worked his way through school to be an RN, then just kept going from there. Nurses are beasts.

"Crying is for girls and babies," Jude says, pulling me back to our conversation, and I shake my head.

"Nah, Captain. Everyone is allowed to cry. It's not a bad thing."

The kid gets quiet, and when we approach his room, arguing voices filter through the hallway.

"—you can't just leave before he gets back," a familiar voice clips. Her words are hushed, but the anger is still obvious.

"He's fine. You can text me what the doctor says." That's the dad. Patrick. He's impatient. Dismissive. He sounds like a dick. "You left work early so there's no sense in me staying."

"I left work early to be here for *our son*, not so you can—" Her voice dips lower, cutting off, and I hear him scoff. I knock hard on the wall beside the door before slowly pushing it open.

"Jude's all finished with his x-rays," I say to the dad, then flick my eyes over to the mom. Her posture is rigid, her arms are clasped across her chest, and there are deep creases between her eyebrows. When she sees Jude, though, she transforms immediately, all smiles and warmth and positive energy. She crouches in front of the wheelchair as soon as I stop pushing.

"Thanks," Patrick says, and we both watch as the mom embraces Jude lightly. "This is my wife, Lyn. She's taking it from here."

"Okay." I nod slowly and watch as the mom pointedly ignores the dad, choosing to fuss over Jude and June instead. "It shouldn't take the radiologist long to review the x-rays, if you want to stay."

"Lyn will pass it on." Patrick walks up to Jude and ruffles his hair. "I'll see you in a few days, bud. No purple."

"Kay, Daddy," Jude says, his voice low, and he watches his dad walk out of the room. He says nothing to his wife, and the prick never even looked at June. When I glance at the girl, I know she noticed.

The door shuts, and I turn to the mom and stick out my hand.

"Mrs. Thompson, I'm Jesse Hernandez," I introduce myself, and when she takes my hand, I note how small hers feels in mine. Her handshake is firm, though, and her palms are slightly calloused.

"It's Calligaris," she corrects. "Jocelyn Calligaris."

"Of course," I rush out. "Excuse me." I mentally kick myself. I should know better. Ivy and Bailey would have my balls if they knew I'd blindly assumed antiquated patriarchal standards. I can practically hear them spouting off about it now and I have to stifle a laugh. "It's nice to meet you, Ms. Calligaris."

"Just Jocelyn is fine," she says, and her eyes sweep over my face, studying me. I straighten up under her gaze, putting every bit of my 6'4" frame on display. Does she recognize me? I ignore the way my heart kicks up under her attention. *She's married, dumbass.*

"Jocelyn," I say, rolling the name off my tongue, then smile. "That's a J."

She arches a dark eyebrow, a confused sort of interest coloring her green eyes. "Yes, it is," she says slowly.

"And Jude and June," I continue, and Jocelyn tilts her head to the side, surveying me.

"Yes…"

"They're J's too." I resist the urge to bounce on my feet and work to keep my grin from reaching manic levels of creepy. "I'm a J."

"I'm sorry?" She shakes her head slightly, so I point to myself, then to her, then to each of the kids as I state our names.

"Jesse, Jocelyn, June, and Jude. We're all J's." My lips twitch with the need to grin bigger. I point toward the door her husband just left through. "He's a P."

She studies me again, plump lips tipped up in a polite smile. Curiosity and probably a little concern mix on her features because I might be acting like a crazy person. A smidge. She probably thinks I'm just learning the alphabet.

Great job, dork.

"Have we met before?" she questions. "You seem…familiar."

So, she *does* remember me.

"Not officially. A few weeks ago, I was at a party next door to your townhouse."

Her eyes flash with recognition, and her full lips curl into a surprised grin. "The boy with no s'mores," she says, and I cock my head.

"Am I?"

"Are you what?"

"A boy."

I don't say any more than that. I just let the implication float in the air between our locked gazes. *A grown man,* I say with my smile. I watch as her cheeks flush slightly, and she blinks. I wonder if she's as flustered as I feel. Her eyes, the same big ones I've been picturing for days, are a clear, piercing green, and they pop brightly from under thick-arched eyebrows. Her black eyelashes are so long that they feather against her eyelids when she blinks. Her sloped nose, her Cupid's bow lips. Tendrils of dark hair that have fallen from her ponytail frame her heart-shaped face, and my eyes drag over her jaw. It's gracile, elegant.

An Elizabeth Taylor jaw.

I want to trace it with my fingers.

A few months ago, Ivy was appalled to learn that I hadn't seen the movie *Grease*, so she planned several viewing parties where she and Bailey made me watch a bunch of movies they'd deemed "iconic" and "necessary." *Grease, The Breakfast Club, Ferris Bueller, Blue Hawaii, Rebel Without a Cause.* We watched almost twenty movies, but when the viewing parties were over, I couldn't stop my fascination. I started working my way backwards—90s, 80s, 70s, 60s—and then fell into a sort of obsession with Old Hollywood. I streamed every movie I could find from the 1930s through the 1950s. I couldn't stop.

Maybe that's why I'm getting Lauren Bacall vibes from the way Jocelyn is looking at me—chin dipped slightly, expressive eyes peering up through her lashes. Why I can't stop seeing Marilyn Monroe. Why I can't stop finding comparisons to Elizabeth Taylor. The eyebrows. The lips. The jaw.

There's just something about her. Something classic, captivating, like the movies, that grabs my attention and doesn't let go. I know why Dylan dubbed her *The Hot Mom*.

"I didn't know you were a doctor," Jocelyn says, pulling me from my thoughts.

Shit. Have I been quiet for too long? Was I staring?

Of course, I was fucking staring.

My fingers itch, and I fight the impulse to reach for her.

"I'm not," I answer quickly, saying the first thing that comes to mind to fill the dead air. "If someone gets hit by a car, you should still call 911."

June laughs quietly from her chair in the corner, but the shocked widening of Jocelyn's eyes and the tiny gasp that escapes her tells me I said the wrong thing.

Fucking Bailey.

Note to self: don't imply your patients aren't in good hands. Maybe also don't mention car accidents. And for the love of god, don't repeat anything Bailey has said. Ever.

"I mean, I can't perform surgery yet," I stutter out, and Jude lets out a tiny squeak.

"I need surgery?" the kid whispers fearfully, and Jocelyn's hand moves to his on the bed.

"No," I say quickly, shaking my head and scrambling to fix it. "I will be a doctor. In a few years. They don't trust me with a knife yet."

Three pairs of already giant eyes widen to freakishly large proportions. What are those squirrel monkey things with the big eyes? Galagos? Bush babies? I got three of 'em staring at me right now.

"A knife?" June whispers, and I start to panic.

"I mean a scalpel. For skin."

"*For skin?*" The terror in Jude's humongous eyes is loud as shit. How are his eyes getting bigger? And now they're welling up with tears. Fuck, I'm gonna make the kid cry.

Fucking pediatrics.

I open my mouth to try and undo the damage, just as a knock sounds and Dr. Rana walks in. Saved by the Doc. Judging from Jocelyn's deep breath, she's just as relieved as I am.

Great job, Hernandez. Awesome.

Note to self: don't fucking talk about knives. Idiot.

"You must be Jude's mom," Dr. Rana says. "Your husband told us you'd be coming."

"Oh, um, ex-husband," she says quickly, "but yes, I'm Jude and June's mom. Jocelyn." She shakes Dr. Rana's hand with the same firmness, and my brain fixates on one word. *Ex*-husband.

"I'm Dr. Parisa Rana, and this is Jesse Hernandez. He's going to med school in the fall, and he's shadowing me today. Mr. Thompson said it was okay for Mr. Hernandez to stay in the room, but is it alright with you?"

Jocelyn's eyes scan over my face, and I try like hell to look the opposite of how I feel—which is like a complete moron. My bedside manner is usually top notch, but I'm crashing and burning with this woman.

"It's fine," she breathes out, and I give her a small smile.

As Dr. Rana goes over Jude's x-rays, I can't keep my eyes, or my thoughts, from wandering back to Jocelyn. Under her bulky jacket, she's wearing grey scrubs, something I didn't notice at first. Is she in the medical field? Nurses wear scrubs. Physician's assistants. Dental hygienists. Do veterinarians? Her nails are short and unpainted; there are no rings on her fingers. No wedding band. *Ex-husband*, she said. She's taller than I remember. I wouldn't have to bend much to kiss her. Just a little raise on her tiptoes, and she could probably slide her arms around my neck easily.

The picture in my head is almost overwhelming.

Her arms thrown around my neck, mine wrapped around her waist, just a tiny bit of tip-toe action, and our mouths fused together perfectly.

I hear Dr. Rana explain to Jocelyn that Jude has an isolated fracture of the ulna. It's simple and stable, so it won't require surgery and won't affect the growth plate. I know all this already because I saw the x-rays. It's a clean break. Sixish weeks in a cast and the kid will be sailing the seas with his cardboard sword once more.

"Alright, folks," Dr. Rana says, "just sit tight in here and someone will be down quickly to get you all set up with a cast."

"Can he do it?" Jude asks, eyes on me, and I grin wide. He's such a cute little bugger. At least now I know I didn't terrify the kid with my word vomit.

"Wish I could, kid," I say honestly, "but it's time for me to head out." Jude's shoulders slump a little, so I add, "Next time I see you, I'll sign your cast, okay?"

With that, he perks up and gives me another nose-scrunching grin. "Kay."

"It was nice to meet you, June," I say to the quiet girl still folded up on the chair in the corner, then I turn and stick my hand out for her mom. "Jocelyn," I say as I wrap my hand around hers once more, "it's been a pleasure."

"Thanks for your help today," she says, her lips quirking up into a small smile, and my gaze latches on to the movement. It's not until Dr. Rana clears her throat, that I drop Jocelyn's hand and step back.

"Anytime," I say honestly, resisting the urge to wink at her. I nod quickly at Dr. Rana, avert my eyes, and then book it out of the room.

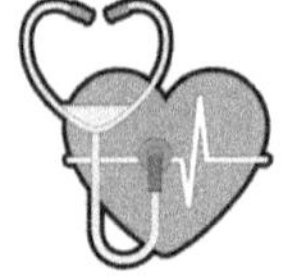

jocelyn

MY LAPTOP SCREEN glows in the darkness from its perch on the arm of our small couch.

My textbook is spread out on the coffee table, my binder of notes lies open in my lap, and I press my fingers to my temples, willing myself to get one more hour of Pharmacology in before I have to crash. If only I could sleep on my books and transfer the knowledge via osmosis.

It was after eleven by the time I got Jude and June to bed, which means getting them up and out the door tomorrow morning is going to be fun. June hates going to school these days—something I thought I wouldn't have to deal with until at least junior high—and Jude is a bear if he gets less than nine hours of sleep. Add in the fact that my patience for the week is already almost depleted, and tomorrow is going to be one hell of a Monday.

I scrub my hand over my face and take a deep breath.

I almost passed out when Patrick called me today and told me he was at the hospital with Jude. My mind immediately shot to the last time, the last call, and ice-cold dread blanketed my body.

Calm the fuck down, Lyn, Patrick had scolded. *He just fell from the counter. He's fucking fine. You don't need to freak out.*

I left work early and rushed to the hospital anyway.

I wanted to be there for Jude. I couldn't stop picturing him scared and in pain. I thought he would feel better if both of his parents were there for him, but I should have known better. Patrick cut out as soon as I stepped foot in the hospital room. The boys and beers have always taken precedence over his family. I shouldn't be surprised.

I look at the clock on my laptop screen. It's pushing two in the morning, and I've got an eight-hour shift tomorrow, plus an assignment due Tuesday. And I've accomplished next to nothing this evening.

It was already late by the time we left the hospital with Jude in his cast, so I grabbed some burgers from a drive-thru and made quick work of their bath and bedtime routines. Then it was laundry, dishes, and a quick, lukewarm shower for myself (because I'd already used up all the hot water) before I could even consider studying. Just thinking about the coming week coats my bones in cement. I'm reaching new levels of exhaustion every day.

You knew this wouldn't be easy, I tell myself. *But it will be worth it.*

I hope.

I stack my study materials on the table, then power down my laptop. I stand and stretch, then make my way toward the stairs in our three-bedroom townhouse. I pad my way up the carpeted stairs quietly, stopping first at Jude's room when I reach the landing.

I pick my way through the toys scattered on the floor of the room, grateful for the glow from his Spider-Man nightlight. He's kicked off his favorite purple blanket and he's sprawled out so that his casted arm and half his upper body hangs off the side of the bed. Even in his sleep, he doesn't stop moving. I maneuver him so that he's back on the bed, then cover his body with the blanket, taking care to lay the arm with the lime green cast on top. I study his little face, chubby cheeks and long eyelashes. I run my fingers through his sandy blond hair, the same shade as his father's, and he purses his lips and swats at me. I have to stifle a laugh, so I don't wake him.

So much about this boy is like Patrick. His impulsive nature. His fearlessness. His curiosity. Unlike June, who is in every way my mini, the only things Jude got from me are his big green eyes and his determination. I'm grateful for that. I'd like to think he got the best of both of us, but only time will tell for sure.

I press a kiss to his forehead, dodging yet another swat, and head toward June's room.

The kids were so excited when we moved in here. The apartment where we'd stayed after the initial separation wasn't big enough for them to have their own rooms. Though this townhouse is smaller than the place we shared with their father, it's a veritable palace compared to the apartment. It's brighter and cleaner too. Quieter.

I was nervous about moving onto this street, but except for the one party the neighbors threw, it's been peaceful. It has been a blessing, which is why I keep waiting for the plot twist.

I push open June's door and take a few steps toward the bed, when I hear sniffling and a rustle of sheets. I tiptoe closer and she lets out a quiet sob.

"June Bug," I whisper, dropping to my knees by her bed and pulling her to me. Her cheeks are wet with tears, and she buries her head into my shoulder while her tiny arms wrap around me. "Junie, what's wrong, sweetie?"

"It's nothing." She hiccups into my hair, and her grip around me tightens. "Just a bad dream."

"Oh, baby," I whisper, and run my hand down her hair.

These tears are my fault. I should have seen this coming. After everything that happened today—the hospital room, the doctors. I should have known it would cause this. I was so caught up in making sure Jude's injury was taken care of that I didn't think about how the whole ordeal would affect June.

"I'm so sorry, June," I whisper. "I'm so sorry. I didn't think..."

"It's okay," she says. "I'm fine."

"You don't have to be," I tell her. "You can be scared. You can cry. Today was a lot."

She doesn't say anything, but her grip on me loosens, and she straightens herself up.

"I'm okay now, Mom." Her voice is clear and steady as she wipes her cheeks with the sleeve of her pajamas. Eight going on thirty. And that's my fault too.

"Why didn't you say something earlier?" I ask. "If you were upset or frightened."

June shrugs. "I wanted to tough it out."

Tough it out. I grit my teeth and breathe once through my nose. That's a Patrick thing.

"You don't have to tough it out by yourself, June Bug." I press a kiss to her forehead, and she lies back down on her pillow. "Next time, please tell me if you're feeling bad, and I promise to try to pay closer attention. We're stronger together, and that means we have to be honest with each other. No more toughing it out alone."

I close my fist and stick out my pinky finger. "Promise?"

Her lips twitch into a smile, and she makes her own fist, then hooks her pinky with mine.

"Promise," she says, then we both lean in and press a kiss to our knuckles.

"Love you, June," I whisper as I tuck her in, then leave one last kiss on her forehead.

"Love you, Mama."

I tiptoe out of her bedroom and into my own, then crawl underneath my fluffy duvet, but sleep doesn't come. When I close my eyes, I'm transported through my memories to a couple years earlier. I hear the phone call. I hear June's muffled whimpers. I smell the antiseptic and choke on thick smoke. I toss and turn for several more minutes before I give up and silently make my way back to June's room. She's fast asleep now, and she doesn't stir as I crawl onto her twin bed and lie down beside her. I listen to her rhythmic breathing, place my hand on her back to feel her steady heartbeat, and close my eyes.

I'll stay just for a bit. Get a few hours of sleep, and then I'll wake up and sneak out before she even realizes I was here at all. Like always.

* * *

"Good morning, Roxanne," I greet as I step through her doorway with the breakfast tray.

I wasn't assigned to the hall Roxanne's room is on for my last few shifts, and things have been so crazy that I wasn't able to check on her. I'm glad to see her again, and I smile when I find that she's already dressed in a pair of red sparkly pants and a black silk blouse.

"You look wonderful today."

"I know." She grins. "You're looking rather beautiful yourself."

I shrug off the compliment. I definitely feel like an extra on *The Walking Dead*, so I'm sure I look the part, as well. I'm running on the fumes of fumes, at this point.

"Take the compliment, Jocelyn," Roxanne scolds, but I laugh it off.

"How was your night?" I set her tray up on the small table by the window. "You're progressing well with your physical therapy."

"Fine, fine," she answers from behind me, but her next words are cut off by someone bursting through the door.

"Roxanne Gunther, you are in trouble," a deep voice calls, and I straighten from the table and whip around just in time to see a large man lift Roxanne in his arms and spin her in a hug. My senses go on high alert, and my heart races in my ears while I try to quickly determine if the scene in front of me is threatening or if it is causing Roxanne pain. Then her raspy laugh breaks through the air allowing my shoulders to relax.

"Put me down, you big buffoon," she forces out between gasps of laughter, and the man carefully and gently sets her back on her feet next to her walker.

"Woman, you had me worried sick," the man scolds, and I watch, fascinated as the muscles in his wide back flex under the fabric of his shirt. "I had to hear from Ralph. Ralph!"

"Oh, phooey on Ralph. That man needs to mind his own damn business. He's such a busybody." She waves a hand at the man and shuffles around him, coming toward the table where I'm standing. When the man turns to follow her, my jaw drops and my eyes widen.

Jesse Hernandez.

Jude's "new friend." The intriguing shadow from the hospital last week. The boy with no s'mores.

The calm, professional demeanor I remember from the hospital last Sunday is gone, and instead, his shoulders are tight, his jaw is rigid, and his brows are etched with concern.

"If it weren't for Ralph, I'd have no idea what happened to you, Rox," he answers seriously. His attention is fully on the smirking red-haired woman so he hasn't noticed me yet. "I showed up today with my box of hats and your house was locked up tight. 'Stang in the garage, mail overflowing from the mailbox—I brought it for you, by the way." He pulls a bundle of envelopes out of his back pocket and hands it to her. "If Ralph hadn't been creepin' from his porch, I'd still be pacing your front lawn. I thought you'd died."

Roxanne snorts. "You know I'm too stubborn to die. Now if you'd thought I'd run off with a lover...." she winks, causing Jesse to let out an exasperated laugh.

"I'm sorry to have scared you, Jesse," she says, then takes his hand and gives it a squeeze. "I really am fine. Just a little trouble with my hip, but I should be out soon. And I'm in good hands."

Roxanne gestures my way, and before I'm ready, the full force of Jesse's attention lands on me. I don't have enough time to transform my fascinated smile into something more appropriate, but I try my best.

"Nice to see you again," I say, and his face breaks into a mischievous grin. It's Cheshire-like, the way it grows and stretches over his face.

"Jocelyn." My name rolls out of his mouth in a way that sounds almost indecent, and I have to fight back a chill. I'm immediately self-conscious, but I can't seem to tear my eyes from the man in front of me.

Man.

Definitely *not* a boy.

"You work here?" he asks, and I lamely gesture to my name badge.

"CNA," I force out. "But RN soon. Hopefully."

"Of all the assisted living facilities, in all the towns, in all the world..." he says, trailing off with a raised brow and a smirk. I snort a laugh and finish the sentence.

"And you walk into mine."

Our eyes connect and stick. I can feel my face heating, feel it creeping from my chest to my neck and ears, but I can't look away. He's got beautiful eyes. He's got beautiful everything. My breaths quicken, and I worry my lower lip with my teeth. His eyes drop to the movement.

"How do you two know each other?" Roxanne breaks in, and when I look at her, her smile is no teeth and all trouble.

"We go way back, don't we, Joss?" Jesse answers, and when I whip my eyes back to him, he's still smiling at me in a way that's charming and playful. He called me Joss. My lips quirk up.

"We do?" I question and watch transfixed as he leans his big body against the wall and shoves a hand in the pocket of his jeans.

Casual. Cool. Confident. Yet still vibrating with restrained energy. He's like neon. I bet if I stand close enough, I'll be able to hear the buzz.

Jesse is tall, well over six feet, and while his defined biceps strain against the long sleeves of his black Henley, he's not bulky. He's lean, and I'm willing to wager his arms aren't the only place on his body sporting defined muscles. He's got a jaw covered in dark, perfectly trimmed scruff, and on his head is black hair cropped close on the sides, leading to a shiny mop of unruly curls on the top. I have the urge to lift my hand and coil a strand around my fingertip. To tug on a curl to see if it springs back.

I'm stuck in the tractor beam of his attention until he turns that disarming smile on Roxanne.

"A while back, Joss's son attacked me with a sword," he deadpans, and I gasp at the same time Roxanne barks a laugh. "A *cardboard sword*," he clarifies before I can protest, "and it's cool because we're buds now. I think it was the beginning of a beautiful friendship."

"Is this the little one?" Roxanne asks me.

"Jude. He's four," I answer, then look back at Jesse. "And I'm so sorry. I didn't know he got you with the sword."

"Nah, it's nothin'," he reassures. "How's the Captain doin, anyway? Rocking the cast?"

"He's well. Pretty proud of his cast, actually." I smile, thinking of how Jude wants everyone to see his lime green plaster accessory. For the last week, I think he's felt a bit like a celebrity. When people ask about it, he preens. Unlike June, Jude doesn't shy away from attention. He seeks it out and eats it up.

"I need to come by and sign it," Jesse states with just a hint of question in his voice. He's seeking permission, without asking for it. I nod.

"Do you live next door?"

"Nah. My friend does, so I spend a good amount of time there." His eyes haven't strayed from mine, locking our gazes together. Shades of brown and green swirl in his irises between thick black eyelashes—eyelashes that people pay good money to have—and they seem to almost sparkle with mirth. I never understood the phrase "his eyes danced" until this moment. Until Jesse Hernandez. This man has dancing eyes.

"Well, next time you're visiting, then," I say, then swallow. "Jude would love if you signed his cast. He actually hasn't stopped talking about you. I've had to stop him from marching over and knocking on the door a few times since the whole sword incident."

Jesse's responding smile does weird things to my stomach. He's so attractive. *College*, I remind myself. He's still in college.

"I don't know if Riggs and Zay can handle ol' Cap'n Meatball," he jokes, and I assume he's talking about his friends who live in the townhouse. "Dylan definitely can't."

Realization dawns on me.

"Those boys helped me unload the moving truck."

Jesse's brow quirks up, his head cocks to the side, and somehow his smile grows more mischievous. He laughs lightly before saying, "*Boys* again, huh?"

I blink, and before I can ask what he means, he continues, "Yeah, they helped you move in. Riggs and Zay, anyway. Dyl probably watched from the kitchen window."

"How wonderful," Roxanne croons, "two of my favorite people in the same room."

Jesse slings his arm around her, dwarfing her entirely, and I take a minute to search their faces, looking for any sort of resemblance. I come up short. Roxanne is petite, as fair-skinned as a person can get, with pale blue eyes and fiery red dyed hair. Jesse is her opposite in almost every way. He towers over us both, with golden skin, jet black hair, and magnetic brownish green eyes. Like a mud puddle filled with pine needles.

"And how do you guys know each other?" I ask.

"I met Roxanne through Knots of Love," Jesse answers. His voice is teasing, as if we're all three in on a secret joke, and I wonder if this is Jesse Hernandez's superpower—giving everyone a sense of belonging. Making you feel welcome. Wanted. I've been in his presence for a collective total of maybe one hour, but he treats me like we've been friends all our lives. I find myself matching his smile, sharing in this amusement I don't quite understand, and I'm not even sure why. It just feels...*right*.

"The non-profit that donates knitted caps and blankets to people going through chemo?"

"That's the one," Roxanne chimes in. "I collect the donations for this area." She pauses and furrows her brow. "Oh hell, I guess I need to contact the main office and let them know I'm out of commission."

"I can take over for you," Jesse says. "I don't mind. My

classes are easy this semester. Basically just coastin' through to graduation at this point."

I file that little piece of information away. A senior. That would make him...

Twenty-two. Maybe twenty-three.

And I'm twenty-eight.

Is five years really that much?

By Hollywood standards, it's not. Five years is nothing to people who can afford to erase the effects of time. I think about June and Jude. About what my body went through to create them. What it's *still* going through to raise them. I think about my full-time job as a CNA and my second job as a nursing student. Third, if you count being a mom. I think about my lack of free weekends, my overflowing laundry basket, and my inability to recall a single popular song other than BTS, and that's only because my daughter is obsessed with them. I think of Patrick. Of the *baggage*.

Good lord.

Five years might not be a lot to some people, but with me and Jesse Hernandez, five years might as well be a century.

From beneath lowered lashes, I study him again. He's so *stylish*. Pristine Jordans on his feet. Grey, tight-fitted jeans that are cuffed at the ankle. Even his haircut is magazine worthy. Meanwhile, I consider it a win every time I take my hair down from the messy bun and Froot Loops don't fall out of it.

I resist the urge to tug at my scrubs, then stifle an exasperated laugh. Because what am I even doing worrying about my appearance? Why does it even matter?

It doesn't.

"—are the biggest donator," Roxanne says, pulling me from my thoughts. "I've never known a person who knits as much and as fast as you."

"Wait," I interrupt, then look at Jesse, "you can knit?"

"He sure can," Roxanne brags. "He's brilliant at it. One of the best who donates through me."

Jesse takes pleasure in my confusion. "That surprising?" he teases.

"Oh, uh," I fumble, "well..." I raise my eyebrows and give an apologetic shrug. "Yeah, it kind of is."

"You think I'd be better suited to, what, play sports? I'm a little short for basketball, but I'm prime height for QB." The humor in his voice is apparent in every dramatic pause, every drawn-out syllable. I shrug again, and he chuckles. "Believe it or not, Joss, organized team sports are not my jam."

I don't believe it. I mean, look at him—he's built like an athlete. He looks like he could have walked right off a court or a field or out of some ESPN player interview broadcast. Muscled and toned and honed to perfection. Plus, that height? The charm? The cocky swagger?

My facial expression must give away my thoughts because he puffs out his chest and sports a positively wicked grin.

"I'm good at many, many things," he says slowly, suggestively, "but sports aren't one of them."

I want to ask him what else he might be good at, but I hold my tongue. I don't have much experience with flirting. Not since I was a naïve sixteen-year-old, and even then, I was bad at it. But if Jesse wasn't an attractive, twenty-three-year-old college student, and I wasn't, well, *me*, I'd possibly, *maybe*, think he might be flirting with me. But probably not.

I clear my throat, suddenly parched, and blink a few times to wet my dry eyes. I scramble for something to say, but all I can muster is an awkward, breathy laugh.

"I'm so happy that you two know each other," Roxanne breaks in and looks at me. "Once I make parole, you'll have to come over and join Jesse and me for a game of Euchre."

"Parole?" Jesse chuckles. "This isn't prison, Rox."

Before Roxanne can respond, I make my way to the door. "I have to finish up my rounds, Roxanne," I tell her with my body already half out the door. "I'll stop back in later but call if you need anything." I smile at Roxanne, then turn to Jesse. "It was nice to see you again."

"It was my pleasure," he says, and just as I turn to walk out the door, he adds, "See you soon, Classic."

jesse

THAT BODY.

Fuck, that body.

I've been thinking about it nonstop. Scrubs have never looked so fucking sexy. Long legs, thick thighs, big hips, a snatched waist, and full breasts.

An Old Hollywood hourglass figure.

Marilyn Monroe.

Sophia Loren's got nothing on Jocelyn Calligaris.

She's classic.

Thank god I'm done with all my med school requisite classes, because I haven't been able to focus on shit. I keep picturing Jocelyn in one of those vintage one-piece swimsuits painted on the side of a fighter plane.

Nose Art Jocelyn. Pinup Girl Jocelyn.

I groan inwardly.

I even tried to sketch it, but I'm shit at drawing, so my fighter plane ended up looking like a dildo and the nose art resembled a three-year-old's sidewalk chalk stick figure. But with big tits.

Kelley laughed for hours when he saw it, but fuck him, because Jocelyn Calligaris owns my brain right now.

I can't even knit. Every time I pick up my needles, I end up zoning out and replaying our encounter in Roxanne's room. The ER exchange has earned a permanent place in my replay reel of fuck-ups. I haven't been that awkward since I was fifteen and stumbling over my own spaghetti limbs.

They don't trust me around a knife.

Seriously, what the actual fuck was that.

What. The. *Actual.* Fuck.

I was supposed to be the knowledgeable medical professional in that scenario, and instead I acted like an incompetent asshat who'd never been around a pretty girl before.

I groan and rake my fingers through my hair. I was two seconds away from dropping some cringey pick-up lines. Or tripping over my jelly legs and faceplanting at her feet.

Thankfully, I found my balls. Got my groove back. Sway in full force.

It's nine in the morning when I knock on Riggs's door. I know for a fact he's at Bailey's because Ivy stayed at our place with Kelley last night, but Zay doesn't need to know that I know.

When there's no answer, I knock again, then check out the townhouse next door while I wait. There's a wooden sunflower propped haphazardly on the porch with the word *Welcome* written on it, but other than that, there's nothing that sets Jocelyn's home apart from any of the others on this cul-de-sac. It's also quiet, probably because it's 9 a.m. on a Saturday.

Do kids still watch Saturday morning cartoons? Nickelodeon Saturday mornings were fucking tight when I was a kid. What was that show with the little dudes who rode skateboards?

"What the hell are you doing here?" Xavier asks when he opens the door. He's wearing a pair of BU baseball sweatpants, and his face is still rumpled from sleep. His hair sticks up on one side, making him look kinda like one of those birds with the crazy feathers on their heads. Cockatiel? Cockatoo? Whatever. Never seen him so disheveled.

"Nice crest, Polly." I push my way through the door and kick off my shoes. "You have a game later. I knew you'd be up."

"At four," he grumbles, following me into the kitchen where I drop a paper bag on the counter. "Dyl's still sleeping. Riggs isn't even *here*."

I pull a bagel sandwich out of the bag and toss it to him. He catches it with one hand.

"Now that our besties are loved up and abandoned us, you and me are besties now, Z." I pull out my own bagel sandwich, then toss the third in the fridge.

"**X**avier," he says, emphasizing the X.

"Eat the food I brought, you ungrateful dick." I smile big, then make my way into the living room.

I pull open the curtains on the big window—the one that just so happens to face Jocelyn's house—and prop myself on the end of the couch. From this spot, I can see Jocelyn's front porch. Could probably see right into her own living room window if the curtains were open, but that's a voyeur-level line I'm not gonna cross.

I have a mission to accomplish, not a creepy obsession.

I'm just watching so I know when I can head over to sign Meatball's cast. I told the kid I would. After scaring the shit out of him and almost making him cry, it's the least I can do.

This definitely has nothing to do with me having a crush on *The Hot Mom.*

Even if I might have a small crush on her.

Once I'm settled, I grab the TV remote off the coffee table, then glance at Zay. He's still standing where I left him, holding the bagel sandwich in one hand and staring at me with a furrowed brow. I unwrap my sandwich and take a bite.

"Saturday morning cartoons," I mumble as I chew and flip on the TV. Zay sighs and disappears back into the kitchen, before reappearing a few seconds later with plates and paper towels. He drops one of each in my lap, then throws himself onto the couch without another word.

Dylan stumbles down an hour later and joins us, and we watch cartoons until movement in front of Jocelyn's house catches my eye, and I turn my full attention to it.

A big, black truck pulls up to the curb and parks, then the guy from the hospital—Patrick, the **ex**-husband—gets out and rounds the back door. When he opens it, June hops out, then the guy pulls out Jude. He then drops two small duffle bags on the ground and pulls out a car seat.

He's dropping them off.

I smile inwardly at my luck—I hadn't even considered the kids might not be home—when Jocelyn comes rushing out the door wearing scrubs and no shoes. She motions for the kids to go inside, then rounds on the ex with her hands on her hips.

When it's obvious they've started arguing, I almost open the window, so I can listen in. But I don't because Dr. Vanessa Hernandez would beat my ass if she knew I was shamefully invading someone's privacy.

Woman's never touched me like that but I still live in fear of the possibility every day. Doesn't matter that she's five-nothing and a buck ten, my mom can be fucking terrifying.

I smile at the thought. *Lil beast.*

The smile falls when I see Jocelyn wrap her arms around her torso and shake her head. Her body language puts me on edge.

But nothing pisses me off more than the hard set of the ex's shoulders and the patronizing look on his face.

His mouth moves again, and her shoulders slump. She presses her fingers to her temples and says something else, then the ex gets back in his truck and peels away. Jocelyn stands outside a few more minutes, idly looking at the ground, then turns and walks slowly into the house.

"Prick," Zay says, and I turn to see that both he and Dylan are watching out the window too. His disgust is more emotion than I'm used to from Xavier, and I nod my agreement.

"Pretty sure he's a cop," Dylan adds.

"Why?"

He shrugs, plopping back down in his chair. "Seen him come by a few times. Random times. Usually at night. Sometimes he's in a cop car."

"You sure it's him?"

"Yeah," he nods and starts scrolling mindlessly through his phone, "never stays long."

I let that sink in. She still sleeping with the ex? I head toward the door.

"I'll see you guys later," I call over my shoulder. "Have fun with your balls tonight." I slip on my shoes and walk out the door.

I'm on the neighbor's porch in ten steps, knocking before I can think it through and looking into June's upturned, blank face within seconds.

"Hey," I greet. "I came by to sign Meatball's cast."

"Hold on," she mumbles, then shuts the door on me. I stick my hands in my pockets and shift my weight from foot to foot. Not exactly the kind of welcome I was picturing.

A minute later, the captain himself opens the door and tackles my legs in a hug. I chuckle and ruffle his hair. This is more like it.

"What's up, *Capi*? I came by to sign your cast." I wave the marker I brought in the air.

"*Capi*," he says with a giggle. "What's a *capi*?"

"You know, like a little nickname. Short for captain, but in Spanish."

"Cool! *Capi*!" He smiles, then grabs my wrist with his un-casted hand and pulls me into the house. The layout is exactly like Riggs' townhouse, but inverted, so when Jude drags me down the hallway, I know we'll end up in the living room. He pulls me to the couch and pushes me down on it, then sits next to me and puts his lime green plaster casted arm in my lap.

"So, where's your mom, Meatball?" I ask, noticing the kitchen is empty of both Jocelyn and June. I gesture to his cast. "This is sick. Is green your favorite color?"

"Upstairs on the phone. My favorite color is purple."

"Yeah? Why'd you go with green?"

Jude shrugs. "Dad says no purple."

The fuck? I'm not even going to ask.

"Alright, you ready?" I survey his cast. The only other signatures on it are his mom's, dad's, and sister's.

"Ready!"

I tap the marker on a blank spot on his forearm. "I'm claiming this spot."

"Kay." He squirms on the cushion next to me.

I scribble on his cast, finishing the last letter in my name just as Jocelyn rounds the corner into the living room. When our eyes catch, she stops in her tracks and her mouth drops.

"Jesse?"

"Classic," I greet with a grin. "Came by to sign Captain Meatball's cast." I lift Jude's arm and give it a little wiggle, making him laugh. Her eyes go from me to Jude then back to me again.

"Oh. Well." She scrunches up her eyebrows and cocks her head to the side a smidge. "Hi?"

"Hi." I laugh, then gesture to her scrubs, making sure not to stare. "You work today?"

"No." She glances down at her body. "I'm supposed to have a clinical, but..." She trails off.

"But...?" I stand up from the couch. Jude does too, and he mirrors my stance. Cute little bugger. I knock him lightly with my leg, and he giggles.

"Well, the kids were supposed to be with Patrick today, and I can't find a babysitter." She worries her lip. She doesn't want to get into it, but it's obvious she's bummed about having to miss a clinical. The hours are probably required for whatever program she's in and missing could really fuck up her grade. I make up my mind a fraction of a second before I speak.

"I can watch them," I offer, and her eyes widen, and she starts to protest.

"Oh, no, that's—"

"Please, Mom! Please?" Jude cuts her off and she narrows her eyes at him. He doesn't take the hint. "Please can he, Mom? I'll be so good. I'll be the most good and I'll make Doonie be nice and I'll pick up all the things when I'm done. He can be here a day an a morrow."

A day an a morrow? I chuckle. I'm gonna need a translator with this kid.

"It's not a problem," I assure her with a smile.

She shakes her head again. "That's very kind, Jesse, and no offense, I'm sure you're great, but I really don't know you."

"You kinda do, though," I reason. "You know a lot about me."

"I do?"

"Sure. You know I'm a pre-med student at Butler and I shadowed Dr. Rana. I also volunteer at Kindred Spirit Hospital, and to be approved for that I had to have a background check done and be up-to-date on all my vaccinations. You know I knit and donate hats to Knots of Love through Roxanne, and you know that Roxanne adores me."

When she doesn't immediately cut me off, I continue.

"Some other notable stuff to help my case... I've been accepted to Harvard Med, which, not to brag, is pretty baller because they only have an acceptance rate of 3.5%. My mom and dad both work in the medical field. I speak conversational Spanish. I have an IQ of 160. I've never had a speeding ticket. I'm an only child. I can play the guitar and the piano, but I'm a horrible singer, and I recently discovered that I have a love of old movies and I kind of envy Cary Grant."

And not in small part because Cary Grant and Sophia Loren had a torrid love affair.

See? Owns. My. Brain.

Jocelyn's lips twitch at the corners, but her face is still scrunched, forming two little backward parentheses between her eyebrows. I put on my best *respectable and trustworthy adult* smile. I really did just tell her basically everything impressive about myself, so this feels sorta like an informal job interview, and just like with a job interview, the stuff I purposely left out nags at me.

"How important are these clinical hours?" I ask seriously, and her face falls.

"Extremely important."

"And you have no one else to watch J-Squared?"

She laughs lightly at the new nickname but shakes her head in confirmation. "No one."

"Then I'm your guy, Classic. I'll watch your minis. You can FaceTime us every hour if you want."

She takes a deep breath, brow furrowed, eyes trained on the ground as she works things out in her head.

"I'm serious. FaceTime us every hour. Every thirty minutes," I reassure, and she sighs.

"Let me talk to the kids first."

"I'm okay with it!" Jude shouts, and I reach down and pat his head like a little puppy.

"It's fine," a small voice adds from the hallway, and when I look toward it, I find June leaning quietly on the wall. Not sure how long she's been there. Jocelyn takes another deep breath. Then she looks at me again. I want to reach up and smooth away those little lines between her eyebrows.

"It's a twelve-hour clinical," she says.

"It's cool."

"I won't be home until late."

"I said it's cool, Joss. I've got nowhere to be." Other than Riggs's game, but he won't care if I miss it.

"You'll have to feed them," she continues.

I smirk. "I think I can manage."

Her vibrant green eyes bounce between mine, and I can see the exact moment she makes up her mind and gives in. I don't hide my smile.

After giving me a brief rundown of info (emergency contact numbers—including her cell, *score*, the location of the first-aid kit, the kids' regular routine, etc. etc. etc.), Jocelyn leaves me with her kids for a twelve-hour stretch of time. I'm nervous as hell.

Once she's out the door, I turn to J-Squared.

"What should we do today, squad?"

"Do you have kids?" Jude asks, catching me off guard.

"Nope."

"Why not?"

I shrug. "Not ready for 'em."

"Why not?"

I shrug again. "Too young for kids."

"Mom was twenty," June pipes up, and when I look at her, her face is pensive. What the fuck do I say to that?

"My birthday is in a couple a days," Jude continues.

"Oh cool!" I say, but when I look at June, she shakes her head no.

"It's not for months," she says coolly, but Jude just keeps jabbering, unfazed.

"Do you have a scooter?"

"No."

"Why?"

"Don't need one."

"Why?"

"Got legs."

"Scooters are funner than legs."

"That's true." He's right. They *are* funner than legs. My legs, anyway, but Jocelyn's legs...

"I have one at my dad's, but I have to leave it there 'cause I can't bring it here 'cause my dad says so 'cause he paid for it and not Mom."

I look at June, and she gives me a curt nod. Man, fuck that guy. I'm sure he does make Jude leave it there. Sounds like something a dick would do.

"Do you have a dog?" Jude continues. I don't think this kid has taken a breath. "I'm gonna have a dog at my dad's for my birthday."

I get another head shake and a scowl from June. "Dad says no dogs."

"Well, I don't have a dog either," I tell him, and he screws his face up in displeasure.

"Do you have a rabbit?"

"No."

"A turtle?"

My lips twitch at the way his eyes have grown in disbelief. "Nope."

"A squirrel?" His voice is shocked, and I shake my head, trying not to laugh. *A squirrel?*

"I don't have any pets at all."

"Why? Don't you like aminals?"

For the life of me, I don't know how to answer. Because I *do* like aminals, so why *don't* I have one? A dog or a turtle or even a hedgehog. I follow a hedgehog on social media. His name is Horace, and his human is always putting little hats on him. It's so cute. I could def see myself as a hedgehog dad.

"What's your superpower?" Jude asks, changing topics. And I thought my brain moved fast.

"My superpower?"

"Mom says everyone has a superpower," June adds, and Jude wiggles in agreement.

"What's yours?" I ask the kids, and Jude bounces up and down.

"I'm *emengenetic!*" he shouts. I raise a brow and look toward June. She sighs loudly. I bet she and Bailey would get along great.

"Energetic," she translates, and I nod. That makes sense.

"And you?" I look toward June, and she rolls her eyes.

"I'm *observant,*" she says flatly.

"That's a really good superpower," I tell her, and her shoulders perk up slightly. "What's your mom's superpower?"

"She's our mom," Jude says, his tone very matter of fact. Very, *duh Jesse, isn't it obvious?* I ruffle his hair. It should have been obvious.

"Can you really speak Spanish?" June chimes in.

"*Sí, princesa.*" I wink at her.

"Is that princess?" Her nose scrunches up and she looks like a tinier version of her mom.

"What's wrong with princesses? Princesses are badass."

Jude giggles, and I wince. Note to self: don't cuss around the kid.

"I don't like dresses and girly pink things and crowns," June says without missing a beat. I laugh at the utter disgust in her voice. Girl must really hate pink.

"Princesses aren't just dresses and pink and crowns. They also do things like charity, foreign policy, diplomacy. They help run whole entire countries, June. That's a lot of responsibility. That's bada— uh, that's cool."

Her face stays scrunched like she's smelled something rancid.

"Not sold?"

She shakes her head no.

"For the record, I think pink is a cool color. But, how about *caballera?*"

She arches an eyebrow. "What's that?"

"A knight in shining armor." *Kind of.* There's no feminine word for knight in Spanish, but I don't tell her that. A smile stretches across her face. The first I've seen from her. I smile back.

"What about me?" Jude asks, giving my arm a tug. "What can I be?"

"Hmmm." I rub my chin and pretend to think. "You can be.... *pequeño pirata.*"

"Penguin Pirate?" he shouts with a giggle.

"Tiny pirate," I correct, and he frowns.

"Strong pirate?" I try again.

"Yes!"

"*Pirata fuerte,*" I announce, and Jude repeats it. "Okay," I redirect, "what do you guys

usually do on Saturdays?"

"Stuff," June says with a shrug, and I watch as she sits on

the love seat, pulls her lanky legs up under her giant sweatshirt, and wraps her arms around herself, doing that same shrinking thing she did at the hospital.

She looks like a Weeble. The ones that wobble but don't fall down. I have to resist the urge to give her a light shove because, realistically, I know that while she'll definitely wobble, she'll also likely fall down. And we don't need another broken bone.

"You wanna do slime?" Jude asks, the "l" sounding very much like a "w", and when I ask what slime is, he gets up and runs down the hall and up the stairs. Minutes later, he's back in front of me with his arms full of tiny colorful plastic containers. He drops them on the coffee table and then hits me with that little nose-scrunching smile. "Slime!"

* * *

The sound of a click wakes me up, and when I open my eyes, I see Jocelyn standing above me holding a heavy-duty looking black camera. She smiles, and in the dark of the living room, haloed by the glow of the television, she looks straight out of a black and white film.

Muted colors and high contrast shadows. Soft and stark. Fascinating.

Classic.

I blink and move to sit up but remember the *pirata fuerte* on my chest. Jocelyn puts her finger to her lips then points to the ceiling, so I slowly maneuver my hands around Jude's body and stand with him cradled in my arms.

I follow Jocelyn through the living room and down the hall-way, careful not to step on one of the many, many toys strewn about the floor. I follow her up the stairs and into Jude's room, then I wait while she tugs back the comforter on his bed. I lay him on the mattress and pull the blanket back over him, dodging quickly when he swats at my head. I widen my eyes at Joss, and she covers her smile with her hand. I narrow my eyes and shake my head, then walk back into the hallway.

Jocelyn comes back out of the room and opens the door across the hall. She peers inside to check on June, then gestures for me to follow her back downstairs.

"How'd it go?" she asks once we're down the stairs.

"Good," I say with a grin. She knows it went well. She Face-Timed almost every hour.

Once we're in the living room, she flips on a small lamp, and I watch her survey the room. When I look around, I feel terrible and also embarrassed. It's a disaster.

"Shit, Joss, I'm sorry," I say, and scramble to start tidying up. "I planned to clean up before you got home, but we fell asleep watching that troll movie."

I start putting the cushions back on the couch that are scattered all about the floor from when we played The Floor is Lava. The coffee table is covered in crayons and construction paper, there are blankets draped over the kitchen table from our fort, and I know there are plastic blocks underneath it. Plus, the sink is not only full of dirty dishes, but also full of slime. And the kitchen counter is littered with empty juice pouches and pizza boxes.

Shit.

Jocelyn's house looks like a kindergartener's version of a frat party.

"It's okay," she says with a tired chuckle. "I've seen it worse, trust me." She pulls the blankets from the kitchen table to fold them, so I start on the coffee table. I put the crayons back in the box and begin gathering up the construction paper, when my eyes catch on handwriting that I didn't notice before.

It's a loopy, slanted hybrid of cursive and print, capitals and lowercase, and it was done by a practiced hand, which tells me it's Jocelyn's handwriting. I peek toward the kitchen. Joss is under the table now picking up blocks, so I look back at the paper.

Underlined at the top of the page are the words "Be A Full Person."

Underneath is a bulleted list that I scan quickly. Most of these things don't make sense to me. Items like "Find MY Music," "Rib Tatt," and "Back to Photography" have me squinting in confusion, but the item at the bottom makes my heart jump right into my throat.

Sex.

And not just *sex*, but SEX!!!

In all caps and with three exclamation marks after it. I'm trying to unswallow my tongue when Jocelyn comes into view, causing me to jump like an idiot and bash my knee into the coffee table.

"Shoot, are you okay?" she asks. "I didn't mean to startle you." She rushes toward me, and I cover the list with a few other pieces of construction paper.

"It's fine," I say, and quickly stand, leaving the stack of papers on the coffee table. "I'll wash the dishes."

"You don't have to do that," she says as I make my way to the sink. "You should head out. I got this stuff."

"Nah." I start organizing the dishes the same way I do at my place. Pots and pans first, then plates, bowls, cups, and utensils last. I plug up the sink and start to fill it halfway with water, just like my dad does. "I was here with them. I helped make the mess. You shouldn't have to clean it by yourself."

I feel her come stand beside me. "You wash, and I'll dry and put away, then?"

"Sounds good." I don't mention the dishwasher that's a few feet away, and she doesn't either.

We fall into a routine—I scrub, rinse, and pass—and the whole time, we talk.

Jocelyn tells me that she's working as a CNA and taking courses online to become a licensed RN, finishing up the program she started but couldn't complete once she got pregnant with Jude. And because, as she says, "life happened." I don't pry. Not because I'm not curious—I am. I fucking am—but because I don't want to say or do anything that could stop her from talking.

She asks me about med school, and I tell her the truth. Something I haven't told anyone. I haven't committed to any of them yet. Sure, it will probably be Harvard. Why wouldn't it be? It's the top med school in the fucking country. But I've got a couple weeks before I have to make the final decision.

"Commitment phobic?" she teases, and I laugh.

"Probably," I say honestly. Not because I'm uncertain of what I want. I am. Medicine is the only thing that's held my attention for longer than a few months, because there is always something new to learn. Med school is the only thing I've ever been sure of, but... Once I commit to a school, that's it.

Official adulthood.

I've thought about taking a gap year, but I know myself well enough to worry that one gap year will turn into two, then three, then I'll end up another former "gifted kid" who squandered their potential on half-explored interests and forgotten hobbies. I wince at the invasion of memories. The windowsill lined with potted plants, the old metal desk, the encouraging words. I hate that my career drive was so influenced by *her*. I feel guilty for considering any of that experience good. God, it was all so fucked up. I want to reach into my pocket, but even that pisses me off.

Kelley says I would have been drawn to medicine anyway because my family is so established in the field. Ivy says it's okay to be grateful for *that* influence because *that* influence was genuine. Expected, even. It's the other stuff that—

I blink out of my thoughts and hand Jocelyn the last piece of silverware, then drain the sink.

"Not ready to fully enter the land of adulting?" Her back is to me when she asks, and for some reason, I'm grateful for that.

I laugh. "Is anyone ever?"

"Some people aren't really given the choice," she replies. Her voice is quiet, flat, and I don't know how to respond. She inhales, then turns to me. "Why do you smell like peanut butter?"

"Huh?" I ask, milliseconds before it dawns on me, and my cheeks heat as an embarrassed smile stretches over my face. "Oh, that..."

She watches me, waiting.

"Well, Meatball wanted to play with that slime stuff, and he kinda got some in my hair."

"*Okay...?*"

"Well, I needed to get it out, right? And Google said the oils in peanut butter were a good way to get slime out of hair, so we used peanut butter."

"You put peanut butter in your hair"—she pulls her lower lip into her mouth and bites down, her eyes sparkling with repressed laughter—"to remove the slime?"

"Yeah," I admit. "It worked too."

"Did you try soap first?" she asks slowly. "Shampoo?"

My face falls. "Don't tell me I could have just used soap."

Her laugh breaks free, deep and full-bodied, and I don't care that I had to slather peanut butter all up in my hair if it means I got to hear this sound.

"I've had to get slime out of Jude's hair several times. June's once, and even mine once," she explains after she's caught her breath. "Shampoo and conditioner work just fine." She swipes her fingers under her eyes, then hits me with a more subdued smile. "Thanks again for your help today." She reaches into her scrubs pocket and pulls out a wad of cash, then tries to hand it to me.

"No way." I throw my hands up and take a step back. "I offered to help. I don't want money for it."

"You have to let me pay you, Jesse," she argues, and steps toward me, arm outstretched. I swat her hand away playfully and dart out of the kitchen. Her answering bark of laughter makes me smile.

"I don't want your money, Classic. I had fun with your minis. If you want to do something for me, let me put your name down as a job reference. I need more peds experience."

She eyes me skeptically. "You already got into med school, Jesse. You don't need to build up your applications."

"On my CV," I correct, referencing the longer, more comprehensive version of a résumé, and she sighs.

"Okay," she relents, and puts the money back in her pocket. "Thank you."

"Same time tomorrow?"

Her eyes widen when I ask. "What? No, that's okay. I don't exp—"

"You got a clinical tomorrow?"

"Yeah."

"You got someone to watch J-Squared?"

"I was going to call Patrick."

I shake my head. Fuck that guy. "Nah. Don't bother with the ex. I'll be here tomorrow." I make my way toward the door.

"You're sure?"

"Totally." I slip on my shoes, then turn back to her. "What's with the camera?"

She opens her mouth, then closes it. Studies me. Then says, "Roxanne loaned it to me. I'm...taking some of her advice."

"What is it?" I crack the door open, and she leans on the hallway wall.

She speaks slowly and clearly. "To be a full person."

The list. Well, okay then. I open the door and step backwards onto the porch.

"See you in the morning, Jocelyn."

"See you in the morning."

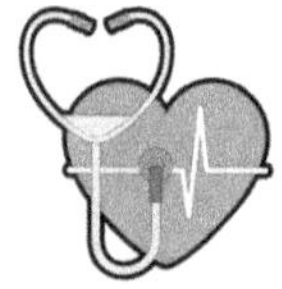

jocelyn

"IS JESSE COMING TODAY?" Jude asks as I place his breakfast plate in front of him.

"He is."

"YES!"

"I'm glad you're excited."

I was a nervous wreck through the first half of my clinical yesterday, but after the fifth laughter and smile-filled video call, I was able to loosen up. I was relieved to hear that the kids had a good time with Jesse. It was the first thing I asked when they woke up this morning, and then I was filled in on all the fun things that took place while I was gone. Even June was happy because Jesse let her put his hair in ponytails while they watched *Frozen*.

"But does he have to cook again?" The look June gives me tells me she really, really hopes the answer is no.

"What's that face for?"

"Mom. He put a bunch of vegetables in a pot and said it was Martian Stew."

I choke on my coffee. "He what?"

June and Jude start talking at once.

"He dumped cans of green beans and peas—"

"—and lime beans!"

"And lima beans into a pot and tried to make it our dinner."

"They're healthy and help our moon systems fight sinuses."

"Viruses, Jude. And he said it was Martian Stew—"

"Martians are green!"

"Yeah, because Martians are green, and the veggies are green—"

"And you'll be 'mart—"

"Yeah, and vegetables help with brain development."

"And big brains make you 'mart."

By the time they've finished filling me in on Jesse's mealtime indiscretion, June looks positively insulted.

"He tried to make *that* our dinner, Mom."

"Did you eat it?" I ask, trying to wrangle my laugh. I'm more curious than anything else.

"Ew. No." June sticks her tongue out and closes her eyes tight.

"We got pizza!" Jude shouts with glee.

Ah. So *that's* why Jesse ordered pizza last night. And here I thought it was just because he wanted pizza for dinner, and not because my children rejected his Martian Stew.

"He is going to have to do dinner with you, but I'll make sure he knows what to make, okay?" I should have done that yesterday before I left, but everything happened so quickly that it slipped my mind.

Martian Stew? What on Earth.

The doorbell rings, and Jude shoots from the table.

"I'LL GET IT!" he yells as he darts toward the front door.

Seconds later, Jesse is sauntering into my kitchen, hand held hostage by Jude, wearing a shirt that says "Ask me about my feminist agenda," red and black Nikes, and joggers. His hair is tousled, and he's got that permanent smirk affixed to his face. I smirk back.

"Martian stew?"

He bites his lip and looks at the ceiling, then glances playfully at June and Jude.

"Snitches," he teases, then puts all his attention on me. "I'm not much of a cook, but I know the food pyramid. It was an honest attempt, at least."

"You could have texted me."

"Didn't want to distract you. Clinicals are important."

I shake my head. "Well, come here, Gordon Ramsey, and I'll give you instructions for dinner before I head out."

My smile carries through the day, despite it being grueling. I enjoy clinicals. I'm good at my job and having the CNA experience helps immensely. But it's still stressful. It's still exhausting. It's still *work*.

I was lucky to get into this CNA to RN bridge program. I can do most of the coursework online, and any clinicals I can't complete at Harvest View, I'm able to do on the weekends with the nursing school at Butler U. If everything goes as planned, I'll be done with the program, have passed my NCLEX exam, and will be a registered nurse by July.

I just have to make it to the end.

I swear, though, Patrick is doing everything in his power to hinder my plans. The crap he pulled this weekend? He knows I need these hours, but that didn't stop him yesterday from feigning illness and dropping the kids at my door an hour before I had to leave the house. I know he doesn't want this for me. He doesn't want me to have any independence from him. He thinks that with the increased pay, I'll be able to rely on him less.

He's right.

It's one of the reasons I gave in and let Jesse watch the kids, despite my anxiety over leaving them. Finishing this bridge program is the next necessary step toward freedom from Patrick.

I tried to get my Bachelor of Science in Nursing a few years ago but got pregnant with Jude and ended up dropping out. I don't regret Jude. I love him. But I wasn't trying to get pregnant. I was taking precautions to avoid it, and I've always had the sneaking suspicion that Patrick did something...

I don't know what. I don't know how.

All I know is, he was real quick to use guilt trips and gaslighting to push for me dropping out of school as soon as we saw two pink lines on the pee stick. The sweet words that dripped from his tongue, honeyed up to sound like concern and love, hadn't fooled me for a long time, but they still affected me. It's like he knew I was trying to find a way out for June and me, and he needed to find a way to tighten the leash. Fortify the lock.

I love Jude, and I will never, ever, tell anyone this.

But I cried for days afterward.

I resented the pregnancy. Resented Patrick. Resented my foster parents and the naïve girl I was back then. Resented how it was always one step forward, five steps back.

When I met Patrick, he was eighteen and charming and beautiful. I was sixteen and awkward, and lonely, and I just felt lucky to be seen.

To be wanted.

Bouncing around from foster home to foster home my whole childhood, by the time I transferred to Patrick's high school, I'd gotten used to being alone. The feeling of being unwanted was a familiar one. But when Patrick set his sights on me the third day of school, it all changed. It was a heady experience, feeling like the center of someone's world, and I was too young to recognize the red flags.

This gorgeous, popular, adored senior wanted *me*. The girl whom no one wanted. Not even her parents. I couldn't believe my luck.

Patrick quickly became my everything.

My *only* thing.

He made sure of it.

It took me years to realize that he wasn't my savior, but my captor.

"Ooof, this day," Demi says, pulling me from my thoughts. She's in my program, so we've done a few clinicals together.

"Yeah, it was rough." I sigh. "I'll be glad to get home. My feet are killing me."

"I can't believe that one guy. Hitting on us while we were putting in his catheter?" She widens her eyes and shakes her head. "Some of the shit we've seen makes me wonder if we'll ever be prepared."

I huff out a laugh. That whole experience was definitely awkward. Thank god, it's over.

"I also think our preceptor might hate me a little."

"Girl, same," Demi says. "We're almost done, though. Eye on the prize. Won't be long now."

"I know. I'm so ready." I'm so close to the finish line that I'm constantly on the lookout for someone trying to trip me up. Someone with buzzed blond hair and a police officer's badge.

Demi and I walk to our cars in the parking lot, the night air is crisp and sets a chill through my bones. I climb in my car and wave goodbye, then hook up my music streaming app.

I've been compiling a playlist from the random songs the app has played me. The more songs I "like," the more curated the music selection becomes. I've found some songs and artists that I really like, and I'm thrilled that basically none of them are country.

It's a strange thing to be excited about, developing a music taste independent from Patrick's influence, but it fills me with pride, nonetheless. For years, I was so wrapped up in him that I didn't know where I ended and he began.

At first it was comforting. It made me feel safe and loved. Like I had something to depend on. But at some point, it changed; I felt stifled. Isolated. *Erased.*

I still don't know if it happened gradually or all at once, but either way, I didn't recognize it until it was too late.

Be a full person.

I turn up the radio and head home.

The house is dark when I pull up, quiet when I unlock the door and step inside. I prepare myself for another disaster like the one from last night—toys and crayons and snacks littering every surface—but I find a tidy, empty living room instead. I turn toward the kitchen and find Jesse knitting at the table. He looks up when he sees me, and the smile that stretches across his face makes my knees wobble. It's painfully unfair how beautiful he is.

"Hey," I half-whisper, setting my bag on the counter. "How were they?"

"Great," he says, and leans back in his chair. "We had a good time. Read about fifty books. Played pirates—I hid the sword under the couch—and we drew some pictures." He nods in the direction of the refrigerator, and I turn to find that it's covered in construction paper art. "All in all, it was a great Sunday."

I scan the pictures, and one jumps out so suddenly that my eyes flash and my breath hitches. To someone unfamiliar with Jude's drawings, it would just look like a bunch of circles and lines with scribbled faces. But I've spent hours upon hours admiring Jude's work, so I know exactly what this picture displays.

In purple crayon on yellow construction paper, Jude has drawn a picture of himself and June smiling happily next to a tall figure with curly hair. Jesse. But what really gets me is that I'm there too, standing next to Jesse, and we're holding hands. I squint at the small brown blob drawn on Jesse's shoulder.

"That's a squirrel," Jesse says, following my gaze to the picture. "Her name is Frank."

"Frank the Squirrel?" I ask, and Jesse just grins.

"Dinner went well," he says. "Thanks for the tips. Can't wait to use my new skills for my roommate."

I smile. "Your roommate likes dino nuggies and mac and cheese?"

"New favorite meal for sure."

When he stands, I avert my eyes back to the kitchen. "Thank you. For cleaning up and everything. I really appreciate it." The sink is empty, the counters are wiped down. It's cleaner than it usually is.

"No problem." I feel him move toward me, stopping just a few feet away. "Just remember to talk me up when you get called as a reference."

I laugh lightly. "Of course."

I hear the sound of paper sliding on the counter, and when I look toward the sound, my face heats and my eyes jump to Jesse's. "Where'd you get that?"

My words bite, but Jesse's smile is smooth, not an ounce of contrition. "Found it in a stack of construction paper yesterday. Today, I saved it from being turned into a portrait of Frank the Squirrel and her little squirrel posse."

I snatch it from him and pull it to my chest. I shouldn't be embarrassed that he's seen my list. There's nothing wrong with it. But it's personal, and maybe I still feel a little guilty about it, about wanting to find some sort of identity outside of my kids. Does that make me a terrible mom? To wish for more than just motherhood?

And the last thing on the list…

My cheeks grow hotter. This man is beautiful, and young, and judging from his confident swagger, has probably no shortage of opportunities to explore sexual urges. To have my inexperience and desire so boldly identified in all caps fills me with a shame I don't quite understand.

"Thanks," I force out, then turn to shove it in my purse.

"That's what the camera is for? Roxanne's advice?" I don't answer, and he continues, "It's like a to-do list? A wish list?"

I sigh and meet his eyes. "Yeah, kind of. Just trying to find myself, I guess."

He nods like he gets it, though I'm not sure how he could, then scans my face. I look away. I can tell he wants to say more. Whether it's to tease me or to ask me questions, I'm not sure, but the look in his eye tells me he's not finished with this topic.

I shift my weight and brace myself. I've never been good with boundaries. I've always been a *grin and bear it* kind of person. Avoid the confrontation. Go along with whatever, just so it doesn't get uncomfortable for everyone else.

But that's how I got to this point, right?

I've always let things happen to me, instead of making them happen for myself, and that's not who I want to be anymore. That's not the example I want to set for my kids. For June.

So, this time, instead of being passive, I take a deep breath and speak up for myself.

"It's personal," I say to the ceiling, then force myself to meet Jesse's eyes. "I'm not really comfortable talking about it."

I watch his face, wait for any signs of anger or disappointment, even straighten my spine to better absorb any snide comments. But I'm surprised when he smiles and nods instead.

"Cool," Jesse says, and his deep voice is genuine. "If you ever do want to talk, I'd love to hear about it." I blink, and his smile grows at my obvious confusion.

"How old are you?" I blurt, and I wince at my rudeness, but he laughs.

"I turned twenty-three in December," he answers, then points to his chest. "Sagittarius Sun, Cancer Moon, Virgo Rising."

Five years. I was right. I study him blatantly. He knows his birth chart, which just makes him that much more fascinating. Then he winks and hooks his thumb over his shoulder.

"I'm gonna head out. See you soon?"

"Yeah," I say slowly. "Okay."

He walks past me, close enough that our arms brush, and the goosebumps that prickle my skin make my heart speed up. I turn and follow him to the door. I tell myself it's so I can lock it behind him and ignore the way my body is drawn to his.

"Thanks again for this, Jesse," I say as he slips on his shoes and opens the door. "I know I probably sound like a broken record, but I really appreciate your help."

"You're very welcome," he says, slipping his hands in his pockets and leaning on the door frame. "Though I should be thanking you for letting me hang out with your crew. Anytime you need someone to watch them, gimme a call."

"Thank you," I say again, then immediately laugh at myself. I cover my face with my hands. "Ugh, just go before I say it again."

He chuckles, and I'm so glad I'm hiding my face because I don't want him to see how red my cheeks have gotten.

"Later, Classic," he says, voice low, and then he turns to walk away.

"Jesse," I call out, and he spins around. "Why 'classic'?"

He smirks. "It fits."

I want to ask what he means, but I can't for some reason. My voice won't work, so I stay silent. I just watch him until he gets to the curb and climbs into his car. Then I shut the door and rest my back against it. Like every other encounter we've had, I take a moment to play it back in my head. God, he's just so *attractive*. And smooth. Jesse is definitely the kind of guy I would have fallen for when I was younger.

I laugh to myself.

When I was younger. As if five years is a lifetime.

Though, I suppose it kind of is, in this case.

Still. If I'd have met him earlier, sooner, I would have crushed hard, and he wouldn't have given me the time of day. I close my eyes for a few breaths and give myself a few seconds to imagine a different reality, then a loud knock sounds through the house and makes me jump.

Several sharp pounds, made undoubtedly with a closed, impatient fist, rattle the door, and I want to growl in frustration. I unlock the door and whip it open before the knocking wakes the kids.

"Patrick," I breathe out, "what are you doing here?"

He's driving his truck and wearing civilian clothes, which fills me with dread. At least when he stops by in uniform, I can trust that he's sober. When he's not working, though? I straighten my shoulders.

"Who was that?" he seethes, and I smell the sweetness of whiskey on his breath. His eyes are droopy with drink but sparking with barely-restrained anger, so I step out on the porch and pull the door shut behind me.

"Who was who?"

"Don't fuck with me, Lyn." He takes a step closer, but I hold my ground. I'm not letting him in the house when he's like this. "Who the fuck was that guy who just left? A new boyfriend? You fuckin' someone else, Lyn?"

"Jesus, Patrick, lower your voice," I whisper harshly. His voice carries on the wind and slices through the night air. "That was the babysitter."

He laughs humorlessly. "Your *babysitter*? You expect me to believe that?"

"Yes, I do. He watched the kids so I could attend my clinicals," I tell him, trying to keep my voice calm and emotionless, but his nostrils flare and his jaw clenches at the mention of my nursing program.

"So, you're just letting anyone watch the kids so you can play at being something you're not?"

"You knew I needed those clinical hours, Patrick, and you bailed on keeping them because of it," I say calmly, firmly. I don't sugarcoat my accusation, but the pride I feel at his shocked expression lasts only half a second before he takes another forceful step forward, causing me to back up against the door.

"Jesus Christ, Lyn," he scolds, his words sharp enough that I have to fight against the need to curve my shoulders inward. "Listen to yourself. You can't make your kids a fucking priority?"

"No, that's not—"

"You care more about this fucking program than your kids."

"That's bull and you know it. I do everything f—"

"You're being a shit mom just like you were a shit wife. You only care about yourself and this fucking bullshit *dream*." He spits out the last word like it's garbage, then moves forward and presses into me, bringing his mouth to my ear. "Maybe I should just take the kids off your hands, then. Maybe that will make you happy. That what you want?"

The threat makes my stomach drop to my knees. It's not the first time he's hinted at taking me back to court, and it terrifies me. More than his closeness. More than the smell of alcohol on his breath. More than anything. Because even though I know he doesn't want full custody of our kids, I can't be sure he wouldn't do it just to hurt me. And he *does* want to hurt me. He wants to break me.

And if he took me back to court, he'd win.

"I don't know why you're bothering with this school shit anyway," he whispers into my hair, crooning like a lover. "You couldn't follow through the last time. You're just setting yourself up for failure. Fucking give up already before you embarrass yourself."

I shake my head, eyes clamped shut. "You're wrong. I could have finished, but—"

"Oh, so now it's my fault?" He rears back, voice lowered to a menacing whisper. "Or is it Jude's fault? Gonna blame everyone else because you're not good enough? You're fucking pathetic, Lyn. Always everyone else's fault when, really, it's just that *you're* not fucking good enough."

The cruelty flows off his tongue like venom from a snake bite, and my body reacts in kind. My spine crumples, and I fold into myself almost involuntarily. He angles his head and peers at me in that way I hate, like he wishes I were shorter, so he could truly look down on me. So my stature would reflect the way he wants to make me feel. Small. Weak. Worthless.

"Or maybe you think you can trick that guy in to swooping in? Saving you from your big bad husband? Gonna latch onto him and drain him for all he's got too?"

My eyes burn and my chest aches. I don't want to cry. I don't want to give him the satisfaction.

"Nobody is gonna fuckin' fall for that bullshit, Lyn. Nobody wants to be saddled with a bitch with kids and a used up, stretched-out pussy." He trails his hand lightly down the side of my rigid body, resting gently on my hip. I grit my teeth and fight back the whimper. "No one is gonna want you, Lyn.

Stop being a fuckin' slut before you embarrass your kids and me."

When the first tear slips through my closed eyes, Patrick scoffs, but he finally steps back, giving me space to breathe. He got what he wanted. I wrap my hands around my belly as more tears fall.

"Fucking pathetic, Lyn. Always so fucking pathetic."

I don't move, don't even open my eyes, until I hear his truck drive away. Then silently, I let myself back into the house and lock the door behind me. I make my way into the kitchen, pour myself a glass of wine, then slide down to the floor.

I broke for him. I always break for him.

Worse still, I shrink myself for him. I make myself smaller, so he can feel bigger. I know it happens, and I know it's wrong, but I still do it. I always have. I'm so scared that I always will.

I was strong once. Long enough to leave him. Long enough to fight through a brutal divorce that drained my bank account, my energy, and what little self-confidence I had managed to fake. My strength was fueled by the pain of June's accident, and I hate myself for it. I hate that it took something so terrible for me to finally find the courage to leave. I hate myself even more that I can't sustain that courage.

I don't know what else I can do. I'm trying. I'm trying so damn hard with everything I have, but what if it isn't enough? What if he's right? And what if this will always be my life? Him breathing down my neck and beating down my door whenever he wants to. Holding the ax of a custody battle over my head. Sharpening it with accusations and lies.

I wipe my tears away with my hands, though they don't stop falling. Not until my wine glass is empty and my head is pounding, and I make my way to my bedroom just a few hours before dawn.

jesse

"J. What the hell is going on in here? Your yarn baskets explode?"

I look up from the floor where I've laid out all of my yarn. Kelley sets down his gym bag and Ivy steps around him, closing the door of the condo behind her.

"Ooooh, are we organizing?" V asks as she tiptoes her way through the yarn piles scattered around the living room floor and sits down in an open space. "I'll help."

"Thanks, V," I say, then return my attention to sorting.

"Didn't we just do this not that long ago?"

I nod. "By weight, but it's gotten a little crazy, so now we're doing color. We gotta consolidate first, though. I've got a bunch of the same skeins started, so you'll have to put those together."

"Why don't you finish one skein before starting a new one?" she asks, picking through my massive yarn stash.

"That's a great question," I mumble, and she lets out a soft laugh. "It gets a little chaotic. I sometimes forget I've started one skein between projects and then I'll just grab a new one. Or I'll buy yarn before I know what I'm gonna use it for, or I'll buy some and forget that I already had the same one at home." I chuckle but don't look up from my task. "The result is this." I wave my hands over the sea of skeins and tangles between us.

"Hmm." She hums, and I glance up just in time to see her and Kelley exchange *a look*. Because Ivy knows. She always knows.

"I'm gonna hop in the shower," Kelley says, and heads down the hall toward the bathroom.

"Don't fall!" I sing out, and I hear his bark of laughter just before the bathroom door shuts. A minute later, I hear the shower turn on.

"What's up, J?" Ivy asks, her voice soft as ever. She glances to the small end table, where the elephant I started knitting for my mom lies unfinished, then waves her hands over the disaster on the floor. "Last time we did this was because...well...has she—"

"No, V," I cut her off. "I haven't seen her or heard from her. It's not that."

Ivy releases a sigh of relief, and her shoulders loosen. "Something else, then?"

I shrug. "A couple things."

"Wanna talk about it?" Her question is genuine, and not at all judgmental. I drop the tangle of yarn I was holding into my lap and scan her face.

"You got time?"

"All the time in the world for you, J."

I watch as she returns her focus to the yarn, giving me space to speak when I'm ready. She knows that whatever I have to say is going to be difficult, and she knows it will be easier without her eyes on me. Ivy *always* knows.

"The commitment deadline is soon," I breathe out. "In a matter of days. I have to decide my future in just a few days."

"Is that a bad thing?" she muses. "I thought you were pretty set on Harvard. Excited for it, even."

"I was." I pause and wait for her to ask another question. She doesn't. "But...I don't know. It's a big deal, you know? What if it's not what I want for the rest of my life? What if I'm doing it for the wrong reasons?"

Silence stretches between us, long enough that I glance at her and find her studying me with a furrowed brow.

"You sure this doesn't have anything to do with *her*?" It's a statement disguised as a question, rhetorical in every way. Because Ivy always fucking knows.

"She said she was proud of me, V," I admit. "Like *she* was the reason I was going to med school. Like I was doing it *for her* or some shit." I scrub my hand over my face, a memory from just a few months ago invades my mind. The fear I felt blends with something worse, something that makes my stomach churn. I lower my voice to just above a whisper. "For a split second, V, I was *happy* to know that she was proud of me," I confess. "I was...*pleased*. Isn't that fucked up?"

"No," she says pointedly, "it is not messed up, J."

I shake my head and sigh. I don't know if I agree with her.

"How old were you when you first knew you wanted to be a doctor?"

"Seven," I say quickly. I don't even have to think about the answer. I remember the exact day. My parents brought me to an awards banquet, honoring the work my mother had done in reconstructive plastic surgery. There were speeches from fellow doctors and former patients, hailing my mom as the best in her field, and I was in awe. I was so proud of her and of the things she'd accomplished. I knew immediately that I wanted to be a doctor. A surgeon, just like her.

Ivy nods knowingly, then catches me off guard by asking, "How old were you when that desire changed?"

"What do you mean?" I ask, confused. "It didn't. It hasn't changed."

"Exactly. Don't diminish your accomplishments, and don't credit *her* when she deserves none. You've wanted to be a doctor since you were seven years old, J. You're the one who has worked your butt off. You're the one who got accepted into not one, not two, but three top med schools. You. And you would have done it with or without her influence."

She pauses to reach out and take my hand.

"You did it *despite* her, even. Despite everything. And it's okay that, for a minute, you were glad to know you'd made her proud. She was important to you once. She's the one who messed up, J. Not you."

I squeeze her hand and give her a smile. I don't tell her about the object in my pocket because I don't want to worry her. I still don't fully understand why I'm carrying it around instead of tossing it in the trash where it belongs. A reminder of what I've overcome, probably, but I don't know that Ivy would see it that way.

Regardless, talking to her has helped calm my overactive thoughts. It always does. Ivy is going to be one hell of a lawyer, but I think she'd make an even better therapist. I tell her as much, but she laughs it off.

"When you've been to as much therapy as me, J, you pick up a few things."

Kelley comes out of the bathroom, auburn hair wet from the shower, and heads into the kitchen. "I'm making burgers," he calls out. "You down, J?"

"Definitely," I call back, then flick my eyes toward Ivy. She's sitting crisscross applesauce on the floor, and she's humming to herself as she sorts through the many skeins of yarn scattered around her. There's a knock at the condo door a few minutes later, and Kelley yells out from the kitchen.

"J, will you grab that? It's Bailey and Riggs. They're coming to eat with us."

I pop up and head to the door quickly, not even bothering to hide the bounce in my step. Kelley has been able to tell that I've been more chaotic than usual. The impending med school commitment deadline is causing me more stress than I'd expected, and Kell knows that having my friends around dulls the buzz. He invited them for me. Big gooey cinnamon roll that he is. If V is the protective Mama Bear of our friend group, Kelley is the nurturing Papa Bear.

"BRIGGS!" I shout as I fling open the door, and Bailey barks out a loud laugh.

"Briggs?" she repeats, then waltzes past me into the condo with Riggs trailing behind her. "What the fuck is a Briggs?"

"It was either Briggs or Railey, and I told him no Railey," Riggs adds, knocking me on the shoulder on the way past. He definitely shot down Railey. Still a little bummed about that.

"Ugh, J, we're back on the ship names?" Bailey groans, flopping down next to Ivy then surveying the floor in front of her. "By color?" she asks Ivy, and Ivy nods.

"We were never off the ship names, B," I tell her, and my smile grows as she starts sorting the yarn skeins with Ivy. "Yours was easier than Ivelley's."

"Ivelley is terrible, J."

"I kinda like it," Ivy chimes in, and I smile.

"Thank you! See, B? You're just a grump."

"You knew he'd do it eventually, Sundance. Just embrace it," Riggs says to Bailey as he kicks off his shoes.

"Briggs is terrible," she grumbles, and Riggs laughs.

"I kind of like it," he tells her, repeating Ivy's statement, and I bark out a *HA!*

"Ugh, go away," she says, without looking up from the yarn, and flips me off. I follow Riggs into the kitchen.

"So, how'd babysitting go, Mary Poppins?" Riggs asks after he hands me a fancy beer, then throws the rest of the twelve pack he brought into the fridge. I don't miss the smirk Kelley gives him from where he's standing at the stove. I roll my eyes at both of them.

"Supercalifragilisticexpialidocious, dickheads." I twist open the bottle and take a drink. "The kids are cool."

"Ah, the *kids* are cool, huh?" Kelley jests.

"I suppose it has nothing to do with *The Hot Mom*, then?" Riggs adds, calling me out.

I don't answer. Just take a pull from my beer, then shrug. "I need the peds experience."

Kelley and Riggs both laugh loudly, and I bristle.

"You're such a fucking terrible liar, Jesse," Kell says.

"I do need peds experience!" I protest, and he shakes his head. I can hear him snickering over the sizzle of burgers in the frying pan, and I try like hell to hide my smile.

"Zay told me you were stalking her house last Saturday morning from our couch, SD. You need peds experience so bad that you're turning in to a window creeper?" Riggs taunts, grinning over his beer bottle like a douche.

"Fuck off, God of Thunder," I grumble, his words bothering me in a way he couldn't understand. "It's not like I'm 'bout to boil some bunnies. Zay's a snitch."

"You tryin' to be a stepdaddy, Hernandez?"

"Call me Odin and I'll be your daddy, Thor," I joke and then have to dart away when he tries to punch my shoulder. Riggs and I are about the same height, but he's built like a brick shit house, so I'm sure catching a fist would hurt like hell. "Watch those meat cleavers, Fabio. I'm not tryna have my ass kicked in the name of funzies."

Riggs smirks just as Kelley hands me the plate full of burger patties, and I set them on our large kitchen island. Then I grab the bag of burger buns as Riggs pulls condiments from the fridge.

"Food," Kelley calls into the living room, and seconds later, Ivy and Bailey are joining us.

We fix plates, grab drinks, then make our way back into the living room. The yarn stash has been tackled almost entirely and is piled by color along the wall. We sprawl out on the furniture, and Kelley tosses me the TV remote.

"No Marvel movies," Riggs commands, and I bite back a retort about self-loathing. The way he narrows his eyes at me says he could have guessed what I was gonna say, anyway.

"And no cooking shows," Bailey adds. "They still give me anxiety."

I snort a laugh, and she rolls her eyes. B and Riggs participated in a baking competition over winter break. It's kinda cool, actually, but it stressed her the fuck out. Now she says she can't watch the competitions without feeling anxious for the participants. She likes to pretend she's not, but this right here proves that B is a big empath softie. She'll murder me if I say it out loud, though. Empath softie with a violent streak.

"We could watch that one—"

"NO!" Everyone shouts, cutting Ivy off, and she frowns.

"You don't even know what I was going to say."

We all answer at once.

"Horror." "Something stabby." "Serial killers." "Creepy shit."

She giggles. "Okay, so you did know what I was gonna say."

"I got it," I say, pulling up one of the programs I use to rent and stream movies. I scroll down to a movie I'd recently rented, but haven't had a chance to watch, and push play.

"Houseboat?" Kelley reads the screen.

I nod. "Cary Grant and Sophia Loren." I put the remote on the coffee table, then pick up my burger. "You're gonna love it," I promise, then take a bite of my burger and settle in for the movie.

. . .

Riggs, Bailey, and Ivy all dip out after the movie, leaving the condo empty except for me and Kelley. It's rare since he and V started dating. I'm not complaining. I love having V around. I prefer the nights when she stays here to the nights when Kelley stays at her place.

I'm not *bad* at being alone, but why would I choose it when my friends are so fucking great? And anyway, having company means having siphons for the energy that's always bubbling under the surface. People to talk to. Things to joke about. Distractions from my wayward thoughts.

We've already cleaned up from dinner, and the girls put away the rest of my yarn stash, so there's no distractions when I finally breech the topic I've been thinking about since midway through the movie. Sophia Loren, man. Jocelyn Calligaris owns my damn brain right now.

It's been a week since I've seen her, yet her image is still in the forefront of my mind.

"That first date you took V on," I begin, then pause. He glances at me and arches a brow.

"Yeah? What about it?"

"It was pretty smooth, yeah?"

"Yeah," he says slowly, voice mixed with satisfaction and bemusement. "I guess it was."

"How'd you plan that?" I try to be subtle, but I've always sucked at it. King of Direct (and often inappropriate) Statements, right here. Kelley's smile grows, and he shakes his head.

"C'mon, J. I had years to plan that date. You know that."

I laugh with him. "Yeah, okay," I relent. He's right. He'd been pining for V for *literal* years before finally making his move. I've only been crushing for a few weeks. "But, like, say I wanted to plan something..." I let the statement trail off and Kelley's jaw drops.

"You want to take someone on a *date*? You?"

I don't take offense to his surprise. Fuck, I'm surprised even. How I went from hooking up every weekend to this, I don't even know. I blame V for ditching me for this ginger douche. I tell him as much and he tells me to eat a dick. I laugh so hard my side hurts.

"Why you asking me?" he questions after I've caught my breath. "You know the girls would be all over this shit."

"That's exactly why I'm *not* asking them," I say pointedly, and he nods in agreement. He gets quiet for a minute, probably mulling it all over in his ginger head, before hitting me with a thoughtful look.

"This for the mom?" I shrug and he asks, "How well do you know her?"

"Not as well as I'd like to know her, ya know?"

I don't tell him that she makes me feel something I haven't felt in a long time. Like I'm interesting. Like I'm worth knowing for more than a night. Worth more than a fuck and some laughs.

He hums to himself. Runs his fingers through his hair. Chews his lip. I'm two seconds away from shaking him and telling him to spit it the fuck out when he finally opens his mouth.

"Well, you gotta remember that the only person I've ever actually planned a date for is Ives, and she's—"

"The love of your life and you want to fill her with jizz so she'll have all your babies," I cut him off, and he laughs out loud, but doesn't even bother trying to deny it. He's whipped and he loves it.

"Well, for me and Ives, our first date was great because it was thoughtful. It was built off our shared history, yeah? So, I guess, consider what you know about the mom, and what you want to accomplish with the date, and then..." He shrugs.

Like *that's it*.

Like, *shrug, that's how you do it*.

Wtf. Maybe I should have asked the girls. Ivy would have given me a pros and cons list, a flow chart, and itemized directions. Bailey would have given me hell at first, but she'd have probably given me a list of what not to do. Much better than some vague statements and a slouchy, one-shouldered shrug.

I open my mouth to push. To beg for something a little more instructive. Direct. I start to protest, but then I'm hit with one of those lightbulb moments.

Consider what I know about her, huh?

I've got an idea.

* * *

The next Saturday morning, I knock on Jocelyn's door. I've been by Harvest View a few times to visit Rox, but every time I'd just missed Jocelyn's shift. Apparently, her schedule isn't consistent because she has to be able to work around her class requirements for her nursing program and the ex's schedule for visitation with the kids.

Or so Roxanne said.

It's not like I asked or anything.

I push my hand into my pocket, brushing my fingers over the cool metal inside, and sway back and forth while I wait for the door to open. I'm debating between knocking a second time or walking away when the door swings open and my breath leaves my body in a woosh.

"Jesse?" Jocelyn greets, questioningly. "What's up?"

It takes me a few seconds, and a few swallows, before I can respond because, good God, this woman is gorgeous. In joggers and a tight tank top, her body calls to me like a siren. Her face is clear of makeup, her hair is wet like she just got out of the shower, and she smells like flowers. Like a field full of fucking flowers, and I want to roll around in it.

I clear my throat and give her a smile.

"Just thought I would come by and see if you needed my services today," I say suggestively, and the color that flushes on her cheeks fills me with pride.

"Oh, uh, the kids are with Patrick," she says softly. "He took them this weekend since he, uh, couldn't last weekend."

More like *wouldn't*. I don't trust that fuck.

"Do you have clinicals today?" I ask, and she shakes her head no. "Work?" She shakes her head no again. "You got any plans at all?" Her lips twitch into a small, shy smile, and she shakes her head no a third time.

"My friends are all out of town," I say honestly. Ivy and Kelley went back to their hometown for the weekend to visit their families, and the baseball team is playing in Ohio this weekend, so Bailey went along to be a supportive girlfriend, even though she hates sports and Ohio. "Let's hang out."

"Hang out..." she repeats, bemused. "You and me?"

I chuckle. "Yeah, me and you. I made you something."

"You did?"

"Yeah. You wanna let me in so I can give it to you?" I hold her gaze, bolstered by the spark of *something* that I see in those glittering green irises. I like that I unsettle her. I like that she likes it.

"Sure," she says quietly, then steps back to let me in the house. "Just go have a seat in the living room. I'll be right back."

I make my way into the living room and sit on the couch while Jocelyn heads upstairs. I pick up a matchbox car that's sitting on the coffee table and drive it over my knees. It's purple, and I know it's one of Jude's favorites. He probably didn't bring it to the ex's house because it's purple. Fuck that guy. What kind of person tells their kid they can't get a cast in their favorite color after breaking his fucking arm? I don't like it. I widen my legs and jump the car between them, reenacting a scene from the Fast and Furious franchise.

A few minutes later, I drop the matchbox car as Joss comes back in the living room with her hair pulled up in a bun and a Bears sweatshirt covering her top half. I want to frown at the oversized mess of fugly cotton now hiding the swell of her breasts and hips from me, but I don't. Instead, I smile and hit send on the message I'd composed on my phone. Seconds later, a ping sounds from somewhere in the kitchen. I wave my phone at her and gesture toward the noise.

"Go check that," I tell her. She squints at me and screws up her lips, amused and curious, then goes to fetch her phone.

"What is this?" She laughs out, then comes back into the living room, sporting a smile that makes my chest tighten.

"At the risk of sounding like a total twelve-year-old," I say jokingly, "I made you a playlist." The text I'd sent her had the link to the playlist I'd thoughtfully curated over the last week. It's eclectic and random, but every song was chosen for a purpose.

"Why?" she asks, smile still affixed on her lips, totally clueless. "Why make me a playlist?"

Why does a boy ever make a girl a playlist? I want to say. But I don't. Because there's just as much confusion swirling in her green eyes as there is delight. My passes have never been so easily ignored before. I'm not good at hiding my interest. I definitely haven't been trying to hide it. But I must seriously be off my game because Jocelyn Calligaris might actually be oblivious to my attraction. Wild.

"Your list," I say, and she arches an eyebrow in question. "Your to-do list to be a full person," I clarify. "One of the things said 'find my music,' so I thought I would help. Give you some material to sort through."

"Oh, wow," she whispers. "Thanks." I watch as she scrolls on her phone, thumbing through the titles. "I appreciate that."

"I'd like to help with the rest of it," I blurt, and she whips her eyes back to me. "With your list. I'd like to help you with your to-do list."

It's not until her face shows shock and embarrassment that I realize she's probably thinking about the last item on the list —sex in all capitals with three exclamation points—and I can't help the wicked grin that curls over my lips.

"I wouldn't mind helping with that one either," I drawl, and her breath hitches and face flushes as my statement sinks in.

Yeah, Classic. That's right. I'm *more* than interested.

"I thought maybe we could take the camera Rox loaned you to the state park today," I continue. "That hits two of your things, right?"

Jocelyn blinks.

"Photography and Being Active," I explain, and her jaw drops.

"Did you memorize my list?"

I smile sheepishly and give a shrug. "I didn't memorize it *intentionally*." I bring my hands up by my ears and mime turning gears. "I have a selective memory but no say in the selection process. I have very little control over what makes it short term to long term storage."

I say it jokingly enough, but it's totally true.

It's why, to my mother's displeasure, I'm not fluent in *Español*. Why I can easily recite every bone in the human skeleton, but barely passed any of my history classes in high school. I could never keep the dates straight. My brain is fucking weird.

I watch Jocelyn bite her lip, then wring her hands together.

"You can say no," I tell her. "If you don't want my help, say no."

She scrunches up her nose and purses her lips, and I laugh softly.

"If you're worried about upsetting me, don't be. I won't be upset. But even still, my possible reaction shouldn't dictate your response. Your feelings come first, Joss."

The wave of emotions I watch pass over her features is fascinating. Uncertainty, concern, apprehension, surprise. And then finally, excitement.

"Okay," she says with a nod, and her smile grows with mine.

"Yeah?"

"Yeah. Let's go to the state park."

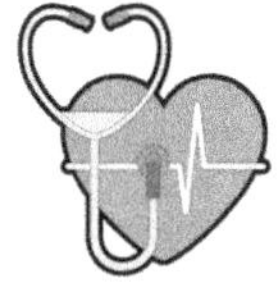

jocelyn

JESSE DRIVES AN OLDER MODEL KIA.

For some reason, that surprises me.

I didn't take much notice of his car when he babysat, but for some reason, I assumed it would be an SUV, maybe something stylish and expensive. But it's not. It's an older model Kia.

Watching him fold himself into it surprises me even more. For being so tall, he's able to glide in and out of the sedan with grace. I'm still not convinced he couldn't be an athlete. Someone who moves with such finesse has to be athletically inclined. *He must be good at many things with a body like that.* The thought heats my blood, and I jump a little when Jesse speaks.

"We're gonna stop at the grocery store and grab some stuff for lunch," Jesse says to me once we're buckled in. "Hook your phone to the Bluetooth and you can be DJ."

It's ridiculous how thrilled I am at that statement. Getting excited over having control of the radio when someone else is in the car is pathetic, right? I take a deep breath and pull up the playlist Jesse sent me. I'll listen to it and save the ones that I like. Surprisingly, I recognized several of the songs he'd included, several of which I've already saved to my own playlist. It makes me giddy to listen to the rest of them.

"I like a lot of these," I say to him as I cue up the music and he pulls onto the road.

"Yeah? Which ones?"

"Christian French. Quinn XCII. Bishop Briggs."

He nods. "Bishop Briggs slaps. Love her voice."

I agree. Her song "Champion" has been one I've played frequently over the last few weeks, but I don't tell Jesse that. Something about it feels too personal, too vulnerable. I don't want him to read into it. I don't want him to read into anything.

"My friend is obsessed with Harry Styles," he says somewhat randomly.

"Yeah? She a fangirl?" I ask with a grin, but Jesse flicks his eyes toward me and smirks.

"*He* is definitely a fanboy," he says. "Grew his hair out long because of *Long Hair Harry*, and now he's thinking of chopping it off to be like *Fine Line Harry*."

I must look confused because he adds, "Harry Styles hairstyle eras. When you have a minute, Google it. But be ready to fall down a rabbit hole."

Jesse pulls into the parking lot of a grocery store, and we grab a basket as we walk in.

"How do you feel about charcuterie?" he asks, and I laugh.

"I love charcuterie."

"Perfect. Let's get stuff for a charcuterie picnic, then. I've already got a cooler and blanket in the trunk."

A pleased smile creeps over my lips. "You planned for this? Were you so sure I'd agree to come with you?"

"Mmm, I hoped for it." He smirks at me over his shoulder, then winks. "Some might say I manifested it."

I laugh again. I've been with him for an hour and it's already the most fun I've had with another adult in a long time. The effects of Jesse Hernandez's superpower are intoxicating.

"Manifestation, huh?"

"Classic, I've been trying to manifest a lot of stuff regarding you lately."

His voice is suggestive, and his gaze is heated. So much so that I have to look away and laugh it off before my brain short-circuits.

This is flirting, right? I'd have to be an idiot to think it's not. The provocative looks, the teasing comments. This is *textbook* flirting.

But...is he flirting *with me*, or is he just a flirty person? I try to remember the last time someone flirted with me. So I have something, anything at all to compare it to... But all I can recall are those early days with Patrick, and nothing ever felt quite like this with him.

Nobody wants to be saddled with a bitch with kids.

No one is gonna want you.

Especially not some young college guy. Not one that looks like Jesse Hernandez. Especially not with everything that comes with me. I give my head a subtle shake, trying to exorcise myself of Patrick's voice, but it doesn't go easily. Not before I'm reminded of every flaw, every insecurity, every little thing that Patrick always made sure to point out.

I hate him. I hate myself more for letting him have this power over me.

"Get outta your head, Joss," Jesse says, then he slings his arm around my shoulders. I stiffen at the touch, the heat and weight of his arm, the unfamiliar closeness, and he gives me a slight squeeze, then steps away. "This will be fun. I promise."

"Yeah, of course," I say, brushing it off. I grab a box of crackers and toss them in the basket. "Cheeses?"

"Cheeses."

. . .

When we get to the state park, we decide to do some hiking before we break out the charcuterie. I grab Roxanne's camera, and Jesse pops the trunk, pulling out a grey backpack with a blanket attached.

"What's that?"

"Only the coolest fucking picnic basket ever. I borrowed it from my roommate." He grins and unzips the backpack. Inside, he puts the stuff we picked up for lunch, packing with a strategic single-mindedness that makes me laugh. He flicks his eyes toward me with a half-smile. "What?"

"You're so focused."

"I'm trying to impress you, Classic, and anything worth doing is worth doing well." He winks, then zips the bag back up and slings it over his shoulder, leaving me speechless. "Ready?"

We choose one of the hiking trails that runs through a heavily-wooded forest and follows a large creek, stopping frequently so I can snap pictures of any and everything. There are blooms popping up along the trail, all sorts of wildflowers that I can't identify, and we're surrounded by the trills of birdsong and the soft babbling of the creek. If this were a date, which it's not, but *if* it were, it would be off to a pretty phenomenal start.

"So, Jesse Hernandez," I say, peering through the viewfinder of Roxanne's camera. I snap a picture of the landscape beyond the creek. "Were your parents big into wrestling?"

He barks out a laugh. "Ah, it's been a while since someone brought up that comparison," he says with a smile, trying to skip a few rocks across the creek's surface. "It's actually a fun story."

"Oh, I'm intrigued." I turn my camera and snap a few pictures of his smiling face. He's balancing on two flat rocks with the sun haloing his body, the light reflecting off the water and bouncing off his chest like sparkles. It's almost comical how attractive he is. "Do tell."

"Well, first, you need to know that I'm technically Jesse Hernandez *Junior*."

"Your dad is also Jesse Hernandez?" He nods. "But not the wrestler Jesse Hernandez," I state, and he laughs again, shaking his head no.

"Nah. My dad is a blond-haired, blue-eyed beast of a nurse anesthetist. Not a 70-year-old pro wrestler from the 80s."

He hops down from the rocks and stalks over to where I'm standing. He gestures for the camera, so I hand it to him slowly and watch as he brings it up to his face and points it at something across the creek.

"My dad's last name was Bakker," he says, the *click* of the shutter sounding between his words. "That's with two K's." He turns slightly, pointing the camera at something else.

"Jesse Bakker." I roll it off my tongue, and he nods, snapping another picture with a *click*.

"When my dad met my mom, she was already pretty well-known. Everyone knew Doctor Vanessa Hernandez was on track to be a powerhouse surgeon. Plus, you know, she is proud of being a Mexican woman in a field dominated by white men. So, when Dad inevitably won her over with his charm and she agreed to marry him, she wasn't too keen on the idea of changing her name." *Click.*

"I don't blame her," I say. I wouldn't have wanted to either.

"Exactly. So, when they got married, instead of hyphenating or anything else, my dad decided to take her name." He pulls the camera down and smiles at me. "He's kinda a huge simp and her biggest fanboy." A laugh bursts out of me at the pride in his voice, and the shutter *clicks* again. "So, my dad became Jesse Hernandez first. Then I was born, and I look exactly like my mother—except she's like five nothing and weighs as much as my biceps." I laugh again, barely registering the *click* of the shutter. "So, they named me Jesse after my father. And I became Jesse Hernandez, Jr." *Click.* "See? A happy accident."

"I like it," I say with a smile. He turns and points the camera at me, and I throw my hands up. "Don't!" I shout, but I hear the *click* anyway.

He meets my eyes pointedly.

"You know you're gorgeous, right?" His question makes me sway on my feet.

"What? No. Stop," I stutter out, and he takes a few steps toward me, until I'm mere feet from him. I start to turn away, but he reaches out and puts his hand lightly on my arm.

"I'm serious, Jocelyn. You're gorgeous."

"Shut up, Jesse." My face heats to burning, and I avert my eyes.

"You're fucking hot," he says, his voice low and playful. I wish he wasn't so playful. I can't tell if he's serious or not. I don't think I'm unattractive, but hot? No. And he's...*him*. I cover my face with my hands and huff; my cheeks are warm to the touch.

"You're a MILF, Classic," he says, and I snort-laugh into my hands, making me even more embarrassed. "A regular Mom I'd Like to F—"

"Okay!" I squeal, cutting him off, and he bursts into belly-deep laughter that I can't help but match. My forehead presses into his chest simply because my laughter is making my knees weak, and his arms wrap around me to keep me steady. That's *all* it is.

I calm myself down then take a few steps backward, widening the distance between us. I need to get a grip, and I need to do it while *not* engulfed in his spicy leather scent. I force a scowl, then meet his eyes. *Click.* He snaps a photo.

"Asshole," I snark, clamping my lips shut to fight my smile, and he winks.

"Your turn," Jesse says, then gestures for me to follow him back to the trail.

"My turn for what?"

"To tell me something about you."

"What do you want to know?" I speak the words before thinking them through, then regret them immediately. I can't act like I'm an open book because I'm *not* an open book.

"What are you comfortable telling me?" he asks, and my shoulders relax. Is he this perceptive with everyone?

"Hmmmm." I think for a moment. "I was named after my dad's mother, but she died before I was born, so I never met her."

"She must have been pretty great, though, if your parents wanted to name you after her."

I follow him as we weave through the trees and make our way over the trail's path.

"Maybe. I don't actually know anything about her. I was put in foster care when I was eight." June's age. The realization rocks me to my core.

"That must have been rough," Jesse muses thoughtfully, and I shrug even though he can't see me.

"It was and it wasn't. My dad went to jail for armed robbery, and my mom wasn't up to mom-ing. She dropped me off at a Friday night fish fry at a Methodist church, and I haven't seen her since."

"Damn, Joss." He halts in his tracks and turns to face me. "That's fucked up."

"Yeah, it kind of is, isn't it?" I laugh, and he eyes me quizzically. "Do you ever have moments where you think to yourself 'wow, I could be way more messed up than I am?'"

"All the fucking time," he deadpans. "Literally all the fucking time."

The connection I feel with him surprises me, like a jolt of warmth through my veins. I can't know for sure, but something tells me he'd understand a lot more than I'm willing to reveal.

My laugh breaks first, followed quickly by his, until we're, once again, giggling like fools, and I have to wipe the evidence from my cheeks. I'm grateful our trail is empty of other people because, otherwise, I'd be feeling extremely self-conscious.

"Have you always liked photography?"

"I took a photography class in high school and really enjoyed it." I was pretty good at it too. Won an award and was featured in the local travel highlights magazine—the one they put in state rest stops and stuff to attract tourists. I don't tell Jesse that. Instead, I lie. "I kinda lost interest, and then let it fall by the wayside."

I didn't realize it at the time, but looking back, I know that Patrick is the reason I stopped pursuing photography. He'd put down my work, criticize it, call it a waste of time and money. I cringe at the memory.

I don't know why you're putting so much effort into this hobby, Lyn. You should just stick to what you're good at.

And so, I stopped.

"I do that with a lot of stuff," Jesse says, then taps at his temple. "Start a hobby and then lose interest and move on to the next thing. Jack of Many Trades, Master of One." He pauses a moment, then adds, "Well, maybe two."

I laugh. "What are the two?"

"I'm pretty good at knitting, and I'm gonna be a boss ass surgeon."

"Two good things."

I halt and crouch down to take a picture of a patch of wildflowers blooming along the side of the trail. Whites and yellows and oranges speckling the green and brown forest floor.

"They're going to be everywhere soon," Jesse muses, and I glance up to find him watching me.

"What are?"

"The wildflowers."

I nod. He's right. By summer, the park floor will be carpeted in wildflowers.

"The unsung heroes of nature." I brush my fingers lightly over the blooms, careful not to touch them.

"How do you figure?"

"They nourish birds, bees, and animals, help to sustain whole ecosystems. They're resilient too. Can grow in even the most unfavorable conditions. Harsh winters, dry spells. You name it, wildflowers can usually withstand it." I stand up and brush my hands off on my jeans. "All while radiating a humble sort of beauty."

"Is that their superpower?" he asks, and I smile, snapping another picture of the patch of flowers.

"I think so, yeah."

Jesse hums, and I meet his gaze. "Sounds like someone else I know."

The look is intense, and my skin erupts in goosebumps at his words. His voice is low and sincere, and his eyes are penetrating. My body warms, and I don't know how to respond, so I stay quiet.

"Did you know that sunflowers turn toward one another on cloudy days?" he asks randomly, when I break eye contact.

"Is that true?"

"No," he laughs, and I look up to find him grinning proudly. "I saw it on Facebook. Can't believe anything you see on there." I shake my head. He's so *playful*. "It's a nice sentiment, though, isn't it? Find the light within your relationships when everything else feels dark."

He catches my eye once more. His are so open, so inviting, and I want to walk closer. Want to close the distance between us and… What? I don't even know. I'm so out of my element. My feet stay rooted to the spot, and his soft smile suggests he understands my internal battle.

"C'mon, Classic," he says, then turns back on the trail. "Let's find somewhere to eat."

"Wow," I breathe out, taking in my surroundings. "Can you imagine how beautiful this will be in a few weeks?"

The clearing that we found is sunshiny and full of blooming wildflowers. Jesse wastes no time laying out the blanket he brought.

"We'll have to bring J-Squared back here," he says absent-mindedly as he unpacks the contents of the backpack. "Bet they'd like to see it once the wildflowers are in full bloom. The colors and everything."

The statement makes me want to cry. Usually, I'm the only one considering June and Jude. I blink away the stinging in my eyes and have a seat across from him on the blanket.

"This looks great," I say brightly, and his full lips quirk up.

"Impressed yet?" He twists off the lid of a bottle of water, then hands it to me.

"Very," I say on a laugh, then roll my eyes at the thought of him trying to impress *me*.

"Hey, I'm serious," he says. "I put a lot of thought into this date. Are you having fun?"

I choke on my water. *Date?*

"Whoa, you okay?" He scoots closer and pats my back

lightly. "I can do mouth to mouth if you need it." His stupid impish smile.

"Date?" I gasp out between coughs, and his smile falters.

"Yeah, Classic. *Date.*" His eyes bounce between mine, his hand still resting lightly on my back. For a second, I see something pass over his face. Uncertainty. Vulnerability. "Don't you feel this?" he whispers, and my mouth drops open.

"I..." I rasp, then lick my lips. Swallow. Try again. "I thought it was just me," I say quietly, and his answering chuckle—low and rumbling—vibrates through me. He reaches out and grasps my hand, then presses it to his chest.

"This feel like it's just you?"

My eyes fall to where his hand covers mine. Beneath my palm, his chest is hard and warm, and his heart thunders rapidly. I flex, pressing my fingers into his skin, and he groans. My eyes snap back to his.

"I'm attracted to you, Jocelyn."

"You are?"

His grin is wicked. "I can put your hand on something else if you need that proven to you too..."

My eyes widen and laughter bursts from me, loud and echoey through the clearing. I can't believe he just said that. And his grin is so proud with his playful, dancing eyes.

"What do you want, Classic?" His gaze falls to my mouth, and I wet my lips. "Tell me what you want."

I want to kiss him. I want his mouth on mine. But that can't happen. None of this makes sense. He's... He's... And I'm—

"Get outta your head, Joss." He tightens his grip on my hand, pressing it harder into his chest, heart beating even faster. You can't fake that, right? "What. Do. *You.* Want?"

"To kiss you," I breathe out, and he wastes no time closing the distance between us.

His lips are warm, soft, and patient. So patient. Surprisingly gentle, but I can sense the energy buzzing just beneath the surface. He runs his tongue along my bottom lip, coaxing me slowly, giving me time to pull away. To change my mind.

I do the opposite.

I run my hands up his chest, around his neck, and plunge my fingers into the mess of curls atop his head. He wraps his arms around me, pulling me close, and deepens the kiss. When I open my mouth and our tongues touch, I swear I feel his body shake. He slides his hands up and down my torso, brushing over my breasts in a barely-there touch that makes me whimper. At the sound, he does it again, then cups one and squeezes.

"Fuck, the things I want to do to you." He growls into my mouth, then moves his lips to my jaw, my neck.

I want his hands everywhere. I will him to slide them under my shirt, down my pants, and I blush hot with the direction of my thoughts. I want it, but I can't bring myself to say it, and as much as I want to touch him, too, my hands stay firmly above his waist. We kiss for minutes or hours, long enough that I'm breathless and dizzy, and his hands have caressed almost every part of my body. Some places I wish he'd have lingered longer. But we don't take it further, and when he slows the kiss, my head is fuzzy, and my heart is pounding.

"This one left them all behind," he whispers when we break apart, eyes running all over my face.

"What?" I ask, and his small smile takes my breath away once more.

"Nothing," he says, and shakes his head. "It's from *The Princess Bride*." He lifts his hand and traces his fingers over my jaw, then lightly over my lower lip.

"I tried to draw you. After that first time I saw you in Rox's room." He traces his fingers back the way they came, lip then jaw then shoulder and down my arm where he takes my hand.

"You can draw too?" I watch as he flips my hand over and runs his index finger over my palm.

"Absolutely not," he says honestly, then meets my eyes. "It was a horrible rendering." I can't hold back my laughter at the look on his face. "I'll never try it again."

"Why'd you try it at all?" I question through giggles, and he smirks.

"Cause you're in here." He taps his temple as he speaks, and the gesture reminds me of what he said earlier. How he loses interest quickly. He has no say in what *stays*. Whatever happens between us, it won't be a big deal for him, and it won't last long. Just a blip on his dating radar.

Dating.

"I can't date you," I blurt out, and he flinches. Of course, he does. Just because he took me on a date doesn't mean he wants to be exclusive. "I mean, I can't really do anything serious right now."

"Yeah," he says after a few seconds. "I leave at the end of the summer, anyway..." He sits up straight, but he doesn't let go of my hand. "But until then, what if we just have some fun?"

"Fun?" He means sex, right? Making out. Having sex. I blush, and his eyes flare.

"Yeah, Classic. *Fun.* I can help you with your list, and we can spend time together. But we won't do anything you don't want to do."

My shoulders loosen. I hadn't even realized I had tensed up to begin with.

I consider his words. His *proposition*.

Oh my god, am I being propositioned?

I stare over his shoulder. Watch the flowers blowing in the slight breeze. What do I even say to this? My heart pounds in my ears. Do I *want* to be propositioned? I bite my lip. By him? Yes. Yes, I do.

My skin tingles at the possibilities, and just as quickly I'm reminded of how different we are.

No one's gonna want you. Especially not Jesse.

I wince at Patrick's voice in my head. My loudest insecurities always sound like him.

"You can say no." Jesse breaks into my thoughts, and when I look at him, his face is a mask. Impassive. "You can say no, Jocelyn. Your feelings come first. What do *you* want?"

What do I want?

"I don't want to say no," I whisper, and his lips turn up into a slow smile.

"Yeah?"

"The kids can't know," I say quickly, and he nods. Then I think of what would happen if Patrick found out, and I add, "*No one* can know. Not Patrick. Not even your friends."

"Okay," he says with a curt nod. "Sure. Keep it quiet. Got it."

"Just for the summer?"

"Sure, Classic." His small smile grows. "Let's see what happens."

He pulls me closer, kisses me again, and doesn't stop touching me. Not while we eat and chat and laugh, and not after, while we lie sprawled on the blanket, surrounded by wildflowers, and watch the sun go down in an explosion of oranges, pinks, and purples.

When he drops me off, it's late, and I don't invite him in. He kisses me goodbye with a promise to see me soon. The house is dark and quiet when I walk through the door. Like always, I miss June and Jude. I always miss them when they're not here. To my surprise, I also miss Jesse. Minutes after he drives away, something deep in my chest aches for him. For his buzzing energy and the easy way he makes me laugh. For the feeling of lightness, of weightlessness, I get in his presence.

Just for the summer. God, this is probably a terrible idea.

After showering and climbing into bed, I take out Roxanne's camera to look over the photos from today. I've captured some great shots of the landscape and flowers, and a small flicker of pride blooms in my chest. My eyes catch on one of Jesse smiling brightly by the creek. The camera captured the sun's reflection off the water's surface, making him look almost otherworldly. Celestial.

Or like neon.

I smile and run my fingers over my lips, replaying the kisses that took place today. It's probably a horrible idea, but I still can't stamp out the giddiness. Can't tame the shameless smile.

I click through a few more shots until I come upon a few of me. I knew Jesse had taken one, but I wasn't expecting to see these others.

So many. By the creek. On the trail. In the clearing surrounded by flowers.

My first instinct is to criticize the photos.

Frown at the way my skin is wrinkled by my eyes. The way my hips ripple and flare. How my belly isn't smooth and flat. My first instinct is to view the pictures through Patrick's eyes, and his voice rages in my head. But I fight it. He shouldn't still have this power over me, where he's conducting my thoughts like his own personal orchestra.

I squeeze my eyes shut and give my head a shake. Is this how I would want June looking at photos of herself? Through this harsh lens of self-loathing?

I open my eyes and look at the photos again.

The setting is beautiful. It was such a perfect day. And I'm smiling so big. Laughing outright in a few, and I can recall the exact moment those photos were taken because I can recall exactly what I was laughing about.

I look pretty. I look weightless. I look *happy*.

My phone pings with a notification on my bedside table.

Jesse: Thinkin bout u

My lips curl upward and a giggle bubbles out of me. I stare at my phone. What do I even say? That he's on my mind? That I miss him? Would that freak him out? I decide to go with honesty.

Me: I'm thinking about you too.
Me: Thank you for today.
Jesse: Always

Another text comes in telling me to sleep well, followed by a few emojis. A moon, a star, a blue heart, a pink flower. I push away every nagging worry and send him back one emoji. An orange heart, because it reminds me of the sunset we watched just a few hours ago.

When I fall asleep, it's with a quiet mind and small smile on my lips.

jesse

IT'S STILL EARLY when I knock on Jocelyn's door.

I probably should have called or texted first.

I didn't exactly think this all the way through. I just knew that I couldn't sleep and couldn't stop thinking about her. I'm jonesin' like a fucking fiend. I just want to get a little more time with her this weekend before J-Squared get back from the ex's —*fucking dick*—because as soon as they're home, it's back to hands off.

She said yesterday that she planned to study all day before the kids got home. I hope she's up for a study break, because shit, those lips. I'm gonna need at least a few more kisses to sustain me through the week.

The door opens slowly, and I'm surprised to see June's face peek around at me. I'm so taken aback to see her that I don't speak right away, and her eyes narrow.

"Dad dropped us off early," she says, answering my unspoken question, then swings the door open and gestures for me to come inside. "Mom is upstairs with Jude."

"Thanks, Junie B. Jones," I say as I trail her through the house. She looks up at me like I'm fucking nuts, and I bite my lip to keep from smiling. "Came by to see if you guys'll need me to watch you at all this week." It's a weak excuse, but I think she buys it. She shrugs, then heads to the kitchen.

I lean on the wall and watch as she climbs up onto the counter and pulls down four plastic, mismatched bowls. She sets them out onto the kitchen peninsula, then fills them with cereal from a box she grabs from the cabinet. Something colorful and no doubt sweet. Looks like knock-off Froot Loops. She gets a gallon of milk from the fridge and pours milk into two of the bowls, then silently slides one of the bowls in front of me, making a scraping sound as it slides, then a sloshing sound when it stops. She puts the milk back in the fridge, hands me a spoon, then climbs onto a stool and pulls the other milk-filled bowl to her. Without saying anything, she starts eating the cereal.

So, I do what anyone else would do.

I sit on the stool next to her and eat the cereal.

"So why you back early?" I ask her between mouthfuls.

She shrugs. "He always brings us back early." *Interesting.* "It's okay," she adds stoically. "I don't like being there anyways."

I'm silent for a minute—this kid is always making me question my words—before saying, "Well, I'm glad I get to see you, Dune Buggy."

She doesn't look at me, but I see her smirk into her bowl before she shoves another spoonful of cereal into her mouth. I'll take it.

I'm midchew when Jocelyn and Jude round into the kitchen. They both stop short when they see me, then Jude launches himself at my legs.

"Jesse!" he shouts. "Are you here to play with me?"

I go to ruffle his hair, but it's been buzzed short and now

feels like soft Velcro. I flick my eyes from him to Jocelyn. She still looks stunned, so I direct my question to Jude.

"What's with the new 'do, Meatball?"

He climbs onto my lap, then reaches over the counter to grab a bowl of cereal while he answers.

"I got a sucker in it." He looks at his mom. "Can I have milk?"

Jocelyn moves to the fridge. "He fell asleep with a sucker in his mouth and apparently woke up with it wrapped up and knotted into his hair," she tells me. I take note of the worry lines between her eyes as she pours the last of the milk into Jude's bowl and tosses the gallon into the garbage. "Patrick cut it out," she winces, then finally looks at me with a *what the actual fuck was going through my head when I married that idiot* expression on her face.

Well, that's how I read it anyway.

She picks up the last bowl of cereal and starts eating it, piece by piece, dry. She doesn't even bother with a spoon. I track her delicate fingers as they bring a colorful O to her lips and place it in her mouth, and then I look away, because I'm dangerously close to getting an erection.

"He had a giant chunk cut out of his hair on the side of his head, so I had to even it out with some clippers." She surveys Jude's head and forces a smile. "I like it. Perfect for summer weather."

"Now my head won't get hot!" he announces to everyone, and Joss and I share a smile.

We finish eating our cereal, me and June on the stools, Jude on my lap, and Jocelyn leaning on the counter across from us. Jude rambles about all the fun stuff he did at his dad's house—rode his scooter, jumped on a trampoline, went swimming, played with *'mote 'introl cars*—but when I glance at June, she gives me a small shake of her head.

Jude's imagination knows no bounds, but it rubs me the wrong way that he had to imagine such simple things. Shouldn't riding his scooter be a reality? Fuckin' ex.

"You guys wanna go to campus today?" I blurt out. "We can get pizza and play frisbee on the quad."

"I'll get dressed!" Jude yells, then scrambles off my lap and darts up the stairs. I realize my mistake a split second later when silence falls in the kitchen. When I glance at Jocelyn, her face is tight.

"Go get dressed, June," she says softly, and June slides off the stool and heads upstairs without a word.

"I'm sorry," I say quickly. "I should have asked you first."

"Why are you even here, Jesse?" she asks, her voice strained. Is she mad? "I said the kids can't know. You can't just show up here unannounced and spring plans on us without talking to me first. We can't give the kids *ideas*. You know how this looks?"

Yeah, she's mad.

"I know. I'm sorry," I tell her honestly. "I just got pissed that Jude had to lie about the fun shit he did at the ex's this weekend, and I spoke before thinking."

"How do you know he lied?"

She cocks her head to the side. She knows the kid made all that shit up; I can tell from the look on her face.

I shrug. "June told me."

She scrubs a hand down her face and sighs.

"I can take them if you want," I offer. "You can get some studying in like you'd planned."

"No," she says quickly, and I'm immediately offended. Hurt, though I know I shouldn't be. She doesn't trust me to take them out of the house.

"You're right," she continues, "they could use something more than television this weekend." She sighs. "But campus? What if we run into someone?"

"We won't," I promise. Those lines between her eyebrows are deep, and I just want to reassure them away. I hate that she's so worried about anyone finding out about whatever this is, but I get it. Kind of. I don't want to cause her more stress.

"It's Sunday, so all of my friends will be prepping for the week," I say earnestly. Riggs and Bailey are probably still recovering from the away game travels, Ivy will probably be studying or interning or whatever, and Kelley uses Sundays to prep his lessons for student teaching. "We won't run into anyone important."

She sighs again. "Just for a couple hours," she relents, then hits me with a serious look. "And no touching. No flirting. No anything that could even hint at—" She gestures between us, and I grin at the tint of pink that stains her cheeks.

"No touching *today*," I whisper, locking her eyes with mine. "But soon, I'm going to touch you, Classic, and I'm not going to stop until you're quivering and spent."

Her breath hitches. I smirk. I like unnerved Jocelyn.

"I'll check on your minis."

I climb the stairs and find Jude's legs poking out from under his bed.

"Dude, what are you doing?" I ask with a laugh, then grab his ankles and pull him out.

"I can't find my sword," he grumbles and flips over onto his back. He is wearing his red and black pirate pants and his pirate vest. He can't find his sword, though, because I hid that shit under the couch.

"Weird," I say, then set him on the bed. "You won't need it today. No swords allowed on campus. If you bring it, we can't eat pizza or play frisbee."

"Awwwww," he whines, then takes off running through his door and toward June's room.

"Hurry, Doonie," he shouts as he bursts through her door. "Pizza!"

She whips around from where she was standing at her dresser and glares at Jude. She's wearing a black tank top and jeans, and she's holding a hoodie. My eyes immediately catch on her left shoulder and arm, and my eyes widen.

"Don't come in my room!" June shouts at Jude, but when she sees me, the anger on her face is replaced with...I don't even know. Terror? Shame? Emotions that I never want to see on a kid's face. Ever. Especially not directed at me. She pulls the hoodie up to her neck and blinks back a few tears.

"Please leave," she pushes out, and the rawness of her voice hits me right in the chest.

I grab Jude and steer him out of the doorway.

"We'll wait for you downstairs," I say with a forced smile, keeping my eyes on hers, careful not to let them drop any lower.

She stays facing us, hoodie held like a shield, but I already saw what she's trying to hide. The bright pink, jagged, angry skin that covers her shoulder and arm, that continues into her tank top.

Scar tissue. Fresh scar tissue.

My body hurts just thinking about how much of her upper body is covered with it, and my medical brain immediately runs through scenarios of what could have caused scars like those.

Every possibility is terrible. Every single one is painful. Terrifying.

June is eight years old, and scars like that....

Jocelyn meets us at the bottom of the stairs, face alert and concerned.

"Is everything okay?" she asks, and when she meets my eyes, hers fill with tears. I swallow back the knot in my throat and open my mouth to speak, but nothing comes. She shakes her head, closes her eyes tightly, and whispers, "Later."

. . .

June doesn't speak to me. She doesn't speak to anyone. She stays silent the whole drive to campus, and I can't help but take note of the fact that she's wearing jeans and a baggy hoodie. I've never seen her in anything other than long pants and long sleeves, come to think of it, and usually both of them are huge on her thin frame.

My fingers flex, making a fist until my knuckles turn white.

When we climb out of the car, Joss and the kids follow me in the direction of the quad, and when we reach the edge of the large open stretch of green grass, I nudge June with my elbow.

"See that big tree, Junie Moonie?" I say to her, and she looks to where I've pointed.

"Yeah?" Her voice is mostly flat with just a tiny note of curiosity. I latch onto that note. That's the string I need to pull on.

"First one to touch it gets to pick where we go for dessert," I tell her, and bounce my eyebrows. Her lips quirk up, but her eyes narrow.

"You'll beat me."

"Maybe." I shrug. "But maybe not."

She flicks her eyes toward the tree, then back to my face.

"On your mark," I whisper, and her big eyes widen, looking back toward the tree, then surveying the quad between it and her.

"Get set," I say a little louder, and when she drops the book she brought onto the ground, I know I've got her.

"GO!" I shout, and we both take off in a sprint across the quad.

It's a beautiful day, so the grassy area is full of students. Lying on blankets, tossing footballs, even some people doing yoga. We run through the crowd, and June holds her own. I thought I would have to trip or fake a cramp to let her win, but nope. All I had to do was underestimate her.

The path June takes is cleaner than mine. With the time I spend having to duck, weave, and juke to avoid disaster, she gains crucial ground. When she slaps the tree with both hands, I'm still ten feet behind her, but I skid to a stop when she whirls on me, knocking me on my ass with the fireballs she's shooting at me from her giant eyes. For a moment, I'm afraid of an eight-year-old.

"You let me win," she accuses, and immediately, I shake my head.

"No," I say honestly, "I didn't. I swear."

She blinks and searches my face for any hint of a lie. Yep, I'm scared of her. I put on my *please believe me I'm innocent* smile.

"You didn't let me win?"

"No. You saw a better path and took it." I wink, nervous as hell. "That observation superpower."

Her eyes narrow even more, then she makes a fist and sticks her pinky out at me. I hook my pinky with hers instinctively. I haven't done a pinky promise since...well...maybe since I was like eight.

"Promise," she demands, and her finger tightens around mine.

"Promise," I say with a nod. Then I watch as she quickly leans down and kisses her fist. She straightens, but doesn't release me, and when she arches a brow, I lean down and kiss my own fist. The smile that breaks out over her face triggers my own. I want to run a victory lap for that smile.

"I want a big ice cream sundae with chocolate and caramel and sprinkles," she announces, and I knock her shoulder as we head back to her mom and Jude.

"Then we'll get you an ice cream sundae with chocolate and caramel and sprinkles, Champ."

"I wanna race," Jude pouts when we get close. Jocelyn has laid out the blanket we brought, and he's camped out on the corner with some matchbox cars, a coloring book, and markers. Pirate hat tilted to the side, but no pirate sword. Because that shit's still hidden.

"We can race later, Meatball," I say, and bend down to grab the frisbee. "You know how to throw a frisbee?"

I spend the next twenty minutes or so trying to teach Jude how to throw one. Trying and failing, but we still have fun. Jocelyn's got her camera up and is snapping pictures, and her laughter does *things* to me. I want to keep her laughing. I want to keep that smile on her face; the one that puts her teeth on display and makes her eyes squint and her nose scrunch up. June and Jude have the same smile. Fucking adorable.

I'm running to catch June's toss when a familiar man bun and ginger coif come into view. I catch the frisbee then freeze, glancing to where the J Squad is waiting for my return throw. When I look back at Riggs and Kelley, I see Bailey's pink hair and Ivy's blonde curls. *Shit.* I'm half a second from dropping my body to the ground and army crawling back toward Joss when Riggs sees me.

"Slipper Dick!" he shouts, and I smile and wave on instinct. Stupid move. I should have ignored them. Maybe they'll just keep walking?

Nope, they turn off the sidewalk and start cutting through the grass right toward me. So, I turn quickly and run away. I can feel them following me, and I have only a matter of seconds to run damage control.

I sprint up to Jocelyn, and her smile falls flat when she sees the apology on my face.

"I'm sorry," I breathe out. "I didn't invite them, I swear. I really didn't think they'd be here."

Confusion flashes over her features, then her eyes trail

behind me. I already know what she sees. A Thor clone, a ginger Ken doll, a punk pixie with perpetual RBF (resting *bored* face, thanks), and a bouncy blonde in Chucks. Damn it. The little parenthesis between her eyebrows returns, and a minute later, a giant hand comes down with a thud on my shoulder.

"Dick, I call you and you run away? Not cool," Riggs scolds, and I turn around to face the group.

"You'll never steal him from me with that behavior, J," Bailey snarks, and I scowl jokingly at her. I laugh and try to subtly stand taller, broaden my stance, in an attempt to keep my friends from noticing the people behind me.

"Whatchya doin?" Ivy asks, and when I look at her, her eyebrow is popped. She can tell I'm hiding something. Fucking Ivy. Then her attention drifts away from me.

"Hi," she says with a smile, eyes trained at my hip, and I look down to find Captain Meatball peeking out from behind my leg.

"You're very pretty," he says to her, and she beams.

"Thank you," she says, flashing me a playful look before focusing back on Jude. "You're a very handsome pirate." He puffs up his chest, and I can't help but laugh.

"Captain Meatball, these are my friends." I point them out. "Riggs, Bailey, Kelley, and Ivy." Then I bite the bullet and turn my body to the side, exposing Jocelyn and June. "Friends, this is Jocelyn, June, and Captain Meatball."

"Oh, yeah, we've met," Riggs says. "My roommate and I helped you unload your U-Haul."

"Yeah." Joss nods. "Thanks again for that." She tries to laugh, but it's tight and uncomfortable. I want to say something, anything, to relieve the tension, but I got nothin'.

"We were going to get some pizza," Kelley says, cutting through the silence. "Texted you but you haven't answered."

"Weird." I got the text. I just didn't reply. I didn't want them asking what I was doing because I'm a shit liar and I didn't want them crashing my party. Fail on all counts.

"We're gonna get pizza too." Jude punctuates every word with a hop, and I smile at him and rub his little Velcro head. When I glance back at my friends, four pairs of eyes are on me and my shoulders tense.

"We came to throw the frisbee," I say, pleading them silently not to ask questions. *Abort your inquisition*, I want to yell. *Go. Away. Please.*

"Cool," Bailey says, then snags the frisbee from my hand and pushes past me. "We'll play too."

She's such a tiny tyrant. She hates frisbee. She hates *people*. Pretty sure she's allergic to social interaction. I turn around to tell her to get lost, but the way June's eyes latch onto Bailey with interest stops me. *Damn it.* They really would get along...

I watch as Bailey says something to June, and June says something back. Bailey laughs, then June laughs. June rarely laughs. *Double damn it.*

I send Jocelyn yet another silent apology with my eyes, and she gives her head the tiniest, almost imperceptible shake. *Sorry*, I mouth, then turn back to V, Kell, and Riggs.

"Wanna play for a bit and get pizza after?"

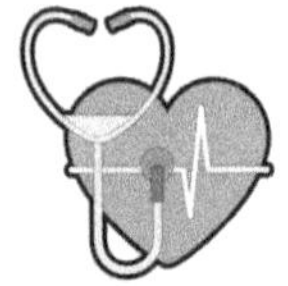

TEN

jocelyn

WHAT THE HELL am I doing here?

I haven't felt this out of place in a long time. I don't spend my Sundays playing frisbee on a college campus with a bunch of college *kids*. God, they are kids, too, aren't they? Jesse is a kid. I let him kiss me...touch me.

I don't even know what to talk about. What do college kids talk about? Even when I was their age, I wouldn't have been able to carry a conversation. At twenty-three, I was potty training a toddler and trying to maintain some sense of dignity within a toxic relationship. Me and these kids? We are not the same.

As Jesse and his friends spread out with the kids to throw the frisbee, I just stand there, speechless, like a fool.

"Hi," the blonde girl says brightly, pulling me from my thoughts. I smooth out my face as best I can and smile back.

"Hello."

"I'm Ivy." She sticks her hand out, so I take it. Her handshake is surprisingly strong.

"Jocelyn."

"Nice to meet you, Jocelyn." Her eyes are bright blue and

130

sincere, but I'm still intimidated and awkward. I smile and nod.

"So, you live next to Riggs and the guys, right?" She asks, looking back toward the frisbee circle, and I let my shoulders relax a bit. "In DuPont Village?"

"We moved in a few months ago." DuPont Village is the name of the cluster of townhouses where we live. "It was nice of your friends to help us unload the U-Haul."

"Riggs and Xavier are so helpful. Plus, Riggs's dad owns the cul-de-sac, so he makes a great welcoming committee."

"Oh, I didn't realize," I say.

"Mhm," she hums, smiling as she watches the frisbee tossed from one person to another. The redhead, Kelley, lifts Jude and spins him in a circle, and Ivy laughs as she watches. "Stanton is Riggs's last name, as in Stanton Property Management, and DuPont Village is actually named after his mom. Odette DuPont Stanton." Her lips twitch downward, and her brows furrow briefly, then she blinks and the smile returns. "So, if you ever need a cup of sugar, Riggs is a good neighbor to have."

"Good to know," I say, then attempt to...make small talk? I do it with patients all the time. I can do this. "What are you studying?" There. That's safe.

"I'm pre-law," she says. "Right now, I'm interning at a law firm. What do you do?"

"I'm a CNA at Harvest View," I tell her, then quickly add, "but I'm in a bridge program to become an RN."

I don't know why I felt the need to tell her that. I'm not ashamed of my job, but I've always struggled with an inferiority complex. It's a knee-jerk reaction.

"Oh wow. That's awesome." She sounds genuine. "I know that must be a lot of work. Doing that, going to school, and raising two kids? You must have superpowers."

I shrug. "Just a mom," I say, and she levels me with a pointed look.

"Jocelyn, there's no *just* about what you do. You're kicking butt."

Before I can respond, the pink-haired girl—Bailey—throws herself onto the blanket with a thud.

"I changed my mind. Frisbee sucks." She pants, covering her face with her arms. "I wasn't made for physical activity."

Ivy smirks, then motions for me to sit on the blanket with her. Ivy sits next to Bailey, and I sit across from them just as Bailey says, "Let's just leave these goons and go get pizza without them."

Ivy giggles and I look away. This conversation isn't meant for me. Great. They're going to start talking, and I'll be the awkward mom person hovering just on the fringe of the circle. I resist the urge to tug at my shirt or smooth out my leggings. I would have worn better clothes if I knew I'd be meeting people. They're both so young and attractive. God, I must stick out like a sore thumb. I reach for the book June brought. Flipping through an eight-year-old's chapter book is less rude than scrolling through my phone, right?

"June is a crack up," Bailey says, and I glance up. She's still lying on her back on the blanket, but her head is turned toward me. Ivy's attention is on me as well.

"Yeah, she's very witty," I say with a smile. "She's usually pretty introverted, though."

"You should have heard her hand Riggs his ass." Bailey cackles with glee. "Oh, it was so good." She raises the pitch of her voice to what I assume is meant to be an impression of June and snarks, "*I thought baseball players were supposed to be good at catching and throwing.*"

My hand shoots to my mouth, and my jaw drops. "I'm so sorry," I start to say, but Bailey and Ivy can't hear my apology over the sound of their laughter.

"You should have seen his face." Bailey gasps between

giggles. "And then she told him to go braid his hair!" She clutches her stomach and rolls on her side, and my own surprised laugh shoots out of me.

"She didn't," I whisper, then glance to where June and Jude are still playing frisbee with Jesse and his friends. The smiles stretching across their faces, *all* of their faces, send bolts of joy through me. I never see June smile that openly. Not anymore, and certainly not with strangers. I probably should be mortified at her rude behavior, but I'm mostly just happy to see her interacting so freely.

"Oh, she did." Bailey props herself up into a sitting position. "I've never seen Jesse so proud either. He about fell over laughing."

"Poor Riggs," Ivy jokes, "he already gets it enough from J."

"You know he loves it," Bailey adds, then looks toward me again. "June is eight?"

"Yeah," I tell her. "She's very mature for her age."

"That's what Jesse said," Ivy says. "He wouldn't stop talking about *J-Squared* the other night. It was *June this* and *Meatball that*. I think he had more fun babysitting than the kids did."

"Why Meatball?" Bailey asks, and I laugh.

"I have no idea," I answer honestly. "Apparently being Captain Jude wasn't good enough because one day, he just started demanding I call him Captain Meatball."

"Told you," Ivy beams, and Bailey rolls her eyes. When I raise my brow questioningly, Bailey explains.

"I thought Meatball was one of J's nicknames." She shakes her head. "He likes to make up weird ass random nicknames sometimes. But V said J's nicknames are never totally random, so Jude probably came up with it himself."

I look to Ivy, and she shrugs with a smile. "Lucky guess."

"So, he's been talking a lot about us?" I say slowly, and Ivy's smile falls.

"Well, that Saturday he babysat, he didn't come to the base-ball game with us, so we asked what he did instead," she says carefully. "So, he told us about babysitting and the stuff he and the kids did. He also asked me for some activity ideas for Sunday because I have a younger brother. That's all."

"He hasn't really said much about you, though," Bailey clarifies. "Just that you work your ass off and you're a great mom. And you're getting into photography."

I flush a little. He said I was a great mom? He didn't say anything else about me, though. Ivy and Bailey didn't mention knowing about the state park date. That's good. That's what I wanted.

I think.

Or maybe he didn't say anything because...

"Are you guys..." I trail off, gesturing between where Bailey sits on the blanket and Jesse stands yards away on the quad. "Either of you... and him?"

I feel like an idiot for asking, but I have to know what I've gotten myself mixed up in.

Ivy studies me with her head cocked to the side, and Bailey stares blankly at me. She blinks a few times, processing, and then her eyes widen.

"You mean us and Jesse...like..." She makes a gagging face. "Ew, no."

"Bailey!" Ivy scolds, and Bailey winces.

"Sorry, no offense," she says to me, and before I can protest that there's no reason at all for me to be offended, no, nope, nothing between him and me either, she clamps her eyes shut and shakes her head again. "But ew. No."

"What Miss Articulate means to say is that we love Jesse. He is *family*," Ivy states clearly, and my shoulders loosen.

"Exactly. Family. Like a big dorky annoying older brother," Bailey says, and I bark out a laugh.

"Is he that bad?" I ask through laughter, and her face softens.

"Nah," she says with a smile.

"Jesse is a really great guy, Jocelyn," Ivy says. "Kind, fun, genuine."

"And loyal. Like a golden retriever," Bailey interjects, and Ivy shoots her hand out and smacks her shoulder, making us all laugh. I trail my eyes back to the quad, where the man in question is currently galloping in circles with Jude on his back.

"Yeah," is all I say.

Conversation flows smoothly after that, moving from small talk to more genuine, interesting topics. I learn how Bailey and Riggs were in a baking competition over her winter break, and how Ivy took the LSAT in October and has already finalized plans for law school after graduation. I tell them about my bridge program, about work at Harvest View, and I touch on my budding photography hobby. I mostly talk about June and Jude, though, and Bailey and Ivy never once make me feel bad about it. They ask questions, they laugh, they crack jokes. I don't feel out of place, or too old, or unwanted. I didn't realize how nice it was to interact with other people outside of a work setting. Other women. Other *adults*.

I'm in the middle of telling a story about Jude's pirate obsession when Jesse runs up to our blanket with a giggling Jude under his arm.

"We gotta do a potty break," he says quickly, and Bailey snorts a laugh from beside me. Jesse sends her a quick glare, then focuses on me. "Potty break, then pizza?"

I try to fight my smirk, but I just *can't*. "Sounds good. Need me to take him?"

"Nah, Classic. We got this. Meet you at the front of the union?" He gestures toward the student union at the end of the quad. As soon as I nod, he takes off in a full sprint toward the building, Riggs and Kelley hot on his heels.

"Those boys are heathens," June says, arms crossed, as she watches them run off. Ivy, Bailey, and I all laugh.

"The woman speaks truth," Bailey announces, then holds out her fist for June to bump it. June does so without hesitation, and the smile on her lips is unbidden.

At the pizza parlor, Jesse takes one of the seats next to me, putting Jude on his other side, and June is sandwiched between Ivy and Bailey across the circular table from me.

It's weird.

I don't like it.

June and Jude are having a blast, though, so I'm apparently the only one with separation anxiety.

Jesse's hand gripping my thigh brings my attention back to the group.

"Outta your head, Classic," his voice rumbles. I meet his eyes. "Are you having fun?"

"I am," I answer honestly. "It's been a good day." He smiles widely, and under the table, his hand slides farther up my thigh. My muscles tighten, and I flare my eyes at him in warning, but he smirks and gives my leg a squeeze.

"It's been a *great* day," he corrects, and wedges his hand between my thighs, resting just centimeters from my apex. "I'm glad you agreed to come out today." He squeezes again, and my breath hitches.

He's been getting bolder as the day went on. A lingering hand on the small of my back. A wink and a heated glance. Brushing a strand of hair behind my ear. Each time, I've given him a weak *cut it out* look that I only half meant, and each time, my heart raced faster. But this, his hand inching up my thigh underneath the table in a crowded restaurant, this is *more*.

I scan my eyes around the table, but no one is paying attention to us. The kids are being entertained by Jesse's friends, and no one has any idea that he's just coaxed my legs wider and grazed his knuckle against the seam of my leggings. Leggings that are much thinner than I realized, judging by the sensations I feel from such little contact.

I slide my own hand under the table and grip his wrist, halting his movements. The smirk is still on his face, and I drop my eyes to his lips just as he drags his knuckle against me once more, this time taking care to press lightly on the sensitive bundle of nerves at the apex of my thighs.

My eyes flutter shut on a small gasp.

I can hear my heartbeat in my ears, my blood heating.

"Jesse," I whisper, and my voice is a plea. He hums in response.

The pizzas being placed on our table makes me jump. We ordered four because, apparently, the guys are, as Ivy said, "bottomless pits." When Jesse brings both of his hands to the tabletop so he can eat, I excuse myself to go to the bathroom.

I weave through tables of people and down a hallway, following the signs for the restrooms. I find them tucked in the back of the restaurant, right next to a small, dark room that holds a few electronic poker and arcade games, and one of those claw machines full of cheap stuffed animals. The only light from the room comes from the glow of a few game machines, and I glance inside curiously before heading into the bathroom.

I study my reflection in the mirror above the sink as I wet a paper towel. I'm flushed, still trying to settle my heartbeat from Jesse's touch. I wring out the paper towel and bring it to the back of my neck. I need to get it together. It's okay. No one noticed. I noticed, but at least no one else did. This whole thing with Jesse is so *strange*. Exciting and new and strange. I woke up this morning thinking the entire afternoon yesterday was a fever dream, but the next thing I knew, he was in my house and eating cereal with my kids. And now we're here, with his friends, at a popular pizza place on campus.

It's not at all the way I thought I would be spending my Sunday.

I was never planning on letting the kids see Jesse in any capacity outside of a possible babysitter, and even then, I'm hoping to never have to ask him to watch them again. But now we're hanging out, with his friends, in *public*. Luckily, Patrick doesn't frequent campus, but if someone sees us and reports back to him? I take my hair out of my ponytail, run my fingers through it, then throw it back up in a bun. This is why I said *no one can know*.

But we're in a group. Jesse and I have mostly kept our distance from each other today, and no one has noticed anything. I think. I hope.

God. It's only been a single day of sneaking around, and already, I'm giving myself an ulcer.

I throw the paper towel in the garbage can, take one last look in the mirror, then head back into the hallway. As I walk past the small room with the arcade games, a familiar hand wraps around my arm and pulls me inside. Within a breath, I am pressed up against the wall between a pinball machine and Ms. Pac-Man with Jesse's arms propped on either side of my head.

"Jesse," I gasp out, my heart beating hard against my rib cage. I look toward the doorway, searching for the kids.

"They're still at the table," he whispers, answering my unspoken question. His eyes bounce between mine. "I just need a minute with you." He cups my jaw and rubs lightly on my lower lip with his thumb. "You want me?"

His question catches me off guard. It's abrupt and raw. Sincere and subtly vulnerable. I couldn't lie even if I wanted to. I nod once, and his mouth is on me instantly.

His body presses into mine, lips urgent and hungry. He slides one of his hands down my body and grips my backside, massaging and then squeezing hard. I gasp, opening for him, and his tongue tangles with mine. When he moves his lips from my mouth to my jaw, then to the hollow of my throat, my nipples peak and my head goes fuzzy. The worries I had seconds earlier—that we're in public, that someone might see—disappear, and all I can think of are his hands and his mouth and his tongue. The sounds he's making, the heady way his body feels against mine, and the undiluted need that flows through me. I dig my fingers into the fabric of his shirt and pull him closer.

"You know how bad I've wanted to touch you?"

His voice dances over my skin. He brushes a thumb over my nipple through the cotton of my top, then cups my breast. I arch into him, and he tugs my shirt down, so he can nip and suck at my collarbone.

"Last night after I left you, this morning before I went to you, today surrounded by everyone. All I wanted was to touch you again."

With one hand massaging my breast, he drags his other down my body and caresses the spot between my legs. I whimper, widening my stance, and he hisses. I'm wet. I know he can feel it, the heat and dampness. Should I be this turned on? Is that normal? He rubs me over my leggings, taking my mouth again in another hungry kiss. His tongue massages mine as his hand works me below, and I find myself moving on him, gyrating my hips and pressing down to increase the friction.

"Fuck," he growls into my mouth, then pulls back and looks me in the eyes. He watches my face as he brings his hand to my waist and slowly pushes it into my pants. He's waiting for me to stop him, but I don't.

When his fingers graze the skin just above my panties, my eyes fall closed in anticipation, and my head drops back against the wall. His hands are magic, and my heart is racing. The room is silent, but for our heavy breathing and the soft sounds of the game machines, as he slips his hand beneath the cotton of my underwear and brushes lightly over my clit.

"Yes," I say on a sigh, and he slides his fingers lower, groaning when he finds my arousal pooling. A harsh breath leaves me as he circles my opening, pressing in just to the first knuckle, then pulling out and returning his attention to my clit. He rubs my wetness over the bundle of nerves in tight, quick circles, and a moan falls past my lips. It feels so different than my own fingers, the touch foreign and exciting.

"Jesus, Classic," he says just before he kisses me once more.

As his tongue attacks my mouth, his fingers sink into me— first one, then two—and he curls them inside me, caressing, while grinding the palm of his hand against my clit. I move on him, back and forth, chasing the sparks that his hand is creating. He bites my lip, sucks on my tongue, moves his hot mouth to the sensitive spot just below my ear, and I tilt my head to the side for him.

I'm so caught up in him, in the sensations, that I don't even flinch when his other hand slides beneath my shirt and bra and pinches my nipple. I rake my fingers through his hair, and his resounding growl sends shivers down my spine while pressure builds between my legs. I bring my hand down between the tangle of our bodies until I can grip his thick length through his clothes. I squeeze his hardness, and he grunts.

"You shouldn't do that right now, baby." His voice is deep,

so deep, and rough. It makes everything about this moment feel hotter, and I writhe on his hand.

"I want to make you feel good," I say, and he kisses me, then speeds up his movements.

"This does make me feel good," he rasps into my mouth, then commands, "Tell me you want to come."

The words fly off my tongue before I can think about them. "I want to come."

It's a plea, whispered and desperate. It doesn't even sound like me, but the look on his face when I say it makes me clench around him. Jesse grabs my leg and hoists it onto his side, then he moves his body as if it's not his fingers inside me, but his cock, thrusting his hips in time with his fingers, grinding and massaging, pushing me toward madness.

"That's it," he purrs, spurring me on. "That's it." He thrusts and curls inside me, presses his hips and erection into my hand, and sounds I've never heard before slip past my lips. "You're going to come right here in this room. In public. People are just a few feet away from us. Does that make you hot, Classic?"

"Yes," I whimper.

"You're going to have to be quiet when you come," he croons, as he moves his thumb to my clit, flicking and rubbing, a sensation wholly different from the roughness of his palm just seconds before. Different, but just as erotic.

"Like that," I encourage, and he stays the course, bringing me right to the edge of my orgasm.

"Come," he commands, then covers my mouth with his as I moan against him, clenching hard with my release, until my legs wobble and my heavy eyelids refuse to open.

My head rests against the wall, while my body is half propped by the pinball machine. Jesse's hard chest is pressed into me and his mouth stays on mine. I feel him smile against my lips, wide and with teeth, and I smile back through ragged pants. Keeping my eyes closed, I open my mouth to speak, but our bubble of ecstasy is pierced by the clearing of a throat.

My eyes fly open, my body tenses, and Jesse's grip on me tightens.

"Uh, guys," Kelley says clearly, "the kids need to pee. We've been stalling, but they're getting antsy, and I don't think the little man can hold it much longer."

"Shit," I breathe out, but Jesse chuckles and scissors his fingers, which are still buried deep inside me. I have to bite my lip to keep from moaning, and I tug on his hair in warning. The fire in his eyes tells me it has the opposite effect.

"We'll be right out," he croaks, and I can hear Kelley's footsteps as he walks away.

Jesse pulls out of me and sucks on his fingers. My jaw drops, and he smirks. This man is shameless. Then he fixes my shirt, straightening the collar where it's been stretched and smoothing out the front. He tucks a few strands of hair behind my ears, then kisses me slowly. It's a kiss I can get lost in if I let myself.

He moves back and gestures toward the door. I brush past him and take a few steps, then turn around. He's watching me, leaning with his arm propped on the pinball machine.

"Are you...?" I nod my head in the direction of the dining room, and he grins again.

"In a minute," he says, then gestures to the large tent in his shorts. "Should probably wait until this isn't as noticeable."

My hand shoots to my mouth, covering my laugh, and my eyes go wide.

"I'm sorry," I say, and watch in awe as he moves his hand downward and grips himself.

"Don't worry, Classic," he says, gazing at me through dark, hooded eyes. "We'll take care of this soon."

ELEVEN

jesse

"YOU CAN'T COME IN," Jocelyn says quickly after unbuckling Jude from his car seat.

I expected this. Actually, I expected worse from her after the shit I've pulled. More heat. More anger. More uncertainty. I broke every assurance I made to her today, and on top of that, I fucking attacked her in the damn game room at the restaurant. I don't regret any of it, but I've been preparing for the consequences.

"I know," I say with a nod. I tell June goodbye as she heads into the house, and I take note of the way she bounces a bit instead of sulks. I think today was good for her.

"Why can't you come and play cars with me? You said you could play cars and I could have the purple monster car and you would play with the black and white broken one and we could race them." Jude tugs on my leg as he pouts, and I rub his head with a smile. The kid played hard today, and his eyelids are heavy. He won't last another hour before he passes out.

"I'll play cars with you soon, Meatball," I tell him. "But not tonight. You got school tomorrow and so do I, and I'm tired. I gotta go do homework. Don't you have homework?"

He giggles. "I'm in *preschool* so I don't *have* homework."

"What!" I say dramatically. "I thought you were in college like me."

"Jesseeeee," he scolds, and I laugh.

"Gonna show all your friends your cast tomorrow?" I ask, and he bounces.

"Yes!" he says excitedly, then stares at his cast adoringly. Not only did Ivy, Bailey, Riggs, and Kelley sign his lime green cast, we also got the waiter at the restaurant and the girl working the counter at the ice cream place to sign it too. His cheeks gotta hurt from smiling so big. Mine kinda do.

"Head inside, Captain," Jocelyn says, and Jude pokes his lower lip out farther. "Go on. Pick out your pajamas. I'll be right in."

Jude hugs my leg, says goodbye, then runs up the stairs and into the house, leaving me and Joss alone in the garage. I turn all my attention to her.

"He's going to be so sad when that thing comes off next week," she muses about Jude's cast. I nod.

"When can I see you again?" I cut right to the point. She's got shit to still finish tonight and I don't want to keep her, but I'm not willing to leave without some sort of plan, either.

"I don't know," she says quietly, and I shake my head.

"Don't do that, Joss," I say. "I'll be more careful from now on. I'm keeping it quiet. When can I see you again?"

She studies me before answering. "I work all week and will be studying most nights. I've got a test coming up."

"Test in what?"

"It's a basic anatomy course. I took it already when I was in my CNA program, but it's the only one of my courses I couldn't opt out of because I took it right before the cut off."

"I can help you study," I offer, and she shakes her head *no* adamantly. I laugh. "Why not?"

"I don't need distractions," she says with a raise of her eyebrow. "And you'd be a distraction."

I don't hold back my grin, and when she flushes, I bite my lip and drag my gaze down her body. Yeah, I'd definitely be a distraction. I step a little closer, making her back up against the car. She glances quickly toward the door leading into the house, then back to me.

"I want a chance to finish what we started today," I say to her, and relish the way her breath hitches and her pupils dilate. I rub my lower lip with my thumb. "That taste I got isn't enough, Classic. I want more."

She sucks her lower lip into her mouth and looks away.

"You don't have to...that's not..." she stutters, and she flushes a deep pink. It stretches from her cheeks to her neck, and into the collar of her shirt. She lowers her voice. "I don't expect you to...." She gestures to her lower half.

My eyes narrow and I tilt my head to the side. What is she saying?

"You don't expect me to...?" I lead, my question equal parts confused and amused. She clamps her eyes shut then takes a breath. She's so cute.

"I don't expect you to *taste* anything," she pushes out, and I hold back a chuckle.

"And if I *want* to?" I ask, bracing my forearms on the car, boxing her in. She still doesn't open her eyes, but her chest rises and falls rapidly as she fights through whatever it is she's feeling. Embarrassment? Is she embarrassed? I smirk.

"I know that you don't...." She takes a deep breath. "I know that guys don't like doing *that*."

I bark out a laugh. This has to be a joke. I swallow another laugh and work to fight my grin. I don't want her to think I'm making fun of her, but this has to be a joke.

"Guys don't like eating pussy?" I ask for clarification. Because...*the fuck?*

She opens her eyes, frustrated, and hits me with a *don't bull-shit me* stare.

"No," she spits, "they don't. I don't want you to think I expect that from you."

My jaw drops, and I gape at her. She's dead fucking serious, and now she's getting pissed at me. For what? Cause she thinks I'm lying to her? Every bit of humor I felt just went up in flames.

"Who told you that, Jocelyn?" I ask sternly, and her head jerks back. She doesn't answer. "Your ex? Is he the one who told you guys don't like eating pussy?"

She still doesn't answer, but she grits her teeth, and I watch her jaw tighten. *Fuck that guy.* "Classic, I mean this with all due disrespect, but fuck your ex. He's a fucking idiot."

Her mouth falls open, but her silence makes me angry. Like she's totally in shock that Patrick the Prick was full of shit. Like she can't fucking fathom that I would be telling the truth about this. Nope. This is not cool.

"I'll be back. Give me an hour. I'll text and you can meet me on the patio." She starts to protest, but I cut her off. "Trust me, Joss," I plead. "Gimme an hour." Then I turn around and walk out of the garage and head straight to my car.

I don't bother going next door because I know Riggs and Bailey are at her place tonight. Instead, I head straight to Bailey's. I also don't bother going through the apartment building to the front door. It's faster to climb up the balcony and go in through the sliding doors. We keep telling the girls to lock those doors, but Bailey still keeps them open when she's home. She says that I'm the only idiot who would climb the second-floor balcony to break in, anyway. She might be right, but I still think she should lock them.

I hop the balcony railing and, sure as shit, the glass door is already open, allowing the cool night air to flow into the apartment. I slide open the screen door and walk toward Bailey's bedroom. I slam through the door and head straight to the bookshelf. She yelps from the bed, but I don't look toward it. I'm on a mission, yeah, but also, I don't want to risk seeing any parts that aren't my business to see. Like Riggs's bare ass. I'd definitely get a complex and be forced to do squats for a year. No way my ass can compare to Thor's ass.

"What the hell, J!" Bailey screeches. "You can't just fucking barge into my room. What if we were having sex?"

I wave her off without looking away from the bookshelf and hear Riggs's deep laugh.

"I need one of your porn books," I say, and thumb through the titles of her expansive romance collection.

"It's not porn, asshole." She growls, and I sigh, frustrated and impatient.

"Yeah, I know. I just said that to piss you off," I say, then rephrase. "I need to borrow one of your feminist novels that depict healthy sexual relationships, promote sex positivity, and empower women." I flash a smile over my shoulder. "And have dudes who like to eat pussy."

She growls again. "You couldn't have texted?"

I shrug and pull another book off the shelf to scan the blurb on the back. "You'd have ignored me." She growls a third time, like a rabid raccoon, and I hear more rustling.

"You maybe got one that has a single mom?" I ask, and a shirtless Riggs steps beside me. He scans the shelves, then reaches up and pulls down a paperback.

"This one'll work," he says, and hands it to me.

"You read it?" I ask as I skim the blurb.

"Yeah."

I glance at him. "It's hot?"

He smirks. "It's hot."

"Cool." I look toward the bed where Bailey sits. She's wearing Riggs's shirt, her arms are crossed on her chest, and she's got a fire-spitting dragon scowl on her face. "You got a highlighter?"

Her nostrils flare. "You're not highlighting in my book!"

"Chill," I tell her. "I'll buy you a new one." She scowls harder and I sigh. "I'll buy you *five* new ones. Gimme your TBR list, and I'll buy the top five titles on it."

She pops a brow. "Ten."

"Deal."

Riggs hands me a highlighter, and I grin at them both.

"Thanks, fam. You may commence your bone fest." I walk out the door and throw an apology over my shoulder. "Sorry for interrupting!"

All I hear is Riggs's laughter as I leave the way I came.

I pull up to the curb outside Jocelyn's townhouse and make my way to the back patio. Most of the lights are off, which tells me June and Jude are probably in bed.

Me: Here.
Classic: Where?
Me: *kangaroo emoji*
Classic: ???
Me: I'm out back. Get it? Outback. Kangaroo?

She doesn't respond, but the patio door slides open quietly a second later, and she steps through it, looking breathtaking in cotton pajama shorts and a tank. She's gonna kill me dead one of these days with how quickly my blood rushes to my dick when she's around.

"Here," I say, keeping my eyes on her face, and hand her the book and the highlighter.

"What's this?" She flips through the book with her nose scrunched all cute like.

"Guys like eating pussy, Classic," I say bluntly. "Guys who are into women like eating pussy, because they want to make that woman feel good. If he doesn't, he's not worth the weight of his dick."

I grab her waist and pull her into me.

"If a guy doesn't get off on the idea of getting you off, he doesn't deserve you." I growl, then press my growing erection against her. Her eyes widen to twice their size. "This is what the idea of tasting you does to me. The thought of burying my face between your thighs and eating you until you scream makes me so fucking hard, you have no idea."

She sucks her lower lip into her mouth, then reaches down and palms my dick, making me groan. I drop my forehead down, thrust my hips into her palm, and rasp into her hair.

"I cannot wait to taste your pussy, Classic."

I let her stroke me through my shorts a few times before I force myself away with a shuddering breath.

"That book," I say roughly, and gesture to the book she's holding, "Read it, or skim it, or whatever, but I want you to highlight the shit that gets you hot."

"What," she gasps in horror, and I smirk.

"You heard me. Anything that intrigues you, anything that turns you on, fucking highlight it. *Especially* the pussy eating." I wink at her. "I think it's time we get started on the last item on your list."

* * *

It's Wednesday when I pull into the parking lot at Harvest View. I'm here to visit Rox, yeah, but I'd be lying if I said I wasn't hoping to see Joss too.

My brain has been working overtime since Sunday. I've tried not to be an obnoxious pain in the ass and have managed to refrain from texting Jocelyn every time she's crossed my mind, so our contact has been minimal, and I'm going through withdrawals. I can't stop thinking about her face when she confessed what her dickbag ex-husband told her.

Guys don't like that.

She was embarrassed and insistent. As if eating her out would be an inconvenience to me. As if I'd be doing it just to do her a favor. Which, that alone—the fact that she obviously doesn't feel like she can ask something of her sexual partners— is a red flag. What else did the ex say to her? What other bullshit did he make her believe? She birthed two whole ass humans for that jerk, and he wouldn't even make her come with his tongue.

As always, Lizzo is right. *Why men great 'til they gotta be great?* The abundance of fuckheads like him in the world is why men ain't shit.

I don't know him. Not really. But I am a literal genius capable of drawing informed conclusions from my astute observations, and I've concluded that he's an epic dumpster fire of toxic garbage.

I'm lost in thought as I round the corner into Roxanne's room, so I don't see the person in front of me until I'm slamming into them and knocking them on their ass.

"Arrghh," the man yells, which makes me want to laugh because he sounds like Charlie Brown with the football, but I still immediately crouch down to help the guy back up.

"Shit, man, I'm so sorry," I say. "Are you alright—*Ralph*?"

Ralph? Roxanne's nosy as shit, meddling, grump-ass neighbor?

"Don't just gape at him, Jesse, help him up," Rox barks, and I spring into action. I've assessed that there are no broken bones and have Ralph back on his feet in a matter of minutes.

"Thanks for stopping by, Ralph," Rox says to him. "I'll be home next week."

He beams at her, which makes me choke on my own spit because Ralph doesn't smile unless he's weeding his flower beds or pruning his begonias, and then he nods at me before shuffling out the door. I stare at her, and she fights off a smirk.

"What?" she questions, feigning innocence.

"Roxanne Gunther, why was Ralph Lowman, the Midwest's grumpiest widower, visiting you?" I prop my hands on my hips. "You guys aren't friends."

She shrugs and walks toward the small table on the other side of the room. "Don't have to like him to screw him, Jesse."

"Roxanne!" I bark out a loud laugh. "Isn't he like ten years younger than you?"

"Watch yourself, boy," she scolds, and I throw my palms up.

"Sorry, sorry. You're right." I stride over to the table and take a seat across from her, then angle the chair so I can see the door. "How long have you guys been...." I raise my eyebrows, and she mirrors the gesture, but she stays quiet. She's not gonna tell me shit, so I chuckle and change the subject.

"You're out next week?"

"I am," she says excitedly. "I've passed physical therapy with flying colors, and they now trust that I can take care of myself and my new hip."

"Congrats! We should have a Euchre night to celebrate. V misses you."

"I miss that sweet girl too," Roxanne says with a smile. "We'll definitely have to plan something."

"And maybe we can invite Ralph." I punctuate the suggestion with a wink, but she blatantly ignores me, which just makes me laugh more.

"Don't you have a class today? Finals coming up?" she deflects.

"Yeah, but I aced the midterm, so I can get a thirty percent on the final and still pass the class with an A," I brag. "Now my Wednesday afternoons are wide open."

"How much studying time did you miss out on so you could figure that out?"

She hits me with *the look.* The same one my dad would give me any time I hyper-focused on one task just so I could procrastinate another. I just grin because I'm immune to that look now.

"Work smarter, not harder, Rox."

"You have the time management skills of a half-eaten pickle."

"Hmm. Weirdly, I want to take that as a compliment. I love pickles."

She snickers and pulls out two decks of cards. She shuffles and deals, and I settle in for a riveting game of Gin Rummy.

"I thought you were coming here to see me," Roxanne says about half an hour later, causing me to cock my head in question.

"Huh? I am here to see you."

"Don't lie to me, Jesse," she chides. "You can't go two minutes without looking at the door. I'm no fool."

I smile shyly, but she scowls.

"Jocelyn is not on this wing today. She came in to say hello, and she will come in to say goodbye, but that's it. So, unless you're planning to stay until after dinner, you won't see her." Briefly I consider wandering the halls until I find her, but Rox shoots that down before it's a completely formed thought. "She is *working,* Jesse. You're not going to go hunt her down and get her in trouble while she's working."

My shoulders slump like a scolded child, and my ears start to burn as Roxanne looks me over with a harsh, speculative expression on her face.

"It's not my business," she begins, and I sit up straight.

Whenever Rox starts with *it's not my business,* she usually follows it with something snarky, wise, and brutal. "And I'm not gonna ask you about it, but so help me, Jesse Hernandez, you better not fuck this up."

My jaw drops. "I'm not fucking anything up," I defend, and she shakes her head.

"You and I both know that there's not much in life you take seriously, Jesse. It's one of the reasons I love you. You don't take many things seriously at all, but you mind my words, that woman better be one of 'em."

I'm rendered speechless at the authority in her tone. Authority and *love,* for me and, if I'm not wrong, for Jocelyn.

"I've got it under control, Rox," I say with a forced smile. We stare at each other for what feels like an hour, then she nods and looks back to her cards. We don't talk about it again.

It's midafternoon when I say goodbye to Roxanne. I decide against finding Jocelyn. Rox is right. Joss is working, and I don't want to cause problems.

I'm in my head the whole walk to the parking lot, only coming out of my thoughts when I notice red plastic glittering all over the ground behind my car. *What the hell?*

My taillight has been busted out. Both of my taillights have been busted, but the bumper and the trunk seem fine. If this was an accident done by another car, there'd most likely be damage to the whole back end.

I spin in a slow circle, scanning the area. A prickle of unease skirts my spine, a feeling I haven't experienced for several months. I don't see anyone watching me. No suspicious cars. Nothing to get all paranoid about, but I still have to fight the urge to brush my fingers over the cool metal in my pocket.

Harvest View isn't in a rough neighborhood, but kids are

dumb everywhere. I look back at my two busted taillights. This looks like something a dumb, bored kid would do. I should know. I was one once. There's nothing I can do about the taillights now. I'll have to get them fixed this weekend.

Resigned, I climb into my car and crank it, then turn on the playlist I made Jocelyn. I've been jamming out to it since I gave it to her. Bailey has a playlist for almost everything, and I never really got it until now. I put some serious thought in to this mix, and it fuckin' slaps. I crank "Summer on You" by PRETTYMUCH and pull out of the parking lot, but I'm not even to the first chorus before red and blue lights flash in my rearview.

Immediately I check my dash display, but I'm not speeding.

Fuck. The fucking taillights. If this ruins my perfect driving record, I'm going to be so pissed.

I flip on my turn signal and pull over, then put the car in park and turn off the radio. While I wait for the cop to come to my window, I pull out my license, registration, and insurance, so I'm ready. I go ahead and roll the window down too.

I hear footsteps moments later, and when I check my side mirror, my stomach falls flat. Because who is striding up to my driver's side door in full police uniform? None other than the ex-husband. The prick who doesn't eat pussy. The jerk who wouldn't let his four-year-old son get a purple cast.

I guess Dylan was right. He is a cop.

"Good afternoon, officer," I say, but he ignores me.

"License and registration." He spits the words robotically, so I hand him the documents and keep my mouth shut. He looks at my license for a long time, but he never does anything to suggest he recognizes me from the hospital. His uniform says Thompson, which reminds me of the way Jocelyn insisted I use her maiden name in the emergency room.

"You know why I pulled you over, *son*?" Officer Thompson asks, and I grit my teeth and force a smile.

"I think it's probably about my busted taillights," I say honestly.

"You think?"

"Pretty sure."

"You knew both of your taillights were out and you still chose to get behind the wheel tonight? You know how dangerous that is, son? Negligent disregard for the law and the safety of the public," he scolds, and his voice oozes condescension that makes my stomach turn. It's broad daylight, and it's not like I'm fucking hammered.

"What were you doing that was so important you had to put yourself and other people at risk?"

There's a hint of suggestion in his voice that I choose to ignore. Even though he's wearing a shiny pair of aviators, I can still feel his eyes on me. It's creepy.

"I only just discovered they were busted. I was at Harvest View, and I think somebody must have busted them out in the parking lot. My place isn't far from here, so I was going to drive home and then get them fixed this weekend."

"You think one of the old folks in the home busted your taillights?" He scoffs. "Maybe they rammed it with their walker? You need to report a crime?"

"No, sir," I say stiffly, his mocking tone grating on my eardrums. If he was anyone else, I'd point out how ageist his attitude is, but I'm not trying to get arrested.

"Maybe we should go round up all the little nurses over there for questioning," he continues, but I stare forward and keep quiet. "You think one of those women did it? Maybe risk breaking a nail?"

Great. Sexist, too. What a gem. I'm not getting into an argument with this guy. It's obvious he's real friendly. Not.

When he realizes I'm not taking the bait, he taps my license on the door frame.

"Sit tight while I run these, son," he commands, then turns and strides back to his cruiser.

I watch him in the sideview mirror until he climbs into his car, and then I rest my head back and watch the rearview mirror. This is the guy Jocelyn was married to? This clown is Jude and June's dad? Officer Asshat? Un-fucking-believable.

It's fifteen minutes before the ex comes stomping back to my window. He hands over my license, registration, and insurance card, and then proceeds to hand me two citations. One for each fucking taillight.

Seriously? Fuck this guy.

"Now, son, this address on your license says Chesterton, but you said you lived not far from here." He speaks slowly, like he's talking to a child. "You're supposed to report address changes to the DMV within thirty days of a move. That's another citation."

"I'm a senior at Butler University," I tell him. "Chesterton is my permanent address."

"So, you still live with your parents." He chuckles darkly, but I can tell he doesn't want me to reply. My fingers tighten on the steering wheel. "And if I were to look into your parents in Chesterton—" he makes a show of glancing back at my license "—Jesse *Hernandez*, would I find everything is *in order?*"

It takes me a second to grasp what he's suggesting, but when I do, my vision blurs and my blood boils. I have to breathe slowly to calm the pounding of my heartbeat in my ears. So not only is this guy a shit dad and a selfish fuck, but he's a racist as well. *Awesome.*

I clear my throat.

"Feel free to look into my parents, Officer," I say clearly and make eye contact. "You can Google Dr. Vanessa Hernandez right now if you don't want to wait to get back to the station."

He stares me down but doesn't speak. He doesn't have to.

The sneer on his face speaks volumes. Then he blinks and flashes me a toothy, smug smile.

"I'm gonna go ahead and follow you back to your place. Just to make sure you get there safely, what with the taillights bein' out and all."

Without another word, he turns and struts back to his cruiser and climbs in. Thirty seconds later, he flashes his brights at me because, apparently, I wasn't moving fast enough. I signal and get back onto the road, and then the dick rides my ass—with the red and blue lights flashing—the whole drive to the condo. He waits at the curb until I'm in the building, and when I step out onto our balcony twenty minutes later, his cop car is still staked out on the street.

For the second time today, my skin prickles, and I know the fucker was waiting for me.

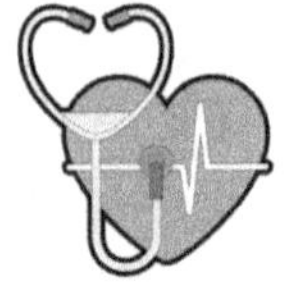

jocelyn

IT'S a little after nine when my phone buzzes from somewhere on the table. I shuffle through the mess of papers in front of me, flipping over pages and pages of notes and study guides, until I find it lying under the flap of my open binder.

Jesse: *Waving hand emoji*

I smile at my phone screen. Jesse and his emojis. I've never used them, or even seen them, as much as I have since Jesse and I started texting. Sometimes his texts can be kind of difficult to figure out, but they're still fun. Like little brain teasers.

Me: *Waving hand emoji*
Jesse: *sleeping face emoji* ???
Me: *book emoji* *computer emoji* *skull emoji*
Jesse: *house emoji* *arrow emoji*

Hmmm. I stare at the screen. Could this one be.... I glance toward the window. I stand up and walk into the living room, then peek out the curtains. Sure enough, Jesse is standing in the grassy area between my townhouse and his friends' townhouse.

He smiles proudly at me, waves, and then points to the patio. I smile back and nod, then move to let him in.

"Hi," I say as he steps into the kitchen. He grabs my hips and tugs me into his body.

"Hi," he says back, and then kisses me, deep and slow, in that soul-quaking way that he does. I pull back to catch my breath, then raise an eyebrow at him.

"I told you I didn't need any distractions," I chide, but it's hollow. I'm happy to see him.

"You've been studying for a week and I've left you alone," he says, then pokes his lower lip out in a pout. I have to bite my lip to keep from smiling. "I figured I could come quiz you."

"Quiz me?"

"Mmmm. I happen to have every bone in the human skeleton memorized," he says, then taps his temple. "I figure I could put my memory to use by testing yours."

I smirk at him. "This test isn't on the human skeleton."

"It's still a good thing to know since you're going to be an RN, because we all know nurses carry the doctors on their backs."

I laugh quietly. The kids are sleeping upstairs, and I don't want to wake them. He steps up to me and traces my jaw with his fingertips.

"I love making you laugh," he says, his voice gruff. "You have the best laugh. I could listen to it for hours." I blush and look away.

"Thank you," I whisper.

"Okay, let's start. You tell me the bone. If you get them all right, you get a prize."

"What's the prize?"

"You'll see." He winks, then places his lips on my forehead. When I don't speak, he whispers over the skin there, "Bone?"

"Frontal," I say, and he smiles. "How many bones in the cranium?"

"Eight."

He brings his lips to my cheeks, then places a soft kiss on each one. I exhale slowly before whispering, "zygomatic."

"How many bones make up the viscerocranium?"

"Fourteen."

He moves his lips from my cheek to my jaw, then drags them over the length of it to my chin.

"Mandible."

"Good," he says against my skin, his hot breath sending goosebumps down my back and arms. He brings his lips to my throat and sucks lightly before moving to nip at my collarbone. He presses a kiss over his bite, and I have to clench my thighs and fists. "Bone?" he rumbles.

"Clavicle," I rasp.

He tugs down the collar of my tank top and licks the spot between my breasts. I let out a gasp and move my hands to his sides, digging my fingers into the fabric of his t-shirt.

"Sternum," I say, and my voice is shaking.

He moves his lips to the swell of my breasts. "I can feel your heart racing," he says, lips ghosting over the surface of my skin. "Are you nervous?"

I shake my head but answer honestly, "Yes."

He drops to his knees in front of me, then takes my nipple into his mouth. I move my fingers into his hair and whimper as his mouth wets the fabric of my thin tank top, cooling then heating the sensitive skin underneath. He sucks my nipple to a stiff peak, then bites. My body jerks toward him, and I have to clamp my mouth shut to keep from moaning loudly.

"That's not a bone," I croak, and he chuckles against me.

"My bad." He pulls my tank top up, so it rests just below my breasts, and my body stiffens. For a moment, all I can think of are my imperfections and how my stomach—my whole body— is probably different from what he's used to.

"*Eres hermosa*," he says against my skin, then kisses down my side. "Absolutely beautiful." He drags his teeth along the skin that covers my rib cage. "How many?" he asks, and I answer immediately.

"Twenty-four," I pant out. "Twelve pairs."

He gives my sleep shorts a small tug, exposing the rounded top of my hips, and bites there. I moan, and he kisses along my belly to my other side and bites that one as well.

"Hip bones," I groan, and he chuckles.

"Try again," he says, then sucks hard on my skin.

I think, digging through my fuzzy memory. "Illium? Illiac crest."

He hums, then moves his mouth downward while grabbing my ass cheeks with his big hands. He sinks his fingertips into my backside at the same time he presses a hot, open-mouthed kiss to the cloth-covered skin at the apex of my thighs.

I watch him with wide eyes as he looks up at me from below, the colors of his irises swallowed up by the black of his pupils, and everything inside me clenches. I've never seen anything as sexy as Jesse Hernandez on his knees for me. My sleep shorts are soaked, the tops of my thighs, warm and sticky, and I'm terrified the evidence of my desire will drip down my legs if I move.

"Pubis?" I whisper, but there's no hiding the raw need in my voice.

Jesse presses his face into my skin and groans.

"Fuck," he says, then uses his hands to widen my stance, pressing his face farther between my thighs. "Fuck, you smell so good."

I tense and flush with embarrassment, but he puts his mouth on my clit and laves his tongue over it, and my brain shuts down everything except my most basic, primal thoughts. Jesse's tongue moves up and down the thin cotton barrier creating the strangest, most deliciously rough friction.

"Oh god," I gasp, and he bites down on my clit. "Oh god," I cry again. Jesse tugs my shorts down my thighs and lets them drop, then grabs one of my calves and maneuvers my leg so it's draped over his shoulder. I wobble and tighten my grip in Jesse's hair. I feel unstable standing on just one leg, but when Jesse puts his mouth on me again, my body bows then stretches until I have to brace one of my hands on the kitchen table behind me and root the other firmly in his ebony curls.

His mouth against my bare skin, with no barriers, is almost unbearable. The sensations are slick and hot and electric. My entire body is at his mercy. When he hums against me, I can feel it all the way in my nipples, which are achingly stiff against my tank top. When he sucks hard on my clit, my throat clenches, and my vision goes white.

And the hottest part of it all? The sounds coming from him. I've never heard such sounds. Every grunt and groan and hum is enthusiastically and erotically carnal.

Animalistic. Intoxicating.

He laps at me with his tongue, sucks with his lips, and kneads my ass with his strong hands, and all I can do is grip his hair and the table and try to control the shock waves jolting through me. When I come, it's with a strangled, silent cry, and my whole body locks up. Stiff as a board one minute, wobbly like cooked pasta the next.

I collapse onto the table behind me and cover my face with my arm while I work to catch my breath and adjust to the world's new tilt. It's not until Jesse chuckles that I open my eyes. His face is glistening with my arousal, and he makes a show of licking his lips.

"Tastes even better than I imagined," he says, then sticks his hand out for me to grab. I bat it away, and he lets out a laugh.

I groan and push myself up on my elbows. My tank top is hiked up over one of my breasts, and everything below is completely bare, but my head is too fuzzy to feel self-conscious. The man just had his tongue shoved so far into my body that he probably tasted my cervix, so the time for being shy is over. At least for now.

I look at him—hair mussed, lips swollen—and I'm hit with a feeling of elation. This gorgeous, brilliant man dropped to his knees *for me*. I'm not ready for this feeling to end.

Slowly, I sit up and then climb off the table. I take a few steps toward Jesse, his eyes tracking my every move. When I start to kneel, he stops me with a hand on my biceps.

"You don't want this?" I ask, and my voice cracks slightly. He kisses my lips.

"I do." He moves my hand to his erection to prove his point. "I *do* want it. But you're not gonna suck me off as repayment for the orgasm I just gave you. I went down on you because I wanted to—because I *needed* to—and I don't expect anything in return."

I smirk in an effort to hide the way my heart squeezes at his words.

"Noted," I whisper, and then I kneel.

I slide my palms up his thighs, reveling in the heated look on his face. I'm not confident in much regarding bedroom activities, but I know how to give a damn good blow job, and yeah, I realize how messed up that is.

I crook my fingers into the waistband of Jesse's basketball shorts and drag them down his legs, purposely leaving his underwear on. I don't break eye contact when I slide my open palms back up his muscular legs, but when I graze over the erection straining his boxer briefs, my eyes widen and drop involuntarily.

I must look comical, gaping at Jesse's giant hard-on, because he chuckles, then threads his fingers in my hair and tugs my head back, so I'm once again looking up at him.

"C'mon, Classic," he says playfully. "I'm 6'4" and boast an *insufferable* amount of swagger. You had to know I'd have a monster cock."

The laugh that bursts from me is so loud that I slap my hand over my mouth, and it takes a minute before I can tame my giggles.

"You are so full of yourself, aren't you?" I tease, and his smile drops away.

"I'd rather you be full of me."

Now it's my turn to smirk. I tug on his boxer briefs and free his erection, then grip and pump it a few times. He hisses, and my toes curl from the sound. I keep my eyes on his as I lick him from base to tip, swirl my tongue around the head, then massage the sensitive skin under the ridge. I break eye contact when I take him into my throat, because swallowing around him takes some concentration.

I know you're not supposed to think about your ex when you're sexing up someone else, but Patrick is nowhere near this big, so all of my tricks have to be altered and tweaked. I pay attention to Jesse's body language. I take note of what makes him moan and tighten his grip in my hair. I've never been so turned on from giving a blow job. When he whispers *yes* and *fuck* and *just like that*, I know without a shadow of a doubt that my memory will be replaying those sounds long after the summer ends.

I'll revisit these memories when I'm alone and lonely, but just knowing that for once I'll be reminiscing actual experiences instead of baseless hopes or fantasies fills me with a spark of excitement. I might not get to keep Jesse Hernandez forever, but I have him now, and I'll never forget the privilege.

"Your test is tomorrow?" Jesse asks later, and I nod.

We're snuggled up on the living room floor under a blanket because, after coming down my throat, Jesse claimed his legs wouldn't work.

"You want to celebrate after?"

I shake my head no. "I actually have an appointment with a tattoo artist."

"Sexy," he purrs into my hair, and I laugh. "Rib tat?" I'm momentarily taken aback before I remember that he has my list memorized.

"Yeah." As I speak, I drag my fingers up and down the strong forearm that's wrapped around me. "I always wanted one, but Patrick didn't like them, so I never got one."

"I'm glad you're doing it. What's it gonna be?"

I grin and press a kiss to his chest. "Secret."

He chuckles, and we sit in a comfortable silence for a bit. My eyes are drifting closed when he speaks.

"Classic, what happened to June?" His voice is a whisper, but I can still hear the emotion in it. The concern. He's not just asking because he's curious. He's asking because he cares.

"ATV accident," I say, then take a deep breath. "It was my fault."

I turn my face, so it's resting on Jesse's chest. I breathe him in, and he rubs his hand up and down my back. I focus on that motion, on his touch, when I start talking again.

"We were with a bunch of Patrick's friends, and they'd all been drinking and riding these ATV trails that one of the guys put all around his property. He owns a farm and a bunch of land just south of here. One of the guys had taken June out on the trails earlier in the day, but that was before they started drinking. I told Patrick, I told all of them, the moment they cracked open the first beer that the kids weren't to set even a finger on any of those ATVs."

The familiar anger creeps up like bile burning my throat, and I clamp my eyes shut and breathe through my nose. My eyes sting with regret anyway.

"When Patrick drinks, he gets stupid, and sometimes, he gets mean. But you never really knew when he would get mean, you know? Sometimes he was sweet and fun, and other times, he'd get ruthless. It was like playing Russian Roulette every time he drank."

I feel Jesse tense, but I don't stop talking. I can't. It's like once I opened the floodgates of this memory, there's no closing them back up.

"When he drank, I'd usually just keep the kids away from him. It wasn't hard, really. He'd be gone most of the time, and then, when he finally stumbled home, the kids were already in bed. But this time we were stranded out there on this damn farm. And he was with his friends, and they were drinking and being loud, acting dumb. It was late, I was exhausted, and then Jude started crying. June was sleeping curled up in a lawn chair with a blanket, so I left her, and I took Jude to the truck. I couldn't carry them both. And Patrick wasn't being scary. He wasn't paying any attention to us at all, so I didn't think..."

I give my head a jerk. I can feel myself slipping.

"It was cool enough outside," I force out, "that I just buckled Jude into the car seat and let him sleep. I needed a breather, so I stayed at the truck with Jude for bit. I was going to go get June. I was going to set us up to just sleep in the truck. It couldn't have been more than ten minutes before..."

I press my palms into my eyes and suck in a breath. "God, I

was scrolling Facebook while my baby girl was fighting for her life."

Jesse tightens his arms around me, and I continue.

"I heard an explosion. I ran toward it. All the guys were yelling. One of them was shouting about calling an ambulance, and I just started screaming out for June. She wasn't in the chair where I'd last seen her. She was gone."

I shake my head at the onslaught of memories. The thick, black smoke that choked me and burned my lungs. The way June's hair smelled like it for weeks. The massive flames. The ambulance. June's tiny little body. Her silent tears.

And Patrick, walking away with nothing but a bump on the head and a hangover. Not even a fucking citation, because him and his boys look out for each other.

"We were lucky. The paramedics said she must have already been thrown from the ATV before it hit the tree, and the helmet and denim jacket she'd been wearing protected her, but she still ended up with road rash type burns all over her back and left side. They had to do skin grafting from her thighs and butt, so she's got scarring all over her lower half too."

"When did this happen?"

"The accident was almost two years ago, and June spent about a year in and out of the hospital. The night of the accident, Patrick was drunk, and I wasn't readily available for him to bully, so he took it out on June. She didn't want to get on that ATV, but she was too afraid to tell him no. As soon as we knew for sure June would survive, I filed for divorce."

And I've been treading water ever since.

"It's not your fault, Jocelyn," Jesse says. He sits up straight and turns me so we're making eye contact, and then he repeats himself. "What happened is terrible, but it is not your fault."

I lean forward and kiss him, and he brushes away my tears with his thumbs. I don't believe him, but it's nice to hear someone say it. Nobody, not Patrick, not his friends, not even his mom, ever told me that it wasn't my fault. They never blamed Patrick, and he was remorseless, so it all fell on me. If I'd have just woken her up or went straight back to get her. Or been more insistent that Patrick go to the farm that night without us...

There are so many decisions I could have made that would have had a different outcome. A better outcome. One that didn't end in June almost dying. But I didn't make a single one of them.

Jesse and I sit together for another hour or so, cuddled under a blanket on the floor in my living room. We make small talk, lighter topics to bring my mind back from the dark spiral of guilt and what ifs. It works for a while. Jesse makes me smile in a way no man ever has, and when he tells me things, I almost believe him.

After he leaves, I head to my bedroom alone, feeling empty and full, all at once.

* * *

I pull into Roxanne's driveway to find that she's waiting on the front porch for me. I don't even have a chance to turn off the car before she's climbing into my passenger seat.

"Freedom looks good on you," I joke as she clips on her seatbelt. She moved out of the facility and back into her house yesterday, but she jumped all over the chance to come to my tattoo appointment with me today.

"Honey, everything looks good on me," Roxanne says with a wink, and I laugh as I pull out of the driveway and back onto the road. "So what are ya getting?"

"There's a picture in the glove compartment," I tell her, and she flips open the door in front of her. She pulls out the picture I printed, studies it, and grins really big.

"I love it," she says.

"Yeah? You don't think I'm, like, too old for something like that? That big?"

Roxanne howls with laughter, and I realize immediately the mistake in my statement. I'm talking to a woman pushing ninety, who wears leather pants, has fire-engine red hair, and drives a classic muscle car. Of course, she's going to laugh at my concern because my worry is dumb.

"Okay, okay," I say with a laugh of my own. "You're right. That was stupid."

She wipes tears from her eyes when her giggles calm, and she catches her breath.

"Honey, unless you're a gallon of milk, age shouldn't be something you fear. You're not a gallon of milk. You're a fine wine. Remember that."

I smile tightly, letting her words wash over me. I don't *feel* like a fine wine. I don't feel like a gallon of milk either, though. If anything, I feel like a gas station bottle of Boones Farm.

"Does this have something to do with a certain 6-foot hunk of energy and bad dad jokes?" she asks pointedly, and I whip my eyes to her with my jaw dropped. "Jocelyn, I obviously wasn't born yesterday," she snarks with a wry grin.

I swing my attention back to the road and bite my lip. What do I even say to that? Oh, well, actually, he babysat my kids and then I gave him a blowie to say thank you? I cringe inwardly.

"It's none of my business," Roxanne starts, "but I think you deserve happiness, Jocelyn, and if Jesse brings you happiness, then that should be enough."

I sigh. "He's twenty-three, Rox. And in college. *College.*"

"Phooey." She waves her hand in the air. "Only for another two weeks, anyway."

My head jerks back. "What? What do you mean?"

"Senior commencement is in two weeks." I see her grin in my peripheral. "Then he won't be a college boy anymore."

I run through the dates in my head. If senior commencement at Butler is in two weeks, then that means that the kids are out of school in....*shit*. I have to remember to call the YWCA and confirm June and Jude's enrollment in the summer program, and then I'll have to text Patrick and make sure he's still paying for half of it.

"When's your program finished?" Roxanne asks, cutting through my thoughts.

"I've got four more weeks. It's not a traditional college calendar," I tell her. "Then I take the licensure exam."

"You're going to blow that test out of the water."

When we pull into the parking lot of the tattoo parlor, I want to squeal with excitement. I'm a bundle of nerves, but it's also thrilling. This is the first real thing I'll be doing to my body that is for me, and only me, no other opinions matter.

"You know, my Marie would have liked you," Roxanne says with a soft smile, then she smacks my thigh. "Alright, let's go get you tatted up, ya hussy."

jesse

"WAKE UP, WAKE UP," I shout into the condo. "Wake up!"

Kelley comes ambling out of the bathroom with a towel around his waist.

"I'm awake, J," he grumbles, and I clap my hands.

"Perfect. Get dressed. Pack a swimsuit. We're going to the lake."

I try like hell to keep from bouncing on the balls of my feet, but I fail. I don't even know why I try to fight it, honestly. Life is just better when you're bouncing.

Kelley's face brightens. "They put the pontoon in early?"

"They put it in early," I confirm, and do a little dance. "An early graduation gift for us and a celebration of me committing to Harvard. Dr. and Mr. Hernandez even had the lake house stocked with food for the whole week, since none of us really have finals."

"I fucking love your parents, J," Kelley says, then nods to his bedroom. "Ives is already here, but you wanna get up with B and Riggs?"

"On it," I say, and then hightail it out of the condo.

I call Riggs and fill him and B in on the news, and they both tell me they're in. Then I head to Riggs's townhouse to grab his cooler and raid his linen closet.

Zay answers the door when I knock.

"Riggs isn't here."

I grin. "I know. He's at Bailey's. I'm here at his behest to acquire the cooler and some towels."

He raises an eyebrow. "At his behest?"

"Gotta remind ya, I'm learned once in a while, Z."

He huffs a teeny, tiny laugh, and moves to the side to let me in the house.

"What are you doin' this weekend?" I ask him as I head toward the garage where the cooler lives. "You wanna come to my parents' lake house? They put the pontoon in and stocked the house with snacks."

"Snacks?"

"Yeah, you know," I say, and motion for him to grab the other side of the cooler. "Snacks. Sustenance. Pizza, pop, chips, cookies. Probably a bunch of stuff for charcuterie, too, because I am trash for a boujee meat and cheese board."

He hits the button for the garage door opener, lifts his side of the cooler, and we bring it out to my car in the driveway.

"You guys leavin' now?"

"Probably in the next hour. It's a ninety-minute drive to the place." We heave the cooler into the trunk of my Kia, then turn back toward the house. "We're probably gonna stay a few days since none of us have finals, but you can drive separate and come and go if you want."

My phone pings in my pocket, and when I pull it out, I find a text from Riggs asking me to grab his swim trunks from his dresser, so I head upstairs to dig through his drawers to find his drawers. Heh.

"Just you guys?" Zay asks when I come back downstairs, swim trunks and towels piled in my arms.

"Yeah. Me, Riggs and B, and Kell and V. That's i—"

I stop midsentence, then glance at the wall. There's nothing on the wall, but it's what's on the other side of the wall that matters. I turn around and head toward the door.

"What the fuck are you doing, man?" The ire in Xavier's voice stops me short. I turn to face him, and find his jaw clenched and his hands fisted at his sides.

"I'm gonna run next door and see if Joss and the kids want to come to the lake," I tell him honestly, which seems to make him angrier. His nostrils flare. "What the fuck is your problem, Z?"

He shakes his head. "For being a genius, you're pretty fucking stupid, Jesse. You can't just fuck around with her. She's not a co-ed. She's different."

My hackles rise and my head cocks to the side as I stare him down.

"You gotta little crush on The Hot Mom, Zay?" I'll kill him. I will beat him to death right here.

He scoffs. "That right there. That's why you shouldn't be messing around with her. You immediately read me as possessive instead of protective. You don't get it."

"What's there to get, Z? Me and Joss have fun together. We're just hanging out until I have to leave in August. She knows what's up."

"Do the kids?" he asks, and I don't answer. "That's great that *she* knows you're leaving in August, but you won't just be leaving her. You'll be leaving them. And I guarantee you, it will hurt those kids a hell of a lot more than you think."

"What are you talking about? I babysat them, Z. That's it."

"Babysat them. Took them to play frisbee. Then took them out for pizza and ice cream. Now you want to take them away for the weekend? It might not seem like a lot to you, but it is to them."

I don't respond right away. I just watch him. Study the genuine frustration in his features, the tick of his jaw, and the rapid rise and fall of his chest.

"Where's this coming from, Xavier?"

He clamps his eyes shut, then rakes his fingers through his hair.

"I was raised by a single mom. Every time someone new came into the picture, I got attached. Every time they left, I was crushed. Trust me, man." He sighs and tilts his head to the ceiling. "It may not seem like it to you, but you're making an impact. You gotta be careful."

My defenses go up, and every stubborn bone in my body sparks. I've never been good at being told what to do. Ever. Caused some serious problems for me in high school.

On impulse, I shove my hand in my pocket, but my fingers don't graze over the cool metal. I pause and run through my morning—I must have left it on my nightstand. The spike of anxiety I feel pisses me off, and I clench my fists. My first instinct is to drive back home and get it, but that's ridiculous. I don't *need* it.

I glance back at Zay and find that he is still looking at me, *scowling* at me, but I don't have time for his shit.

"Just mind your business, Z," I say as calmly as I can. "I know what I'm doing."

"Yeah, okay." The contempt in his voice, in his features, is painfully obvious. I flash a smile.

"You comin' to the lake or what?" I ask, trying to diffuse the tension. I fucking hate when people are pissed at me. He scoffs. I get very few laughs out of Xavier, and it's a gut punch to know that one of them is sardonic.

"You're so fucking smart, Jesse. What do you think?" Then he turns and disappears into the townhouse.

I walk myself back to my car and dump the towels and Riggs's trunks in the back seat, then stare into the distance. Zay is just being paranoid. He doesn't ever talk about his family or childhood or anything like that, but it's obvious he's projecting. Dude's just on some bullshit that has nothing to do with me. Joss's kids are fine. I'm not crossing lines. I'd never do anything to hurt them.

I turn slightly and look at Joss's house. The urge to run up and knock on the door is strong, but I shouldn't spring something like this on her. Not again. Especially not if there might be some truth to Zay's concerns...

Instead, I take out my phone and hit call. It rings several times before she finally answers.

"Hello," she says quickly, and she sounds out of breath.

"Did I interrupt something?" I say with a chuckle.

"Oh, sorry, no. I couldn't find my phone. It was in the couch." I hear rustling, muffled music, and chatter. Then I hear the click of a door, and everything goes quiet. "What's up?"

"What are you guys doing this weekend?"

She pauses. "Nothing. Why?"

"We're going to the lake. I was wonderin' if you and J-Squared wanted to come."

She pauses again, and I worry my lip. I speak before she can decline.

"My parents have a lake house. Four bedrooms. And since the weather has been hot and I'm graduating next weekend, they put the pontoon in the lake. Kinda like an early graduation surprise for me and my friends. The house is stocked with food and there's a slide off the boat. The kids would love it. And there's a pretend ship wheel that Meatball would have a fucking blast with."

She sighs. "I don't think that's a good idea, Jesse."

My heart sinks. Right. I'm about to give in, tell her she's right and hang up, when my legs are attacked by *mi pirata fuerte.*

"Jesse!" Jude yells, followed by "Jude!" shouted from the porch by June. Then, "what's going on?" comes through the phone. Two seconds later, Joss is on the porch behind June, and they're both staring at the tiny pirate latched to my calves.

"I wanna drive the ship," he says, and I shoot my eyes to Jocelyn on the porch.

"I didn't tell him," I say into the phone, and I watch as she drags her hand down her face.

"He probably overheard you," she says quietly.

I see June say something to Joss, and Joss pulls the phone away from her face, so she can respond.

"I wanna drive the ship, Jesse," Jude says again, and I tear my eyes away from Jocelyn and June's conversation, so I can look down at him.

"We'll see, buddy." I give his Velcro head a rub. His cast is off and he's wearing a little camo short and tank set. He's fucking cute.

"You want me to come?" he asks, and he turns those big eyeballs on me. "We can play together." I groan inwardly, then look back at Jocelyn. Why's he gotta be so damn cute?

"I'd really like it if you guys could come," I say into the phone, and I watch her take a deep breath. She's fighting a smile. Even from where my car is parked in Riggs's driveway, I can see her lips twitch, and my chest warms.

"Okay," she whispers, "but just for the day."

$\cdot \quad \cdot \quad \cdot$

I texted Bailey, Ivy, Kelley, and Riggs and told them to head to the lake house without me, so they are already there by the time I pull up with Joss and the kids.

I grab the bags from the trunk with one hand, hoist Jude over my shoulder with the other, and motion for Joss and June to follow me inside.

"Slipper Di—" Riggs greets, but stops short when he sees the tiny ears accompanying me, "—iiinosuars...Slipper Dinosaurs," he corrects, then flashes me one of those *yikes that was close* grimacing smiles.

"Slipper Dinosaurs!" Jude says with a giggle, and Riggs smiles wide-eyed at me. I look beyond him into the house and see my friends all studying me with varying levels of amusement.

"You guys remember Captain Meatball, my emotional support pirate," I say as I put him down on his feet. "He's gonna help me be brave on the boat today."

"He's a 'fraidy cat," Jude says, and hooks a thumb in my direction, making everyone laugh.

"And Jocelyn and June," I say, turning to the side to reveal the rest of the J Squad standing in the foyer.

"Hey, guys!" Ivy greets with a smile. "You're just in time. We're about to head down to the dock."

The tension in my body loosens. It's not that I thought my friends would be weird about me bringing Joss and the kids, but I didn't exactly give them a heads up. The welcoming smiles on their faces tell me I had nothing to worry about. My friends are fucking awesome.

"You guys go ahead," I tell them, and turn toward the hall that leads to the stairs. "Grab the cooler from my trunk too. I'm gonna show J Squad where they can put their stuff."

I lead Joss and the kids upstairs to the bedrooms. I show them where everyone is sleeping, where the bathrooms are, and the empty bedroom where they can put their stuff and change. I head into my room and change into my trunks, and when I come back out, Jude is waiting for me.

"Mom said you can take me to the ship and Doonie will come with her later," Jude says, bouncing from foot to foot. I glance toward the spare room. The door is open, and I can hear the hushed sounds of talking. I don't want to interrupt.

"Alrighty, *Capitán Albóndiga,*" I say while kneeling, so he can climb onto my back. "Let's get you to the ship."

The trek to the dock takes twice as long as usual because I have to stop and answer Jude's questions about everything. He makes me give him a tour of the house, and of the deck, and of the patio under the deck, then of the trees in the back yard. My mom has several fancy birdhouses hanging around the yard, and Jude makes me take him by every single one. By the time we get to the pontoon, my friends are already sprawled out and lounging with the music playing.

I glance back up to the house, but Joss and June still aren't outside, so I turn to the group.

"Can you guys fit him with a life jacket?" I ask, and Ivy is up before I finish speaking. Jude giggles and jabbers as she puts the life jacket on him. I look at Kelley. "Can you show him the ship wheel and keep an eye on him for a minute? I'm gonna go check on the girls."

"Sure thing," Kelley says, then turns to Jude. "C'mon, Captain, let's see how you handle this baby."

I make my way back down the dock, then up through the yard. The house is quiet when I enter through the sliding doors, so I go up the stairs to see if the girls are still in the bedroom. When I reach the landing, it's quiet, but when I come up on the door, the conversation is clear.

"Not a single one of those people out there is going to care that you have these scars, June. They won't laugh at you.

They're kind," Jocelyn says, her voice soft and fierce at the same time.

June stands in the middle of the floor in a bathing suit, a hoodie clutched in her arms, and Jocelyn kneels on the floor in front of her with her back to the door. I go to step away, but June flicks her eyes to me, pinning me to the spot, then looks back at her mom.

"They're ugly," June says, then squeezes her eyes shut. "Dad said so, too. He can't even look at them."

Seriously. *Fuck. That. Guy.*

"Well, your Dad is wrong on this one. He has his own reasons for feeling the way he feels, but they have nothing to do with you."

Joss reaches out and brushes June's hair off her shoulder, then takes her by the hand.

"Those scars are a testament to what you've been through and survived, June. It's evidence of what you've conquered. You're so strong. Here and here." Joss taps on June's temple, then on her chest. "These scars aren't ugly, June Bug. They're armor."

June looks from her mom to me, and I smile, hoping like hell the tears in my eyes don't fall.

"*Caballera,*" I say softly.

Joss whips her head toward me, but I keep my eyes on June. The side of her mouth hitches up in a whisper of a smile.

"*Caballera,*" she repeats. We're all quiet for a breath, then June's face screws up. "Cole says girls can't be knights."

"Who the fuck is Cole?"

"Jesse," Joss scolds, and I wince. *Whoops.* "Cole is a boy in her class," she clarifies.

Ah, of course he is. Little twerp. I look June right in the eyes and hit her with some no-bullshit facts.

"You know how many guys there are in this world, June?"

"No."

"Approximately 3,970,238,390. If this one can't see you for what you're worth, fuck 'em. You don't need him. *He's* not special. *You* are."

I hear Jocelyn choke on a laugh, but I don't look away from June. She narrows her eyes at me and stares me down. Assessing, just like she did on the quad when she thought I'd let her win the race. I keep my face open, earnest.

"How do you know that number?" she finally asks, and I break out in a grin.

"Girl, I got a lot of shit in this head. Stick around for a while and I'll share some more with you."

When June smiles, it's all white teeth and giant laughing eyes, and I feel like a million bucks.

"I promise you that no one down there is going to think your scars are ugly, Junie Balloony." I say it with my whole fucking chest and mean every word.

June looks from me to her mom. "Can I bring my hoodie?" she asks, clutching it tightly.

"Yes, of course," Jocelyn says immediately.

"Okay."

Joss still has to change, so I head back downstairs to give them privacy. I gather stuff for s'mores while I wait, thankful that my parents are fucking awesome and always stock the pantry with the good shit.

I'm loading the s'more ingredients into a reusable shopping bag when Joss and June step in the kitchen. When I look up from the bag, all the air is sucked from my body and I have to legit force myself to close my mouth. I look like Roger Rabbit any time he sees Jessica. Eyes all bugged out, jaw on the floor, tongue lolling to the side.

But what the fuck.

Jocelyn is gorgeous, and I'm losing feeling in my legs from

all the blood rushing to my cock. She's a knockout in sweats, but right now? In a black and white polka dot swimsuit, in that vintage style with a sweetheart neckline and a little fucking bow right at the dip by her cleavage.

Fuck. She's all hips and tits and the space at her waist where I know from experience my hands fit perfectly. It takes all my strength not to reach out and grab her.

I catch her smirking at me because, no doubt, she saw me gawking, so I don't even try to hide it.

"M-I-L-F," I mouth, and she turns bright red. I chuckle and shake my head, then turn to June, holding out the bag of s'mores stuff. "Here, June Bug. You'll be the hero of the party if you walk up with this." She rolls her eyes and fights a smile, but she takes the bag from me.

As we approach the pontoon, laughter and music float on the air, and I find myself growing stiff, on edge. Searching for my friends' eyes, preparing to go on the defensive if necessary. But, once again, I find that my concerns were unwarranted.

No one even looks at June's scars. No one asks. They treat her the same as they have been. The way June's face brightens, and the way her laughter comes more freely, makes me love my friends even more than I did before. And I didn't think that was possible.

When Bailey fits June for a life jacket and they all cannonball off the back of the pontoon into the lake, I do what I've been dying to do since this morning. Since weeks ago, to be honest. The desire to touch Jocelyn is constant, insistent. I wrap my arm around her waist and tug her into me.

"You have no idea the things you do to me just by existing, Classic," I whisper into her ear, marveling at the goosebumps that pop up on her skin. "You have no idea the things I want to do to you."

I expect her to gasp, to pull away, but instead, she pushes her ass into me, making me groan.

"Like what?" she rasps. When she tilts her head to the side, giving me the perfect view of her heaving chest and easy access to her throat, I pounce. I press an open-mouthed kiss to her neck, then suck, before moving back to her ear. The feelings I get when she's near are addicting.

"Stay tonight." I growl. *Plead*. We only have until August. "Stay tonight and let me show you."

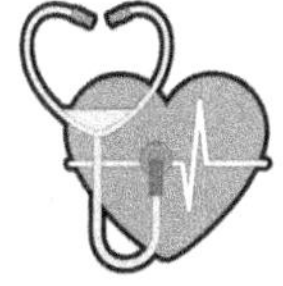

jocelyn

STAY TONIGHT.

Jesse's words echo in my head throughout the day. Through all the laughter and fun, his words tease me. Tempt me.

It's been a wonderful day, and I cannot wait to go back through the pictures I've taken. Watching Jesse, Kelley, and Riggs toss Jude around in the water like a beach ball was one of my favorite parts, and seeing June not only shed her sweatshirt proudly, but engage animatedly with Jesse and his friends made my heart swell so much, I worried it would burst. There are so many superpowers amongst this group that I can't even keep track.

"Meatball," Jesse shouts, dragging me from my thoughts. "Look what I got." He holds up a bag of marshmallows and a stack of chocolate bars. From beside him, June holds a box of graham crackers. Jesse winks at me. "The boy with no s'mores no more."

"'MORES!" Jude shouts. He bounces on the picnic table bench next to me, wrapped in his Spider-Man towel with lake water still dripping off his eyelashes. "I want 'mores!"

"How can you want more of something when you haven't

had anything yet," Jesse jokes, and Bailey groans from her place on the sun lounger.

"No more movie quotes," she says dramatically. "I'm begging. Find a new fixation, please."

"You're killing me, Smalls," Jesse says, then bounces a marshmallow off her head.

I laugh, recognizing the line from *The Sandlot*, and send a questioning look at Ivy across the table. She shakes her head with a grin.

"He gets on these kicks," she says, then shrugs as if it explains everything.

It does.

He hyper-focuses, pays intense attention for a short period of time, then loses interest. He basically told me so himself. *Jack of many trades* and all that. *I'm* his current kick, and just like with the movie quotes, he's forcing his friends to put up with me.

I fight against the harsh voice that creeps up, spitting inevitable truths. This won't last. It's just a passing fancy. Scratching an itch. You're nothing special.

No one's gonna want you.

Especially not Jesse, a gorgeous twenty-three-year-old college student who is bound for Harvard Med in a couple of months. Not his friends, all young and successful in a way I have never been, on the cusps of lives I'll never experience, with loves and relationships I'll never understand. These five are so close that they're more than friends. They're family. It's obvious in every interaction. Me and the kids, we're just visiting.

I look toward June, now sitting on the lounger next to Bailey, breaking graham crackers into s'more-ready squares. And Jude, sandwiched between Kelley and Riggs, as Jesse pushes marshmallows on a stick for him. Am I letting them get too comfortable? We've never had *people* in our lives before. Patrick never allowed it.

Is it going to cause irreparable damage when this group of superheroes inevitably moves on without us, or is this interaction good for the kids? Is it healthy for them—for *me*—to see how relationships and friendships are supposed to work? To feel like they're part of something, even if just for a moment.

I've been a mom for eight years now, and I feel like I'm still figuring this all out as I go. Trial and error and crossing my fingers that I don't accidentally facilitate lasting trauma.

A hand covers mine on the picnic table, and I glance up to find Ivy watching me. Her gaze sharp and astute. She gives me a soft smile and a hand squeeze.

"We are *all* very glad you're here, Joss," she says to me in a voice smooth and warm like sunshine. "The day wouldn't have been half as fun without you and the kids." She grins impishly. "No wonder Jesse can't stop talking about you."

I laugh awkwardly in protest, but she shakes her head. "I'm happy you're here, Jocelyn. And so is he."

I bounce my green eyes between her blue ones. "Thank you," I say quietly, and she nods.

When she gets up to help make s'mores a few seconds later, I consider what she said. I consider the whole day. Every heated look and intentional touch. Every chill. Every blush. If I can only feel like this until August, I should take advantage of it.

After tucking June and Jude into the queen-size bed in the spare room, I kiss them each goodnight and tell them I'll be back in a little while. I don't worry about them waking. They've had a busy day and could barely keep their eyes open at dinner.

I wander downstairs in search of Jesse and find him putting things away in the kitchen with Kelley. I can hear the rest of them in the family room laughing. When Jesse sees me, I motion for him to meet me in the hallway. He mumbles something to Kelley then follows me out of the kitchen.

"Hi," I say awkwardly. He smirks at me, then leans on the wall and drags his eyes up my body, lingering on my hips, then my chest.

"Hi."

We stare at each other for a moment, him undressing me with his eyes and me trying my best not to pant. I can do this. Just be cool. Confident. *Now or never.*

"Do you, um, want to go upstairs and show me your room?" I say, wincing at how juvenile I must sound. He doesn't laugh, though. He doesn't mock. He just smiles.

"Did you read that book?" he asks in a low voice.

I nod. "Yes."

"And highlighted the parts that turned you on?"

I swallow and nod again. "Yes."

His grin is wicked. "Fuck yeah, I want to go upstairs with you, Classic."

I laugh, and when he sticks his hand out for me, I take it and let him lead me up the stairs. We tiptoe past the other guest rooms and sneak quietly into the room where he's sleeping. I watch him close and lock the door, then he turns and stalks toward me.

I back up on instinct, and he halts.

"Just so you know," I stammer, "I, uh, I know you've kind of already seen, but I have stretch marks. Like, quite a few of them." I grimace. *Shut up, shut up.*

He takes one step forward and keeps his eyes locked on mine. "Your body made two whole ass humans, Joss. Those stretch marks are sexy as hell."

I gape, and he takes another step toward me. I step backward, bumping into the wall and plastering myself there.

"My left breast is bigger than my right breast," I blurt, then shoot my hands to my face. Why. *Why* am I like this?

"That's fine," he says evenly. "Everything on my left side is bigger than everything on my right side."

I peek through my fingers at him. "Really?"

"Yeah." He nods seriously. "It's why I jack off with my right hand, so my dick looks bigger."

A loud laugh bursts out of me, and he grins proudly.

"I can't believe you just said that," I say through giggles, and he takes the opportunity to close the distance between us.

He grabs my waist and presses his body into mine. My laughter stops and my breath hitches when I feel his hardness against my belly. The only light in the room is from the moon glowing through the window, so I can't see the greens swirling in the brown of his irises, but I know they're there. I know they're heated and being rapidly devoured by the black of his pupils.

"I'm not—" He cuts off my words with his lips, and I open for him immediately.

When his tongue tangles with mine, we both moan, and I melt into him. I grip onto his shirt and pull him even closer, until every possible inch of his body is touching mine. He runs his palms up and down my sides, gripping onto my backside, then my breasts. He slides his hand up my shirt and tugs down the cup of my bra, pinching and flicking my nipple. I clench my thighs, growing wetter with every swipe of his tongue over mine, every pinch and flick and squeeze from his talented hands. He moves his mouth to my jaw, nipping at the bone, then to my neck where he sucks and bites.

"You take care of everyone else," he whispers against me. "Let me take care of you tonight. Let me treat you the way you should have been treated all along."

My heart jumps and my breath catches at his words. Every

inch of my body quivers with need for him. For the way he makes me feel in every way.

He leans back and tugs my tank top up. I raise my arms and let him pull it over my head, then he drops his mouth to my nipple and sucks as he unlatches my bra. He takes his mouth off me only long enough for me to drop my bra on the floor, then he returns to my chest. Licking, sucking, nipping. Peppering me with marks so delicious I can't think straight.

He drops to his knees in front of me and pulls down my shorts and panties. I kick them off and thread my fingers through his hair. The sight of him on his knees before my naked body brings back memories of the night in my kitchen, and wetness floods my thighs.

He runs his fingers down the new tattoo inked onto my side and studies it. A large anatomically correct rib cage bursting with vibrantly colorful wildflowers. I don't tell him the meaning, that I chose it partially because of what he said in the wildflower clearing at the state park. *Sounds like someone else I know.* Wildflowers are resilient and humble in their beauty and strength. Admirable in the way they sustain and nurture. I want that. I want to believe that my heart, my soul, is like a wildflower. I want it so badly that I sat for three hours while it was inked permanently onto my skin.

A reminder. A talisman. A manifestation for my future.

Jesse's fingers trace over the tattoo, over every rib bone and flower bloom, and goosebumps appear in the wake of his touch.

"This is perfect," he says. "*Mi flor silvestre.*" He presses a kiss to the image. "And so fucking sexy."

He drags his lips from the tattoo to my stomach, bites at my hips, slides his hands up and down the backs of my thighs, gripping and squeezing at the flesh there. Jesse looks up at me and holds my eyes as he presses a kiss to the skin just above my clit.

"What do you want, Classic?"

I blink, unable to voice it. He kisses me again, a little lower, but still not where I wish he would.

"Tell me what you want," he says again. "Tell me what turns you on. Tell me what you want to do with me."

When I don't answer, he stands. I whimper at the loss of his breath on my skin, but it's quickly replaced by his fingers. He brings his lips to my ear and swipes his fingers through my arousal, then rubs light, lazy circles on my clit. I press into his hand, and he chuckles.

"You want my fingers inside you, Classic? Hmm?"

"Yes," I breathe out, and he slides two fingers into me. I moan and move on him. He chuckles again and bites my shoulder.

"What about my tongue?" He scissors inside me, then uses his thumb to press on my clit. "You want me to eat your pussy? Lick your clit until your legs are shaking? Until I'm drinking your cum?"

I jerk my head in a nod. "Yes," I croak.

He drags his free hand up my body and wraps his fingers around my throat, squeezing in a way that makes me clench around him, and he lets out a pleased hum.

"Classic, you are soaking my hand," he rumbles, working my clit and thrusting into me. "I can feel it dripping down my wrist."

He pulls back and squeezes my throat again, then marvels at whatever he sees on my face.

"Fuck," he growls, then kisses me deeply.

His fingers work me while his other hand pulses on my throat, pushing me closer and closer to the edge.

"You're going to come on my hand, and I'm going to spread you out on that bed and eat your pussy until you come again. Then I'm going to sink my cock so deep into this sweet cunt that you see stars when I fuck you."

"Oh god. Please," I rasp, already on the cusp of orgasm. He keeps pace, not changing a single thing, until I'm moaning my release into the crook of his neck. I don't even have a chance to catch my breath before he's lifting me up, placing me on the bed, and burying his head between my thighs.

I lose track of my movements, my words. I don't have time to be self-conscious about my body or my lack of experience. All I care about is how good Jesse is making me feel in this moment, and how I can get more of it. I become greedy and insatiable, panting out wishes and pleas, moving against his mouth until I'm coming hard a second time.

Cold air assaults my sensitive skin when he stands, and I watch with rapt attention as he pulls his shirt over his head, then drops his shorts to the ground.

I can't help but stare at Jesse's immaculate body as he walks to the nightstand and pulls out a condom. He's all lean muscle and sculpted perfection. A sinful portrait. Temptation embodied.

I want to run my tongue over every inch of him. I want to feel him in my mouth again. Want my jaw to ache sweetly as I open for him, my throat to wrap and contract around him as he thrusts deep. I need it.

I sit up and crawl to the edge of the bed. "I want you in my mouth."

"Yeah?" His voice is the sexiest, deepest rumble of desire. He grips his length and strokes, and I press my thighs together. He smirks. "Then you're going to have to choose. You can have my cock in your mouth or in your cunt, but you can't have both."

My eyes fly to his and I see the madness there. The carnal need. He is hanging on by a thread.

"I'll give you whatever you want, Classic," he growls. "You just have to tell me."

I swallow. Lick my lips. Bring my hands to my nipples and

massage in an effort to relieve the ache. He groans and his grip tightens on his erection.

"Classic," he warns. "Mouth or pussy. Where do you want me?"

"Put on the condom," I tell him. He smirks, rips the condom wrapper open, and glides the latex down over his shaft with quick, practiced precision.

"Lie back," he commands, but I don't budge. Emboldened, I shake my head slowly, thinking back to the things highlighted in the book he loaned me. His grin is feral. "Use your voice."

"I want to be..." I whisper and close my eyes, once again feeling insecure. "Can I be..."

"You want to ride me, Joss?" he asks, reading my mind.

"Yeah," I say without opening my eyes.

Jesse's hand wraps around my throat once more.

"Look at me." He growls, and my eyes snap open. "Never be embarrassed to tell me what you want." He moves his thumb to my bottom lip and pulls it down. "There is nothing sexier than hearing you say how you want me."

I blink and nod, then grab his shoulders and push him down onto the bed. Watching him lie back on the mattress makes every part of my body ache. He teases me, sliding his hand roughly down his abs then gripping the base of his erection.

"There's no wrong way to fuck me," he says with a smirk. "Climb up here, slide down on my cock, and use me until you're coming all over it."

I bite my lip and climb on top of him, then rise up on my knees as he positions himself at my entrance. Briefly, I reconsider. I've never done this before. I haven't had sex in two years. He's...huge. I might be in over my head.

"Go as slow or as fast as you want," he says softly, pulling me from my thoughts. I drag my eyes from the place where our bodies are almost joined to his face. "If it feels good for you, it feels good for me. And if you want to switch it up, just let me know, and I'll flip you under me and fuck you senseless, missionary-style."

I laugh. His smile is so playful that I can't help it, and my worries are forgotten. His gaze turns heated once more and he rubs the head of his erection over my clit.

"Either way," he says, then slides himself through my slick folds, "we're both coming tonight."

I bite my lip and bring my attention back down, so I can watch as he swipes his erection up and down through my swollen, sensitive skin. When he moves himself back to my entrance, I lower myself slowly.

We both moan at the contact, and he whispers a curse when I'm fully seated. He slides his hands to my thighs, his grip almost punishing. I breathe through the sensations, adjusting.

"Jesus," I pant out, and wiggle my hips back and forth. "*Jesus*," I cry again when my clit grinds on his pelvis. This is unlike anything. Deeper. Fuller. *More.*

"Does that feel good, Joss?" Jesse asks, his voice strained, then he grips my hips and pushes up into me. "Fuck, the way you're squeezing my cock is torture, Classic."

He presses his thumbs into my lower belly as I move, and I release a deep moan.

"That's it," he says when I speed up. "Use me, baby. Use me to make yourself feel good."

I plant my hands on his chest then move my hips up and down.

"Fuck, I wish you could see yourself." His eyes bounce from where I'm moving on top of him to my heavy, aching breasts. "You're fucking beautiful." One hand still gripping my waist, he brings the other to my chest and massages, then tweaks my nipple.

"Yes," I say, and he does it again. "Suck it," I tell him, and I feel his growl deep inside my body, shuddering from every point of contact.

He leans up on his elbows and takes my nipple in his mouth, and I release a harsh breath. I move faster on him, alternating between up and down and back and forth, until I find a rhythm that does exactly what I want it to. I chase that feeling, with Jesse's hot mouth attending to my breasts and his thick length stretching me and hitting places previously untouched.

"I'm going to come," I tell him, and he hums around my nipple. I clench from the sensations. "Oh my god, I'm going to come."

My voice is a rasped, muffled cry. When he bites down on my nipple, I explode, every muscle in my body contracting in response. My toes curl and my back bows, and my fingernails dig so deeply into Jesse's pecs that I break skin.

"Shit yes," he groans and jackhammers into me. He moves one hand to my throat and grips my waist with the other, then fucks me hard from below. He grunts as he thrusts and tightens his grip on my throat. His movements grow frantic until he loses all rhythm, and he groans out a prolonged *fuuuck* as he follows me over the edge.

I drop down on top of him, and our hot, sweat-slicked bodies move together as our chests heave to catch our breath. Jesse brushes my hair out of my face and over my shoulder, slides his open palm down my back, then smacks my ass cheek with a loud *whack*. I yelp, then fall into a fit of breathless giggles when he tries to massage away the hurt.

"How do you feel?" he asks me, pressing a kiss to my forehead. I think it through. How do I feel? Exhausted. Sated. Deliciously sore and still tingling in some places. My thigh muscles will be worthless tomorrow. With my head lying on Jesse's chest, I can hear his heart thrumming rapidly, and his breaths still haven't evened out. *I did that to him.*

"Powerful," I say after a moment, and his chest vibrates with a long hum.

"I think that's the best compliment I've ever received."

* * *

I wake up sandwiched between Jude and June. Jude's foot is dangerously close to my face, and June's breathing is still deep and even. I cleaned myself up and crept back into the kids' bedroom sometime before dawn, and they haven't stirred. Not once.

I wriggle myself out of the tangle of limbs and check the time on my phone. It's still early, but it's later than either of these kids usually sleep. The lake really kicked their butts yesterday. I glance at their sleeping faces and smile.

When I stand from the bed, my thighs ache in protest, reminding me of the work they did last night, and I smile for an entirely different reason. *Jesse.* I tiptoe to the door and slip into the hallway. I glance toward Jesse's open door, but the room is empty, so I make my way quietly down the stairs.

The smell of coffee wafts over to me as soon as my feet hit the landing, and the sounds of soft music and easy movement come from the kitchen. I head that direction, noticing Ivy and Kelley standing together on the deck outside. She's holding a mug and he's holding her. Riggs and Bailey must still be sleeping, because when I step into the kitchen, Jesse is alone and singing softly to himself as he pours pancake batter into a pan.

He glances at me from his place in front of the stove and a smile takes over his entire face. He looks behind me quickly, then places the spatula he was holding on the counter and pounces on me.

"They still sleepin?" he asks between kisses, and I nod a yes. "Fuck, it took everything in me not to drag you back into my room last night." He wraps his arms around me and holds me tightly against his body. "If I don't have you again soon, I will die."

I snort a laugh and press another kiss to his lips. "You won't die."

"I will. I will die," he jokes.

"Well, we might all die if you burn the house down," I say, and gesture to the stove where the pan has started smoking.

"Shit." He darts back to the stove and flips the pancake onto the counter, then flashes me a sheepish grin. "First pancakes are supposed to be terrible anyway."

I shake my head to tease him, but his eyes widen with mischief. He reaches toward a Bluetooth speaker on the counter and turns the volume up. I recognize the song from the playlist he made for me. "Magic in the Hamptons" by Social House.

As the music plays, he starts to sing along, slowly dancing his way toward me.

"You look so *classic*," he sings, intentionally changing the lyrics, "come through with that magic." I can't take my eyes off him. His deep voice and the playful way he moves have me both turned on and amused. When he's in front of me, he grabs my waist, coaxing me to sway with him, and sings into the crook of my neck. "And know that I'm 'bout to smash it, it's true."

I laugh out loud, and he turns us in a circle, singing every word. He takes my hand, spinning me out, and I'm mid-twirl when Jude bounces into the kitchen with June trailing behind him. Jesse doesn't miss a beat. He scoops Jude into his arms, grabs June by the hand, and shuffles back toward me, so we're all dancing in a circle in the kitchen.

Jesse makes a show of singing and swinging his hips with Jude in his arms, and June's laughter brings tears of happiness to my eyes. When the song ends, Jesse already has another cued.

"This one is for you, Juniper Mae." He waggles his brows at June just as "Butter" by BTS comes on, and she squeals with excitement. Our dance party grows when Ivy and Bailey join in, and Jesse hands Jude off to Kelley, so he can finish making the pancakes.

By the time breakfast is ready, my cheeks hurt from smiling so big. Add that to the ache in my lower body, and this has been one of the best weekends of my life.

I choose to ignore the fluttering in my chest.

It's late afternoon when we get back to the townhouse. Jesse takes Jude's car seat from his Kia and hooks it back into my Camry as I bring the kids' bags into the house. June and Jude head upstairs to their rooms, and I sneak back into the garage, just as Jesse is shutting my car door.

I wrap my arms around his shoulders and kiss him. It starts light, but deepens quickly, until I have to physically drag myself away from him. I shake my head slowly.

"We can't do that here," I say, and he shrugs.

"Can't blame me for trying." He steps forward and kisses me again. "When can I see you?"

"I work all week and have to prep for my final exams," I tell him honestly. "You graduate next week, right?"

"Getting that degree," he says with a grin.

"I'll call you tomorrow," I say, giving his chest a shove. "Go back and enjoy the lake with your friends."

"Wait. Gimme that book back." His smirk is suggestive and heats my blood. "I need to do some studying of my own."

I don't say anything. I just turn and hustle into the house. I grab the book from my bedroom, then bring it back to Jesse in the garage. I hand it to him, he thumbs through it briefly, then winks. He takes a few steps toward the open garage door.

"You're my hardest goodbye, Classic," he says dramatically, and I roll my eyes.

"Go." I shoo him with my hands, but when he's almost to his car, I call out to him. "Jesse." He stops in his tracks and turns to face me. "Why 'classic'?"

Even from the distance, I can see his smirk. When I asked this question last time, all he said was *it fits*. I hold my breath, half expecting the same answer. He leans back on his car. Cool and confident. Unbothered.

"Classic," he says clearly. "Noun. A work of enduring excellence. A perfect example."

My smile stretches slowly as he continues, and I feel my face flush.

"Adjective. Serving as a *standard* of recognized value. Exemplary. Timeless." He runs his hand through his curls, his eyes never leaving mine. "It was your looks, first. Your body. Marilyn Monroe, Sophia Loren, Elizabeth Taylor. You're an Old Hollywood, classic beauty, Joss. And so fucking sexy."

He pauses, and I watch him bite his lower lip. It's too dark to tell for sure, but I swear I can feel his eyes on me, dragging from my face to my toes and back. When he speaks again, his voice is deep and raspy.

"After I got to know you...now..." My heart races faster in the quiet, wanting more yet dreading it. Needing it. Needing *him*. "Now, Classic, everything about you. It just fits."

I'm speechless for a moment. No one has ever seen me before, let alone seen me like *that*. Like the way he sees me. My eyes sting and I fist my hands to calm the tremble.

"Thank you," I push out, unable to hide the cracks in my voice.

He nods, then blows me a kiss. "We'll do this again soon," he says, then climbs in his car and drives away.

I close the garage door and head back into the house, taking a moment to catch my breath and clear my head. The way Jesse makes me sway on my feet, the way he makes my heart pound and my breaths quicken. I don't think I'll ever get used to it.

I don't know if I want to.

I'm heading up the stairs to get the kids bathed and in pajamas when there's a knock at the door. A smile stretches over my face, and I jog back down the stairs.

"Miss me already," I tease as I swing the door open, but it's not Jesse on the other side. My shoulders tense.

"Lyn. We gotta talk," Patrick says, and my defenses shoot up at the tone in his voice. Veiled authority. Mock concern. Manipulation. Then my eyes catch on the person behind him. A woman. She's beautiful. Maybe in her forties, with short, light brown hair and brown eyes. She gives me a small smile, and something about it makes me nervous.

"Who are you?" I ask her, but Patrick answers.

"That's what we gotta talk about."

jesse

THE WEEK PASSES without much from Jocelyn.

My calls go unanswered. My texts receive single-word responses, if any at all.

It makes me anxious. Concerns about being discarded nag in my mind. I do everything I can to keep my worries from consuming me.

I manage to finish knitting the elephant for my mom. I play some cards with Rox and Ralph. Instead of getting my transcripts in order for Harvard, like I'm supposed to, I clean out my entire email inbox and spam folders, which takes three hours. I make appointments to view some apartments in Boston. I spend fifty bucks on moisture-wicking athletic socks because of an ad I saw on social media, then spend a few hours trying to figure out how to return them, because why the hell would I spend fifty bucks on socks? I play some guitar. I watch *Houseboat*. I watch *Houseboat* again.

I do everything I can to give Jocelyn space. Maybe she was feeling overwhelmed after our weekend at the lake. I get it. It was a lot. She might need time to process.

But by the day of graduation, my patience is shot.

All through commencement and dinner with my parents, a day that should be filled with excitement and pride over my achievements, I can't stop stressing over Jocelyn. I mean, I should be gassed the fuck up. Today, I graduated undergrad with honors when I *literally* barely survived high school. But do I feel any of that pride? No. Instead, I keep wondering if I did something wrong to piss Jocelyn off. If she's cooled on us. The old feelings of inadequacy flood my body until I'm itchy and ready to crawl out of my skin.

Joss sent me one text this morning. A little emoji man wearing a cap and gown followed by a firework emoji. No words. Nothing. I've never hated emojis until now. When Mom and Dad leave to head back to Chesterton, I go straight to Jocelyn's.

I'm surprised I made it as long as I did, to be honest.

The house is dark when I pull into the driveway, but I know she's home. The kids should be with Deputy Douche Canoe this weekend, and unless she picked up an overnight shift at Harvest View, she should be off work.

I climb out of the car and stalk toward the door, closing the distance in three strides. I knock twice, and the door opens seconds later. Jocelyn stands in the entryway and smiles tightly.

"Hey," she says, then takes a step to the side, "come in."

I follow her through the house and into the kitchen, where she sits on one of the stools at the island.

"Congrats," she says, cutting through the silence with forced brightness. "College graduate, next stop Harvard Medical School. That must feel great, yeah?"

I don't have the patience for small talk and false niceties.

"What's goin' on, Joss?" I ask bluntly, and she takes a deep breath. Those little lines between her eyebrows are back and I grit my teeth. I hate seeing them. "Just fuckin' tell me."

"Patrick came to see me on Sunday," she says slowly. "After you dropped us off."

"Okay?"

I dropped them off around four in the afternoon. It's a little weird that Sherriff Shit for Brains would show up that late on a Sunday, but I don't say anything. The comments Dylan made a few weeks ago— *Comes around a lot. Random times. Usually at night*—invade my head, and I have to physically bite my tongue.

"Jesse...who is Sandra Huntington?"

Every muscle in my body stiffens, and ice shoots through my veins.

"How do you know that name?" I ask slowly, fighting against the urge to run. To hit something.

"Patrick brought her here—"

"She was here?" I cut her off, my voice rising. "She was here in this house?" I spin around, eyes jumping from each window to the patio doors, looking for...I don't even know what. A pair of cold brown eyes peering inside? "Joss, she's fucking nuts."

"So, it's true?" she says, and when I swing my attention back to her, she's stark white and her eyes are double in size.

"What's true?" I ask.

"That you had an affair."

The comment stabs right into my chest, and I bark a sardonic laugh.

"Is that what she told you?" I cock my head to the side. "Is that what Mrs. Huntington and your brilliant ex-husband told you? That she and I *had an affair*?"

She sucks her lip between her teeth and bites down. Instead of talking, she nods.

"What else did they tell you about my life, Joss?" My voice is hard, mocking. Cruel. I'm losing my grip on my control. My thoughts swirling rapidly, half-formed and confusing. Am I defending myself? Is she thinking the worst of me? I can't tell if I'm more hurt or more angry. Do I feel betrayed? Nervous?

When Joss doesn't speak, I ask again, "What did they tell you, Jocelyn?"

Her voice is a whisper when she finally speaks, but each word jolts through me as if it were shouted through a megaphone. I have to brace myself, so I don't flinch.

"That you had an affair. You liked her because she was older. You...you *seduced* her. She lost her job. She left her husband for you. Lost her kids. And you...you didn't want her after that."

"And you believed them?"

"I didn't," she rushes out. "But the way you just acted. I thought..."

"You thought what? That I have some sort of mom fetish? An Oedipal complex? That I like to prey on older women?"

She shakes her head no, but she doesn't speak. Doesn't protest. It guts me, and I clench my fists and breathe slowly through my nose.

"Jocelyn," I say tightly, "did they tell you when me and Mrs. Huntington had our *affair*? When did I supposedly seduce her?"

Joss shakes her head and wipes tears from her cheeks.

"You know how I know Sandra Huntington, Joss? She was my freshman year guidance counselor. In high school."

"No," she says on a gasp, and more tears fall.

"Yeah," I bite out. "I don't know what other bullshit they told you, but a fifteen-year-old high school student can't *seduce* their thirty-year-old guidance counselor. If you don't believe me, you can check the court records. They didn't think so either when they charged her with felony unlawful sexual activity with a minor."

"Oh my god, Jesse." She covers her mouth with her hand

and stares at me. I can tell from the pain in her eyes that there is more.

"What else did they tell you?" I grit out. "What other parts of my life did your ex dig through?"

She closes her eyes. I know what she's going to say before she says it.

"Rehab."

Fuck her ex. Fuck him straight to hell.

"I suppose they didn't tell you the specifics, though, did they?" I scoff when the look on her face tells me I'm right.

"I told them I didn't want to hear any more."

It's silent for a minute. Our ragged breathing the only sounds, and they're deafening in the small kitchen. My skin is crawling with memories and insecurities.

"I was fourteen when I met Sandra Huntington," I begin. Joss starts to speak, but I cut her off. "I was fourteen and fucked up. My head was a mess, I was failing classes. I hated school because I couldn't focus. My parents are great, but they were working a lot, and I was just... I was fucking fourteen years old."

I rake my fingers through my hair.

"It was Mrs. Huntington's job to find me a tutor. Put me in programs to help me learn better, right? Well, she figured I probably had ADHD, and she started mentoring me. Tutoring me. Helped me find these tricks for better managing my symptoms. My grades started to improve. She hooked me up with an after-school science program. After a while, I was doing really well, and I was grateful to her. I spent a lot of time in her office. Spent time with her after school."

I glance at Joss to find her watching me intently, pity on her face, and I have to look away. I can't stand her looking at me like that, but I can't stand her not knowing the truth either.

"She started giving me meds. Mostly Adderall, but some

other stuff too. To help me focus, right? To help me *'calm down.'* Then one day, things became physical..."

I remember the exact day things went too far. I remember everything about her office, the way the sun was low and shining through the potted ferns she had resting on her windowsill. She was wearing a skirt and blouse I'd never seen before, and I remember thinking she must have forgotten to do some of the buttons because when she moved, I could see right down her shirt. I remember trying hard not to look, but she always seemed to move herself right into my line of sight. And then she put her hand on my thigh. Slid it up. *Do you like what you see...*

I squeeze my eyes shut and fight back the memory. The same one that randomly invades my consciousness, that I'll stress over for days, thinking of all the things I should have done, should have said. So much could have been avoided if I would have just done a few things differently that day.

I don't say any of this out loud. I can tell from the twist of Jocelyn's features that she is hurting for me. I don't want to cause her unnecessary pain. Just because the memories plague my thoughts doesn't mean she needs to be burdened with them too.

"First, it was just her touching me, and I was a horny fucking kid and I looked up to her. It felt...weird, you know? But I fucking *worshipped* her at that point. She'd done so much for me. Believed in me. Helped me. Then she made me touch her, and then..."

I shrug, letting her assume the rest.

"How long?" she whispers, and I give her a sinister smile.

"Until the end of my junior year," I answer. "And it only ended because I had to be admitted into Lake Serenity Wellness Facility for abusing Adderall. I ended up having a mental break-down and confessing everything to my therapist. They arrested

Mrs. Huntington, and I felt terrible. I didn't want to get her in trouble. I thought she cared about me."

I scoff.

"And then it came out that I wasn't the only one. There were three of us, and I realized that she'd taken advantage of me, you know? I was just a vulnerable, confused kid, and she used me."

I don't get into the mess of emotions I felt before realizing that I was the victim of a predator. I don't tell her how I was crushed because I thought I was in love with her. I felt betrayed and not good enough. I was jealous of those other boys, my classmates. One was even someone I considered a friend. I don't tell her how, even after years, I still struggle with those feelings of inadequacy and guilt. Sandra Huntington made me think I was important to her, made me feel like someone worthy, but in the end, I wasn't. In the end, I was just someone to use.

A fuck and some laughs.

They had to extend my stay at Lake Serenity after I found out about the others.

"I'm so sorry, Jesse," Jocelyn whispers. "I'm so sorry."

I reach into my pocket and pull out the ring, then put it on the table in front of her.

"And since I'm cutting myself wide open tonight, this is a ring Mrs. Huntington gave me. She had it made. It's like a fidget spinner that I could wear. I wore it every day from freshman year until I was sent to Lake Serenity."

Jocelyn stares at the ring like it's a rat, with equal parts fear and disgust.

"I don't keep it because I'm in love with her, or because I miss her, or because I romanticize the way I was groomed and sexually assaulted," I say bluntly. "She's a *predator*. I keep it because fuck her. That bitch didn't ruin me. That was the darkest time of my entire life. When I went to Lake Serenity, I thought I was literally losing my mind. I thought I was going to die, and that was all her fault. I keep this stupid piece of metal as a reminder of what I'm capable of overcoming. So, I can't get used again."

My hands are shaking. My whole body is shaking, and I'm having trouble catching my breath. I close my eyes and count.

"How could you believe them, Classic?" I choke out, my teeth clenched. Rehashing all of this doesn't hurt half as much as her doubt.

"I didn't," she pleads. "I swear, I didn't."

"Then why the fuck has it been radio silence?" I yell, and I immediately regret it when she winces.

"Patrick said he'd tell the Dean at Harvard. He has... He has a restraining order. I didn't believe what they said about you; I knew there was some sort of explanation for everything. I don't trust anything Patrick says ever. But I also can't underestimate him. He has connections. He knows people. He has your discharge papers from the facility. He has a restraining order, I saw your name, and he said if I have any more contact with you, he will take it to the Dean and get your acceptance revoked."

"Jesus Christ, Jocelyn. Fuck your ex. Seriously, he is the worst kind of person." I drag in a deep breath. This guy was going to use her human decency and kindness against her. She was trying to protect my future from a lie. "That restraining order was against Sandra. I filed it months ago."

"What?"

"Sandra came back around last summer and basically started stalking me. She got out of jail, and I guess her ex-husband and kids want nothing to do with her, so she came crawling to me. *I* filed that restraining order. Sandra Huntington is not allowed within 500 feet of me, my family, my friends, or any part of campus."

"And the Dean?"

"Fucking let your dumbass ex try." I let out a genuine laugh this time. "Dean Hollis knows everything about my past. I talked about it at length in my interview. Harvard Med doesn't fucking care that I had to go to kiddie rehab or that I've got a crazy stalker. All they care about is that I'm honest and that I've got the highest MCAT score in the country."

"That prick," she whispers, scowling at nothing. "She was here. He brought her into my house with my kids."

"Stay the fuck away from her, Jocelyn," I command. "I'm serious. If she comes back here, call the cops."

"Patrick *is* the cops, Jesse."

"I don't care. Call the cops, then call me."

"Okay," she says, pain and shame etched in her features. I hate seeing her brow furrowed. "God, I'm so sorry, Jesse."

"It's not your fault your ex-husband is an evil troll," I say lightly, then pull her in for a hug. She sniffles into my shirt, tightening her grip on my waist. "But you gotta trust me, Joss. I'm an adult. You're a great mom, but you're not *my* mom, okay?"

I *need* her to trust me. I've struggled my whole life to get people to take me seriously, to see me as worthy and capable. I don't want to have to do that with Joss. I can't. I need her to know I'm *more*. Because I am.

She nods, her head leaning on my chest. "Okay."

I lean down and brush my lips over the skin of her neck, letting my shoulders relax. I was finally starting to feel seen, appreciated. I don't want to lose that. I close my eyes and breathe in her floral scent.

"I missed you all week," I whisper, letting my mouth ghost over her skin. She shivers, and my lips pull into a genuine smile.

"I missed you too."

"I graduated today," I say. "I wanted to celebrate with you."

"Mmmm," she hums, then runs her hands up and down my back. She pulls away and looks me in my eyes. "Celebrate how?"

I grin. I need all of this bullshit in the past.

"Well, you see…" I say, "I've been studying up on your high-lights. I got a few things we can try…"

* * *

It's barely dawn when I wake up in Jocelyn's bed, her naked body pressed up against mine. My dick is so hard it hurts, and when I move, it brushes against the comforter, and I have to stifle a groan.

The shit this woman has asked me to do to her.

Sure, this week fucking sucked, and yesterday was terrible, but we more than made up for it last night. Good god, I've hit the jackpot. Smart as fuck, gorgeous as all hell, breath-play curious, and down for butt stuff. Just thinking about it makes me even harder, and I have to bite back another groan.

Jocelyn stirs beside me, turns slightly, and drags her leg up over my waist. When she makes contact with my dick, I jerk on instinct, and she wakes.

"Is everything okay?" she asks sleepily. Her sleepy little voice kills me.

"Baby," I whimper, then take her hand and move it to my dick. "I'm so hard."

She giggles, then cups my shaft, stroking it.

"Poor baby," she mumbles. "What can I do?"

"Welllll," I say, then quickly flip us so I'm between her legs and suspended above her. Her laughter turns into a moan when I swipe the head of my dick through her pussy, the tip so sensitive my vision sparks white. She hums and tilts her hips upward. "Let me sink into this sweet pussy. It'll be fast, but I'll make you come on my tongue after."

The moment she moans her approval, I'm snagging a

condom from the strip I left on the nightstand and burying myself to the hilt in her heat.

"Fuuuuck me," I pant out. "Heaven is being balls deep inside you."

She laughs, causing her inner walls to clench on my dick, and I groan. I pull out to the tip, spit on her pussy, then slam back in. I perform exactly how I promised. I fuck her hard and fast, spill my release into the condom, then eat her until she's writhing on my tongue and begging for mercy.

"Three," I say after collapsing next to her and catching my breath.

"Three?"

"Mmm." I turn on my side and press a kiss to her lips. "Jack of Many Trades, Master of Three." She raises a brow in question, and I smirk. "Knitting, surgery, and—" I grab her ass cheek and squeeze "—dat ass."

She squeals and falls into a fit of laughter, and I bask in the sound. I want to record it and listen to it on repeat. I want to learn record producing and sound mixing, just so I can make a whole album of it. I want to store it in my brain and keep it safe, so I can play it back and listen to it anytime I want to. Long after she's gone.

Not for the first time since she and I started this whole thing, I resent Harvard. A few weeks ago, August seemed so far away. Now, it's not far enough. The thought of having to say goodbye to Jocelyn and the kids makes my stomach clench. Makes me feel lost in a way I haven't in years.

I looked it up. Harvard Med is exactly 953 miles from Jocelyn's townhouse. It's a fourteen hour and fifteen minute trip, without stops or traffic.

By the end of the summer, I will have to move 953 miles away from Joss, June, and Jude. Fourteen hours and fifteen minutes from three people who have somehow become permanent fixtures in my mind. In my chest. When I think about it, it hurts.

To shut my brain up, I roll back on top of Jocelyn and take her lips in a long, deep kiss. I get lost in the tangle of our tongues, the breathy moans and whimpers she makes.

"My wildflower," I whisper against her skin, dragging my lips just to watch goosebumps erupt at my touch. I could stay in this bed with her all day. Forever. The realization knocks me on my ass, and I kiss her again to erase it. But it doesn't go away, it just flashes brighter. I pull back and rest my forehead on hers.

"I'm going to go make coffee," I whisper.

"Okay." She smiles, then brushes one more light kiss to my lips. "I'll be down in a minute."

I crawl out of the bed, pull on my boxer briefs, and make my way downstairs. I'm fixing up the coffee pot when I hear the *click* of a shutter behind me. I turn quickly and find Jocelyn leaning against the counter, wearing a silk robe and holding her camera.

"Did you just snap a picture of my ass, Classic?" I joke, and she smirks and shrugs.

"Something to remember you by."

I laugh off the sting of her statement. Just a fuck and some laughs, but not worth keeping.

I spend the day with Joss. I go with her to the grocery store to do the shopping for the week, I fold a load of the kids' clothes while she finishes up a homework assignment, and I slip out the back door minutes before Patrick shows up to drop off the kids.

Despite last weekend, she still thinks it's better that the kids don't see us *together*. We still need to keep up appearances. Keep things quiet. Especially around the ex. I don't like it, but I do it anyway.

I knock on Riggs's patio door and Zay opens it for me. We haven't exchanged words since last weekend.

"Hey," he says, then moves to the side to let me in. "Riggs is upstairs. I'll get him."

He turns down the hall, but I stop him.

"Z," I call, and he looks over his shoulder at me. "I'm sorry."

"Yeah," he nods, then disappears up the stairs. A minute later, Riggs comes into the kitchen, but Zay isn't with him. Fine. That's how he's gonna be, then.

"Sup," Riggs says, and I cut to the chase.

"Has B told you about my stalker?"

The look on his face tells me she hasn't. She has no reason to. By the time Riggs came into the picture, we all thought Mrs. Huntington was taken care of. I take a breath.

"So basically, last summer, right before school started, I had some issues with a stalker, and I had to file a restraining order. I'll explain everything in full, but right now, I need you to come with me to my lawyer's office, so we can amend the restraining order and put your townhouse on the list of places my stalker can't go near."

He nods, then raises an eyebrow. "What about Joss and the kids?"

I sigh. "Her ex is a cop and an epic douche. If I name her on the order, he'll probably start shit, but since she's your neighbor, I'm hoping this will protect her by proxy."

"Unless she's at work or the kids are at school," he says pointedly. I nod. I've already considered that, and as of right now, I got nothing. When I don't say anything, he stands. "You think this stalker is dangerous?"

I think it over. "No, but I don't want to take chances, you know?"

"Alright, let's go."

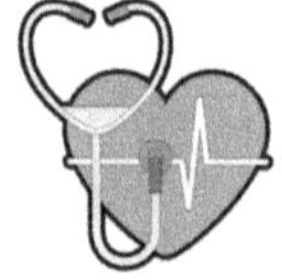

jocelyn

"MOVE YOUR BOOTIES, SQUAD," Jesse bellows into the house, and Jude's laughter echoes down the stairs.

"He said booty!" Jude squeals, and Jesse winks at me.

"Every time," he says with a proud smile. "Every single time."

Jude comes bounding down the stairs with June in tow. I take a moment to appreciate the smiles on their faces, especially June's. She's wearing a sweatshirt, but I can see the thick strap of a tank top underneath. The fact that she's layering at all is a huge step. She doesn't always take the sweatshirt off, but sometimes she does.

I've been making Jesse keep his distance from the kids. I've mostly been seeing him when they're at school or Patrick's, but since their summer break started, it's been harder for him and me to...well, sneak around, I guess.

Today, we're taking the kids to a soccer day camp on campus. It's free, Kelley and Riggs are hosting it along with some of their friends. Jude's been missing Jesse, and June has mentioned Bailey and Ivy a few times, so when Jesse told me about the camp, I couldn't say no.

"Can we get ice cream after?" June asks as she climbs into the car. Jesse glances at me, and I nod.

"I think we can manage that, June Bug," he says, then finishes buckling Jude in and slides himself into the passenger seat. "One scoop per goal you score."

June smiles, and I shake my head with a sigh. I should have given him some parameters.

We pull up to the soccer intramural fields, where the camp is being held, and unload. Ivy and Bailey greet us at the registration table and give the kids their name badges and team t-shirts. I'm actually surprised at how organized it all is. They have the kids split into groups by age, Ivy tells me, and they made sure to put Riggs with Jude and Kelley with June.

"That was really thoughtful," I say with a grin. "Thank you."

"Of course," she chirps happily. "Anything for J-Squared. They're the whole reason we're doing this, anyway." My jaw drops, and she smirks.

"Numbskull didn't tell you?" Bailey quips with a laugh.

I look at Jesse, wide-eyed, and he gives me a sheepish smile. He opens his mouth to speak, but then halts, turning his attention to June. She's standing with her arms crossed, staring at something on the field, and she's got a small scowl on her face. I track her line of sight and recognize a lanky boy around her age.

"June, is that Cole?" I ask, and she mumbles out a yeah.

"Girls-can't-be-knights Cole?" Jesse butts in. "That Cole?"

"Yep," June says.

Jesse nudges her arm with his. "3,970,238,390 guys, *Caballera*" She glances up at him, mouth still set in a scowl. "He's not special." Her lips twitch into a grin.

"But I am," she says, and Jesse winks at her.

"You are."

The kids head out onto the field with their coaches, and I sit on the sidelines with Jesse, Ivy, and Bailey. Jude is having a blast, and he only acknowledges us once, when he brings his pirate hat to us because it keeps falling off his head when he runs. Ivy is now wearing it proudly, and I snap a picture with Roxanne's camera.

June takes a little longer to get into it, but pretty soon, Kelley has her scoring goal after goal, and all the kids on her team are clapping for her. When she brings her sweatshirt over for us to hold, I have to choke back tears.

"June! You're kicking ass," Bailey tells her, and we all start laughing. Bailey winces. "Oh shit— I mean shoot. I mean you're kicking *butt*."

"Nice save, B," Jesse teases. Bailey squirts him with her water bottle, and June runs back onto the field, smiling without her sweatshirt. I snap some more pictures.

"Hey guys, can you keep an eye on J-Squared," Jesse asks Ivy and Bailey. "I gotta talk to Joss about something." They agree without question, and Jesse nods for me to follow him. I narrow my eyes and tilt my head to the side, but he doesn't explain, so I stand and trail behind him.

He cuts through the parking lot, until we're out of sight from the intramural fields, then takes a stone path to a small courtyard between two brick buildings. It's Saturday and summer session, so campus is quiet, and the courtyard is empty. There are two stone benches on either side of the grassy area and some sort of tree with large, pink and white, waxy looking flowers. It's beautiful.

Before I have a chance to speak, Jesse pushes me up against the tree and takes my lips. The kiss is slow and deep, and I immediately forget everything except the feel of his mouth on mine and the floral scent of the tree surrounding me.

He pulls back and takes a deep breath, and I smile at him.

"What was that all about?" I ask, and he moves his lips to my neck.

"I don't like not being able to touch you whenever I want to," he says, pressing soft kisses up and down my tender skin. "And your laugh makes me hard." He presses his hips into me as evidence. I push on his chest with a laugh, and he groans playfully.

"Stop it," I say. "My laugh did not do *that*."

"Yes, it did," he insists, then licks up my neck sloppily, making me laugh even more. He groans again, louder this time, then moves my hand from his chest to his erection. "See?"

I squeeze him, and his chest rumbles with a growl.

"Let me touch you," he says, and I shake my head.

"How is that going to help *this*?" I ask, stroking him once over his shorts.

"It will. Trust me." He brings his hand to the hem of my sundress, slips his fingers under and grazes the skin on my thigh. "Outta your head. Let me touch you," he says again, then slowly walks his fingers up, up, up, until he's gently stroking me through my panties.

I flutter my eyes shut, breathe out my permission, and get lost in the sensations of his fingers and lips. It doesn't take long before I come with a choked cry, and he kisses me again.

"My two favorite sounds," he whispers against my lips. "When I make you laugh, and when I make you come."

He takes my hand and leads me back the way we came but stiffens and shoves me behind him the moment we leave the courtyard.

"Jesse," a familiar voice says, and I glance around him to see Sandra Huntington. Her eyes flick from him to me and back. "I just want to talk."

After knowing what I know about her, I'm shocked by just how *normal* she looks. Her hair is highlighted and styled, her face accented with light makeup and mauve lipstick. She's wearing a pair of dark wash jeans and a flowy tank top. She's pretty. Fit. She looks like someone I'd see in the school pick-up line. She could be one of June's teachers. From appearance alone, I never would have guessed what a sick person she really is.

"No," Jesse says, "you're violating a restraining order by being on campus."

Sandra looks at me again. "You're going to let him ruin his life?" she accuses, anger tinting her features. Her voice, even angry, is light and smooth like silk.

"Don't talk to her," Jesse barks at Sandra, but she ignores him.

"Do you even know how hard he's worked?" She raises her voice and takes a step forward. Jesse moves us back, then fumbles with his phone. "He's brilliant. You're going to ruin it for him. He's going to—"

"Shut up, Sandra," Jesse shouts, and she jumps. He speaks into the phone, telling someone about the restraining order violation.

"You're going to get me arrested," she shrieks, as if Jesse doesn't already know the consequences of her being here. He scoffs and tells the person on the other end of the phone his location. Sandra gives me one last scathing glare.

"You're going to ruin his life," she hisses, then she turns and walks away.

It takes me over an hour to stop shaking. Thankfully, Patrick isn't one of the cops that shows up to take Jesse's and my statements, but I know both of the officers. No doubt word will get back to Patrick quickly. Jesse convinces me that it's safe to take the kids out for ice cream, and by the end of the afternoon, the encounter with She Who Must Not Be Named is all but forgotten.

"I'm sorry about today," Jesse says for the millionth time

after we get back to my house. The kids have headed inside, leaving Jesse and me alone in the garage.

I give his forearm a quick squeeze. "It's not your fault," I say honestly.

It's *not* his fault. I'm nervous and worried and confused. I keep thinking about how much worse today could have been. What if she'd approached my kids? Is she dangerous? What if the cops don't find her and arrest her? I'm a ball of anxiety, but none of it is Jesse's fault. The woman is obviously unhinged. Still...her words keep bouncing around in my head.

"What did she mean? That I was going to ruin your life?"

Jesse shrugs. "She probably still thinks your ex's threat about Harvard is real."

"And you're sure it's not? You're sure you're good?"

I can't help but worry. Patrick doesn't make empty threats. He's ruthless and manipulative. I have no doubt in my mind Patrick would ruin Jesse if he could, especially if he knew the full extent of Jesse's and my relationship. As of right now, Patrick still thinks Jesse is an occasional babysitter. A kind neighbor. Nothing more, and I have to keep it that way.

"I promise, Classic," Jesse says, tugging me in for a hug. "I'd like to see him try, actually. Harvard practically turned cartwheels to get me to commit. They aren't going to drop me on the ramblings of some two-bit Barney Fife on a power trip."

I huff a laugh into Jesse's chest. "Shouldn't you be taking this a little more seriously?"

"No," he says firmly. "I shouldn't. Your ex ain't shit, and I'm not going to waste precious brain space on him." He presses a kiss to the top of my head, and I fight the urge to melt into his embrace.

"Well, at least we only have to deal with it for a few more weeks," I say, then force a tight laugh. Jesse's body stiffens.

"Yeah," is all he says.

We haven't talked about the date, how August is coming up on us like a freight train. We avoid it, ignore it, but it's always there hovering in the back of my mind. We've got an expiration date. Until then, I'm making the most of the time we've got left.

"What's your week like," he asks as he releases me.

"Same as usual." I work and then I do homework, though my bridge program will be finished soon, so all my work now is for final projects and studying for a few exams. "The kids will be at the summer program at the YWCA all week, and then Patrick should have them Friday through Sunday."

"I leave for Boston Friday to check out some apartments," he says, then grins. "Come with me. We can make a weekend out of it."

For a few seconds, I actually consider it, but then reality crashes over me.

"I can't," I say sadly. "I've got to use that time to finish up my coursework, and I picked up two shifts. Plus, I can't leave the state without the kids. I'll worry too much."

"You can find someone else to pick up the shifts, and you can do your coursework in the hotel. The kids will be fine for a weekend."

"Jesse, I just can't. I'm sorry." I avert my eyes and hope he can't see what else I'm thinking. It's not just that I can't, it's that I *won't*. This is going to be painful enough on me when he leaves. I don't need to make it harder.

"Okay," he says with a pout. "I'll bring you back a souvenir."

He kisses me goodbye, and I close the garage door behind him.

* * *

The week passes slowly, and I try not to count down the days until I get to see Jesse again.

I go to work. I come home. I cook dinner. I wash dishes. I study. I do laundry. I shower. I sleep. I wake up. I go to work.

Wash, rinse, repeat.

Texts from Jesse brighten my days, but the moment the kids leave with Patrick on Friday afternoon, that familiar feeling of loneliness settles in. Jesse's presence has masked it in the recent weeks, but with him in Boston, I'm reminded quickly of my impending future. He will be at Harvard, doing whatever it is that first-year med students do, and I'll be here, doing what single mothers do. Working, cooking, cleaning. Fighting to remain functional. Wash, rinse, repeat.

I'm on track to finish my bridge program at the top of my class. Then, all I have to do is pass the licensure exam, and I'll be a licensed registered nurse.

At the very least, that means less dependency on Patrick and more leverage if he ever follows through on his threat to take me back to court. I have no family and, right now, very little savings. Patrick comes from money, and his family is fairly influential in the small town where we grew up. On paper, he's an upstanding citizen, with a stable career as an honorable police officer and a strong family support system. On paper, I can't even compete. If he takes me back to court, he'll win. Hands down. But once I finish this program and start working as an RN...

I drag a hand down my face, then pull my hair out of my ponytail, only to throw it right back into a bun. How is it that I'm both longing for and dreading the future?

I get home from work late in the afternoon on Sunday. I talk to Jesse for a bit via text, and I smile as he sends me pictures of the random things he's done over the weekend. Drank a beer in America's oldest continuously operating tavern. Ate "the best damn clam chowder in New England." Toured the Harvard campus. Shopped Faneuil Hall Marketplace.

Each picture makes me both happy and sad.

When six o'clock rolls around and Patrick still hasn't dropped the kids off, I give him a call. It rings and rings and rings. I call the police station and ask if they've heard from him. They say no. I call his mother, even though she hasn't spoken to me since before the divorce, and it goes straight to voicemail. By seven, I'm ready to jump in my car and head straight to his house, but the sound of his truck pulling into my driveway fills me with relief.

I run to the front door and swing it open, only to be wrapped in a frantic hug by June. She sniffles into my shirt, and I pull back to see that her face is splotched and tear-streaked.

"I'm sorry," she whispers, and I hug her back to me. I look up and watch, confused, as Patrick takes Jude out of the truck, who then runs to me and latches onto my leg. Patrick struggles to remove Jude's car seat—he refuses to keep one in his truck and insists on borrowing mine—then drops it on the lawn. When he turns toward me, the look of anger in his bloodshot eyes tells me everything I need to know.

"Go upstairs," I say quickly to June. "Take Jude. Go into your room. Turn on some music and lock the door." She doesn't respond, just takes Jude's hand and drags him inside the house.

I stand and try to pull the door shut before Patrick reaches the porch, but he grabs me roughly by the forearm and yanks. The smell of alcohol chokes me and makes my eyes water.

"You drove them drunk?" I hiss out, trying to tug my arm from his grasp. His grip tightens, and he shoves me backward into the doorframe. I grunt and shove back. "Let go of me," I say through my teeth, but he opens the door and pushes me backward and inside.

I land on the floor with a thud, and seethe as he steps into my house and slams, then locks, the door.

"Get the hell out of my house, Patrick," I say sternly, trying like hell not to raise my voice. I don't want to scare the kids. I don't want to piss him off any more than he already is.

"Shut the fuck up, Lyn," he slurs, then shoves me out of the way with his booted foot. I push myself up and follow him down the hall and into the living room. He's mumbling profanities under his breath, and I take note of the way he wobbles with each step.

He's not just drunk. He's completely smashed.

He drove like this. He drove like this with my children in the car. Fear and rage war inside me.

"You can't even walk straight," I say, my voice shaking. "You could have killed them."

Visions of the ATV accident flash through my mind, but this time, it's Patrick's truck. This time, it's both of my children. I jerk my head to chase away the thoughts.

"Shut the fuck up, Lyn," he says again, raising his voice with each word, until he's shouting. "You're a slut. You're an ungrateful, good-for-nothing whore."

Spit flies from his mouth as he speaks, and I'd be terrified if it weren't for the fact that his eyes can't focus, and he can't stand without swaying. He won't be conscious much longer. But even with bleary eyes and slurred speech, the hatred is loud and clear.

He hates me. I wonder if he always has. He doesn't see me as a person. He sees me as a possession, and he hates that he's not able to control me right now. It's why he insists on still calling me his wife, despite the fact we're divorced. Why he calls me Lyn, knowing I don't like it.

He never wanted to love me. He wanted to own me.

"Patrick," I say calmly, "how about we call Travis to come give you a ride home?" Travis is one of his friends. Another cop. Travis is a decent guy, but he's loyal to Patrick, so we can never be friends.

"You fuck him too?" he spits at me. I bite back my anger. I divorced him, so I didn't have to endure this abuse anymore, but he just won't go away. "You fuck Travis like you fucked that kid?"

My stomach drops, and I stare at him. He wheezes a wet, gurgling laugh, then pulls an envelope from his pocket and throws it at me. I try to catch it, but he's drunk as a skunk and has shit aim, so I only graze it with my fingertips before it falls to the floor and the contents spill out.

He rages on about something, but his voice fades quickly. All I can hear is my heart pounding in my ears and all I can see are the pictures scattered on the floor. Four by six glossy finish images, some grainy and out of focus, some vibrant and sharp, have me falling to my knees as I sort frantically through them.

No.

No.

They're all of me and Jesse.

All of them.

In the grocery store. In the parking lot of the state park. On the quad with his friends. In the game room of the pizza parlor. There are a few of me and Jesse in this kitchen that seem to have been taken from outside on the patio. My breasts are exposed, and he's on his knees in front of me.

The pictures blur as my eyes well with tears. My most intimate, precious moments lie littered on the floor in front of me like trash. Each one more explicit in nature, each one a slicing violation of my privacy. A slicing violation of my dignity.

"How could you..." I whisper, just as my eyes catch on another photo, more recent, and I reach for it. Jesse and I in the courtyard on campus, pressed against the trunk of a tree covered with pink and white flowers. My eyes are closed, my mouth is open, and he's...

It all makes sense. I drop the picture, just as my hair is

yanked hard, and I'm pulled back up to my feet and pushed against the wall. His shove is weak, but I trip over my own feet and slam into the wall, pain shooting down my spine and neck from the impact.

Patrick wraps his hand around my throat and squeezes, and my thoughts strangely jump to Jesse. His hands always feel liberating, because I know their purpose is to make me feel good, and I know that I'm always in control. With Patrick, it's a stark opposite. As his fingers attempt to tighten, his intentions are clear. Pain. Perhaps worse. He wants to hurt me. He wants me powerless. For the first time ever, I fear he might actually want me dead.

My vision sparks, and I know I should try to yell, but who will hear me? June and Jude? I don't want them to see this. I don't want them to hear a struggle. They'd never be able to unsee their father holding their mother against a wall by her neck. They've heard enough yelling to last a lifetime.

I wrap my hand around Patrick's wrist and pull. His grip, like his shove, is weak, and it loosens enough that I can breathe a little better.

Patrick's eyes are drooping rapidly. There's an eternity between each blink. He's minutes, if not seconds, away from falling over. That's why I decide not to fight him. Why I don't yell. I don't want to stoke his adrenaline. It will just make it worse. It will scare June and Jude, who are likely huddled in the closet upstairs. I've been here before. I just stare into his blood-shot eyes and hope he passes out before I do.

"You're going to listen to me," he threatens. "You're going to do what I say, or I will fucking kill you, Lyn. I will fucking kill you."

jesse

MY PLANE DOESN'T LAND in Indianapolis until 11:35 p.m. I text Joss, but she doesn't answer, so I go to the condo and entertain Kelley and Ivy with tales of my weekend in Boston.

I'm up and out the door immediately the next morning. I'm itching to talk to Joss. To tell her my idea. I had a realization this weekend. An epiphany that happened between touring apartments and sending texts to Jocelyn. I'm not ready to let go of her and the kids. I don't want to. I want them to be part of my life permanently, so I made a decision. One I'm hoping she embraces.

I'm buzzing with excitement from the possibilities. It's early, but I know she's off today, so the kids probably won't be going to the YWCA. I'm going to try and convince her to let me take them all to the state park. The wildflower clearing must be an explosion of blooms by now, and I bet I could teach June how to skip rocks.

I'm lost in my head, making plans for the day, when I turn on the cul-de-sac. My face falls into a frown as soon as I see the big, black truck in the driveway.

What the fuck is Colonel Cunt Nugget doing here?

I pull up to the curb and cut the engine, then stride to the door. I knock twice, step back and wait. The door swings open, and on the other side, smiling a smarmy, skeezy, thin-lipped grin, is the fucking ex.

The first thing I notice, after the shit-eating grin, is that he's shirtless. His hair is wet, like he just got out of the shower. Then I drop my eyes to find that he's wearing a pair of *my* joggers. The one's I let Joss borrow at the lake and never got back. My nostrils flare, fury sparking under my skin with accusations. *Comes around a lot. Random times. Usually at night.* My knee-jerk reaction is to assume the worst, to expect betrayal, but I pull back. My impulse control is shit, but I'm not self-destructive anymore.

This is Jocelyn. She wouldn't do that. She doesn't want him. I don't know why Lieutenant Lame Ass is here, but I trust my girl. I force a smile and let myself find humor in the way he's had to bunch my joggers up at the ankles. He's too fucking short to wear my pants.

"Hey, man," the ex says. "We don't need a babysitter today."

This dick.

I stand at my full height and make a show of looking down my nose at him.

"I came to talk to Joss."

His lip curls on a snarl. "Lyn's busy."

"I can wait." I force a grin, then point to his ankles. "Maybe you should roll those up, so you don't trip on 'em. Seems your little leggies aren't quite long enough."

I watch in amusement as his left eye twitches. I debate making a comment about it, but Jocelyn's voice steals my attention.

"Is someone at—" She appears over the ex's shoulder, and the color drains from her face when she sees me. "Jesse."

"Can I talk to you?" I ask her, and she nods. She pushes roughly past the ex, then shuts the door behind her.

"What's goin' on?" I ask, and follow her as she walks off the porch and to the road. When she reaches my car, she leans on the hood and stares at the ground.

"Classic," I say slowly, dread collecting like bile in my throat. "What's going on?"

Finally, she looks at me, and her big eyes are hard. Emotionless. Exhausted.

"I'm being blackmailed," she says, voice flat. I don't know what I was expecting her to say, but it wasn't that. I wait for more, but she doesn't continue.

"By the ex?" I ask, and she nods.

"And by Sandra fucking Huntington."

I choke. "What?" I croak out. I can hardly believe what she's saying. It doesn't make sense. "I don't understand."

She clamps her eyes shut and tightens her hands into fists.

"Patrick has pictures of us." My skin starts to crawl. "I don't know if he was having Sandra Huntington follow us, or if he just happened to capitalize on her stalking habits, but these pictures are bad, Jesse."

I start running things through my head. Surely, she can't mean what I think she means.

"What kind of pictures?" I ask, and Jocelyn sighs.

"Pictures of us, you and me, doing...stuff. And they're graphic. In a few of them, I'm almost entirely naked."

I'll fucking kill him. I turn to head back to the townhouse, but she grabs my wrist.

"You can't go in there, Jesse. Are you not listening to me? I'm being blackmailed."

I whirl on her. "Blackmailed how?"

Her facial expression answers for her, but I let her speak.

"I have to play by his rules. I have to stop seeing you. If I don't, he'll send the pictures to the Dean and get you expelled, and—"

I bark out a laugh, cutting her off.

"Fuck him, Classic. Seriously. I told you, he can't do shit to me."

"You didn't see these pictures, Jesse."

"I don't fucking care. Let him try." I take her hands in mine. "You know what I came by to tell you this morning? I found us a house in Boston. I've already signed the lease. You, me, and J-Squared."

Her jaw drops, but I plow forward.

"I even looked into schools. We'd be in the district of a great public school, or there's a Montessori school right down the block, and it's only a twenty-minute commute to the hospital, where you can work as an RN."

The twin worry lines between her eyes are deep as she stares at my chest, and I squeeze her hands.

"Classic. Are you listening to me?"

"You want me to come with you to Boston," she states, voice flat.

"Yes." I force a smile, willing her to smile back. This isn't going how I pictured it would. "It will be great. The kids will love it there. You'll love it there. You—"

"I can't follow you to Harvard," she spits out, and it's like a punch to the gut. "I can't uproot my life, my kids' lives, to follow you to Boston. That's *your* life, Jesse. It's not mine."

I swallow back the pain of her rejection. She didn't even consider it. Not even for a second.

"I want it to be *our* life, Jocelyn." She shakes her head rapidly. "Why not? Because of him?"

"He's going to take my kids," she rasps, pain lancing with each word. "Do you get that? Those pictures. My relationship with you. If I keep seeing you, he's going to use it against me, and he's going to take my kids."

"No," I deny. That's not possible. "No way."

"Yes. Yes, Jesse." She clamps her eyes shut. "He's not just threatening to send those pictures to Harvard; he's threatening to take me back to court. To use my relationship with you, and those pictures, and Sandra Huntington, to prove I'm unstable and unfit. He'll say I'm putting my kids at risk by dating you, and he will use all of this to make you seem terrible. And he *will* win, Jesse."

"We'll fight him," I say, and she makes a noise somewhere between a chuckle and a sob. I don't know how to fix it. I want to fix it and I can't.

"There's no 'we,' Jesse. I am going to fight him, but you can't be involved."

"Why the fuck not? I told you, I don't ca—"

"But I do," she cries. "I care. I will not be the reason you don't get to go to Harvard Medical School. I *cannot* be that reason."

"That's my decision to make."

"It's not. I don't want your help."

"I'm in love with you, Jocelyn," I confess, but she refuses to look at me. Refuses to acknowledge my words.

"You're going to go to Harvard, you're going to become a brilliant surgeon, and in a few years, you won't even remember us."

"Are you fucking hearing me, Joss? I said I'm in love with you." Why isn't she listening to me? Why is she making me fight like this? She loves me too. I know she does.

"No, you're not." Her tone is sharp. A slap to the face.

"Yes, I am."

"Well, I'm not in love with you."

"Bullshit." She's lying. I can tell.

"Sometimes love isn't enough," she argues quietly, and I shake my head in protest. "You're naïve," she insists. "You just don't—"

"No," I cut her off. "You're not turning this into an age thing. You're five years older, but that doesn't mean you know better. You don't have the market cornered on heartache, on pain. I've been just as broken, as beaten down, as you feel now. And I'm telling you— love *is* enough. Our love, this, you and me, is enough."

I reach out and take her hands, pressing them to my chest, hoping she can feel my heartbeat. She squeezes her eyes shut, and I watch her face crumple with despair. My chest hollows.

"I can't lose my kids, Jesse," she whispers. "I can't. And you can't lose your future. We're liabilities for each other. We won't succeed if we're together."

"You can't let that fucking drunk ass bully win, Joss."

"He already has!" she shouts, stepping away from me. "He always does. You know what he did last night when he dropped them off? He was so drunk he couldn't walk a straight line. He drove the kids here and he was black-out drunk. He could have killed them. Ten more minutes and he would have passed out while driving, and they'd all be dead. And then he pushed his way into *my* house, threatened me and pushed me around and scared the shit out of *my* kids. And you know what happened when I called his partner, another cop, and asked for help? He told me to get him some coffee and let him sleep it off. In *my* house."

"Did he hurt you?" I ask, fear gripping me, and she shakes her head, exhaustion evident in her every movement.

"No. He yelled and threatened, tried to knock me around a bit, then vomited all over himself and passed out on my kitchen floor." She looks up at the sky and lets the tears fall freely down her cheeks. "How the fuck did I end up here?"

"We'll get through this," I say softly, but when I take a step toward her, she takes a step back. The sounds of her feet on the pavement snap through my head like a bullwhip. She's retreating from me. I'm losing her.

"There's no we anymore, Jesse. There can't be."

"Let me help you."

"You *can't.* You cannot help. You'll only make things worse. I don't need a savior, Jesse. I need to handle this myself."

"Don't do this," I plead. I try to make my voice strong, try to hide the cracking, but I'm failing. This can't be happening. An hour ago, I was picturing our life together and now...

"You don't know him, Jesse. I do. I've been under his thumb since I was sixteen. He doesn't make idle threats. He will ruin your future, and he will take my kids from me, and he will use our relationship to do it. He has money and influence, and I have nothing to fight him with."

"Then let *me* fight him."

"This isn't your fight," she says through gritted teeth. "You don't understand the risk or what's at stake. This is *my* responsibility. *My* mess. *My* kids. *My* life. Not yours."

I let her words hit me, one after the other, until I feel raw. I don't have a say in any of this. They are her kids. It's her life. There's no room for me in it. She doesn't trust me, and I'm not worth the risk.

"We just...we're in two very different places in our lives," she says quietly. "You've got your whole future in front of you with endless possibilities. I have to fix the things I fucked up in the past before I can move forward."

She sniffs, wipes the tears from her cheeks. I drag in a shaky breath and move closer.

"You're going to go to med school, you're going to achieve your dreams, and it's going to feel so good, Jesse. It will feel so good, and this summer will barely register as more than a blip in your memory."

"You're wrong," I say, my throat and eyes burning. She's so wrong. I push a strand of her hair behind her ear. Then I take her hand and press it to my chest once more. "Nothing will ever feel better than you, Classic. Not for me."

She forces a sad smile. "Maybe if we'd met at a different time. A different place."

I close my eyes and breathe past the hurt.

"It wouldn't matter the time or place. I'd love you the same in every single one of them."

* * *

"You're sure you want to go now?" Ivy asks, laying my yarn skeins carefully in a moving box. "You still have a few weeks until you have to be in Boston. This is our last summer together."

I pull a drawer from my dresser and upend its contents into another box.

"No point in prolonging it, V," I tell her flatly. "I want to get settled in the area. I won't know anyone. It's not like we won't still keep in touch."

"Don't say that," she scolds. "Don't say it like we'll only be talking once every few weeks or something. I still expect to hear from you daily."

I huff a small laugh. "Of course. I'll keep you all updated in the group chat."

"You better," she grumbles.

Bailey pokes her head in my bedroom, holding an air fryer. "Is this yours or Kelley's? He says he can't remember."

"If it's up to me, then it's mine," I say with a grin, and Bailey rolls her eyes before disappearing back the way she came.

"Have you talked to her?" Ivy asks quietly, keeping her eyes on the box in front of her.

I should have known she'd know.

"Not since she ended things last week," I answer honestly, and I don't bother to force false lightness into my tone. I know I haven't been fooling anyone. They all know I'm miserable despite the fake as fuck smiles and half-hearted jokes.

"Does it have anything to do with *her*," Ivy spits, referring to Mrs. Huntington. Ivy hates her. It's a good thing she didn't see Sandra at the intramural field or V might have caught a charge. Sandra has been arrested and charged, which is a weight off my shoulders, and my lawyer said I should be able to give written testimony instead of having to appear in court.

"Not exactly." I consider what to tell her. I don't want to betray Jocelyn's privacy, but I also don't want to lie to my friend. "Jocelyn's ex-husband is a nasty person. She's got to get that stuff figured out, and our lives are too different."

Ivy hums. "Did you tell her how you feel?"

I smirk. Ivy probably knew how I felt about Jocelyn before I did.

"I did, V," I tell her. "I gave Classic my heart, and she didn't even give me a pen."

She groans playfully at my movie reference then throws her arms around my middle and gives me a hug, telling me she didn't see through my deflection. I hug her back, swaying side to side slightly, and soak it in. I don't have to say it. She knows.

Yeah, V. It fucking hurts. It really fucking hurts.

Ivy doesn't say anything for a while, and we pack boxes in silence. I finish up the dresser and move on to the desk while V tackles the closet. When we're done with that, and my room is nothing but an empty box with a stripped bed and bare walls, we go to the kitchen and join Bailey, Kelley, and Riggs.

With all of my belongings packed in boxes or tossed in

laundry baskets, and Jenga-stacked into a small U-Haul trailer, we order Chinese take-out and have one last meal together before I have to hit the road.

"I can't believe you're leaving," Bailey grumbles into her lo mien. "I thought we would have a few more weeks."

"Awww, are you gonna miss me, B?" I tease, and she snorts.

"More like I'm going to miss being able to do Labor Day at your lake house."

I mock gasp, then use my chopsticks to fling a piece of broccoli at her.

"Children," Riggs warns, and B and I both flash him our best *I didn't start it* face.

It feels good, the laughter and normalcy, but it aches, too. This is my family, my support system, and I'm leaving them in a matter of hours. I wasn't planning to leave for Boston early, but after five days of pacing and obsessing, I decided I have to get out of the same city as Jocelyn Calligaris. Knowing she's so close is driving me mad. I have to leave before I do something outrageous like ditch Harvard entirely and stand outside her house with a boombox over my head blasting "Nothing Feels Better" by Pink Sweat$.

We're cleaning up from dinner when a loud knock sounds on the door. I open it and find Xavier is standing in the hallway.

"What's up, Z?"

"You're leaving?" he asks, and I raise a brow. He's agitated. Angry. It's obvious his patience with me is fucking gone; I just don't know what I've done this time.

"Yeah. Bout to get on the road now, actually." I smirk and throw my arms out wide to dissolve the tension. "You here to give me a hug goodbye?"

"Did you tell *them* goodbye?"

I drop my hands to my sides, finally understanding.

"She doesn't care, Z."

"Jesse, for fuck's sake, I'm not talking about Jocelyn. I'm talking about June and Jude. Do *they* know you're leaving?"

"No," I admit, and guilt floods my stomach.

"Those kids care about you, Jesse. If you leave without saying goodbye, it's going to fuck them up. They'll take it personally. They'll wonder what they did to make you leave."

I nod. Fuck, why didn't I think about that?

"You're right," I rasp.

"I'm sorry that you got your heart broken but grow the fuck up and go give those kids the goodbye they deserve," he says, then just turns around and walks away. A total mic-drop moment, and I'm left feeling like an asshole in the hallway.

"Hey, guys," I call into the kitchen, as if my friends didn't just witness the whole exchange. "I got something to do."

I don't bother unhooking the trailer, I just jump in my Kia and head toward Jocelyn's. The closer I get to her townhouse, the harder my heart pounds. I even consider pulling over and doing one of the deep breathing exercises Ivy is always recommending for anxiety. I go to stick my hand in my pocket, then remember that I trashed the ring a couple nights ago. I don't miss it, but old habits are hard to break.

I pull up to the curb outside Joss's house and heave a sigh of relief that a certain big, black truck isn't parked in the driveway. I take a few beats to compose myself, then bite the bullet and walk to the house.

"Jesse," Jocelyn says, surprised, when she opens the door. Her eyes run over my face. "What are you..." Her attention snags on the U-Haul at the curb, and then snaps back to me. "You're leaving?"

"Yeah, figured I'd go ahead and give Boston some time to acclimate to me," I joke, and try to hide the way my body yearns to pull her closer, to hold her. Kiss her. I fist my hands and shove them in my pockets. She's so pretty that I have to look away.

"You were supposed to be here until the end of August," she says. I shrug. I don't know what to say to that. I have to leave or I'll go nuts? I can't stay here because you broke my fucking heart? I don't think now is the time for that.

"I, uh, I was actually hoping I could say goodbye to J-Squared?"

I flick my gaze back to her face, just in time to see her lip quiver and her eyes mist, but she opens the door wide.

"Come on in," she says. I don't step into the house, though. I can't.

"It's okay. I'd rather talk to them out here if that's alright." The heartbreak on her face kills me because it matches mine, but she nods quickly.

"I'll be right back."

She disappears into the house and returns moments later with June and Jude. Her face is now an impassive mask.

"Hey, squad," I say brightly, and June zeroes in on the U-Haul.

"Are you going somewhere?"

"Yeah, Doonie. I gotta leave for medical school today."

She screws her lips up to the side and doesn't take her eyes off the U-Haul when she says, "so they'll finally trust you with a knife?"

I chuckle. "Exactly."

"Can we come too?" Jude asks, excitement in his voice.

"Not this time, Meatball."

His little face falls, and his big eyes grow bigger. When he speaks, his voice is a whisper.

"Will you come back?"

I flick my eyes to Joss. Her face is tight as she watches, and I can't read it. Not a hint of emotion, and fuck, it hurts.

"I dunno, kid." I don't want to lie to him. I don't want him holding on to that lie, only to be let down later. "But I wanted to come and say goodbye to you guys and thank you for spending so much time with me."

"I don't want you to leave," Jude whispers again, and I hear a small hiccup, a cry maybe, escape Jocelyn. I don't look at her. I can't.

I rub Jude's fuzzy little head and force yet another fake as fuck smile.

"I don't really want to leave either," I tell him honestly.

"Then why are you?" June asks, and when I look at her, her face is the same as her mom's. Blank. Tight. Emotionless. Only her big eyes give her away, but with time, she'll probably master those too.

"I want to become a surgeon. I can't do that without going to school, so I have to go."

June nods, and a sniffle from Jude has me crouching down in front of him. He's trying to wipe his tears away, obviously embarrassed, so I grab his hand gently and hold it in mine.

"It's okay to cry, Jude," I say softly. "It's okay to cry."

I brush a tear off his cheek, and he reaches up and brushes a tear off mine.

"See?" I say, "even I cry."

"I'm gonna miss you."

"I'm gonna miss you, too, kid."

I don't even want to think of how different my life will be tomorrow, with June and Jude and Jocelyn permanently behind me. The aching in my chest is enough to make breathing difficult.

"If you come back, you have to visit," June demands.

"Okay."

"Promise," she says, and sticks out her pinky.

Fuck, these kids are making this so hard. I reach out and hook my pinky with hers.

"Promise." She leans forward and kisses her knuckles, so I do the same.

If I don't leave now, I'm going to lose it. When I glance at Jocelyn, she reads it on my face. One nod is all I get.

"Alright guys," she says. "Let's let Jesse get on the road."

We say goodbye, and I give hugs. June holds me a little tighter than I expected, so I pull back and look her in the eyes.

"You're the special one," I tell her. "Those boys ain't shit." Her lips twitch into a small smile. I'll take it.

When they finally go into the house, after just a simple wave from Joss, I drag my feet back to my car. I do deep breathing. I wipe the tears from my eyes and tell myself I'll wait until I get back to the condo before I lose it. But then *mi pirata fuerte* comes running back out the front door calling my name.

Joss is standing in the doorway, so I crouch down and get eye level with Jude.

"What's up, Captain?"

"I got this," he says, and hands me a paper. I flip it over and find a picture of me and Jude from the day at the lake. One Joss must have taken. He's sitting on my lap, and I'm fixing him a s'more. We're smiling so big, and his face is smudged with chocolate. The picture is creased heavily down the middle, like he's been carrying it around with him. "So, you can have your *'motional import pirate* for in case you need to be brave."

Bwave. Jesus, this kid.

"Thank you," I say, tears falling freely again.

He reaches his tiny hands up and puts them on either side of my face.

"Will you still do your superpower?" he whispers. I swallow.

"What's my superpower, Jude?"

"Loving us."

The truth of his words hit me hard. *Loving them.*

Fuck, and I do love them.

I love them so damn much that leaving them is putting me in physical pain. I don't know exactly when it happened, but I fell for June and Jude just as quickly as I fell for Jocelyn. Just as quickly, and just as hard. My inhale is shuddered and sharp.

They've become so important to me in such a short period of time, and now I have to say goodbye to them. The hardest fucking goodbye.

I pull Jude into a hug and hold him tight.

"Yeah, buddy," I rasp. "I'll always do my superpower."

"Good," he says, then turns and runs back into the house.

I don't look up. I keep my eyes fixed on the ground as I round the car and climb in, then crank it and pull away from the house. I don't make it three blocks before I have to pull back over and break down.

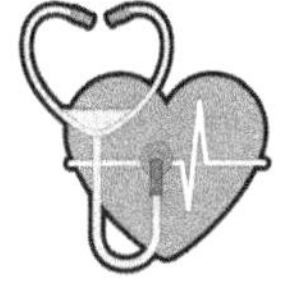

jocelyn

"GOOD MORNING, MERYL."

"Mornin', hun."

I brush past her and unload my bag into my locker, then reach for the last shift's notes.

"Or should I say...morning, Registered Nurse!" She pops out a noise maker and blows in it, then tosses some stringy paper confetti at me. I laugh and blindly grab at my head to remove it from my hair.

"Not an RN yet, Meryl. Still have to pass the licensure exam." I uncap my five-hour energy and drink it, then check to make sure I brought a second one. I'm going to need it.

"Honey, you got that exam in the bag," she tells me with a grin. "The real question is, are you going to stay here with us, or are you going to leave us?"

"If Harvest View will pay me what I'm worth, I'd happily stay," I tell her honestly, and she rolls her eyes. We both know that's a long shot. I think my next step is to get a job at Indianapolis General.

"You should be more spunky," Meryl muses, eyeing me

suspiciously. "Where's that smile you'd been sporting? The pep in your step? It was here a few weeks ago and then, poof, it's gone."

I avert my eyes and shrug. "Just tired I guess."

Just tired and not at all heartbroken.

But just like with my bitter, creamer-less coffee, I choke it down and hope that eventually, I'll adjust to the new pain in my chest. I worry that ignoring it won't make it go away.

"Well, there is a light at the end of this tunnel, hun." She places a hand on my shoulder and pats gently. "After that licensure exam, you'll get some time to breathe."

Right. Time to breathe.

I wish I could say that I'm successfully moving forward, putting one foot in front of the other, and not stressing over what's behind me. But if I said that, I'd be a liar.

I check Jesse's social media every night. In the last few weeks since he's moved, he has posted a couple pictures of Boston and one of him in a pub with a group of people that aren't Ivy, Kelly, Bailey, or Riggs. He seems happy. Or as happy as one can seem in a filtered, square photo posted on the internet.

I tell myself I want him to be happy. I tell myself this is for the best.

But I also tell myself I'm full of crap because a part of me hopes he's feeling even a fraction of what I'm feeling. If he feels what I feel, then at least I know it was real, even if it didn't last.

I zombie through my shift.

New patients. Old patients. Small talk. Biohazardous materials.

Just another day in the life.

I miss him. I miss him terribly. But I have to focus on what's in front of me.

After work, I put on the playlist I've created of my new favorite songs. Some are from Jesse's mix, yeah, but most are from my own searching, and all have been approved by me.

It feels good. I roll the windows down and let the summer air kick around my hair. I turn the volume up. I sing along. I do my best not to dwell on the fact that tonight, after I've tucked my kids into bed, I'll hold my breath as I open social media and search his name, and I won't exhale until I see that there isn't a picture that tells me he's replaced me.

I don't want to think of how I will feel on the inevitable day that I do see that picture.

I pick the kids up from their YWCA summer program, and we swing through a drive-thru for dinner because I'm exhausted and don't feel like cooking. I set the kids up in the kitchen with their dinner and start on a load of laundry when there is a knock at the door.

"Ivy," I say with surprise as I open the door. My stomach twists. "Is everything okay? Is Jesse—"

"Everything is fine," she says quickly. "Sorry for worrying you. I just wanted to stop by and give you something."

"Oh." I stand up straighter. "Sure."

I'm about to move to the side and let her in, but she holds out her hand and gives me a business card. I take it and flip it over. It's for Pierce, Pierce & Associates, a law firm in downtown Indianapolis. I look it over, then raise an eyebrow at her.

"Forgive me ahead of time, Joss, because I might cross a few lines here," she says with a small laugh. "I've come to consider you a friend. No matter what went down with you and J, I like you. We all do. You and the kids." She takes a deep breath, her kind eyes never leaving mine. "If you ever want to take legal action against your ex-husband and secure a custody settlement that is in the best interest of you and your kids, I know the family practice lawyer at Pierce, Pierce & Associates would be willing to help you."

I shake my head. "Did Jesse—"

"Jesse didn't say anything," she rushes out. "I promise. He doesn't like your ex, but the rest...Well, I pay attention, I guess. And I made an assumption. Like I said, I'm probably crossing some lines."

"No," I assure her. "No, it's fine." I hold my hand out to give back the card. "But I couldn't afford PP&A during the divorce. I probably can't now. I'm still waiting to hear back from my lawyer."

I called him last week. Twice. He hasn't gotten back to me yet, but I'm determined to see this through. Patrick has crossed too many lines, and I'm not going to sit by and watch him destroy everything I love any longer. I can't. I will not lose my children. I've managed to make up excuses to keep the kids from going to Patrick's since the drunk driving incident, but I know, without legal representation, I won't be able to hold out much longer.

"PP&A has income-based fees. And since you are friends with Kelley, I know Christina will take your case."

"Kelley?"

"His mom is Christina Pierce," she clarifies. "PP&A is his parents' law firm. It's where I intern. At least until I move to Chicago for law school."

I stare at the business card. It's heavy and embossed. It feels expensive. Pierce, Pierce & Associates is one of the best law firms in the state. I glance back at Ivy.

"Thank you," I tell her honestly. "I'll give them a call tomorrow."

"I'll tell Ms. Pierce."

Somehow, her smile is both kind and professional, and it

puts me at ease in an instant. When she leaves, I put the business card on the fridge with a magnet and go about the rest of my evening. It's hard to feel hopeful about anything right now, but I'll call tomorrow. It has to be done, and I'm harnessing every ounce of courage in my body so I can see it through.

Patrick Thompson's reign of terror needs to end. He's done enough damage.

He will not win. Not again.

* * *

Three nights after my first meeting with Christina Pierce, my phone rings. It's almost midnight on a Thursday. I don't have to guess who it is.

I let it go to voicemail.

It rings again immediately.

I texted Patrick yesterday and informed him that, once again, he can't have the kids this weekend. He didn't care, which is no surprise. But judging by the constant calling, I'm guessing it, somehow, made it back to him that I've been to PP&A. I don't know how he finds this stuff out, but he does.

I let the phone ring out again, then stare at it in silence for a full minute. Then two.

Maybe he's given up. Passed out drunk at his house and won't bother me again tonight.

My relief is short-lived when I hear the familiar rumble of his truck pull into the driveway. Quickly, I glance at the patio doors to make sure the blinds are drawn. I know it's locked because I haven't unlocked it since I saw those pictures that had been taken of me and Jesse through the glass. Then I rush to the front door and click the deadbolt just before the handle jiggles.

The knocks start once he realizes the door is locked.

One set of three calm, normal raps. Followed by louder, quicker pounds.

"Let me in, Lyn," he slurs on the other side of the door.

I don't answer, and he bangs on the door again.

"Open the door, Lyn!" he shouts. The door starts to vibrate and shake, as if he's kicking it. "Let me the fuck in, Lyn," he repeats, his words louder, muffled only by the assault he's leading against the door. "Open the fucking door!"

I hear a crack and frantically scan my eyes over the frame. Then I hear another. He's going to break it down.

"Patrick," I yell through the door, "go home. You're drunk."

"Don't fucking tell me what to do," he shouts. His kicks and pounds haven't stopped. Jesus Christ, he's actually trying to break the door down.

"I'll call the cops," I threaten, holding my phone tightly in my hand. My arm is shaking rapidly. So much so that I worry I'll lose my grip. He laughs, and it's manic and careless.

"Fucking call 'em." The doorframe makes another cracking sound. "Don't make me shoot this fucking door down, Lyn."

He's not kidding. He doesn't make empty threats. My heart is in my throat as I unlock my phone. I can't let him in this house.

"I will fucking kill you," he screams, each word punctuated with a loud, cracking kick at the door. "I will fucking kill you, Lyn!"

"Mom," a voice cries, and I look up the stairs and find June and Jude's terrified faces peering down at me. The threats and kicking haven't stopped. Patrick is still hurling threats at the door as I peer up at our children. Their skin is stark white, their eyes round with fear.

"It's going to be okay," I tell them in my most reassuring voice as I dial 911. "Go in my room and lock the door, then hide in the closet." I put the phone to my ear. "Go."

I watch as June grabs Jude's hand and tugs him away.

"I'm calling 911," I yell through the door. One last effort to get him to stop, and he goes quiet. The operator answers on the other end of the phone, asking me about my emergency, and as I open my mouth to speak, three gunshots sound, one right after another.

Glass shatters, a framed picture falls off the wall and crashes to the floor, and I run halfway up the stairs, watching in horror as Patrick starts kicking the door again. There are chunks of wood littering the hall, but I can't tell where they came from.

The operator asks if she heard gunshots, and I tell her yes. She asks if I've been hit, and I run my trembling hands over my body. I don't feel pain, but I don't feel much of anything outside of fear, and I can barely get enough air in my lungs to answer her.

"I don't know," I say honestly, trying to focus on the phone call and not on the abuse being shouted at me from the other side of the door. "Please hurry."

Outside the door, I hear more voices. Another shot. A crashing sound and grunts. There's no way the cops could be here already. I stand and creep down a few steps, just as another knock sounds—it's softer, but no less urgent.

"Jocelyn?" the voice calls, and I recognize it. "Jocelyn, are you okay? Can you open up?"

I rush down the stairs and unlock the door. When I crack it open, I see Riggs's roommate Xavier standing on the porch, shirtless and in sweats. For some reason, his bare feet catch my attention. There is glass covering my front porch and he's standing here in bare feet. I scan for blood and find some. Smeared on the ground. On the sides of his feet.

Xavier's voice is calm as it floats into my consciousness over the sounds of my own rapid breathing and heartbeats. He's asking me if I'm okay. If the kids are okay. He says he's called the police.

"I've called them too," I mumble, then glance at my hand.

I don't know where my phone is. I don't think I hung up with the operator. Where is my phone? I move my eyes from my hand back to Xavier's feet, but my attention snags on the yard beyond.

There's a heap there.

A body.

Two bodies.

I gasp and move to step forward, but Xavier puts his hands on my shoulders, stopping me.

"Don't come out here yet," he says. "Riggs is fine. Your ex-husband is knocked out, but we're not taking chances."

I look back to the yard and let my eyes adjust. Riggs is looking at me, and his body and hands are restraining Patrick. Patrick, whose eyes are closed and head is lulled to the side.

He looks dead. I couldn't be so lucky.

Two cop cars and an ambulance arrive. Patrick is arrested. I'm checked for injuries. I'm questioned. Riggs and Xavier are questioned.

"I'm pressing charges," I tell Travis. "He needs to be punished for this."

To my surprise, Travis nods. I thought for sure he would take Patrick's side and try to talk me out of it. Just like he did with June's accident. When Travis was one of the officers to answer my 911 call, I was prepared to have to fight tooth and nail to keep this from being swept under the rug. Instead, Travis agrees with me.

"I know, Lyn," he says solemnly, and I can hear the guilt in his words. "It should have been handled a long time ago."

I don't point out that he's one of the reasons it wasn't handled a long time ago.

"Jocelyn," I correct him. "My name is Jocelyn."

Before Riggs and Xavier leave, I thank them for their help, then make them swear not to say a word to Jesse about any of it.

"I can't do that, Joss," Riggs says. "I can't keep something like this from him."

I clamp my eyes shut. "This is going to be a shitstorm, Riggs. I don't want Jesse involved. I can't deal with all of this and him too."

I watch as Riggs and Xavier exchange a glance.

"I know your loyalty is to him," I say with a defeated sigh. "I know I'm asking a lot. But this isn't his problem, and you know he will treat it like it is."

I want to throw up when those words leave my mouth. I know, without a shadow of a doubt, that Jesse would drop everything—med school, his future—to come back here and check on me. I want that. I want it so badly. And that's exactly why I can't let it happen.

He cannot lose his future because I've messed up mine.

"I won't offer the information," Riggs says finally. "But if he asks about you..."

"Okay." I nod. If that's the best he can do, I'll take it. "Thank you. Both of you. Thank you so much for what you did tonight."

Xavier pulls me in for a hug and a few tears fall from my eyes. I don't want to think of how differently tonight could have gone if they hadn't intervened. They were here a full seven minutes before the police showed up. That seven minutes could have cost me my life.

Riggs gives me a hug, then says goodbye to June and Jude, who are huddled together on the couch under a blanket. I'm worried how they're going to process this. Will they have nightmares? Will they struggle with this night for years? Should I look into getting them a therapist?

"I'll have somebody come over first thing in the morning to

fix the door," Riggs tells me. First thing in the morning is just a couple hours away. He puts a big hand on my shoulder. "I'm glad you're okay. You'll get through this."

When the guys leave, and it's just me and the kids once more, I pad my way to the couch, climb under the blanket, and curl up next to them. I hold them close, and we turn on a movie. Something light and fluffy with catchy sing-along songs and corny jokes. We don't move from the couch all day. I order pizza. We eat ice cream. We don't talk about what happened.

I will. I *will* talk to them about it tomorrow.

But right now, we just need peace.

* * *

There's a knock on our new door.

When I open it, Bailey and Ivy are grinning at me from the stoop.

"Hey," I say, smiling but confused. Ivy beams. Bailey smirks. It's fitting. "What's up?"

"Welllll," Ivy says, then holds up two reusable Target bags. "I know you've got today off, and the kids are at the YWCA program. We thought maybe you'd want to take a break from studying and hang out with us."

I cock my head to the side. I've been talking more to Ivy lately since Christina Pierce took my case. Usually the occasional text, sometimes a phone call. She's come by to check on me twice since Patrick was arrested, but her and Bailey showing up at my door with goodie bags is new. I don't hate it.

"Sure?" I step to the side and let them in the house.

"She's leaving for Chicago soon and I'm staying behind," Bailey states as we head to the kitchen. "Figured it was only right that we get a few hang outs in together before it's just you and me."

I blink at her. *Her and me?*

"Oh, should we invite Rox?" Ivy chimes in, and I nod. Why the heck not?

"Tell her to bring her cards. Maybe we can play something."

Ivy sends a quick text.

"She said she's on her way," she announces, then starts unpacking the stuff in her Target bags. Crackers, cheese, fruit.

"Charcuterie?" I ask, and Ivy hums and gives her shoulders a little shimmy in response.

I get excited, and then remember I don't have the buffer of Jesse anymore, and immediately feel anxious. Anxious and sad.

"I'm working on being more honest," I say, and Ivy and Bailey both look up from their tasks. I swallow. "I'm working on being more honest, and I just...I need you guys to know that I might be bad at this."

"At what?" Ivy asks softly.

I gesture between us. "This," I say. "I've never really had..."

"Girlfriends?" Bailey states flatly, and I chuckle.

"No." I shake my head and clarify, "Friends. Period."

"Oh," she says. Then blinks. "Well." She shrugs. "They're overrated."

Ivy gasps and swats Bailey on the shoulder. I laugh. Bailey rolls her eyes and gives Ivy a shove.

"'Cept this one. She's pretty okay. I'll share her with you."

I laugh again. These two.

"Okay," I say with a smile. "Thank you."

When Roxanne pulls up in her Mustang twenty minutes later, Ivy and Bailey have constructed a pretty impressive cheese board. My brow furrows when I think about the last time I had charcuterie, and I try my best to dodge the memory.

"The party is here," Roxanne sings as she lets herself in the front door. "I brought rosè."

Ivy and I exchange a glance. It's 10 a.m. Looks like we're turning this into a brunch party.

Roxanne and I have grown closer recently. She calls to chat. We'll meet for coffee. She still hasn't told me about her daughter Marie, but I have a feeling she passed away. Rox will tell me when she's ready. Or maybe she won't. Either way, I'm grateful for the friendship I've found with her.

Rox rounds into the kitchen with a bottle of wine in each hand, wearing bedazzled skinny jeans and an off the shoulder t-shirt with Def Leppard on it. She catches me eyeing the shirt and grins.

"You like it?" She glances down at her shirt as she sets the wine on the counter. "That bassist was talented with his hands but shit at giving head. Couldn't believe I had to teach a rock star how to find the clitoris."

I bark out a laugh just as Bailey starts coughing. Ivy pats her on the back awkwardly, and Bailey waves her hands in front of her face.

"Sorry," she chokes out. "I inhaled some cheese." She clears her throat and takes a sip of water, then turns to Roxanne. "The bassist for Def Leppard went down on you?"

Rox scoffs.

"Barely."

She waits for me to finish laughing before she asks me where my wine glasses are. I wince.

"I only have one," I tell her sheepishly. I used to have more. I just don't know what happened to them.

"That's fine," Roxanne tells me. "Tastes the same out of coffee mugs." I point to the cabinet that has the mugs, and she pulls one down for each of us. She pours rosè into each mug, then bluntly asks me about Patrick.

I sigh.

"He's been charged with willfully discharging a firearm at a house, which is a felony, and he's on leave from work." *Paid* leave, I don't add. "Christina thinks his lawyer will plead it down to a misdemeanor."

"That's gotta be good for your custody case, though, right?" Bailey asks, popping another cheese cube in her mouth. I shrug.

"Christina thinks so." I take a sip from my mug, then stare at the pink liquid in it. "So far, he's respected the restraining order. Not so much as a text. But his family has money. I'm not expecting him to go away easily."

"You're asking for full custody?"

I nod. "And supervised visits. If I could ask him to terminate his rights, I would."

"Why can't you?" Bailey asks, thinly-veiled anger in her tone. I don't know her whole story, but I get the feeling she doesn't have the best relationship with her parents. Moments like this, I'm sure of it. I take another sip of wine and leave the question unanswered. I was abandoned as a child by my birth parents. I don't wish that for my kids.

"How's the photography," Ivy asks, changing the subject. I shrug at that, too, then give Roxanne a smile.

"You can actually have your camera back, Rox, since you're here."

"Why? You get your own?" She narrows her eyes at me when she asks, and I look away.

"No. Just too busy for it."

"Well, I don't want it. It's yours now." I start to protest, but she cuts me off. "When's the last time you used it, Jocelyn?"

I don't answer. I don't want to say it. I haven't touched the camera since Patrick accosted me with the blackmail pictures. I hate him for it. The irony of the whole thing. How he's once again tarnished the hobby for me, and this time, he's done so with pictures of his own.

"He's taken enough from you, Joss," Roxanne says sternly.

"Don't let him take this too. Not again." I make eye contact with her, and the fierceness on her face has me sitting up straighter. "Quit letting him win."

I don't say anything at first. I just nod. Take a bite of cheese. Take another sip of rosè. We all sit in silence while I work out the tangle of thoughts in my head.

"I've made so many mistakes," I whisper finally. "I worry I won't be able to fix them all. How do you move forward from shit like this?"

I was just a kid when Patrick and I met. I didn't know any better. I'm still paying for that.

"Your desire to grow and improve is admirable, but it can also be a terrible burden," Ivy says softly. "You can't keep applying that critical lens to your past—sometimes you just need to be proud of how far you've come."

I'm weighing her words when Rox lets out a long whistle.

"Damn, girl," she says, and Ivy laughs.

"I can't take credit for that one. That's all Dr. Joyner."

"Who is Dr. Joyner?" I ask, and it's Bailey who answers.

"Her therapist."

"Hmm." I glance at Ivy. "I've been thinking about getting the kids in to see a therapist. A counselor or something. Someone better equipped to help them process this whole mess."

Ivy nods. "Christina can help. She's got some great contacts."

"I'll ask her about it."

"Perfect," Roxanne interjects with a loud clap. "Now that that's all squared away, who wants to play poker?"

It's a good day. I enjoy the company of these women, and I can't remember the last time I actually felt like I had *real* friends.

Today I do.

I pretend like my life isn't a mess, like I'm not about to dive into a custody battle with my alcoholic and abusive ex, like I'm not completely and utterly heartbroken, and I allow myself the freedom to laugh and joke and relax with my new friends.

And thankfully, no one mentions the 6'4" elephant in the room.

I don't think I could pretend I was okay if they did.

jesse

"EARTH TO JESSE," Anjali sings, then snaps her fingers in front of my face. "Where'd you go just now?"

"Sorry." I blink a few times and flash a smile. "I think my brain is just tired."

The sounds and smells of the surrounding café rush back into focus, and I have to shift in my seat to adjust.

"I get that," Anj says after taking a sip of her latte. "I keep having to remind myself to trust the process, but good god, the process feels brutal."

Anjali is also a preclinical student, which is just saying we're both in our first year at Harvard Med, and she's in my society, which is kind of like HMS's version of Hogwarts houses. She also happens to live in my building.

I opted to not move into the house I'd found for me, Joss, and the kids, but I missed my chance to get a spot in the dorms with most of the other first year med students. Initially, that didn't bother me, but I didn't consider just how lonely I'd be living on my own. Three weeks after moving to Boston, I had no roommate and didn't know any of my neighbors, so I was climbing the walls and strongly considering getting a cat. The day I recognized Anjali leaving the building, I swear the clouds opened and angels sang.

She hasn't been able to get rid of me since.

I still think I might get a cat, though. And I want to name it Steve Carell. I'm not sure why. It just feels right. I'll make a game out of fitting as many Steve Carell quotes in a day as possible. With just *The Office* alone, the possibilities are endless.

"Can you believe we've been at this for, like, almost two months?" Anj says, cutting back into my thoughts. She's talking to me, but her eyes are on the computer screen in front of her.

"Honestly? No," I tell her, and click to the next lecture slide. "But sometimes I have moments where I'm like...how is it not fall break yet?"

She hums her agreement and clicks the trackpad on her laptop.

Our classes are flipped, so we have to do all the readings and course lecture videos prior to class, then during the actual class, we get to do group discussions and work through clinical cases. I really like the way it's set up. Anj and I spend most of our time at this café doing class prep together, but really, it's her doing prep and kicking my ass every time I zone out.

Which is often.

It's taken me a few years, but I've found strategies that work for me when it comes to managing my ADHD. I keep to a routine. I live out of a planner. I try my best to stay organized. I have an app on my phone that I use specifically for task and time management, complete with alerts, reminders, and check-lists. I curb excess energy with the gym or knitting, and I meditate as needed. But like anything else in life, the difficulty of managing the symptoms varies, and right now, the outside stressors are making everything more challenging.

Boston is cool, but aside from my relationship with Anjali, I'm lonely. I miss my family. I miss my old condo. I miss Indiana, which is something I never thought I would ever say. I miss the familiarity and the comfort of home. Surprisingly, though, moving my entire life to a new state and starting medical school hasn't been the hardest thing to acclimate to. I've assimilated fairly quickly.

But the breakup?

That has threatened to derail me on more than one occasion.

Some days are better than others. On the good days, I'm on top of my shit. I'm social. I'm kicking ass in class. But more often than not, I'm just going through the motions. And sometimes, like tonight, I can feel myself slipping. I miss Jocelyn and the kids, and it's all I can think about.

I'll waste whole chunks of time stressing over the breakdown of everything with Joss—what I did wrong, what I could have changed, how I could have been more careful. So much of it was my fault. It was my involvement with them that put her at risk. If it weren't for my past...

I grit my teeth. No matter how many times I try to beat them back, the same old insecurities reappear.

I wasn't good enough for her. I screwed it all up.

I can't stop seeing her face the day we said goodbye. I can't stop hearing Jude's voice when he said he would miss me. And June's hug. I can't stop remembering the way it felt when she released me and stepped back.

I realized I loved them moments before I lost them.

Those thoughts are like despair quicksand, and on nights when they're the most vicious, I'm fucking grateful for Anj, because she can throw me a lifeline in the form of a shin kick or a finger snap.

Ivy and Bailey would love her.

I've kept my promise. I check in with the group chat daily, and I've FaceTimed with each of my friends at least once since I got to Boston, and no one ever mentions Joss. It's like an unspoken agreement. I don't inquire, and they don't divulge.

Jocelyn Calligaris is Fight Club.

"Hey," Anjali says, punctuating her word with a swat to my shoulder. "You're doing it again." She sits up straight and hits me with *the look*. "Should we call it a night?"

I glance at my computer. "I still have ten slides." I screw my lips up and scowl.

"A change of scenery, then?" she suggests, and I smile.

"Let's get food and go back to your place and take turns reading the slides out loud."

"Why my place?" She powers down her laptop and slides it into her bag. "Your place is closer."

I snort a laugh. "By one floor." My apartment is on the fourth floor, and Anjali's is on the fifth. "Your apartment because mine is a disaster and the couch is covered in yarn skeins." I never realized just how much Kelley cleaned until I moved into an apartment on my own.

"Okay, Grandma Jesse," she says, and slings her backpack over her shoulder. "It's your turn to buy."

The next morning, I'm waiting for Anjali on the sidewalk outside of our building to head to class. She takes forever and always leaves right at the last minute. I used to think I was pushing it until I met Anj.

While I wait, I scroll through my socials. I don't go on a lot, and even when I do, it's to post and bail. I rarely scroll—it makes me miss home too much—but Rox just made an Instagram profile, and she cracks my ass up. Best part of my month was when she sent me a friend request.

"Ready," Anjali says, informing me of her presence as I type in Roxanne's IG name… @StangBangGranny76. I try not to think too hard on why she chose it.

"One of these days we're going to be too late, and they'll lock us out," I scold as I fall into step beside her, and I hear her scoff.

"Please. You can't rush perfection."

I side-eye her and snicker, and she swats me in the stomach. Talking 'bout *can't rush perfection* when she's wearing yoga pants, a Stanford Med t-shirt, and Adidas slides with toe socks. Her hair is always in one of those bun things, and she never wears a stich of makeup.

"You just didn't want to get out of bed," I tease, and she nods shamelessly.

"Exactly. My bed is perfection."

I turn my attention back to my phone as Roxanne's profile loads. Her latest picture is of Ralph kneeling in his flowerbed, and the caption says, "Honey Bee." I snort and double tap.

The next picture takes a minute for me to process. I don't even realize I've stopped walking until Anjali punches my arm.

"Dude," she says. "You're getting worse. You sure you don't want to go see Student Health? Talk to someone? Get on something?"

I shake my head without looking up from my phone.

Kelley is in a bounce house with Jude. But Kelley and Ivy are in Chicago, so this doesn't make sense. But the picture looks like it was taken at the cul-de-sac.

"Can't do drugs," I mumble as I check the date. A week ago.

She scoffs, no doubt about to launch into her lecture on the validity of ADHD meds and erasing the stigma, but I cut her off.

"I got nothing against ADHD meds for other people, Anj. I wasn't introduced to them in a healthy way and now I don't trust myself with them."

I scroll. Three more similar pictures.

Anjali says something else, but I don't hear her.

The next picture is of Jocelyn and Zay. They both have on party hats and big, blue, heart-shaped sunglasses. Zay is smiling. Big. Jealousy stirs in my chest.

Anjali kicks my foot as I stare at the third picture.

"We gotta move, Jesse." I wave her off.

It's a birthday cake with one of those edible fondant photos of BTS on it.

Nine candles.

June is smiling behind it.

"I gotta go," I say as I shove my phone in my pocket and head the opposite direction of our class.

"What the hell!" Anjali yells after me. "You can't just skip class, Hernandez! This isn't undergrad!"

"Take notes for me, Thakrar," I shout over my shoulder before breaking into a run. "You're the best!"

I can't believe I missed her birthday. I can't believe no one told me it was her birthday. Seriously, what the fuck? How could they not tell me?

I hop the transit bus that'll take me to the mall. While I ride, I scour every recent photo on all of my friends' social media accounts.

Nothing.

Not a single picture, story, status. Nothing to suggest they celebrated June's ninth birthday a week ago without telling me. Nothing to suggest they even see Jocelyn and the kids at all.

Before I can think better of it, I go to Jocelyn's profile. I haven't looked at it in a month. When I first got to Boston, I stalked it. Multiple times a day. It wasn't until Anjali asked me if she should be concerned about my "creepy obsession" that I stopped.

The breath is sucked right from my lungs as soon as her

profile loads. There aren't many pictures of her. Mostly June and Jude, and my chest aches with longing. I miss them.

Jude's little buzz cut has grown back. There's a back-to-school photo for both of them, and I can't hold back my proud grin when I notice that June is wearing a short-sleeved shirt. There's a picture of June on a soccer field. One of Jude smiling with his face and hands covered in paint. Then there's a photo taken in the wildflower clearing in the state park. It's the only recent photo that has Jocelyn in it too. Her, June, and Jude stand in the field, surrounded by wildflowers, with big, toothy smiles on their faces.

My first thought is I should have been there.

My second is who took this fucking picture.

My third is that I can't do this to myself again.

The bus pulls up to the mall, and I close out of the app. I head straight to the bookstore, ask a clerk for recommendations that a nine-year-old would enjoy, and buy everything she suggests. I grab two of those teeny bopper magazines that have BTS on the cover too.

I check out and head to the UPS store. I box everything up, write a quick Happy Birthday note, and overnight it to June. Then I take out my phone and shoot a text to the group chat.

Me: Don't ever let me miss another birthday.

I watch multiple chat bubbles pop up, typing dots appear, then they go away. It happens several times before one of them finally sucks it up and hits send.

Ivy Bean: Okay.

No apology, though I guess they don't owe me one. They

were doing what they thought was best. I drag my hand over my face. Tug on my hair. Sigh.

She's happy. Her and the kids. They're happy.

I need to let myself be happy too.

Even if it hurts.

Two days later, my phone rings, and my stomach nearly falls to my feet when I see the Caller ID. I'm so busy staring at it that it almost goes to voicemail.

"Hello," I say quickly, heart in my throat.

"Jesse?" a familiar voice says. "It's June."

My smile is immediate.

"Hey, June Bug!"

"Thank you for the books," she says excitedly. "Mom got me another bookshelf because I ran out of room."

"I'm glad you like them." I swallow and try to stop smiling like an idiot. "How was your birthday party?"

"So much fun. We put up a bouncy house, and I had friends come over. Granny Roxanne made me a cake with BTS on it. I got my own practice soccer net and new green cleats, and I got to have a sleepover."

I've literally never heard June this excited before. She's talking a mile a minute.

"Soccer, huh?" I say, playing dumb. "You play soccer now?"

"Yeah, and I'm really good."

"I bet you are," I say with a grin. "Probably better than all the boys."

"Yup," she says proudly, popping the p.

I ask her about school, and she rambles on about her teacher and her friends. She mentions that little twat Cole, but I hold my tongue. I listen to her talk for a while, and then I hear Jude in the background begging for a turn.

"Jude wants to talk to you," she says with an annoyed sigh, and I chuckle. "But Jesse..."

"Yeah, Joanie Baloney?"

She giggles, then clears her throat. When she speaks again, it's a whisper.

"Are you still doing your superpower?"

An anvil straight to the heart. Like one of those Looney Toons scenes. These kids, man. Even 950 miles away, they wreck me. I have to swallow several times before I can speak.

"Every single day, June Bug."

She's quiet. I hear a small sniffle. A little laugh. Then, "here's Jude."

I have to pull my shit together really fast once Jude gets on the phone. His conversation is harder to follow. Enjoyable, but confusing. He's still very concerned with whether or not I have *aminals*. When I tell him I might get a cat, I can hear him bouncing with approval. When I hang up with him, my call log tells me I was on the phone for almost two hours, but it wasn't long enough.

My phone pings with a text before I can set it down.

Classic: Thank you.
Me: Of course. Thank you for letting her call me.
Classic: They miss you.

God, that text fucking hurts. I wait a few seconds, willing her to follow it up with the words I want to read. That *she* misses me too. But they don't come.

Me: I miss them.
Classic: Maybe they can call you again?
Me: I'd love that.
Classic: *orange heart emoji*

Me: *orange heart emoji*

Before I go to bed, I log out of all my social media accounts. I don't trust myself. I'll log back in once I get my head straight.

* * *

"Anj!" I shout into the apartment. "Hurry up, would you? We're going to miss our ride."

"Stop yelling," she grumbles, and I hear her heels clopping on the floor as she comes down the hallway. "I keep telling you. You can't rush perfection."

She makes a show of posing against the wall, arm up, hip out, lips on full pout.

"Daaaamn," I say dramatically. "You look hot. Like a ray of fucking sunshine." She laughs and offers me her hand, so I take it and give her a twirl. "We'll definitely be the hottest couple there."

She turns around and pushes me toward the mirror on the wall, then hooks her arm in mine. I study our reflection, her in her yellow dress and me in my charcoal grey tux and yellow tie. We look good.

"How big are those heels?" I ask her, noticing she reaches almost to my shoulder. "There's not a whole two feet between our faces anymore."

"*Please*," she teases, "you are not that tall."

"I'm 6'4"," I protest, and she rolls her eyes.

"Yeah, you and every guy on every dating app, but I'm pretty sure you're barely 6'1" on a good day."

"Hey, miss lady." I point an accusatory finger at her. "Just what are you doing on dating apps? Do I need to have a looksee through your phone?"

She rolls her eyes, then takes her phone out and holds it up.

"Smile," she says with a grin. "We need selfies."

Anjali snaps about thirty pictures, and then we head downstairs to meet our ride.

I'm practically skipping with excitement. I didn't go to dances in high school.

I prefer not to think about what I did instead of attend dances.

When I found out HMS was hosting a formal, it was like my chance at a redo. Anjali has been humoring me and let me do the whole nine. I matched my tux to her dress, got us corsages, rented a limo, and made a reservation at the Olive Garden. I even did a fucking promposal with balloons and a handmade posterboard sign.

We're doing formal Midwest high school style, and we're doin' it right.

Tomorrow starts fall break, but tonight we party.

Anj switches out her phone with mine once we're in the limo and takes a few more pictures.

"There," she says when she hands it to me. "Pictures for the memories."

I can't fight the downturn of my lips or the furrow of my brow. *Pictures for the memories.* I stare at the photo on my phone screen. I look happy. Anjali looks beautiful. It's going to be a fun night, but fuck, I miss Jocelyn. I wish she was here. I wish I was having this experience with her. She'd be in a dress sure to make us *late* late, and I'd feel her up in the limo. I'd make her laugh all through dinner. We'd dance all night. And at the end of the evening, we'd go home to June and Jude, and it would be...perfect.

I squeeze my eyes shut and breathe through the thoughts, until Anjali places a soft hand on top of mine.

"Hey," she whispers, and I meet her eyes. "Let's have fun, okay? Let's give you the experience you should have had."

I nod and smile. She's right. I gotta quit hanging on to what I wish could have been. Jocelyn said it herself—another place, another time, maybe it could have been different. But we're here and it's now, and this is how it is.

She's in Indiana. I'm in Boston.

I'm going to become a brilliant surgeon. It's going to feel so good.

And in a few years, this heartache will be nothing but a blip in my memory.

As I post the picture of Anjali and me to my social media and plaster on a happy face, I know it's all bullshit.

TWENTY

jocelyn

Me: The coast is clear.

I SEND the text the moment I'm certain June and Jude are fast asleep.

A reply doesn't come, but there's a soft knock on the door ten minutes later.

I open it and let Bailey inside.

"I brought emergency supplies," she says with a grim smile, holding up a box of wine, and a large, repurposed butter tub. I chuckle softly and follow her to the kitchen.

We don't say anything as she grabs coffee mugs from the cabinet and fills them with Pinot Grigio, then she breaks open the butter container and pulls out several delicious looking cookies.

"These smell amazing," I say, then grab one and take a bite. "Oh my god, they taste amazing," I mumble through a mouthful.

"Thanks," she says with a proud smile. "Caramel toffee, but I played around with the way I creamed the butter and brown sugar. I think it makes them softer."

I flash her a thumbs up and take another bite. "You did great. They're phenomenal."

We move into the living room and take seats on the couch, and as soon as her legs are crossed in front of her, Bailey levels me with a pointed look.

"Be honest," she says clearly. "How'd it go?"

I sigh, close my eyes, and drop my head back on the couch.

"It was brutal," I confess. "He was able to use the pictures."

"WHAT!" she shrieks, then immediately covers her mouth. We freeze and look at the ceiling for a few seconds. When no sounds come, she exhales. "Sorry. But seriously, what the fuck? How can he use those? They were taken by a literal stalker who is now in jail."

I shake my head.

"His mom is saying they paid a private investigator. There is no proof Sandra Huntington took them."

"That's bullshit."

"They're also using those few weeks I wouldn't let him see the kids. Saying I purposely am trying to keep them from him to turn them against him."

She blinks. "You wouldn't let him see them because he drove drunk as a skunk and put their lives in danger. That's not even hyperbole. That's fact."

I shrug. "My word against his."

"Jesus Christ, he is the lowest kind of scum. Congealed garbage juice at the bottom of a dumpster."

I laugh because it's a better alternative than crying. I'm so tired of crying.

"What about the arrest? The gun? He shot three bullets through your door, Joss. Riggs had to replace the whole thing and replaster part of the wall. That should render everything your ex says null and void."

"You'd think," I say. "But his parents have money, and money talks."

"What does Christina say?"

"She says not to worry. To trust her, and that Patrick doesn't have a leg to stand on. She says everything they're throwing at me is just a dog and pony show, trying to distract from the reality that he's not a good person, and that it won't work."

"And do you trust her?" she asks, her head cocked to the side as she studies me with concerned eyes. I take a moment to think about it. My lawyer, Christina Pierce, is brilliant. Not only is she representing me in this custody mess for free, but she also found youth counselors for June and Jude, and got me in touch with a therapist who works primarily with domestic violence survivors.

When she first suggested it, I was adamant that I didn't need it.

Therapy, sure. But therapy for domestic violence survivors? That wasn't me. I insisted I wasn't a survivor of domestic violence. Patrick never abused me. He was just a dick.

Then Christina pointedly and clearly set me straight. The way I was treated by Patrick, in every single way, was abuse. He *is* abusive. When he yanked me around by my hair, pinned me to the wall, and made threats, those were acts of violence. Just because he didn't break skin or leave bruises on my body didn't make them less severe.

"I do," I tell Bailey earnestly. I *do* trust Christina. "She hasn't given me a reason not to. But it doesn't make this any easier." I cringe. "Seeing those pictures again was hard."

Sure, they were censored, but you can't censor the memories. That night with Patrick, when he hurled those photos at me and I watched as they scattered on the floor at my feet, is burned in my brain. I have nightmares about it. Having to relive it today was terrible.

"I'm sorry, Joss. This whole thing is bullshit. It's all bullshit."

I nod. "Yeah." I run my finger over the rim of my coffee mug and change the subject. "Jesse's been texting."

She sits up straight. "Really? About what?"

"Random stuff," I shrug. "Emojis and photos mostly. June called to thank him for the birthday gift a few weeks ago and the communication lines have stayed open. It's been...nice."

"Does he know about..." She waves her hand around in front of her and I shake my head.

"I haven't told him. So, unless one of you guys—"

"We haven't. We promised we wouldn't unless—"

"Unless he asked about me." She jerks her head in a nod, and my stomach twists. "He hasn't asked about me."

"I think maybe it's just too hard for him, you know?"

"Yeah, maybe."

This is what I wanted, him in Boston pursuing his dreams. Him living *his* life and not being dragged down by mine. This is good. I'll be fine. I have too much to worry about to be dwelling over a broken heart, anyway.

"Jocelyn..." Bailey starts, then trails off.

"What?"

"Are you sure he knows? How you feel, I mean? Does Jesse know you're in love with him?"

I don't bother denying it. Bailey isn't stupid.

"It doesn't matter, Bailey." I shrug. "He's got his life, and I've got mine. He needs to go to Harvard Med. He can't ruin his future for me."

"Don't you think that should be his choice to make?" When I look at her, her lips are tight, and her eyes are narrowed. "He's a grown man. You know that, right?"

I gasp, jaw dropped wide in shock, but her gaze doesn't let up.

"Yes, I am well aware that Jesse is an adult," I defend. "You think I'm trying to parent him? I'm not. I'm trying not to let my tidal wave of a fucking life pull him under and drown him like it has me."

I can feel my eyes start to sting with unshed tears, but I stare at the wall and will them away.

"I can't be the reason he loses everything," I whisper.

"I think that's the problem," Bailey says softly.

"What is?"

"You're considering yourself a loss instead of a gain."

I open my mouth to speak, then close it. I have no words for that.

It's hard to see myself as anything worth *gaining*. The only person who has ever made me feel that way was...*Jesse*.

"You know," she starts, "part of the reason you ended things with Jesse was because Patrick threatened to use the pictures and Jesse against you, right?"

I nod. "Yeah."

"Well, Patrick's done it. You ended things with Jesse and your ex still used those pictures. The damage is done, and according to Christina, it's really not much damage at all."

"Okay..." I raise a brow, and she raises one right back.

"I just wonder, at this point, if keeping your distance from him is really what's best for either of you. That's all."

She gets up quietly and moves into the kitchen. I hear her rustling around and refilling her mug. While she's in there, I mull her words over in my head. She's right. A relationship with Jesse is no longer the danger it was when he left. Sure, he's in Boston and I'm here, and I do want him to stay in Boston because it's where he needs to be to achieve his dreams, but maybe...

Out of curiosity, I open my social media and go to his profile. I haven't been to it in a few weeks. I've refrained. I couldn't handle more things to be sad about on top of all the Patrick crap. Last time I checked it out, his feed was full of pictures of food, lifestyle type shots of him studying, and cats. So many cats.

When his profile finally loads, though, it's a slap to the face. I feel like somebody kicked me in the stomach with a steel-toed boot.

The very first picture I see is one of him and a gorgeous girl. He's wearing a grey tux and his yellow tie matches her elegant yellow dress.

He's smiling. A real, sparkling teeth, all the way to his dancing eyes, Jesse Hernandez smile full of humor and mischief. He looks so beautiful it hurts.

And she's smiling too. I recognize that smile. It's the one people get when they're in the throes of experiencing Jesse's superpower.

She's very pretty, this girl. Petite, with rich brown skin and long dark hair. Her eyes are lined with dark black and sparkling gold, and her lips are the deepest of reds. When the picture starts to blur, I blink to clear my eyes of the tears. Then I notice that he's posted some new story videos, and against my better judgment, I click on them.

I wish I wouldn't have.

His deep voice and his playful laugh feel so real. He's dancing. He's singing. Sometimes he's by himself, sometimes he's with people I've never seen before, and most of the time, he's with the pretty girl in the yellow dress. It's a whole string of short videos of him at what looks like a formal dance. Like prom or homecoming. I never got to go to dances in high school. Patrick didn't like them. He'd promised me we could go to senior prom, but he ended up breaking that promise.

On the last slide I see the girl's account is tagged, and I click on it, but her profile is set to private. The bio tells me she's in her first year at Harvard Med, though. I laugh darkly. I told him our lives were too different. Now he's found someone who fits his better. I laugh harder, until my side aches, and my face is drenched in tears.

"It won't always feel like this," Bailey whispers from the couch next to me. I didn't even realize she came back. I have no idea how long she's been sitting next to me. I glance at her and see her phone is open and on Jesse's profile too.

"The universe is really trying to make me hate pictures," I muse.

"Fuck the universe," Bailey spits, and her voice is full of so much venom that it starts me laughing all over again.

A couple hours later, Bailey leaves, and I find myself rage-cleaning the kitchen, so I don't fall victim to my sadness and heartache.

I declutter the countertops before wiping them down, then empty and wipe out each drawer in the kitchen. I've finished four drawers and am starting on a fifth when a familiar piece of construction paper catches my eye. I pull it out and study it.

My list.

Be a Full Person.

It feels like a lifetime ago when I wrote this, but it's actually been less than a year. Six months, maybe? It's crazy how fast things change. At first, my shoulders slump and I go to throw the list away, but something stops me.

I read the items off the list out loud, and by the time I reach the end, my lips have curled into a soft, bittersweet smile. I've accomplished every one of them. Every single one of the goals I'd written for myself, I've achieved or completed in one way or another. Something like pride surges through me.

I might not be where I want to be, but I've come a long way

from where I was, and I'm not giving up. My heart may be aching, but it's still beating; and my life might be difficult, but for the first time in almost twenty-nine years, it's mine.

The realization is liberating.

I fold the list in half and put it in my back pocket with the intention of keeping it safe in my bedroom. Proof of progress. An artifact of hope.

jesse

"YOU'RE AN ASSHOLE," Bailey's voice grates from the phone screen, her face furious. I recognize the background. She's at Riggs's place. Well, now her place too, I guess.

"Good morning to you, sunshine," I grumble. I pull my phone farther away from my face to check the time. "Bailey, why the hell are you video calling me so early on a fucking Saturday?"

"Oh, I'm sorry. Were you out late last night?" she asks sweetly, and her innocent smile causes me to sit up straight. I don't trust sweet Bailey. Either she's been body snatched and is now a pod person, or I'm about to get my ass reamed.

"What do you need?" I raise a brow and her smile falls into a scowl.

"How is it that one week ago you FaceTimed Riggs drunk and crying about how much you miss Jocelyn, and then last night you're out yuckin' it up with some rando in a yellow dress?"

"Uhhhh," I mumble. "She's not some rando. That's Anjali. And since when do you say *yuckin*?"

"That's not the point."

"No, the point is that Riggs is a dick and was gossiping about my vulnerable moment."

"He did not *gossip*. I was literally sitting right next to him the entire time you blubbered on FaceTime." Her eyeroll is epic. Like, lose your eyes in the back of your head epic. "It's not my fault you're incapable of seeing anyone else when my boyfriend is around."

"It's the man bun," I say absently, and she shrieks.

"Jesse!"

"Bailey! Stop being such an Aries."

"I'm not an Aries, you weirdo."

"It's your moon sign, and you're projecting."

"How do you even know that?"

"I just do," I say with a grin.

She growls at me. "This has nothing to do with Zodiac signs."

"Be a lot cooler if it did." I shrug and bite my lip to keep from laughing.

"JESSE," she shrieks again. "Stop trying to piss me off!"

"Sorry. It's the Sagittarius in me." I wink, which just pisses her off more. She drags a hand down her face in frustration.

"Just please focus," she says with a sigh. She's relentless. There's no distracting her when she's like this.

"Okay, sorry. What should I be focusing on?"

"On Jocelyn," she whines, and I huff.

"Yeah, no. Wrong. I've spent too much time focusing on Jocelyn. I need to focus on what's here in front of me in Boston."

"You are literally the dumbest genius I have ever met."

"Pfftt. Like you've met any other geniuses."

"Are you still in love with her?" she asks, and I sigh.

"Yeah, I am. You know I am."

"Well, she's in love with you," she states, and I throw myself back down on my bed with a groan.

"She's not, B. She told me so herself."

"She is, and you're a twat for just giving up so damn easily."

"Did you just call me a twat?" I laugh.

"The twatiest of twats." She shakes her head. "And if I were there, I'd totally smack you upside the head."

"Aw, B, you know you're not fast enough for that."

"Jesse, I'm serious. You just took off at the first minor hiccup."

"I didn't *just take off*, Bailey. I went to med school, which Joss told me to do. And I would hardly call my former abuser and her psycho ex teaming up to blackmail her a 'minor hiccup.'"

"Jesse," she groans, giving me pause.

"What is with you, Bailey? You used to be firmly Team Yeet or Get Yeeted. Now you're a simp."

"Ha. I am *not* a simp. If anyone is the simp in this relationship, it's Riggs."

I laugh just as Riggs' face pops into the screen, and he flashes me a smile.

"Proud simp, right here," he says, and then disappears, but not before I notice that he is wearing an apron covered in flour.

"What's he doing?"

"Makin' cinnamon rolls."

"With the cream cheese icing?"

"Of course." She grins, and my stomach growls.

"I'm jealous."

"Could come back for fall break and have some," she says, dragging out the last few words in a song. I chuckle and shake my head, about to tell her again that I've made my decision, and I'm staying in Boston for fall break, but the expression on her face stops me short.

"What?" I ask, and she scrunches up her nose. "Bailey, seriously, what?"

"Look, I'm just saying that Jocelyn has a lot going on right now, and I think it would be good for both of you if you came here to visit for fall break."

"What do you mean she has a lot going on? Is she okay?"

"Just come home, Jesse." Her shoulders slump, and she sighs.

"Why?"

"Because she's in love with you too, ya big dummy. She told me so herself."

The ground drops out from under my feet. I shake my head a bit and hit her with a glare.

"What did she say?"

"Oh my *god*, Jesse. What are we, in 8th grade? I said, are you in love with Jesse? And she said, yes. And I said, does he know that, and she said, it doesn't matter blah blah blah he can't ruin his future for me blah blah blah. But here's the thing, Jesse. That woman is a freaking saint, and she would do everything— I mean *everything*—by herself, just so she wasn't a burden on someone else. She would never ask you for anything, but if you love her like I think you do, like you *say* you do, then you wouldn't make her ask. So, stop being so fucking boring, get on a god damn plane, and come get your fucking girl!"

We stare at each other for a moment, her with smoke coming out of her ears and a frown, and me gaping like a moronic fish out of water. Then, when I finally process her speech, I hang up. I'll probably get my ass handed to me later, but at least she'll be able to do it in person.

I use my phone to book the next flight out, which is in two hours, and rush around my apartment tossing shit in a duffle. I'm halfway down the hall before I have to turn back.

"Steve," I call, running around and looking under furniture and in closets. "Steve, my son, come out, come out. Time to go see your Auntie Anjali."

I find Steve in the back of my closet on top of a pair of white and green Jordan 4s. I keep telling him not to lie on my shoes, but this cat gives zero fucks.

"C'mere, son." I scoop him up and carry him out of the apartment and up the stairs.

I knock on Anjali's door, and she answers immediately.

"You're up early," she greets with a smile.

"Me?" I joke. "You're the one who usually sleeps until noon."

She rolls her eyes, then zeroes her attention in on Steve. She pops a brow, and I give her my best, innocent and charming smile. She doesn't budge.

"Can you watch Steve this week for me?"

"Why? I thought you were staying in town for break."

"Change of plans," I hedge, but she gives me *the look* and I cave. "I'm going back to Indy. She loves me."

Anjali's face transforms into a giant smile, and I smile back.

"Jocelyn?" she asks, and I nod. "I knew it."

I jerk back and scoff. "How'd you know?"

She shakes her head. "I swear, for being a genius, you're not very smart."

"Why do people keep saying that to me?" I throw my catless arm out and drop it back down, and Anj laughs.

"Love makes people dumb," a voice calls from inside the apartment, and then Cam, Anjali's partner, who goes to Stanford Med, walks into the room.

"Hey," I say with a smile. "I thought you couldn't be here until tomorrow?"

"I didn't think so either, but I was able to move some stuff around and got in about six this morning."

"Sweet." I lift up Steve. "Do you mind?"

"Definitely not." Cam steps forward and takes my black and white floof of fluff. "Have a safe flight."

I hand Anjali my keys, give her a hug and Steve a goodbye head pat, and then rush out of the building.

When I finally land and turn my phone back on, I have one text from Bailey. The fact that there is only one makes me afraid to check it.

Ball Buster: I swear if you're ignoring me for any reason other than being on a plane to Indiana, I will make you regret it. It will be painful. You will rue the day you hung up on me.

I shudder. That girl is terrifying.

Me: *plane emoji* *corn emoji* *orange heart emoji*
Ball Buster: YOU BETTER NOT BE LYING TO ME!!!
Me: *praying hands emoji*
Me: *Aries emoji*
Me: *middle finger emoji*
Me: *running man emoji*

I put my phone on silent.

She's going to murder me.

The only rental car the place has is a tiny-ass compact, but I take it because I'm on a mission. I feel like one of those clowns at the circus getting in and out of the damn thing, though. I chuckle. I guess now I know how Shaq felt in *Kazaam.*

On the drive to Joss's house, I get nervous. I don't even

know why I'm so nervous. I love her. She loves me. The rest should be cake, right?

Fuck.

I pull into the driveway and cut the engine. My first impulse is to run up and knock but being impulsive hasn't always worked in my favor. Instead, I pull out my phone and send Joss a text.

A car emoji and a house emoji.

And an orange heart emoji.

Two minutes pass. Then five. Then ten. With every second that goes by, my breaths grow shallower and my jaw tighter. I can see her car in the garage. My patience is shot. I've spent hours on a plane to do this. I'm gonna do it.

I fling myself out of the car and march up to the door. Just as I reach the steps and raise my hand to knock, the door swings open and there stands Joss, wrapped in a towel and dripping wet. Like she was in the shower and didn't take the time to dry off. My eyes devour her, starved for her. I *need* her.

I close the distance.

"Kids?" I ask between heaving breaths.

"Next door," she says, and then I'm on her.

When my lips touch hers, for the first time in months, I lose it. I shuffle her back inside the house, kick the door closed behind me, and tug the towel off her wet body. My eyes eat up her bare skin as my eager hands rush to touch every inch of her.

"Fuck," I pant out, moving my lips from her mouth to her neck to her chest. I bite the swell of her breast, lick downward and around her nipple. She gasps when I grip her ass and moans my name when I slide my fingers in her already wet pussy. "Fuuuuck," I groan again, thrusting my fingers in and out.

I move my mouth back to hers and walk her backwards a little more until we're at the stairwell.

"Lie," I tell her, and she does.

She lowers herself to the stairs, body naked and glistening from the shower, hair wet and sticking to her skin. I want to commit her image to memory. I want to keep her naked and laid out on this stairwell forever.

"If you don't want this, tell me now," I growl out, dragging my eyes from her body to her face. "If you want me to leave, tell me. Otherwise, I'm going to fuck you on these stairs."

The wait feels like an eternity before she speaks.

"I want you," she says, her voice pointed and sure and full of desire for me. I drop to my knees and go straight for her pussy. I lick with the flat of my tongue, once, twice, three times, then suck her throbbing clit into my mouth.

I don't toy with her. I don't play. I don't have the patience for that.

I suck hard and use my fingers to thrust and stroke her insides. I need her to come. I need her to come fast and hard.

"Oh my god," she cries, and bucks into me. I use my forearm to pin her back down and I don't let up. "Jesse, oh my god."

"You taste so good," I murmur against her, scissoring my fingers and pressing my thumb on her clit as I talk. "You know how many times I jerked my dick thinking about your taste? Fantasizing about having my tongue inside you again?"

She moans as I replace my thumb with my tongue. I remove my forearm from her hips and grab one of her hands that's white knuckling the edge of the stair. I bring her hand to my head and fist her fingers in my hair.

"Pull," I growl, and she does.

She tugs at my hair, and when she starts to quiver and shake, I bring my free hand to her neck. I tighten my hand around her throat, just enough force for her to feel me, and suck hard on her clit until she comes with a rasped cry.

I stand quickly and take off my shirt, then remove my pants.

I spit in my hand and stroke my throbbing cock twice, then drop down on top of her. I brace myself with one arm, so I don't crush her, take her mouth in a deep kiss, and use my other hand to guide myself to her pussy and push inside.

Her cry matches mine as we come together, the feeling both blissful and torturous.

"This pussy is mine," I growl against her lips, thrusting hard. "No one else."

"Yes," she breathes out as she hooks one leg around my waist.

She meets my thrusts, quick and deep, her hands gripping tight on my arms.

"Play with your clit," I tell her between kisses, and she brings one of her hands between us. "I want you to come again around my cock."

"Harder," she says, so I thrust harder. I slam into her in a steady, rhythmic motion, gritting my teeth against the impact, holding off my own release until she has hers. "I'm almost there," she moans, and seconds later, she clenches around me so tightly my vision blurs and I lose my breath.

I let her ride out her orgasm, then pull out quickly. I rise onto my knees and stroke myself hard and fast, keeping my eyes on Jocelyn's face as she watches.

"I'm going to come all over you."

My voice is a low, rough rumble, waiting for her to decline my threat. When she whispers, *please*, I fucking lose it, and shoot thick streams of white all over her chest and belly with a long groan.

"You made a mess of me," she says airily, and I chuckle and admire my handiwork. I've painted her in stripes of glossy white. She's never looked so fucking sexy. I lean down and smash my naked chest to hers, wiggling, and she laughs out loud. I love that sound. I've dreamed about her laugh for months, but nothing compares to hearing it in person.

I stand and pull her up, then throw her over my shoulder as she shrieks. I give her ass a playful smack.

"Looks like you need another shower, then."

And I carry her to her bathroom.

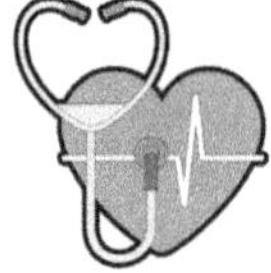

jocelyn

I SIT with Jesse on my bed, both of us wrapped in towels and eyeing each other hungrily.

After taking me on the stairs, he washed every inch of my body with a care that nearly broke my heart. His whispered words and promises, filling me with both hope and dread. Finally, after minutes of silence, I break it.

"Why are you here?" I ask, and his grin makes me pause.

"I'm here because I'm in love with you, and you're in love with me. The rest we'll figure out."

I chew on my lip and take a deep breath before speaking. "What about the girl? In your photos."

"She's just a friend. Her partner goes to Stanford, so she and I went to the formal together. But she's just a friend, Joss. Nothing has ever happened there."

The relief I feel is immeasurable, but that's only one of our obstacles. The smallest.

"But Boston?" I question. "Med school? My situation hasn't changed. I can't move there with you."

"I know," he says with a nod, and I raise an eyebrow. His grin grows. "Look, I don't know the specifics of how this is going to work. I just know that it has to, because I'm not willing to try and silence my love for you anymore. I want to love you loud. I want everyone to know about it."

"Jesse," I sigh, fighting back tears. I want so badly for this to work. I want to believe that it can. But...

"Do you love me?" he asks, and I freeze. "No bullshit, Classic. Do you love me?"

I close my eyes and speak the truth. "Yes."

"Do you trust me?"

"Yes," I say instantly.

He takes my face in his hands, and when I open my eyes, I'm staring right into the most beautiful swirls of brown and green.

"Now is our time," he says. "This is our place." He presses a kiss to my lips, tasting the tears I hadn't realized I'd cried. "Loving you is my superpower, Classic. Let me be great at it."

His kiss is passionate and full of love. The kind of love I never thought I'd feel. The kind of love I never thought I deserved.

He wraps his arms around me and pulls me close, until our bodies are touching at every possible surface. He places one hand on my face, strokes his fingers down my jaw, then tugs lightly on my lower lip with his thumb.

"Nothing feels better than this, Classic. Nothing will ever feel better than us."

An hour later, two hours past when I said I would arrive, I let myself into Riggs's townhouse carrying the dish of now cold green bean casserole.

I've been looking forward to the Friendsgiving potluck they'd planned. Ivy and Kelley drove down from Chicago for it, and Roxanne and Ralph will be here soon. I've never been to a Friendsgiving before, but every other Thanksgiving dinner I've been to was tense, cold, and anxiety-inducing. I'm looking forward to making new memories, for both myself and my kids.

I walk through the living room, where June and Jude are currently watching a movie, then round the corner into the kitchen. I'm met with four pairs of curious eyes. Eyes belonging to people I've come to think of as family. I smile shyly as I set the casserole dish on the counter.

"Sorry I'm late," I say, and take note of the smirks on Ivy and Bailey's faces just as I hear laughter and screeching coming from my kids.

"JESSE," Jude yells, and I let out a soft laugh as I watch Jesse scoop both my kids up and spin them in a circle with a roar.

"We told you, fuckers," Bailey says with a laugh, and I turn back just in time to see Kelley and Riggs slapping money into Ivy and Bailey's outstretched, waiting hands. I raise an eyebrow at them, and Ivy giggles.

"They really need to learn not to doubt us," she says with a sly smile. I open my mouth to say something, just as Jesse's arms wrap around my waist and he rests his chin on my shoulder.

"*Hola, familia*," he says, his lips tickling my ear. "Y'all thought you could have Friendsgiving without me?"

Bailey barks a laugh.

"Puh-leeze," she groans, "it's about time you came to your senses. Your denial was giving me migraines." Bailey and Ivy both laugh, and Jesse gasps playfully.

"You tiny hypocrite," Jesse says, then points to Ivy. "You too. You're both tiny little evil hypocrites."

Ivy pushes a strand of blonde hair behind her ear then checks her nails.

"I have no idea what you're talking about," she sing-songs. "I have never in my entire life refused to see what was right in front of me, instead choosing to bury myself in fear and denial in an attempt to ignore my very obvious feelings for someone else." She glances up from her nails and shrugs. "You must be mistaking me for someone else."

Kelley chuckles and Riggs snorts. Bailey flashes them both a scowl then turns her attention to Jesse. "Me either."

"Tiny little lying hypocrites."

"What am I missing?" I ask, bouncing my eyes between the two couples in front of me.

"Oh, I'll tell you all about it," Jesse says, giving my side a squeeze before walking around me and into the kitchen. "I've got enough stories of these four being boneheads to fill a whole book. Shit, to fill two whole books."

"Three, if you count yourselves now," Kelley says with a grin.

I still feel lost, but I don't have a chance to ask any more questions before the rumble of a car outside announces the arrival of Roxanne. June runs to the door, and minutes later, Roxanne and Ralph are joining us in the kitchen. Ralph sets down the dishes they brought, and Roxanne embraces Jesse in a hug.

"Bout time you came to your damn senses," she scolds him, and he winks at me over her head.

Riggs and Kelley start pulling dishes from the oven, stove, and fridge, spreading them out on the counters and setting them on potholders and uncovering the containers as they go. The townhouse fills with delicious smells, and Ivy hands out plates. I call June and Jude into the kitchen. June fixes her own plate and I fix one for Jude, which is basically just potatoes and a few pieces of ham.

"Hey," Jesse says, looking up from one of the dishes on the counter. "Who made my *frutas en tacha*?" His brows are furrowed, and his lips are in the cutest little pout. "This is my Friendsgiving contribution."

"You waited until the last minute to decide if you were coming home or not, and I didn't want to take chances, so I called your mom and got the recipe," Bailey says matter-of-factly. Then she adds with a sigh, "It's probably not as good as yours, though."

Jesse's frown transforms into a grin immediately.

"Did everyone hear her say that? Can you say it again? I want to record it."

Bailey rolls her eyes and leaves the kitchen with a huff, ignoring the muffled laughter of her friends. Throughout the rest of the afternoon, we eat and laugh. Riggs sets up a bean bag game in the yard, and at one point, everyone moves to the cul-de-sac to kick around a soccer ball. If every holiday came together just like this for the rest of my life, it would be perfect.

A few hours later, I'm helping Jesse do the dishes when Roxanne comes into the kitchen to throw some garbage in the trash can. She gives me a one-armed hug, then pats Jesse on the shoulder.

"Glad you're here, Jesse," she says. "The arrest and the custody bullshit has been wearing our girl down, and it's nice to see her smiling again."

My eyes go wide as Jesse turns to me, questions and concern on his face.

"He doesn't know?" Roxanne says, looking between me and Jesse.

"I haven't had a chance to tell him yet," I say quietly, not taking my eyes off of him. His nostrils flare, his eyes narrow, and he calmly turns off the water and takes my hand.

"Excuse us, Rox," he says, pulling me past her. "We have some stuff to talk about."

Jesse takes me through the garage door and into the yard, bypassing everyone in the house. Silently, we walk hand and hand to my townhouse, and as soon as we step through the front door, he has a seat on the stairs. I sit next to him.

"What was she talking about?" he asks, and I take a deep breath.

I tell him everything. I start with the night he left. The visit from Ivy. The first meeting with Christina Pierce. When I tell him about the night Patrick was arrested, the anguish on his face breaks my heart. He stares at the wall, the door, as if searching for the since-repaired bullet holes.

"I should have been here," he says, and I shake my head.

"No," I say quickly, "it wouldn't have changed anything."

"I should have fucking been here, Jocelyn."

I don't argue again, I just push forward, until I'm up to date on the custody stuff. He sits quietly for several moments.

"I'm sorry you've had to go through this by yourself," he says, staring at the ground, hands fisted in his lap.

"I haven't," I say. "Not entirely."

"I never should have left. I should have been here for you," he says again.

"It's not your problem, Jesse. I don't want my mess to affect you."

He shakes his head.

"You gotta stop trying to make my decisions for me, Jocelyn. I'm an adult. I make my own choices. I choose you, and everything that comes with you. J-Squared. Endless laundry. Deputy Dildo, even. If I have to put up with him to have you and the kids in my life, I'll do it."

"Did you just call my ex-husband Deputy Dildo?" I ask, trying to hold back my laugh. He grins.

"That was funny, right? I call him a lot of things in my head. None of them are nice."

I laugh out loud, and Jesse slings his arm around my shoulder.

"I'm here. Don't push me away again. Your mess is my mess. I want it. Let me have it."

"So, are we going to do this? Like, a long-distance relationship for the next four years?" I ask, holding my breath. I don't bring up after that. Residencies and fellowships and whatever else goes into becoming a surgeon. It's overwhelming.

"Yeah," he says. He's so sure. I try to soak it in. "We'll talk daily and spend breaks together. We'll make it work. And you won't have to do everything on your own."

I start to protest, but he cuts me off.

"No, Classic. Trying to do everything by yourself isn't commendable. It's dumb."

I blink, then bark out another laugh. "Did Roxanne tell you that?"

"Of course. I suppose she's told you the same thing?"

"About twenty times."

"Well, she didn't get to her age by being stupid. I think we should listen to her."

"I think you're right." A thought hits me. If this is going to be real, if we're going to do this... "I think we should tell the kids."

Jesse nods, and it feels good to be on the same page as my...partner? Boyfriend? Whatever he is, we're in sync. It's new for me. I like it.

"Let's do it tonight," he says. "After Friendsgiving. I don't want to waste any more time."

Later, when we're sitting in my living room after the festivities have ended, I give Jesse a look. One that says, *let's do it now.* He grins.

"Hey, guys," I begin, hoping the brightness in my tone overshadows my nerves. I've spent the last couple of hours planning what I'm going to say, but I still feel unprepared. "Jesse and I want to talk to you about something."

"Kay," Jude says, bouncing a little on the couch cushions as he speaks.

"What's up?" June asks. Her eyes flick between me and Jesse, then settle on where our hands are clasped. She raises an eyebrow but says nothing.

"Well, I wanted to let you know that, even though Jesse is in Boston for medical school, he and I will be, um…" I stutter, my mind going blank. "We're going to…"

Jesse squeezes my hand and gives me a small smile.

"Your mom and I are going to be dating," Jesse says bluntly. "You know what that means?"

"Like, you'll be boyfriend and girlfriend," June answers, then glances at mine and Jesse's joined hands once more.

"That's right," I tell her. "So, you'll probably see us holding hands or being more affectionate sometimes."

"You're going to kiss!" Jude giggles, and I smile at him.

"Yeah, we are, kid," Jesse says with a chuckle. "Is that okay with you?"

"Yeah," Jude says, and June shrugs. "Sure."

"So," June continues slowly, "does this mean you'll be coming back?"

I look at Jesse as he nods. "I'm going to come back to visit whenever I can. But I still have school in Boston, so I won't be able to see you all the time."

"So just for school breaks and stuff," June clarifies.

"That's right."

"I also want you guys to know that we're not trying to replace your father. Patrick is still your dad," I add.

"That's right. I'm going to be dating your mom because I care about her, just like I care about you two. But I know that Patrick is your dad."

Jesse's voice is clear and steady, and his grip on my hand is firm. I study his face as he speaks to the kids and marvel at the sincerity I see there. He does care about them, I know it, but I love hearing him say it.

"I'm not trying to replace him, okay?"

"Okay," the kids say in unison. Jude is smiling, but June purses her lips and furrows her brow when she answers.

"Are you sure that's alright, June?" I ask her, and she nods slowly.

"It's just…" she pauses, then looks to Jesse. "We don't care, you know, if you do. Replace him, I mean."

I startle. Open my mouth to speak, then close it. I don't really know how to respond to that. When I look at Jesse, he's grinning.

"Thank you, Junie Pontoonie," Jesse says. June rolls her eyes. "That's nice to hear."

"Okay, well, I'm going to go read," June says suddenly. "I'm glad you're boyfriend and girlfriend finally. I knew you were but now we can say it."

I bark out a laugh and June smirks. Then she hops up and heads upstairs.

"I knew too," Jude says. He's wearing a big grin, and when I look at Jesse, he's sporting a matching one.

* * *

The next few months are both blissfully wonderful and heartbreakingly difficult.

Jesse and I text constantly and talk on the phone at least once, but usually more than once, a day. He stayed in town for the whole winter break, leaving only for a few days to visit his parents in Chesterton. He wanted me and the kids to meet his parents, but I said no. Not yet. I'm not ready. I could tell he was hurt by that, but we didn't talk about it. We avoided any heavy topic and spent the break focusing only on things that made us smile. The pictures I took of him and the kids having a snowball fight have to be some of the best I've ever taken.

Jesse sent me flowers when I was hired as an RN at Indianapolis General Hospital, celebrated with me via FaceTime when I was awarded full custody of June and Jude, and listened patiently and lovingly as I worked through my confusing emotions when Patrick gave up his parental rights because he didn't want to pay child support.

"I never want them to feel unwanted," I told him through my tears, heartbroken for my children that their dad so willingly gave up on them. Full of guilt over not choosing a better man to have children with. "I don't want them to look at this whole thing years later and wonder why they weren't enough."

I know those feelings too intimately. I know how painful they are.

"They'll never feel unwanted, Classic," he told me. "They've got a superhero of a mom who loves them unconditionally, and they have me. We'll love them, and we'll remind them every single day that they're perfect. That they're more than enough."

I let his words wash over me, and I pretend he isn't 950 miles away talking to me through a phone.

For spring break, the kids and I flew out to Boston. Jesse introduced us to his new friends and took us on a tour all around the city. When I told him it was my first time leaving the Midwest, he did everything in his power to make it a memorable first vacation for all of us. Jude fell in love with Jesse's cat, Steve, and June declared that she wanted to go to Harvard Med to become a surgeon just like Jesse. *After* winning the FIFA Women's World Cup, of course. The whole week was full of moments that filled my heart with happiness, but the goodbye at the airport effectively broke it in half.

Every time I see him, I want to hold on to him for a little longer. Every time, it's harder to keep myself from begging him to stay. Every goodbye, every see you later, every 'just one more kiss' breaks something inside me, and I don't know if it's reparable.

Will these cracks heal once we are finally able to be together? Or will I continue to chip away until I inevitably shatter? Can I make it through three more years of this? Can I make it through *this* year? Can he?

Jesse tells me I'm it for him. He speaks of nothing but love and the future and our life together. But he's still in Boston, and I'm still in Indiana, and I've never known of a love to survive both time and distance. I've never known of a love to survive anything, period.

But I'll keep answering the phone with a smile each time he calls and welcoming him into my home with open arms when he visits, and I will keep pretending he's not 950 miles away every time he whispers that he loves me over the phone.

I'll close my eyes and imagine that he's lying in bed beside me, and I'll push through one more day of having him but not *really* having him. Because nothing feels better than Jesse Hernandez's superpower, and if the alternative to this is never feeling it again, I'll choose him every time.

* * *

"I miss you," I whisper into the phone, my eyes drinking in every inch of his beautiful features.

"I miss you most." His smile is sad.

"Tell me about classes."

"I've already told you everything," he says slowly, his voice tired. I can hear the weariness, and I know it's not just because we're pushing past midnight for the third day in a row. His eyes droop closed, but he still holds the phone propped up, so I can see him. So he can see me when he drags his eyes back open. "I study. I go to class. I study some more. I scold Steve for sleeping on my Js. That's basically all I do."

"Hmmm."

"And I miss you. Constantly." He yawns, making me yawn, and we both laugh softly. "Tell me about you and the kids."

"I've already told you everything," I repeat his words. "I work, I chauffer, I do laundry. Jude insists he's a pirate. June talks about soccer. And we miss you. Constantly."

"Sometimes, I imagine what it will be like when I'm done here and finally with you. I'll dream about it and it's always so real, but then I'll try to touch you, kiss you, and suddenly, gravity tugs heavily and I can't lift my arms or move my feet. When I call out for you, my voice won't work."

"That sounds terrible," I say, my voice cracking. I don't tell him I've had similar dreams, but I actually prefer the dreams where I can't touch him to the ones where I can. At least the sad ones are easy to wake up from.

"It *is* terrible." He hums. "Sometimes I also have dreams that I have a flesh-eating disease or one of those brain-eating bacteria that you can get from contaminated water."

"Oh my god." I giggle, then giggle some more, and his sleepy smile warms me up from the inside. I long to kiss him. "Those dreams sound worse."

"They're not," he says, frown lines replacing the smile I was just admiring. "I'd take brain bacteria over never being able to touch you again. Every time."

I sniff. Blink back tears.

"Is this ever going to get easier?"

He's silent; his eyes closed. He's quiet for so long that I think he's fallen asleep. It wouldn't be the first time we've fallen asleep on the phone together. Just as I'm about to whisper *I love you* and hang up, he opens his beautiful brown eyes, stares right at me, and delivers the saddest news I've heard in a long time.

"I don't think it will."

I take a deep breath, then release it slowly.

"I'll talk to you tomorrow?" I say, trying to force some levity into my voice.

"Yeah," he mumbles. "I love you."

"I love you."

"You'll always be my hardest goodbye, Classic." He flashes me a slow, tired smile. "Sleep tight."

"You too," I whisper.

When the call ends, so does my composure, and I spend yet another night crying into my pillow until I finally fall asleep.

jesse

MY PLANE LANDS at Indianapolis International Airport at 2:23 in the afternoon.

I make the walk from the terminal to the rental car lot on autopilot. I could do this trip in my sleep, truth be told. I feel like I've spent more time in the air between Boston and Indiana than I've spent actually on the ground in either state recently.

"Mr. Hernandez," Luce, the clerk at the rental car desk, greets me with a smile. "Back again? I feel like we just saw you last weekend."

I smile as he types on the computer, probably pulling up my reservation.

"That's because you did just see me last weekend," I say with a chuckle. "But this might be the last time you'll see me for a while."

He raises an eyebrow. "Is that a good thing or a bad thing?"

"I'll find that out soon enough," I say with a sigh. He hands me the keys to my rental, tells me good luck, and I thank him before heading to my car.

I'm jittery the whole drive from the airport. I haven't seen Jocelyn since spring break last month, and my fingers itch to touch her, but I'm nervous. She doesn't know I'm coming, or why. I'm afraid of what she'll say when she finds out.

The last few times I've been in town, I've stayed at the Hilton. This time, I make my way to Riggs and Bailey's townhouse. Bailey moved in after graduation. She got a job at an accounting firm in downtown Indianapolis, and Riggs works from home doing some sort of business real estate stuff for his dad's company. Zay moved out a few months ago—something weird went down with his family and Riggs is staying tight-lipped about what he knows, if anything. Ivy and Kelley are in Chicago, but I'm glad Joss still has Bailey and Riggs in case she ever needs anything.

The two times I've come to visit Jocelyn and the kids since fall break, I've stayed at Riggs's at Joss's request. She thinks it's better for the kids. She never said it out loud, but I could tell she was worried about them getting "too attached," in case things between us didn't work out.

She still doesn't trust me with them.

I scoff at the irony. She didn't seem too worried about me getting too attached, though.

I pull my rental into Riggs's driveway and glance next door. I know Joss is at work and the kids are at the YWCA program since their school let out for summer last week, but the urge to run over and knock still hums in all my limbs. I hop out of the car and jog up the walk, knocking four times on Riggs's door. When he swings it open, the look of shock on his face sets me laughing.

"What the hell are you doing here?" he asks with a grin, shuttling me inside and shutting the door behind me. "Don't you have, like, two more weeks of class?"

I nod. "Yeah. Academic year ends June 24th."

"I mean, I'm not complaining. I haven't seen you since Christmas, but, like, why *are* you here?" I follow him down the hall and into the kitchen, where he proceeds to pour me a glass of water. "I thought we were planning a big weekend at the lake to celebrate you surviving your first year of med school."

"I still plan to celebrate that," I say, taking a sip of the water. "I just have a few loose ends to tie up this weekend."

He narrows his eyes at me, and I look away. He and Anjali are the only ones who know how badly I've been struggling with this whole long-distance relationship thing, and he only knows because I told him. Anjali knows because she's witnessed my constant crashing and burning.

"What do you mean *loose ends*? What loose ends could you possibly have to tie up before you move back to Indiana for the summer?" I swallow and stare at my water glass. "You are moving back for the summer, right?"

Finally, I make eye contact.

"That's kind of what I need to talk to you about."

A few hours later, after Bailey came home from work and I filled her in on *everything*, I find myself sitting awkwardly on their couch as they stare at me.

"And your parents are cool with this?" Bailey asks, and I hide my wince.

"They are now." She raises a brow in question, and I sigh. "Mom wasn't at first. She was about ready to send my ass back to Lake Serenity, thinking I was having some sort of breakdown."

"That sounds more like the protective Dr. Vanessa Hernandez I know," Bailey says with a small chuckle, and I smile. She's not kidding. "So, what changed her mind?"

"My dad." I smirk. My dad, the hopeless romantic. He's a sap for a love story. As soon as I told my parents about Jocelyn, he was on my side. Mom took some convincing, but ultimately, Dad won her over.

Bailey nods, but her assessing gaze doesn't relent.

"Quit looking at me like I'm an alien," I say, and Bailey blows out an exasperated breath.

"We're just shocked, is all," she says. No bite. No snark. It worries me.

"You think I'm doing the wrong thing," I state, and Riggs shakes his head.

"No, we don't think you're doing the wrong thing," he says diplomatically. "We know how hard this relationship has been on you and Joss the last few months."

His statement all but confirms what I suspected. I'm not the only one who has been complaining to friends about how much long-distance sucks ass. I nod.

"I'm going to go talk to her, but I think it would be better if the kids don't see me."

Just saying that hurts. I want to see them. I want to hug them and joke with them and hear all about everything, but I need to respect Jocelyn's wishes. That has to be one of the hardest things throughout all of this, keeping my distance from J-Squared. I fucking love those kids, but Joss still doesn't trust me not to hurt them. Not fully.

"We'll go over there and watch the kids and send her over here. Good?" Riggs suggests, and I nod. He stands up and makes his way toward the door, but Bailey hangs back. She looks at me for a minute like she wants to say something, but instead of speaking, she just steps forward and gives me a quick, tight hug.

"I got your back always, J."

"Ditto, B," I say with a grin, and she turns and walks away.

After they leave, I pace, and I avoid every single urge to peek out the window at the house next door. It feels like an hour before I finally hear the front door open.

I hold my breath and listen to the pad of footsteps grow closer and closer until the most beautiful woman I've ever seen in my whole life is standing in front of me.

"Jesse," she says happily, then rushes to me. I wrap my arms around her and draw her to me, holding her, breathing her in. "I thought I wouldn't get to see you for a few more weeks," she says, and I can hear her voice cracking. I pull back and find she's crying, so I reach up and wipe the tears from her face.

"What's wrong, Classic?" I ask her, caressing her cheek with my thumb. I'm so tired of hearing pain in her voice and knowing I'm the reason for it.

"I'm sorry," she says with a pained laugh. "I don't know why I'm crying. I'm just happy to see you." She presses her face to my chest and hugs me tightly. "How long are you here for?"

I rest my cheek on her head.

"I go back Sunday morning."

"Okay," she whispers, almost to herself. "Two days now, then in two weeks, I'll get you for the summer." She steps back and sniffles. "I'm such a mess. I'll be right back."

I watch Joss walk in the direction of the bathroom and hear the water turn on. She's back in a matter of minutes, looking refreshed and calm.

"Sorry," she says again, as if she should have to apologize for having emotions. "What are your plans while you're here? Why are you here? Your classes are over so soon. Don't you have a lot of work to complete?"

"Well," I start, and then stop and gesture to the couch. "Let's sit."

She freezes and her face goes blank.

"Sure." She sits robotically on the couch, a whole arm's

length from me, and folds her hands in her lap. "What's up?" she says to the ground.

"Classic, look at me," I say, needing her eyes on me for what I'm going to say. She doesn't budge. "Joss," I press again. "I have something important to talk to you about and—"

"Just say it then," she says quickly. "Just get it over with, please."

"Get what over with?" I can't understand the clench of her jaw or the expressionless mask on her face. She was radiating with warmth and happiness thirty seconds ago, and now, she's as cozy as a glacier. "Jocelyn. Get what over with?"

"You're gonna end it. Right?" she says calmly. Her voice is so even that if I wasn't paying attention, I'd think she felt nothing. But her hands are shaking, and her eyes are hard, and I know she feels everything. Before I can interrupt, she continues, "Long-distance is too hard and you don't want to be tied to us anymore and you're here to end it. I appreciate you not doing it over the phone, but just say it quickly and get it over with please."

I can't help it. I laugh. She couldn't be more wrong. She couldn't be more off base if she tried.

"Classic," I say with a scoff, "when the hell are you going to get it through your head that I'm not going anywhere? I'm in love with you, remember? I'm not here to end it with you."

"You're not?"

She looks so confused, so lost, that my heart breaks a little. She's so used to people letting her down. I won't be one of those people.

"No," I say more softly, then scoot closer and take her hands in mine.

"But you were so...subdued. So somber... And you just show up out of nowhere unannounced. And you're not acting like yourself..."

I squeeze her hands and release another tired laugh.

"I'm subdued because I'm fucking exhausted. I've been traveling back and forth between Boston and Indiana for the last month, trying to convince the Dean at the IU Med School to let me transfer here."

"What?" Her voice is so tiny that I almost can't hear it.

"Yeah," I say with a sigh, "and I came here unannounced because Dean Clark finally gave me the go-ahead, but I was going to let you make the final decision."

"What? You're...you're transferring here? For med school. Here. For year two?"

"And three and four, hopefully. As long as you want me here."

"As long as I want you here?"

Bless her, she's in shock.

"Joss, I know you don't like when I spring things on you. I'm sorry. I would have said something sooner, but I didn't want to get your hopes up. I didn't tell anyone. Not even the guys. It's almost unheard of for a med school to let you transfer at all, let alone after only your first year. I wasn't sure I could pull it off. I only told my parents because I had to get my mom on board to help argue my case with the deans. I found out yesterday that Dean Hollis at HMS and Dean Clark at IU have decided to approve my transfer request, so I came here as soon as I could to make sure you were okay with—"

"Yes," she shouts.

"But you don't—"

"I don't care. Anything that will bring you here, with me, in this same state, is okay with me." She crawls on my lap, her smile addictive and infectious and every kind of intoxicating.

"You're not going to try and talk me into staying in Boston because Harvard is one of the top medical schools in the country?" I ask, putting my hands on her hips and fighting a smile.

"Nope." She presses a kiss to my lips. "You're a grown adult." She kisses me again and runs her hands up my shirt. "You can make your own decisions."

She pulls my shirt over my head, moving her lips to my neck, then hums against my skin. My eyes fall closed and my breathing kicks up.

"You know that if I do this, you're stuck with me, right?" I say it teasingly, but I'm totally serious, and I roam my hands up and down her thighs. "You're never getting rid of me. Or Steve."

She giggles and takes my mouth again.

"I'm good with it," she says, then bites my lower lip.

"And you're okay with me living on the cul-de-sac?" I ask, and she jerks backward.

"What do you mean?"

"Riggs's dad is hooking me up with one of the townhouses on the cul-de-sac."

"Why? Live with me."

Her eyes widen the same moment mine do, then we both laugh. I'm giddy. I'm so damn giddy.

"What if," she amends slowly, "you live in the other townhouse for a few months, and we gradually warm the kids up to you moving in with us?"

"That sounds perfect." I peel her shirt over her head and pepper her neck and chest with kisses. "Two weeks," I promise. "Two more weeks, and then we won't have to say another goodbye."

"No more goodbyes," she repeats, presses a kiss to my lips, then stands. I watch in awe as she shimmies out of her shorts and panties, then takes charge. "We have to make this quick," she says with a laugh as she removes my pants, then drops to her knees in front of me.

Jocelyn takes my cock into her mouth without hesitation, and I hiss and drop my head back on the couch.

"Fuck, Classic, I've missed this mouth," I grit out, trying not to lose myself completely to the soft, warm, wetness of her tongue gliding up and down my shaft and swirling my crown. When I pull her hair back and wrap it around my fist, she hums around me, making me shudder. I take a few moments to watch her bob up and down on my dick, to marvel at the way her cheeks hollow and expand. When she catches me watching her, she smirks around my cock, then pulls her mouth from me slowly.

"You can just watch if you want to," she teases, "but I was kind of hoping you'd want to do a little more than this."

"Yeah?" I question with a grin. "Like what?"

She licks up my shaft once more, and I tighten my hold on her hair.

"I want to ride you," she says coyly, but I don't miss the way her cheeks tinge pink when she adds, "and I want you to do that thing...with your fingers..."

Fuck me, my dick is a fucking stone pillar.

I pull her up and capture her lips, gripping her hips with both hands as she straddles me.

"I don't have a condom," I say between kisses, then grunt when she takes my dick in her hands and lines me up with her entrance.

"You can finish in my mouth," she says, then sinks down onto me, leaving me breathless in more ways than one.

We moan in sync at the contact, and I have to grit my teeth to keep from losing my vision. When she starts to move on me, I run my hands up and down her sides roughly before grabbing onto her ass cheeks, spreading them apart, and squeezing. I thrust hard into her a few times, and a strangled *yes* falls from her lips.

"I dream of this body," I grind out before taking one of her nipples into my mouth and sucking, reveling in the whimper it elicits from her. I press kisses all over her chest and neck. "I dream of fucking you, of you fucking me. I dream of tasting you. Do you dream of me, Classic?"

"Yes," she answers breathily as she glides up and down on my cock. "Every night. All the time."

I move my hand behind her and rub my fingers along her pussy lips, swollen and soaked as she rides my cock. My fingers graze my throbbing dick as I gather her wetness and drag it to the tight hole above. She drops her head down onto my shoulder and moans in pleasure the moment my fingers caress her there, rubbing her arousal around the tight ring of muscle.

"You like it when I play with your ass, baby?" I ask, and she moans a plea in response. I take my other hand off her hip and bring it to her mouth. She opens for me immediately, greedily sucking my fingers between her lips and coating them in her saliva. I pull my fingers out of her mouth. "Spit," I tell her, and she does. The excitement I see in her eyes is enough to make me blow early.

Joss stops moving on me as I bring my hand down and slowly press one of my wet fingers into her. She accepts it eagerly, and her pussy clenches around my dick in a way that makes my head spin. I pulse my finger in and out gently a few times, and her mouth falls open in a silent gasp.

"More," she pleads. "More, Jesse."

Gently, I add a second finger, and her whole-body shudders with the action.

"Fuck, Jocelyn." I slowly pulse my two fingers inside her, and when she clenches around me again, I wrap my free arm around her waist and thrust my hips.

"Jesus Christ," I groan. "I'm going to finger fuck your ass while my cock beats up your pussy, okay, baby?"

She nods frantically. "Yes. Please, god, yes."

Her voice is desperation and desire. Pure sex and need.

Our bodies are plastered together, connected in such erotic and intimate ways that even the slightest motion feels rapturous. I pump my hips up into her, thrusting deep into her pussy while my fingers work her from behind. I suck on the tender skin on her neck, run my teeth along her collarbone, and feel her inner walls start to spasm.

"Rub on your clit for me, Classic," I tell her, and lean back just enough so she can reach her hand between us. Moments later, she's coming with a loud cry. Before her orgasm ends, I flip us over so she's on her back on the couch and I'm hovering over her, and I pound into her hard and fast. When I'm seconds from coming, I pull out just in time to shoot my release onto her lower belly with a long groan.

She laughs lightly as I pant, trying to catch my breath.

"You were supposed to come in my mouth," she says. I shrug sheepishly.

"I couldn't. It was too far away."

She laughs harder, and I stand up and move into the kitchen to grab some paper towels.

"I'm serious," I joke. "It's because you're so tall. You got that long torso. It's like a mile between two of my favorite holes. I just couldn't make it in time."

She squeals with giggles as I clean her off, then I help her up and back into her clothes before putting on mine.

"So, no more goodbyes, huh?" The smile on Jocelyn's face is a work of art. Contentment and happiness and trust and hope. I take her hand in mine and squeeze.

"No more goodbyes," I reassure her. "As long as we don't tell Bailey or Riggs about this." I gesture to the couch where I just defiled her in multiple ways. "If they find out, you might have to say the ultimate goodbye, because Bailey will definitely murder me in cold blood."

She grimaces and nods. "Deal."

I kiss her lips softly, then press my forehead to hers.

"I'm so fucking in love with you, Jocelyn."

Her smile ghosts over my lips before she says, "I'm so fucking in love with you, Jesse."

I take a step back, then tug her by the hand toward the door. I can't fucking wait to see the kids and tell them the good news.

No more goodbyes.

* * *

Two Weeks Later

"I think that's all of it," Kelley says, taking a swig from his water bottle.

Kelley and Ivy drove down early yesterday from Chicago, just to help me move, and tomorrow, we're all heading to the lake house for some much-needed family time. I've been back "living" in the Midwest for twelve hours, and already, I feel more at home than I have in my whole year at HMS.

Part of it is familiarity, sure. But a bigger part is probably the hot mom who lives next door.

"Thanks for coming to help," I tell Kelley, and he brushes me off with a smirk.

"Don't even mention it." He takes another sip from his water bottle, then uses his shirt to wipe some sweat from his forehead. It's a toasty ninety-one degrees this June morning in Indiana, and we're all feeling it. "How long until you think we'll be back here moving you into Joss's?"

His smile is sly, thinkin' he's slick.

"I'll probably be over there in a few months," I tell him honestly. "But I doubt I'll need help moving anything. Half this stuff I'll sell or donate, and most of the furniture belongs to

Riggs's dad. All I'll be bringing with me are my clothes, my yarn, and my fur son, Steve." I nod to Joss's house next door and add, "Everything else I need is already in that house."

"I'm happy for you, J," Kelley says, and I don't even bother trying to temper my grin.

"Thanks, man. I'm happy for me, too."

Little feet come pounding over to us, and I look up just in time to see June skid to a halt. She's been chomping at the bit for Kelley to take her to the soccer fields and kick the ball around with her. The girl eats, breathes, and sleeps soccer, and since Kelley is a soccer coach, she asks him to play with her every time he's here.

"Are you done? Can we play now?"

She's got a dirty soccer ball under her arm and is already wearing her cleats and shin guards. Kelley flashes me a smile.

"Lemme go grab my cleats and tell Ivy I'm leaving, and then we can go," he tells her.

"Yes! Thank you, thank you, thank you," she sings, hopping with each word.

It's amazing how much June has transformed from the little girl I met in that ER room. Her confidence has grown so much that sometimes I can't even believe she's the same kid. She is, though. She's still just as sharp, just as observant. But now, she's not afraid to take up space.

When Kelley leaves, June turns those keen eyes on me. She looks just like a tiny version of her mom.

"Are you here for good, then?" she asks, and I nod.

"I am." She narrows her eyes at me, and I laugh. "I am, Doonie Zoonie. I swear it."

"And what about your superpower?" Her voice is hushed, so I lower mine to match.

"Never stopped, June. It's why I'm here. So I can do it better."

"So you can be part of our family now?"

These kids, man. They won't stop until I'm well and truly wrecked. I clear my throat and smile.

"You want me to be?" I ask, and she cocks her head to the side.

"Do *you* want to be?"

I bark out a laugh, and she smirks.

"I do," I tell her honestly. "I really, really do." And to seal the deal, I stick my pinky out for her. She hooks mine with hers immediately, then we both press kisses to our knuckles.

"Good," she says with a smile. "I want that too." She starts to walk off, then turns around. "If you can't find Steve later, that's because Jude has stolen him and is hiding him in his bedroom closet."

My laughter echoes off the other houses as she skips her way to Kelley's waiting Jeep, then they zoom off to kick soccer balls at the intramural fields.

"What's so funny?" Joss asks as she slides her arms around my waist from behind.

"June just told me that Jude has taken Steve hostage."

"Oh no," she says, giggling into my back. "That poor cat."

"No, Steve loves it. He's been more Jude's than mine ever since spring break." I spin around so we're chest to chest and wrap my arms around her. "It's one of the main reasons I moved back. Steve was getting depressed without his emotional support pirate."

"Oh, Steve was, was he?" She smiles up at me, and I get lost in the happiness emanating from her green eyes.

"Mmhm," I say, pressing a quick kiss to her lips. "He was. Cried about it every single day. Was getting annoying, honestly."

She hums. "And what would Steve have done if Jude

suddenly decided he liked, oh I don't know, zombies instead of pirates?"

I shrug. "Upgrade to an emotional support zombie, probably."

Her laughter is light and airy.

"Well, I am so glad you were able to help Steve and give him what he wanted." She kisses me again, then lies her head on my chest.

"So, what now?" she asks, but it's not a fearful question. It's excited. Like she can't wait to see what's next for us. She's ready to turn the page and dive headfirst into wherever our story takes us. I recognize it because I feel the same.

"Now, Classic, we love loud."

jocelyn

WE LOVE LOUD.

The summer is in full swing when Jesse and I take the kids back to the state park for a day of hiking, pictures, and picnics. Jude is in full pirate regalia and walking Steve on a leash. June is in her summer soccer tank top and carrying her soccer ball under her arm. She also made sure to have Jesse pack her a book in the picnic backpack.

We take the same path Jesse and I took last spring, the one that follows the large creek, and I marvel at the beautiful wild-flowers framing the trail. We stop at the same rocky shore so Jesse can teach June and Jude how to skip rocks, and I manage to snap some of the cutest pictures of him with the kids. They're standing barefooted at the shallow edge of the stream with the sun haloing their bodies, their faces are sporting lively smiles, and the light is reflecting off the water onto their chests like sparkles.

They are so beautiful. I want to preserve this moment in time, so I never forget it.

When we get to the wildflower clearing, it's an explosion of blooms, and I snap a few photos as June sets to work making flower crowns for us, and Jesse lays out the picnic blanket with Jude.

I brought June and Jude here last summer after Jesse left because I knew it would cheer them up, but it gutted me. Every minute I spent in this field last summer chipped away at my already broken heart, and I had to force myself to focus solely on June and Jude and their joy. We made flower crowns, had a picnic, and used the timer on the camera to take a family photo. It was a good afternoon, but Jesse's presence was missed terribly.

This time, everything about being here is better. The kids' laughter is louder, the smiles are bigger, and I swear even the sun is brighter and the flowers are more colorful.

Everything just feels better when Jesse is around.

After enjoying our charcuterie picnic (pb&j for Jude), I sit with Jesse on the blanket as June and Jude kick around the soccer ball. June is trying to coach Jude, but it doesn't come naturally to him, and the patience my girl has for her little brother is a wonderful thing to witness. At times like this, I think maybe I'm doing a pretty okay job at this whole mom thing.

Sometimes I wonder if June and Jude's relationship would be different if Patrick hadn't been, well, how he was. Maybe they're bonded more because of the negative experience.

Or maybe I'm just desperately trying to find something good in something bad.

Maybe I'm trying to find a reason to feel less guilty.

The kids have seemed largely unaffected by Patrick's absence in their lives. I'm sure the counseling has helped, but something tells me they were happy to hear they'd no longer have to see their father. I have conflicting feelings about that.

Travis told me that Patrick moved back to our hometown and is working for the township police department. I didn't ask how that was possible, what with his arrest and the misdemeanor charge. I'm just relieved that I won't have to worry about running into him anymore. I'm glad my kids can grow without the fear of their estranged father showing up unexpectedly.

"What are you thinking about?" Jesse asks, his low voice tickling my ear from how I'm reclined against him.

"Them." I nudge my head in the direction of June and Jude, and I feel Jesse's responding hum vibrate in his chest. I sigh and focus on the solidness of his chest at my back, feeling content and happy in his arms.

"They're pretty awesome, right?" I can hear the smile in his voice. "You're doing a great job."

He has no idea how deeply I feel that compliment. I savor it and swallow back the knee-jerk reaction to protest. A trauma response, my therapist calls it. Instead, I smile and accept his words.

"Thank you."

I'm getting better every day at loving myself, flaws and all, but when I struggle, Jesse helps me without even realizing it. He shows me how I deserve to be loved, by myself as well as by others. He reminds me that I'm more than enough just how I am.

He runs his palm down my arm, then gently threads his fingers with mine. I feel his chest move with a swallow and his heartbeat kick up against me.

"Have you ever thought of having another one?" he asks in a whisper, and my breath hitches.

I have.

Never with Patrick. But now, with Jesse, the thought crosses my mind frequently. I've never brought it up. He's only just moved back. He'll start his second year of medical school soon. He's still living in the townhouse next door. The thought of another marriage sends me into cold sweats, but the idea of a baby, with Jesse's curls and big brown eyes... It's something I find myself daydreaming about.

I clear my throat before answering carefully. "If I have?"

His hand tightens around mine.

"With me?" he asks timidly, and I nod slowly.

"Is that okay?" My voice cracks with uncertainty, and I wonder if he can feel my heartbeat thrumming rapidly in time with his. He presses a soft kiss to the crook of my neck.

"Hop up," he says. "Time to go."

I whirl on him, relieved when I find a mischievous grin on his face. My lips turn up into a confused smile.

"What? Why are we leaving?"

"Classic, the woman of my dreams just told me she wants to have my baby," he says pointedly. "We need to get home so I can knock her up."

My laugh is sudden, and my jaw drops as I look him over. He's beaming. He's gorgeous. And he's absolutely serious.

"Jesse, I didn't mean *now*," I say quickly. "You're still in med school. I haven't even been working at the hospital a whole year, yet. We can't have a baby right now."

I love my job at Indianapolis General, and I've been considering the idea of getting my Master of Nursing next. I've just started a small savings account to take the kids to an amusement park on their spring break, and we're all still settling in to the dynamic of Jesse being back in town. We can't throw another kid into the mix. Not *yet*, anyway...

"Okay, you're right." He screws his lips up to the side and nods. "Just know that I'm ready. As soon as you're ready, you let me know."

I raise a brow. "And if I said I wanted a baby tomorrow?"

"I'd say we better stop with the butt stuff because I'm not wasting a single swimmer until you're pregnant with my kid."

I can't hold back my giggles.

This man is ridiculous.

Ridiculous and brilliant and absolutely beautiful.

And mine.

"I'm serious though, Classic," he says, looking at me with the most sincere, captivating swirls of brown and green. "I'm ready when you are. Okay?"

"Okay."

His kiss is soft and gentle, and full of more love than I ever thought a kiss could hold. It's a kiss I've waited my whole life for and didn't even realize it.

When he pulls away, I glance back at June and Jude, their laughter like music on the breeze. It's overwhelming in the best way, this contentment. This happiness.

Nothing feels better than this.

JUNE

CHRISTMAS IS in a few weeks and Jesse is still living next door.

I thought him and Mom would come to their senses by now.

He's here every night for dinner, and back every morning for breakfast. Some mornings, I'm pretty sure he never left. They think they hide it, but I still notice.

It's my superpower, anyway.

We even had Thanksgiving with Jesse's mom and dad, and his mom said that me and Jude could call her *abuela* if we want to. *Abuela* means grandma in Spanish.

Mom's been happier. Smiling more. Laughing all the time. Me and Jude are happier, too. Mom watched us like crazy after Dad decided he didn't want us anymore. She thought we would be sad, but we weren't. We didn't want him anymore, either.

Especially not now that we have Jesse.

Well, we *almost* have Jesse.

I thought of telling Jude my idea and letting him tell the grown-ups, but that didn't work out well last time.

No. I need to do it myself.

Tonight is pizza and movie night, and it's Jude's turn to pick the movie. He's still upstairs with Steve the cat, but he'll probably pick *The Grinch* again.

When Jesse knocks on the front door, I run to let him in. I fling it open, and he's standing on the porch with two pizza boxes in his hands.

"Hey, Monsoon June," he says with a grin, and I roll my eyes.

"Hi, Jesse."

I smile with my mouth closed because I lost another tooth last week, one of the side top ones, and now I have a hole in my smile. I don't like how it feels or looks. I'm tired of this baby teeth junk. I'm ready to have all my grown-up teeth so they all match.

Jesse follows me to the kitchen and puts the pizzas on the table just as Mom finishes setting paper plates out on the counter.

Now or never.

"We need to talk," I say in my best mom voice. They both look surprised.

"Sure, June Bug," Mom says. "What's up?"

I take a deep breath.

"It's almost Christmas," I begin, "and I want us to be a family for Christmas."

"We are a family," Mom says with a little laugh. Her eyebrows are trying not to scrunch, though, and Jesse has his head cocked to the side. Silly grown-ups.

"Yeah, I know, but I want us to all be a family here together."

"What do you mean?" Jesse asks, but I can tell from the way his mouth is twitching that he finally gets it. When he winks at me, I know for sure.

"I think it's time Jesse and Steve just moved in here with us."

Mom's mouth drops open, her eyes are wide, and Jesse is smiling like a dork.

"I know that he sleeps over all the time anyway," I say, and Jesse laughs out loud. I shrug and look at him. "When you don't sleep over, at breakfast, your hair is wet from showering at your own house. When you do sleep over, at breakfast, your hair is all crazy curly and dry."

Jesse laughs again, so I shrug again.

"Just move in and then you can shower here in the mornings too."

Also, when Jesse sleeps over, Steve stays sleepin' in Jude's room. I don't say that though. Steve basically lives here already anyway.

"June, honey..." Mom starts, but then she doesn't finish. She just kind of looks at Jesse, and then they do that thing they do when they talk with their eyes.

It makes me nervous. I haven't figured out how to read that yet.

"Jesse, if you move in now, this weekend, then you can be here before my school is out for winter break, and we can all wake up together Christmas morning. Like a family."

I suck in a breath before I drop the big one.

"Mom, you said when you find people with the right superpowers then you find your family. Jesse's superpower is loving us, just like yours. Don't you guys want to be a family together?"

Jesse clears his throat, him and Mom do the eye thing again, and when she nods, my shoulders relax.

"I'd like to be part of your family, June Bug," Jesse says finally.

This time when I smile, I don't even care that my tooth hole is showing.

"Can we move you in this weekend?" I ask.

"I'm okay with it," Mom says. Her smile is big, too, just like mine, only she's not missing a tooth.

"Good," I say happily, and reach for a paper plate. I load it up with pizza and grab a cup of milk. Just before I walk out of the kitchen, I have another thought. I might as well say this one, too.

"Oh yeah," I say to Jesse over my shoulder, "I think me and Jude should call you Dad pretty soon. You know, once you're moved in and stuff. Okay?"

Jesse has to swallow a few times before he answers me. My plate is hot, and I want to set it down.

"Okay," he says, and his voice is super scratchy. He must be thirsty.

"Cool. Get some milk and then come watch the movie," I tell him, then I go claim one of the tray tables Mom already set up for us in the living room.

I've never been this excited for Christmas before. Mom was always pretend-happy, and Dad was always grouchy, and some years, they got into big fights.

This Christmas will be different.

I know this year will be the best one yet. Mom will be happy, and we will be happy, and Jesse will be here. Our first Christmas as a family.

And every Christmas after, too.

The End

Want more Jesse, Joss, and J-Squared?
Keep flipping for an exclusive extended epilogue.

321

extended epilogue

APPROXIMATELY ONE YEAR LATER

Approximately One Year Later

KELLEY

It's well after midnight when my phone chimes from the bedside table, waking me from sleep.

Usually, my phone is on Do Not Disturb this late, but recently I changed my settings for the group chat. There's only one reason I would be getting a text from the group chat at this time of night.

Quickly, I sit upright and reach for my phone, noticing that Ivy has woken up and is doing the same. We see the message at the same time.

"It's time," she squeals, then hops out of bed and rushes to the bathroom just as I pull up Riggs's contact. He answers on the first ring.

"You ready?" Riggs asks by way of greeting. I can hear movement, and Bailey talking in the background. "We can be there in thirty."

Bailey and Riggs live on the north side of the city, so it makes sense for them to pick us up on the way. I glance toward the bathroom. The light is on, and I can hear Ivy rustling around.

"Thirty minutes?" I call out to her, and she pops her head around the doorframe with a wide smile.

"We'll be downstairs!"

"Thirty minutes is good," I tell Riggs. "Just pull up out front. We'll be waiting."

Ivy comes rushing out of the bathroom dressed just as I finish pulling on my shirt. She grabs the bag we've had packed at the ready, and I pull up my email and shoot a quick message to my principal. I've had my school on standby, as well. They'll take care of finding my sub for the rest of the week.

I chuckle. Jesse's kid would decide to grace us with their presence in the middle of the night on a Tuesday. Work week, be damned.

Ivy and I reach the lobby of our condo just as Riggs pulls up in his Audi. Bailey pokes her head out the window, purple hair piled on her head in a messy bun matching Ivy's, with a smile stretching over her face.

"It's time!" she squeals, and Ivy does a little dance.

We're in the back seat and cruising down the interstate minutes later.

"I made a playlist for this," Bailey says, and fiddles with her phone just as "Baby Love" by The Supremes comes on.

I shoot a text to the group chat with our ETA—even though four of the six members are already in this car, and another one is likely indisposed from, you know, being in labor, leaving only Jesse as the intended recipient—and we fill the two hour and forty-minute ride from Chicago to Indianapolis with munching on the cherry turnovers Bailey brought and making bets on what Joss and Jesse will name the baby. We already know it will be a J name, but they've been tight-lipped on any possibilities.

It's after three a.m. when we pull into the parking lot of Indianapolis General and park in the long-term visitor lot, and it takes us only five minutes to find the waiting room for labor and delivery thanks to Ivy having looked up the hospital map online.

Jesse's mom and dad are sitting on the chairs when we barge in. Jesse's dad is next to a curled up, sleeping Jude on a two-seater chair, and Jesse's mom is sitting next to June, both reading books. June jumps up immediately and starts giving out hugs.

"We're having the baby," she says excitedly, her voice low so as not to wake Jude.

"I know!" I tell her, matching her excitement. "We came as soon as we heard."

Ivy looks at Dr. Hernandez. "Any news?"

Jesse's mom smiles. "He was just out here about ten minutes ago. Jocelyn is doing well, and we should have the little one within the hour, so you guys are just in time."

"And Jesse?" Bailey chimes in with a raised brow, and Jesse's dad chuckles.

"That boy is a mess. Started a whole new sentence before finishing the last one, pacing, bouncing. I've never seen him so excited, and that's saying something."

"Dad spun in three circles before remembering which way the doors were to go back to Mom," June says with a giggle. "And he'd only just come out of them!"

The room fills with quiet laughter, and the energy is palpable. Nervous excitement and impatience. This baby is already so loved.

When Jesse FaceTimed to tell us Joss was pregnant, we were a little shocked.

I didn't even know you were trying to have a baby, Ivy had said, and Jesse grinned. *Well, we weren't trying to* not *have a baby,* he replied.

He's since knitted the kid about a dozen matching blanket, hat and booty sets. It will definitely be the warmest baby in all of the Midwest.

We take seats, Bailey hands out turnovers, and then we wait.

Not for long, though.

* * *

JESSE

"He's here!" I shout as soon as I set foot in the waiting room. "Eight pounds, eleven ounces and twenty-two inches long. And he's got a head full of curls."

My family cheers, and I'm immediately engulfed in hugs and back pats. Ivy and Bailey are crying, and everyone is sporting big smiles. My heart is beating so fast, my limbs vibrating with excitement. This is the best day of my life.

"Congrats, man," Riggs says, pulling me into a hug. "We're so happy for you."

"How's Joss?" my mom asks as she tugs me from my friends and wraps her arms around me. "How's she feeling?"

"She's good, Mom. She's tired, but she did so good." I have to swallow back the crack in my voice. I didn't think I could love Jocelyn more, but I was wrong. My heart is near bursting with pride and awe and so much love for my girl and our baby boy. She's amazing. He's amazing. I'm so fucking lucky.

"I'm going to take the kids back to see her first," I tell them. "And then you guys can come back, okay?" Everyone nods in agreement, and I stick my hands out for June and Jude to clasp. "C'mon, squad. Ready to go meet your little brother?"

"Yes," Jude says, wiping sleep from his eyes. There is a strange crease on his cheek, probably from how he was lying in the waiting room chair, and his hair is sticking out in all directions. But his smile, the smile June is also wearing, gets me right in the chest.

"Can I hold him, Dad?" June asks as I walk them through the hallway of the hospital to Jocelyn's room. "I'll be so gentle."

I squeeze her hand and give her a smile. "I think he'd like that."

"Can I too?" Jude asks.

"Yes, definitely." We round the corner and I slow us to a stop. "Okay, remember that your mom and your brother are tired, so be soft and move slowly, and the baby is small, and we need to protect him from germs, so you have to wash your hands in the sink before you can hold him."

Two pairs of giant eyes sparkle up at me as June and Jude nod. I laugh lightly, then open the door to Jocelyn's room. The kids walk in slowly, though it's obviously more difficult for Jude. He moves as if wearing weighted boots. Like every step is carefully restrained and it's taking all of his concentration not to break out in a run.

I feel that.

Jocelyn smiles sleepily from her place on the hospital bed as the kids take turns washing their hands in the small bathroom. Her hair is mussed, features are soft from exhaustion, but her big green eyes are bright. She's so perfect, my girl. My Classic. I've never known a more beautiful person. And now that she's holding my son? She glows.

"Hi, guys," Joss says quietly once the kids are at her bedside. "Want to meet your brother?"

"He's so cute," June coos, beaming at her new baby brother. "He's got hair just like you, Dad." June speaks to me, but she never takes her eyes off the baby. Like looking away from him is impossible.

I feel that, too.

"His nose is so little," Jude says. He reaches out like he's going to boop the baby's tiny nose, but June smacks his hand away. Jude huffs. "Why's his mouth doing that thing? That little fishy sucking thing?"

"Sometimes babies do that," I tell him. "June, if you want to hold him, go ahead and sit down in the chair."

She moves to the chair so fast that I have to stifle a laugh, and Jude posts up beside her like a little bodyguard. Jocelyn and I share a look, one full of amusement and love, and my heart skips. I don't know if I could be any happier.

Before lifting the baby from Jocelyn's chest, I press a kiss to her forehead. My strong girl. My wildflower.

June has been practicing how to hold a baby, so when I place him in her arms, she's a natural.

"Hi, Baby Joel," she whispers, and I smile at Joss.

"You guys decided on Joel, then?" Jocelyn asks the kids, and they both nod without looking away from the baby.

"Baby Joel," I say, the name feeling familiar and welcome on my tongue. "I like it."

For a while, I was worried Jude would win and we'd have to name the baby Jack Sparrow or Blackbeard, but it seems June has talked some sense into him. I thought he would have grown out of his fascination with pirates by now, but it's still going strong. We took them to a big amusement park not too long ago and he made me go on the Pirates ride with him five times. I don't see his love waning any time soon.

"And the middle name?" Jocelyn asks.

"Sparrow," Jude chimes in, and June snorts a laugh. Well, we almost avoided a pirate name, it seems. My kids are at least good at compromise.

"Joel Sparrow Hernandez," Jocelyn says, and when I glance at her, her green eyes are sparkling with unshed tears, and her lips are molded into the smile that makes my knees weak. "I love it."

"I do too," I say honestly. I really, truly love it.

After the family has been in to visit, my parents take June and Jude back to the house and my friends go check into a hotel. My parents plan to stay in town for a while, and I know my friends will be here at least through the week before they have to get back to their responsibilities and jobs in Chicago. I love that they're here, my family all together, exactly how it should be, but I'm glad to spend a little alone time with Classic and Joel. The love of my life, and my legacy.

I lie on my side in the hospital bed with Jocelyn's back pressed to my chest and Joel swaddled on the bed next to her. It's a tight squeeze, but Joss says she's comfortable, and there's no place I'd rather be.

I reach out and brush my fingers through Joel's mess of curls. He's asleep, big eyes closed, and eyelashes fanned over his chubby little cheeks, and my heart could burst from the love I feel.

My boy is going to have his mom's eyes. It's everything I've ever wanted.

It's almost overwhelming, these feelings. If you would have asked me two years ago if I'd be a dad to three kids and head over heels in love, I'd have told you hell no. But now? I wouldn't want it any other way.

"Can you believe we made this?" Jocelyn whispers, and I press a kiss to her temple.

"He's amazing," I tell her. He is. The adorable little nose. The big eyes and Cupid's bow lips. He's the perfect blend of Jocelyn and me. "You did all the work, though. You're amazing, Classic. I can't even believe how lucky I am."

I hear her sniffle, and when she speaks, her voice is scratchy and full of emotion.

"*We're* lucky. I didn't know people like you existed until you infiltrated my life and knocked me off my feet."

"Knocked?" I joke. "Not swept?"

She chuckles. "Maybe swept."

I get choked up because everything she's saying is how I feel. I didn't know I was capable of giving this kind of love, and I didn't know I was deserving of receiving it. Not until Jocelyn. Not until Classic and our three beautiful kids.

"I love you," I tell her. "I love you so much. I love our life. I didn't know how badly I wanted this. Thank you for giving it to me."

She tilts her head to mine, and I capture her lips, slow and deep, breathing my love, my adoration, my awe into her. She slows our kiss and moves her gaze back to Joel.

"He's perfect," she whispers.

"He is. Just like you."

I feel her soft chuckle. Doesn't matter how many times I tell her she's absolutely perfect to me, she still doesn't quite get it. I'll keep telling her, though. Every single day, I'll tell her, and one of these days, maybe she'll understand just how deeply I mean it.

Jocelyn yawns, and I press another kiss to her temple.

"Sleep, baby."

"I don't want to stop looking at him," she whispers as her heavy eyelids drift closed.

"I feel that," I whisper, bouncing my attention between Joss and Joel.

I feel everything.

And nothing has ever felt better.

I know most of you have been waiting for Jesse's book, and I can only hope that you all feel that I gave him the HEA he deserves. Our lovable joker, our loyal best friend, our knitting genius. He deserves big, big love, and I believe I gave him that.

But as much as I love Jesse, it was Joss's story that stole my heart.

Jocelyn's story was inspired by several women I know and love, including my own mother. I'm sure many of you know someone who can relate, even a little, to what she goes through, because it's a harsh reality that too many women face. I think it's important to see the strength and courage in her growth, quiet as it may be sometimes. Remember that healing usually isn't loud or marked by huge, epic milestones. It's gradual, and every single subtle inch is worth celebrating.

There is so much beauty in her resilience. There is so much beauty in **you**.

I ask that you give Jocelyn grace. Give yourself grace. Give every woman who has ever been mistreated grace, and celebrate every step forward, no matter how many steps back may have preceded or followed. We deserve to look at our past experiences and be proud of how far we've come.

And June. Her story is something that is so dear to me, and it's a plot line that I'm extremely proud of. She's the embodiment of hope and strength. So even though June is not a main character, I hope you watched her closely. Her character growth is a wonderful thing to witness.

I hope you love the J Squad as much as I do, fam.

Thanks again for indulging in my imagination with me.

acknowledgments

Goodness.
Book three.
What the *actual* frick.

I'm not quite sure how I got here, but I'm certain I owe so much of the progress to some very important people. I'll try to keep it brief, but if you know me, you know I tend to ramble... Read it all or skim for your name. It's all good.

First and foremost, to **my mom**. For every sacrifice, every hug, every word of praise and every lesson taught, thank you so much. For better or worse, I am who I am because of you. Always blessings.

To **my husband**, without whom, writing and publishing would be a whole hell of a lot more difficult. I love you. You're my rock and my person and I wouldn't have it any other way. Thank you for giving me so much goof-ball material to use as Jesse inspo, for always making me laugh, and for loving me so well. Second on this list, first in my heart. *Awww.*

To my **ARC readers, bloggers,** and **bookstagrammers,** thank you so much for picking up *Nothing Feels Better.* For all you've done to help promote this book, and every book in this series, I am beyond grateful. Your support and enthusiasm mean so much to me, and I would not be writing these acknowledgements in MY THIRD WHOLE ASS BOOKBABY if it weren't for you all.

To **Murphy Rae**, for being a friggen photoshopping baddie, thank you. This cover? Seriously? I'm so in love with it.

To my editor, **Rebecca** at **Fairest Reviews Editing Services,** thank you so much for your thorough attention to detail, and for never complaining to my face about all the times I mess up lay/lie and raise/rise. You're a saint and a gem and I know I'm a mess but please god don't leave me ever because I need you.

To my proofreader, **Sarah** at **All Encompassing Books,** for being my champion, my final set of eyes, and my friend, thank you. I love you so fucking hard.

To my beta team, **Caitlin, Dawn, Haley, Brook, Brianna, Jenna,** and **Kara,** for being a bunch of opinionated, encouraging, honest little freaks, I am forever grateful. Extra special shout out to **Brianna** for campaigning so hard for on-page butt stuff. I know the readers appreciate your tenacity as much as I do.

To **Marisella**, thank you so much for all your guidance and suggestions regarding the Spanish language and Mexican culture. Jesse is better because of your influence. *Te aprecio amiga.*

Thank you to **Haley, Hayley,** and **Ruth** for answering my endless questions, and for providing guidance and information regarding nursing, nursing school, and the application process/student life/academic practices at Harvard Medical School.

To **Josh, my childhood babysitter**, for actually attempting to make my brother and me eat "Martian Stew." I am forever traumatized, but at least I got a funny book scene out of it. Also, thanks for not fucking my mom... *right?*

Big thank you to my **daughter, B,** for inspiring many of the Jude scenes. *Arg, Captain.* You'll probably never read this book, and if you do it won't be for a long ass time because you are only four but know that you made Jude the character he is, and I love him because I love you.

To Quinn XCII, Christian French, Social House, Lil Yachty, and Pink Sweat$ for carrying my fucking playlist and fueling so many scenes in this book. And to Harry Styles, because I am in love with you forever.

That's it for now, my dudes. Read some great books, and I'll be back soon.

-J-Brit

Brit Benson writes real, relatable romance novels that depict epic love. She likes outspoken, independent heroines, dirty-talking, love-struck heroes, and plots that tug on every emotion.

Brit would almost always rather be reading or writing. When she's not dreaming up her next swoony book boyfriend and fierce book bestie, she's getting lost in someone else's fictional world. When she's not doing that, she's probably marathoning a Netflix series or wandering aimlessly up and down the aisles in Homegoods, sniffing candles and touching things she'll never buy.

Brit currently resides somewhere near the Blue Ridge Parkway with her husband, daughters, dogs, and an obscene number of books.

facebook.com/britbensonbooks

instagram.com/Britbensonwritesbooks

goodreads.com/authorbritbenson

pinterest.com/authorbritbenson